LAUREN HANEY

A CRUEL DECEIT

A MYSTERY OF ANCIENT EGYPT

AVON BOOKS

An Imprint of HarperCollinsPublishers

This is a work of fiction. Names, characters, places, and incidents are products of the author's imagination or are used fictitiously and are not to be construed as real. Any resemblance to actual events, locales, organizations, or persons, living or dead, is entirely coincidental.

AVON BOOKS
An Imprint of HarperCollins*Publishers*
10 East 53rd Street
New York, New York 10022-5299

Copyright © 2002 by Betty J. Winkelman
ISBN: 0-380-81287-8
www.avonmystery.com

First Avon Books paperback printing: September 2002

Avon Trademark Reg. U.S. Pat Off. and in Other Countries, Marca Registrada, Hecho en U.S.A.
HarperCollins ® is a trademark of HarperCollins Publishers Inc.

Printed in the U.S.A.

10 9 8 7 6 5 4 3 2 1

Acknowledgments

I wish to thank Dennis Forbes, Editorial Director of *KMT: A Modern Journal of Ancient Egypt*, for being so generous with his time and knowledge. I also wish to thank Tavo Serina for his thoughtful suggestions when critiquing the manuscript in its rough form.

Thanks are also due to my agent Nancy Yost and my editor Lyssa Keusch for guiding me and Lieutenant Bak through the publishing world.

Last but certainly not least, I owe a special thanks to Dr. W. Raymond Johnson, Field Director, Epigraphic Survey (Chicago House in Luxor, Egypt), Oriental Institute, University of Chicago, for answering my innumerable questions about the Beautiful Feast of Opet, the temples involved, and Waset as it probably looked during the dual reign of Maatkare Hatshepsut and Menkheperre Thutmose. Any mistakes are mine.

CAST OF CHARACTERS

From the fortress of Buhen

Lieutenant Bak	Egyptian officer in charge of a company of Medjay police
Sergeant Imsiba	Bak's second-in-command, a Medjay
Sergeants Pashenuro and Psuro	Medjay sergeants lower in status than Imsiba
Commandant Thuty	Officer formerly in charge of the garrison of Buhen
Troop Captain Nebwa	Thuty's second-in-command
Hori	Youthful police scribe
Kasaya	A Medjay policeman

Members of the household of the governor of Tjeny

Pentu	Governor of Tjeny
Taharet	Pentu's lovely young wife
Meret	Taharet's attractive sister
Sitepehu	High priest of the lord Inheret
Netermose	Pentu's aide
Pahure	Pentu's steward

Those involved with the mansion of the lord Amon

Amonked	Storekeeper of Amon
Hapuseneb	Chief priest of the lord Amon

Ptahmes	Aide to Hapuseneb
User	Overseer of Overseers of the storehouses of Amon
Nebamon	Overseer of a block of storage magazines containing valuable ritual items
Woserhet	Scribe responsible for the distribution of food known as the "reversion of offerings"; an auditor
Ashayet	Woserhet's wife
Tati	Woserhet's indentured servant, a scribe
Meryamon	Priest who gathers objects from the storehouses of Amon for use in the sacred rituals

Other individuals in Waset

Djehuty	Chief Treasurer
Maruwa	A Hittite merchant who imports fine horses into Kemet
Irenena	Maruwa's concubine
Mai	Harbormaster
Captain Antef	Master of the seagoing vessel on which Maruwa ships the horses
Lieutenant Karoya	Officer in charge of the harbor patrol, a Medjay
Commander Minnakht	Master of the royal stables
Sergeant Khereuf	Chief of horse trainers at the royal stables
Thanuny	Auditor in the royal house
The red-haired man	An unknown quantity
The swarthy man	Another unknown quantity
Ptahhotep	Bak's father

Plus various and sundry priests, scribes, soldiers, guards, and townspeople

The gods and goddesses

Amon	The primary god during much of ancient Egyptian history, especially the early 18th Dynasty, the time of this story; takes the form of a human being, with the ram as his symbol
Mut	Amon's spouse, a mother goddess, always shown in human form
Khonsu	Son of Amon and Mut, moon god, depicted as a youth wrapped in mummy bandages
Amon-Kamutef	An aspect of Amon in ithyphallic form, literally "bull of his mother"
Osiris	God of death, ressurection, and fertility; usually depicted as a wrapped mummy
Maat	Goddess of truth and order; represented by a feather
Hapi	Personification of the Nile
Re	The sun god
Khepre	The rising sun, shown as a scarab beetle
Thoth	Patron god of scribes, depicted in the form of an ibis or baboon
Inheret	God associated with war and hunting; represented by a man carrying a spear and rope, wearing a headdress of four tall feathers

The lord Amon's mansions

Ipet-isut	The great northern mansion, known today as the temple of Karnak
Ipet-resyt	The smaller southern mansion, called today the temple of Luxor

Both of these temples, as well as the sacred precincts in which they stood, were considerably smaller during the dual reign of Maatkare Hatshepsut and Menkheperre Thutmose than they are as we see them today.

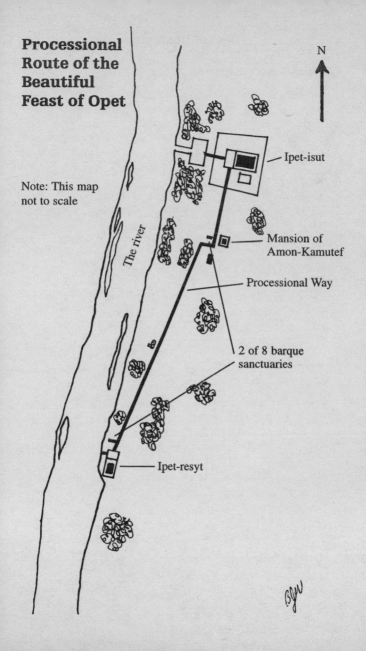

Processional Route of the Beautiful Feast of Opet

N

Note: This map not to scale

The river

Ipet-isut

Mansion of Amon-Kamutef

Processional Way

2 of 8 barque sanctuaries

Ipet-resyt

A CRUEL DECEIT

Chapter One

"Stop! Thief!"

Two men raced along the busy street, darting around the many people ambling among piles of produce on the ground or looking at offerings displayed in open stalls. The man in the lead carried a squawking goose under his arm; the other brandished a short wooden rod.

"Help! He'll slay me!" the man with the bird screamed.

"Stop him!" the other yelled. "He cheated me!"

"It's my goose. I bought it for fair exchange."

"The wheat you gave me was moldy."

"You added bad grain when my back was turned."

The response was lost to the angry cackling of the goose.

The merchants within the stalls and those seated with their mounded produce, the people filling the street, many idly browsing rather than shopping, stopped to gape at the pair. Individuals peered out from the interconnected two-story white-plastered buildings behind the market. Sailors on the ships moored along the waterfront ran to look. A stream of men and women had even begun to follow, unwilling to miss an assault should the pursuer catch his quarry.

At the first angry yell, Lieutenant Bak hurried to the railing of the large, broad-beamed cargo ship on which he stood. Though the heavily laden vessel rode low on the water, its deck rose well above the muddy escarpment, thanks to the floodwaters that lapped the roots of the few tough

1

grasses and bushes that survived untrodden. From where he stood, he snatched glimpses of the pair speeding through the milling throng. A northerly breeze cooled the sweat trickling down his chest, dried the thin film of moisture coating his broad shoulders, and ruffled his short-cropped dark hair and the hem of his thigh-length kilt. He thought to give chase, to thwart a confrontation and see justice done. But crime along the waterfront was none of his business. The harbor patrol was responsible here. Still . . .

He glanced at Sergeant Imsiba standing to his right and Troop Captain Nebwa to his left. Both men nodded and, as one, the trio hurried toward the gangplank, a wide board joining deck to land.

A sharp whistle rent the air, stopping them before they could leave the vessel. The signal was familiar, one often used by Bak's company of Medjay policemen. Within moments, a unit of armed men raced out of a side lane and down the busy street. All were Medjays and each carried the black-and-white cowhide shields of the harbor patrol. They quickly encircled the man with the goose and his pursuer, disarmed the one and took the squawking evidence from the other, and led them away. The patrol officer, also a Medjay, walked along the line of stalls in search of witnesses.

Bak, Imsiba, and Nebwa moved a few paces away from the gangplank and grinned sheepishly at each other. They were no longer at the fortress of Buhen on the remote southern frontier, where such activities were theirs to resolve. They were in the capital city of Waset, where other men were responsible for upholding the laws of the land, thus satisfying the lady Maat, goddess of right and order.

Imsiba's smile broadened and he clasped Bak's upper arms, not merely as his second-in-command, but with an affection close to that of a brother. "I've missed you, my friend." The big Medjay was half a hand taller than Bak, a few years older, dark and muscular. His eyes were quick and sharp, and he moved with the ease and grace of a leopard.

Bak returned the greeting, nearly overcome with emotion. "I can't begin to say how happy I am to see you again." He transferred his smile to the men and women crowding around them on the deck: his company of Medjays; Imsiba's wife and Nebwa's and their children; four other women wed to Medjays; his spy Nofery; and, shouldering a path through the circle, Commandant Thuty. "Not a day has passed that I haven't thought of each and every one of you."

Sitamon, Imsiba's lovely wife, stepped forward to greet him with open arms, after which he knelt to hug her son. He took Nebwa's wife, small and dark and shy, into his arms, with her small child between them. A moist-eyed Nofery, obese and no longer young, swept forward to tell him how little she had missed him and to cling to him as if he were her long-lost son. His Medjays surged around him, clasping his hands, clapping him on the back, in every way letting him know how much they liked and respected him.

Greetings over, the Medjays and women spread out over the ship, gathering their belongings. The deck, piled high with equipment and supplies, was too cramped for anyone to remain on board when other quarters were available. Bak had found a small building where his men could dwell as long as they remained in Waset, and had arranged to get food and other perishable supplies from the quartermaster of the local garrison. Thuty's wife, who had come ahead of her husband, had arranged housing for Nebwa, Imsiba, and their families and the four Medjays' wives.

"We feared you'd forget us." Nebwa, his smile wide and warm, teasing, laid a hand on Bak's shoulder. "How long has it been since you left us behind in Buhen? Two months? Time enough to grow accustomed to the good life, to turn your back on the likes of us." The hard-muscled, coarse-featured troop captain, second-in-command to the commandant, was a man in his early thirties. He wore a rumpled kilt, his broad beaded collar hung awry, and his hair needed combing. His appearance was deceptive. He could be crude at times and tactless, but he was a most competent and experienced officer.

Commandant Thuty, who had been the first to greet Bak when he boarded the ship, drew the trio to the bow, well out of the way of the Medjays and women hustling around the deck.

Bak noticed that the crew and passengers on the large and graceful traveling ship moored at the water's edge in front of them were equally busy. The sailors were preparing the vessel for a long stay, while a white-haired man and two young women ordered servants about and checked storage baskets and chests soon to be carried away by waiting porters. A nobleman, he guessed, and the members of his household. If the four feathers painted on the prow, symbol of the lord Inheret, god of war and hunting, told true, they had come from the provincial capital of Tjeny. All were chattering like swallows, clearly happy to reach Waset and all the good things it had to offer.

Climbing into the forecastle for a better view of the waterfront, the commandant eyed the long row of vessels moored end to end and, farther along the river's edge, tied together side by side four and sometimes five deep. Bak, Nebwa, and Imsiba could see almost as well from the bow. Naked masts rose above vessels of all sizes, the decks of most empty of cargo and passengers. Fittings squeaked, loose lines flapped, a sailor fishing from a deck whistled a merry tune. Sharp-eyed squawking crows settled on yards and masts to bask in the sun and keep an eye open for an easy meal. A pack of dogs fought, snarling and mean, over a furry object too dirty and tattered to identify.

"I've never seen the harbor so crowded," Thuty said. "There'll be a better than usual turnout for the Beautiful Feast of Opet, I'd guess." He was short, broad, and muscular, with heavy brows and a firm chin. The long voyage with few responsibilities had relaxed the normally hard set of his mouth.

"Yes, sir," Bak nodded. "Many men have been drawn to the capital in the hope of seeing the lord Amon and our sovereigns, Maatkare Hatshepsut and Menkheperre Thutmose, the two of them together." To find the royal pair in one place was a rare occurrence, but a measure of the importance of the Opet festival and the rituals the dual rulers would perform throughout the week, reaffirming them as the divine offspring of the lord Amon.

Imsiba eyed the crowded market, smiled. "Not to mention a desire to participate in the festivities."

"Eleven days of revelry." Nebwa chuckled. "There'll be many an aching head and upset belly, I'll wager."

The sound of women's laughter carried on the air, reminding Bak of the ship moored in front of them and the many other fine traveling ships arriving in the capital. "As for men of wealth and import, our sovereigns will be holding audiences from the second day through the tenth, giving them an opportunity to offer obeisance." His voice grew wry. "Few will wish to be counted among the missing."

"Don't be impertinent, Lieutenant." Thuty's gruff demeanor was eased by a twinkle in his eyes. "I'll be down on my knees among them."

"You, sir?"

"My new task as commandant of the garrison in Mennufer is an important posting. I'll now be rubbing shoulders with men of note."

Bak detected the hint of cynicism, as he was meant to, and smiled. "Will the rest of us remain in Waset throughout the festival? Or will we go on ahead to Mennufer?"

Thuty scowled in mock disapproval. "Do you think me a man who'd deprive you of the opportunity to take part in the merrymaking?"

"I wasn't sure, sir," Bak's smile broadened, "but I had the foresight to obtain quarters for my Medjays for the length of the festival and beyond."

The commandant tried to look stern, but a laugh burst forth to destroy the effect.

"Thuty? Is that you Thuty?"

A portly, bald man of middle years hastened down the gangplank spanning the gap between the shore and the traveling ship moored in front of them. He wore the long kilt of a scribe and the broad collar, bracelets, and armlets of a man of wealth and consequence. Passing a young scribe, an aide Bak assumed, and four porters with a carrying chair standing at the foot of the gangplank, he hurried up the waterfront to stand beside the prow of the cargo vessel.

The commandant, smiling with delight, dropped off the forecastle and strode to the railing. "Djehuty? By the grace of the lord Amon! I never thought to see you outside the walls of the royal house."

The man chuckled. "I'm not wedded to our sovereign; I'm a mere servant."

"A servant of great import." Thuty turned to his companions and introduced the man, adding, "Djehuty holds the wealth of Kemet within his hands. He's the Chief Treasurer of our land."

The impatient commands of an overseer sent laden porters filing down the gangplank of the traveling ship. The white-haired man hurried across the deck to watch, while the two women—his daughters, most likely—continued to flutter around the baggage. Their fine, stylish clothing and exquisite jewelry, the large number of servants, reinforced Bak's guess that this was a nobleman's household.

The man followed the final porter to the shore and walked along the water's edge to join Djehuty. He was as thin as the treasurer was plump, of medium height and lanky. A large bald spot showed through his otherwise thick white hair, and his eyes were a surprising blue, bits of sky transported to earth.

Djehuty introduced the commandant, explaining who he was, where he had come from, and where he was bound. "Thuty, this is my friend Pentu, resident of Tjeny and governor of the province." Tjeny was a very old city several days' journey to the north. Although no longer as important as in the distant past, it was the capital of the province in which lay Abedju, the center of worship for the lord Osiris and the location of many ancient and revered tombs.

"Like you, I've known him for years," Djehuty went on. "Since first we came to the capital. Barely more than babes, we were, torn from our provincial homes to learn to read and write in the royal house. We clung together then in our loneliness. Now we're men of substance, still close in spite of the different paths we've trod."

Thuty in turn introduced his companions, then asked Pentu, "You've come for the festival?"

"We have. This promises to be an exceptional year. As the flood was neither too high nor too low, the crops will be abundant. Maatkare Hatshepsut has much to celebrate. She . . ." His eyes, drawn by the patter of leather sandals on wood, darted toward the traveling ship and the two young women walking down the gangplank.

As they approached along the waterfront, Bak could see that they were both in their mid-twenties, close to him in age. Their dark hair brushed their shoulders, and their skin was the exquisite shade and texture of the finest ivory. One was taller than the other and slimmer, but their facial features were very much alike, not beautiful by any means, but certainly handsome.

Whatever Pentu had intended to say was lost forever, as if the sight of the women had torn the thought from his heart. He strode forward to meet them, took the hand of the taller of the two, and looked at her with an intense and utter devotion. "Are you ready, my dear?"

"More than ready, my beloved." She smiled prettily. "As you know, I find sailing to be quite tedious."

She was his wife, not a daughter. Bak kept his face blank, hiding his surprise.

"I sent for a carrying chair. Will you ride or would you prefer to walk?"

Bak exchanged a quick glance with Nebwa and Imsiba. They, like he, had assumed the Chief Treasurer had come in the chair.

"We'll walk, at least part way." She glanced at her sister, who smiled, then beamed at Djehuty. "It was so nice to see you again, sir. Too brief, of course, but we hope to correct that. Our house here in the city will be ready for guests within a day or two. Do bring your worthy spouse."

"Your husband has already invited me and I've accepted," the treasurer said, smiling his assurance.

Male and female servants laden with baskets and bundles hurried down the gangplank and gathered around the carrying chair to await the women. Acknowledging their presence with a glance, Pentu's wife said to her husband, "You won't be long, will you, dearest?"

"I'll catch you before you reach the house."

Another quick smile and she turned away to walk up the street through the market. Unbidden, the servants and porters fell in behind. Shoppers and browsers stepped aside to let them pass and closed in after them, blocking them from view. Not until his wife vanished from sight did Pentu again become aware of the men with whom he had been talking.

Bak, Nebwa, and Imsiba, feeling they had no place among three such lofty individuals, slipped away as soon as they could reasonably do so. They walked through the market, weaving a path through the throng and the mounds of produce, peering into stalls, thoroughly enjoying a carefree reunion.

The number of merchants had doubled over the past few days, Bak noticed, and the number of shoppers and browsers had quadrupled, swollen by those who had come from afar to attend the Opet festival. The opening procession would not take place for another week, but thanks to the uncertainties of travel and the much larger than normal market, many celebrants came to the city well ahead of time.

The world around them hummed with voices and laughter. The high-pitched twittering of monkeys mimicked the squeaking of fittings, masts, and yards on the vessels moored along the water's edge. The slow cadence of drummers marking time for the oarsmen on passing ships echoed the louder beat of musicians playing for gifts they could trade for food. The fishy-musty smell of the river, the rancid odor of unwashed bodies, the smell of animals and their dung mingled with the aromas of spices and herbs, perfumes and aromatic oils, braised and roasted fowl and beef and lamb. Men and women from the land of Kemet, garbed in fine white linen or the roughest of fabrics worn by the poor, rubbed shoulders with individuals wearing the bright-colored woolen robes of the north or the leather kilts of the south.

Nebwa and Imsiba, both doting fathers, stopped to explore a woodcarver's stall, drawn by colorful hanging birds whose wings moved up and down when touched by the breeze. Bak stood off to the side to wait and to watch the passing crowd.

He gradually became aware of a new sound, one out of place in a busy market. The whinnying of horses. Not close enough to catch the ear of people distracted by the abundance around them, barely audible to him. He raised his head, listened intently. Sometimes the sound vanished altogether in the closer, louder buzz of humanity. Sometimes he heard it distinctly. The animals were unsettled, fearful. Their anxious neighing, their alarmed snorts, some distance away and not always clear, were unmistakable to a former chariotry officer such as he. They must be looked at, helped.

He peered into the woodcarver's stall. "Nebwa, Imsiba. I'm going on ahead. I hear horses in trouble."

Nebwa, intent on Imsiba, who was haggling for a bird, took an instant to register the words. "Where?"

"Somewhere to the north."

"We won't be long."

Bak worked his way to the water's edge where the crowd was thinner. He ducked around sailors and porters who stood in his path, jumped over mounds of cargo and ships' fittings when no other way was open, and broke into a fast trot when the route was clear. He slowed twice to listen, to make sure the horses were ahead, not in a side lane he might unwittingly pass. Both times he heard them, and each time their neighing was louder, more distraught. Other people had begun to notice. Most simply raised their heads to listen, a few took tentative footsteps toward the sound, a handful hurried along after him.

He sped past the last few market stalls. The street ahead was nearly empty. Most people leaving the market had taken the eastbound streets and lanes to reach their homes. The few who had come northward had gathered at the water's edge and, talking anxiously among themselves, were looking toward the last ship in line. Baskets overflowing with produce and bulging linen and string bags sat on the ground around their feet. Two boys of eight or so years, one with a yellow puppy in his arms, stood with the adults. Hearing the rapid patter of sandals, they all turned to see who had come.

"Do any of you know anything about horses?" one of the men asked. He pointed toward the foredeck of the ship, a great seagoing cargo vessel, with a broad hull, tall mast and sweeping yards, and what had to be a massive sail furled against the lower yard. "Look at them. If something isn't done before long they'll kill themselves."

"I once was a charioteer." Bak spoke automatically, his attention focused on the animals on deck.

Sixteen horses, blacks and bays, each tied securely within adjoining stalls erected in front of the deckhouse. The animals' neighing was loud and unnatural, sharp with alarm.

They flung their heads wildly, trying to rear up, to tear themselves free of the bounds that held them in place. Their hooves pounded the wooden deck, their flanks slammed against the plank walls of their stalls. Something on board that ship had frightened them, and that fear was building upon itself, driving them wild.

"What the . . . ?" Nebwa slid to a halt at Bak's side.

Imsiba ran up to join them, frowning. "Something's very wrong, my friend. A snake, do you think?"

"Horses are valuable animals," Nebwa growled, "much too costly to leave untended."

"If most of the crew were given leave," Imsiba said, "and only two or three remained, a viper would set them running fast enough."

"Summon the harbor patrol," Bak told the boys. "Ask if they've any men who know horses. We must lead them off that ship as quickly as possible, and we could use some help."

"Yes, sir." Wide-eyed with excitement, the one boy shoved the puppy into his mother's arms and together they raced away.

Bak dashed up the gangplank which, he thanked the gods, had been left in place. Nebwa and Imsiba followed close on his heels. They stopped at the top and looked around, searching for the reason for the horses' panic. Other than the animals, they saw no sign of life. No sailors, no guards, no ship's master. Nothing but mounds of cargo lashed to the deck, none of which looked as if it had been disturbed by a man bent on theft, but all of which could hide a reptile.

A more likely place of refuge for a snake was the bow, where a dozen bags of grain were stacked in front of the forecastle beside a large mound of sheaved straw and hay. A stack of empty sacks, as well as loose grain and bits of straw and fodder littering the deck, spoke of a lengthy voyage during which a considerable amount of feed had been consumed by the horses.

Nebwa spoke aloud what they all were thinking: "Who, in the name of the lord Amon, would abandon a shipload of horses with a snake on board? You'd think they'd at least have left a man to stand watch at the gangplank while the others summoned help."

"We must first tend to the horses. When they're safe, we can seek an answer to that question." Bak's eyes raked the deck, settled on a tunic someone had flung onto the forecastle railing. He scooped it up, swung around, and eyed his two friends, neither of whom had any knowledge of horses. "Find a dead end lane in which we can hold these animals, Imsiba."

"Yes, my friend," the Medjay said and hurried off.

Bak turned to Nebwa. "If I can calm them one at a time, can you lead them to Imsiba?"

"Just tell me what I must do," the troop captain growled, eyeing the animals with undisguised mistrust. He had grown to manhood on the southern frontier and had dwelt there always. He had never been near a horse in his life.

Thanking his friend with a grim smile, Bak walked slowly to the closest stall, speaking softly to the horse inside, a bay mare with a white blaze between her eyes. She looked to be carrying young. Nebwa stood a couple paces away, scanning the deck, ready to lash out with his baton of office should a snake slither through the loose straw spread on the floor of the stalls.

Bak had no idea how tame the mare was—or any of the other horses, for that matter. The ship was built and fitted like a vessel of Kemet, but since far more horses were imported than exported, he suspected they had been brought from some distant land. Which meant the mare had been on board for some time. As far as he was concerned, no sane man would ship a wild horse for any distance at all. Therefore, he had to assume she was fairly tame, at least partly trained, and somewhat trustful of man.

Throwing the tunic, which smelled of sweat, over his shoulder, willing himself to forget the snake, to concentrate on the one horse and ignore the others, the noise they were making, their terror, he held out a hand. The mare pulled away, whinnied with fear. He forced himself to be patient, to speak softly, gently, revealing no hint of how anxious he was to get her out of that stall, how much he feared the other animals would work themselves into so frenzied a state that one or more would break a leg or knock down a wall and do serious damage to itself and another.

Slowly, oh so slowly the mare began to calm down. He sensed that the horse in the next stall was also growing quieter, a good sign that no snake was close by. Again he held out a hand, offering friendship. The mare whinnied in fright, but did not back off. He cautiously leaned over the wall and reached for her rope halter. She jerked away. He remained where he was, leaning toward her, hand held out between them, and continued to speak to her, to cajole her. At last she turned her head and warily sniffed his hand. Soothing her with gentle words, he caught hold of the halter, eased her head around, and rubbed her muzzle.

In no time at all, she allowed him into the stall. He hated to blind her, but decided he couldn't trust her outside the enclosure and especially on the gangplank. He flung the tunic over her head. Talking all the while, he led the trembling mare out of the stall, across the deck, and onto the gangplank. She snorted and held back as she felt the slope beneath her hooves, but she obeyed.

Nebwa, who had spoken not a word throughout, followed them onto the shore, staying well clear lest he frighten the horse. A unit of harbor patrolmen awaited them at the bottom of the gangplank. The officer who stood at their head ordered the men back, giving the mare plenty of room and no reason to fear. With solid ground beneath her feet and Bak's soothing voice filling her ears, her trembling subsided. He tore the tunic from her head and handed her over to Nebwa who, talking to her as gently as Bak had, led her to the mouth of a narrow lane where Imsiba waited.

The patrol officer came forward and identified himself as Lieutenant Karoya. He was a tall, slim young Medjay who had a tribal tattoo on his left upper arm. "Well done, sir."

"I hope some of your men know horses, Lieutenant. We've fifteen more to take off that ship."

"I've three men who can help. All served as archers in the regiment of Amon and were assigned to chariotry companies." Beckoning the trio, he studied the ship and its excited cargo. "Have you any idea what's frightening them, sir?"

"A snake, we think. We'll need three or four men with cudgels to keep watch."

A half hour later, Bak led the last animal off the ship. "Now," he said to Karoya, "let's see what made those horses so afraid." He let his eyes travel over the empty stalls and the hay and grain at the bow. "The lord Amon alone knows what we'll find."

The young officer nodded. "I saw the ship arrive this morning, a couple of hours before you summoned me, but I paid no heed after that. With so many people coming early for the festival and the market so busy . . ." He smiled ruefully. "Well, you can imagine how it is, sir. Many vile criminals have come to prey upon the law-abiding."

A harbor patrolman took the horse from Bak and led it to the mouth of the dead end lane. There several other members of the harbor patrol were preparing to lead the calmed and willing animals to the garrison stables, where they would be cared for until their owner could be found. Nebwa, whose lofty rank would cut short any official resistance, would go with them.

Bak suggested that he, Karoya, Imsiba, and a half dozen harbor patrolmen conduct a sweeping search of the deck, beginning at the bow. After the young officer sent the rest of

his men off to keep an eye on the market, they crossed the
gangplank and walked forward.

While his mates stood by, brandishing their cudgels, one
of the harbor patrolmen took up the long pole used to probe
the depths of the river so the vessel would not run aground
and prodded the sheaves of fodder and hay in front of the
forecastle. A low moan sounded from within the mound.
Bak and the others looked at each other, startled. The patrolman cautiously dug away the straw. In moments, he exposed
two sailors bound tightly together. Both were senseless, but
one had begun to come around.

Bak exchanged a worried glance with Imsiba and Karoya.
No snake had attacked these men. They had no doubt been
left to guard the cargo. If the horses, as valuable as they were,
had not been taken, what else of value had been on board?

Leaving Imsiba to bring the sailors to their senses and the
patrolmen to continue their sweep of the deck, Bak hurried
sternward. The smells of hay and manure dwindled as he
walked alongside the deckhouse, a lightweight, portable
structure built of slim poles walled and roofed with colorful
reed mats woven in a chevron pattern. In air less pungent, he
caught a whiff of an all-too-familiar metallic odor. Muttering an oath, he swept aside the mat that covered the doorway
and looked inside. The interior was gloomy, heavily shadowed, but the man on the floor lay in the long slab of light
that entered through the opening. Bak had no doubt he was
dead. His throat had been cut, the wound deep and gaping.
His head and upper body lay in a pool of drying blood.
Smelling death, the horses had panicked.

"Karoya!" he called.

Taking care not to step in the reddish puddle, he knelt beside the body. The weapon was nowhere in sight, but it had
to have been fairly long and very sharp and the man who
wielded it strong.

Karoya pounded up the deck. He peeked inside, spat out a
curse, and tore several mats off the wall to allow more light

to fall on the scene. The body was that of a man of about forty years. His light brown hair was held back from his broad, clean-shaven face in a single thick braid that lay coiled in the blood. He wore a long-sleeved, knee-length tunic fastened at the shoulders with ornamental bronze pins. A gold signet ring adorned the middle finger of his right hand; he wore several plain gold bangles on his left wrist and an amuletic pendant around his neck.

"A man of Hatti," Bak said.

"Maruwa, he's called." Karoya swallowed hard, looked away from the body. He appeared close to being sick. "I should've guessed when I saw the horses that he'd come back to Kemet."

Bak pretended not to notice the younger officer's discomfort. "You know him?"

"I've seen him here at the harbor, but that's all. He came regularly—every six months or so—to bring animals from the land of Hatti to revitalize the bloodline in the royal stables."

The shadow of a man fell over the body. "What's going on here?" he demanded. "That's Maruwa! What's happened? Where are his horses? Where are the sailors I left on guard?"

Karoya caught the man's arm and forced him back, away from the deckhouse. "This is Captain Antef, sir. Master of this ship." He stared hard at the seaman. "Where have you been, sir? Where are all your men?"

The captain, a once-handsome man going to fat, stiffened his spine, pulled his head back, and stretched to his greatest height. "I did as I always do, as regulations require. I went to customs to report our arrival, to give them a copy of the manifest and arrange for an inspector to come aboard as quickly as possible." He glared at Bak. "Who are you? What's happened here? Did someone steal Maruwa's horses, slay him?"

By this time, the search party had realized something was

wrong other than a snake and they, too, had come to the deckhouse.

"Where are the members of your crew?" Bak asked the captain.

"Why should I tell you? I don't know you. As far as I know, you've no business here at all."

"Answer the question!" Karoya snapped.

Antef flung a resentful glance at the Medjay officer. "I left two men on guard and permitted the rest to leave the ship. I saw no reason for them to remain. Maruwa said he'd stay behind to look after his horses, and the rest of the cargo was of no exceptional value."

"When did you last see Maruwa?" Bak asked.

"I bade him good-bye as I left the ship. He was on deck, tending the animals."

"How long ago was that?"

"Two hours at most. Probably less."

"The men told us they were struck from behind and that's the last they remember," Bak said. "They had no idea how long ago, but sailors on a nearby ship last noticed them and Maruwa about a half hour before the horses began to fret."

Mai, the harbormaster, paced the length of his second-story office and back again to stand before the broad opening in the wall that looked out upon the harbor. He stared at the ships and the people wandering through the market, but the grim expression on his face told the men who stood before him that his thoughts were with the dead man. "The reason for the slaying could not have been a theft gone wrong?"

Karoya shook his head. "The most valuable of the cargo, the horses, were there, and according to Captain Antef . . ." The young officer glanced at the ship's master, standing between him and Bak. ". . . Maruwa was wearing the only jew-

elry he brought on board. All the pieces were made of gold.
A thief could've taken them with ease."

"But did not." The harbormaster was a tall, stout man with
a fringe of curly white hair. Lines of worry cut deep into his
brow. "Nothing else was disturbed?"

"I saw no sign that the cargo had been rifled by men in
pursuit of wealth that wasn't there," Antef said.

Mai gave the captain a thoughtful look. "I've never known
you to transport cargo that didn't pay for itself."

Antef stiffened, indignant. "Belowdecks, we carried copper ingots and stone ballast. On deck we carried grain, hay,
and straw for the horses in addition to leather goods and
woolen textiles popular with the people who come from less
temperate lands to dwell in Kemet. All of sufficient worth to
give a profit, none valuable enough to kill for."

Mai dropped onto a low chair placed so he could keep an
eye on the harbor and at the same time look at the men with
whom he spoke. "If not theft, then why mark Maruwa for
death? He was as diligent and industrious as any man I've
ever met."

"Politics." Antef's response was prompt and certain. "He
may've gotten himself involved in Hittite politics, and we all
know how dangerous that can be."

"Antef could well be right." Mai took a deep drink of beer
and set the jar on a low table beside his chair. "Hittite politics are like quicksand: deceptively placid when left untouched, but slippery, avaricious, and deadly when trod
upon."

Bak, seated on a stool before the harbormaster, whom he
had met some weeks earlier, sipped from his own jar of beer.
He licked the thick, slightly gritty foam from his lips. "Did
you know him well, sir?"

"Evidently not as well as I believed." Mai, who had
thrown aside formality after Antef had gone, grinned like a
boy caught with his fingers in a honey jar. "He discovered I

like olives, the ripe black ones cured in brine. Each time he imported horses, he brought several jars to me." He reached for his beer jar, hesitated. "You didn't happen to find any on board, did you?"

"No, sir," Karoya said, with a hint of a smile. He occupied a stool beside Bak. "I'll have my men look. If they see them, we'll bring them to you."

"I'd be most appreciative." Mai drank again and rested the jar between his thighs, all hint of humor vanishing. "I thought Maruwa unconcerned with the politics of his homeland, but perhaps I erred."

"He never spoke of such things?" Bak asked.

"Never." Mai looked out at the harbor, his expression sad. "I've heard from other men who've traveled to that far-off land that its politics are always volatile, with bad blood among various factions, some loyal to the past king, some to the present king, and some agitating for a new king. As a result, few men hold the throne for long, and when they're unseated, all who share their power are also deposed." He laughed harshly. "If they're lucky. Many are slain and their families with them, so they say."

Karoya shuddered. "A cruel, harsh land, sir."

A long silence ensued while the three men thanked the gods that they lived in a land where murder was an offense to the lady Maat and, while not unheard of at the highest levels of power, was not as common as in less enlightened lands.

"The horses will have to be moved from the garrison to the royal stables," Bak said. "I'll speak with Troop Captain Nebwa, and he'll see the task completed."

"Good," Mai said, nodding approval. His eyes darted toward Karoya. "Maruwa was slain here at the harbor, Lieutenant, so his death falls under your jurisdiction. You must do all you can to snare the slayer."

"I'll do my best, sir."

The harbormaster's eyes slid toward Bak. "How long will you remain in Waset, Lieutenant?"

"We'll not sail until the Opet festival ends."

"I know I've no business to ask before gaining the approval of your commandant, but would you be willing to assist Karoya, should he need your help?"

"I'd be glad to, sir."

Later, as Bak walked along the waterfront after bidding good-bye to Mai and Karoya, he admitted to himself how disappointed he was that another man held the responsibility for tracking down and snaring the one who had slain the Hittite merchant. He knew he would be at a disadvantage in searching for a killer in an alien community in a city he no longer knew well, but the challenge tempted.

Chapter Two

The processional way was lined with men, women and children who had come from near and far to participate in the Beautiful Feast of Opet. This, the grandest of the many festivals held throughout the year, celebrated their dual sovereigns' renewal as the divine offspring of the lord Amon. They were awaiting the initial procession of the festival, soon to make its way from Ipet-isut, the great northern mansion of the lord Amon, to the smaller southern mansion of Ipet-resyt. The long parade of gods, royalty, priests, and dignitaries offered the best opportunity through the eleven-day festival not only of adoring at close hand the lord Amon, his spouse the lady Mut, and their son the lord Khonsu, but of seeing the most lofty individuals in the land of Kemet.

The muted sounds of night had been torn asunder by the marching of the soldiers who had appeared at daybreak to spread out along the route. The soft sporadic laughter of a few half-awake individuals seeking the ideal spot from which to view the procession had become a roar of excitement. Now, as the lord Khepre, the rising sun, attained his second hour in the morning sky, the few had swelled to many. The multitude of people jostled for position along the broad, slightly raised causeway, which was paved with crushed white limestone. Clad in all their finery, whether the rough linen of the poor or the most delicate of fabrics worn by the nobility, and wearing their most elegant jewelry, they

21

stood shoulder to shoulder, all equally intent on sharing this most wondrous of occasions with the greatest of gods, his divine spouse and son and his two earthly children.

Acrobats and musicians performed, entertainers sang and danced, among temporary booths erected along the processional way on ground still damp from the ebbing flood. Hawkers walked back and forth, calling out their wares: dried meat and fish, fruits and vegetables, sweet cakes, beer and water, perfumes, oil for rubbing on the skin, flowers for the hair or to throw in the path of the gods, trinkets to remember the day, and amulets for protection. The smells of cooked meats, perfumes and flowers, and fresh bread vied with the odor of manure dropped by chariot horses held by grooms in a nearby palm grove, awaiting the time when, led by their noble masters, they would join the procession. While soldiers held the crowd off the causeway, police walked among the spectators, searching out thieves and troublemakers, returning lost children to their parents, hauling off beggars and men besotted by too much beer.

The hot breath of the lord Khepre and the receding floodwaters, which lingered in immense low-lying natural basins all across the valley floor, filled the air with an uncomfortable heat and dampness. Not the slightest breeze stirred. Sweat collected beneath broad collars and belts, wilted the ringlets on wigs and naturally curled hair, and made unsightly splotches on dresses and kilts. Hawkers gained more in a day than in a month, trading sweet-smelling flowers and perfume to overpower the stench of sweat, water and beer to ward off thirst.

The mood of the spectators was light, forgiving, expectant. All looked forward, each in his own way, to eleven days of piety and merrymaking.

"Lieutenant Bak." Amonked, Storekeeper of Amon and cousin to Maatkare Hatshepsut, laid a congenial hand on Bak's shoulder and looked with approval at the company of Medjays standing beside the barque sanctuary of the lord

Amon. "You've a fine-looking unit of men, a credit to the land of Kemet."

Bak smiled with pleasure. "I wish to thank you, sir, for arranging for us to participate in today's activities. Never would I have expected such a splendid position along the processional way."

The sanctuary, raised on a platform above the earth on which it sat, was long and narrow. A square-pillared portico open on three sides stood in front of a small enclosed chapel. When the procession reached this point, the barque of the lord Amon would be placed upon the stone plinth inside the portico, where it would be visible to all who stood nearby. This was the first of eight similar way stations where the divine triad would rest on their daylong journey from Ipet-isut to Ipet-resyt.

The Medjays, though relaxed while they awaited their gods, stood tall and straight and proud. They wore their best white kilts and held black cowhide shields so well brushed they glistened. Spearpoints, the bronze pendants hanging from their necks, the wide bronze bands that formed their armlets and anklets were polished to a high sheen.

Amonked gave an unassuming smile. "If a man has a bit of influence and can use it for a good cause, why shouldn't he?"

He was rather plump, of medium height, and his age somewhere in the mid-thirties, but he looked older. He wore an ankle-length kilt made of fine linen, an elegant broad beaded collar, and matching bracelets. The short wig covering his thinning hair gleamed in the sunlight, testifying to the fact that it was made of real human hair.

"Shouldn't you be in the mansion of the lord Amon, sir?" asked Sergeant Pashenuro. "Are you not to be a part of the procession?" The short, broad sergeant, second among the Medjays to Imsiba, had come to know Amonked several months earlier.

"I'm on my way to Ipet-isut now, but I'm in no hurry. I'm not serving as a priest this season, so I can't go into the inner

chambers, nor can I help carry one of the gods' barques."
Amonked took a square of linen from his belt and patted
away beads of sweat on his face, taking care to avoid the
black galena painted around his eyes. "I saw no reason to
stand in the outer court for an hour or more, waiting, while
our sovereigns make offerings and pledge obeisance to their
godly father."

Bak offered a silent prayer of thanks to the lord Amon
that, even on an occasion as important as this, ordinary soldiers and police were not expected to wear wigs and large
amounts of jewelry. The heat was close to intolerable and
would worsen as the day went on. "Must you join the procession as it leaves Ipet-isut? Can you not wait here and join
your lofty peers when they reach this sanctuary?"

Amonked smiled. "A most thoughtful suggestion, Lieutenant, one I accept with gratitude."

Bak exchanged a glance with Pashenuro, who hurried behind the sanctuary and returned with a folding camp stool,
one of several brought for use by Maatkare Hatshepsut,
Menkheperre Thutmose, and the senior priests while the
deities rested.

Ignoring the curious glances of the spectators standing on
the opposite side of the processional way, Amonked settled
himself on the stool. After inquiring about Bak's father, a
physician who dwelt across the river in western Waset, he
talked of the southern frontier and the fortresses along the
Belly of Stones, of the people he had met several months
earlier. He played no favorites, speaking with officer, sergeants, and ordinary policemen with identical good humor
and respect.

When the gossip faltered, Bak asked, "Have you heard
anything of Maruwa, the man we found slain at the harbor
last week?" He knew Amonked would have no official reason
to be involved, but he also knew the Storekeeper of Amon
was one of the best-informed men in the southern capital.

"Nothing." Amonked lifted the edge of his wig and ran

the square of linen beneath it. "According to the harbormaster, Lieutenant Karoya has diligently questioned every man on Captain Antef's ship and anyone else he could find who might've seen or heard anything out of order. Either all who were near the vessel were blind and deaf, or the slayer took care not to be noticed."

"The more time Karoya allows to go by, the less likely he is to snare the wretched criminal."

"Evidently he's well aware of the truism."

Bak smiled at the gentle reminder that he had verged on pedantry. "He may already be too late. If the slayer is a man of Hatti, he may well be on his way to his homeland."

"Karoya shares your fear. He claims never to have reached so dead a dead end so early in an investigation."

"He believes, then, that Maruwa was slain for a political reason?"

"So far he's found no sign that the merchant was the least bit interested in politics. But he wouldn't, would he, if Maruwa was some kind of spy?"

Bak's eyes narrowed. "Spy? Where did that idea come from?"

Amonked shrugged. "I'm not sure. Karoya perhaps?"

"I doubt he's the kind of man to garb another man in bright, sensational colors without due consideration—or some kind of proof. I admit I don't know him well, but he seemed far too cautious, too sensible. As is Mai. No, I'd look somewhere else for the source of that tale."

The sharp blast of a distant trumpet pierced the air, announcing the lord Amon's departure from his earthly home. All eyes turned north toward Ipet-isut, and the many voices grew quiet, anticipatory. Movement could be seen at the large, south-facing pylon gate being built by Maatkare Hatshepsut into the tall, crenellated wall that surrounded the sacred precinct. About half completed, the two towers rose slightly above the lintel recently placed over the doorway. The facades of both towers were hidden behind long, broad

ramps made of mudbricks and debris up which materials
were transported.

Bak spotted the glint of gold and the white kilts of several
men exiting the distant gate, holding high the royal standards. Musicians followed, the beat of their drums and the
harsher sounds of sistra and metal clappers setting the slow,
measured pace of the procession. A dozen or more priests
came next, some perfuming the air with incense while the
rest purified the way with water or milk. A breath of air
stirred the long red pennants mounted atop tall flagpoles
clamped to the front of Ipet-isut's entrance pylon, much of
which was concealed behind the enclosure wall. The hush
broke and voices rose in expectation.

Maatkare Hatshepsut and Menkheperre Thutmose walked
through the gate side by side. Bak noted the glitter of sunlight on gold, garments as white as a heron. Priests sprinkled
aromatic oils on the path before them, while honored servants waved ostrich-feather fans over their heads. The crowd
went wild, cheering the royal couple whose task it was to
stave off chaos and preserve the stability of the land.

"Ah, yes." Amonked sighed. "Now the long day has truly
begun."

The music grew louder, fueling the spectators' excitement. A dozen priests followed their sovereigns, golden cen-
sors glittering through clouds of incense, crystal drops of
water flung from shining lustration vessels to purify the
earth over which the greatest of the gods would be carried.

The lord Amon appeared in the gateway, enclosed within
his golden shrine, which stood on a golden barque carried
high on the shoulders of priests. The long arms of the lord
Re reached out, touching the shrine, blinding the eyes of all
who glimpsed its far-off radiance.

The procession slowly approached the sanctuary.
Amonked rose to his feet and, taking the stool with him,
stepped off to the side, out of the way. Bak ordered his men

to stand at rigid attention, checked to be sure all was as it should be, and pivoted to face the processional way, standing as stiff and straight as they.

Following the standard-bearers, the musicians, the priests, Maatkare Hatshepsut and Menkheperre Thutmose walked up the processional way in all their regal majesty. The regent who had made herself a sovereign wore a long white shift, multicolored broad collar and bracelets, and a tall white cone-shaped crown with plumes rising to either side above horizontal ram's horns and the sacred cobra over her brow. She carried the crook and the flail in one hand, the sign of life in the other. She looked neither to right nor left. Too far away to see well, Bak imagined her face set, an emotionless mask.

Beside her, walking with a youthful spring in his step, was Menkheperre Thutmose. The young man wore the short kilt of a soldier, which displayed to perfection the hard muscles of his well-formed body. His jewelry was similar to that of his co-ruler. He wore a blue flanged helmetlike crown adorned with gold disks. The royal cobra rose over his brow, and he carried the crook and the flail and the sign of life. Bak imagined eyes that never rested; a young Horus, very much aware of his surroundings.

Behind the priests who followed, and wreathed in a thin cloud of incense, came the golden barque of the lord Amon, balanced on long gilded poles carried high on the shoulders of twenty priests, ten to a side. A senior priest walked before the vessel and another followed behind. Golden rams' heads, crowned with golden orbs and wearing the royal cobra on their brows, were mounted on stern and prow, with elaborate multicolored broad collars and pectorals hanging from their necks. A gilded shrine stood on the barque, its sides open to reveal a second, smaller shrine mounted on a dais. This contained the lord Amon, shielded from view within its golden walls.

Spectators shouted for joy and threw flowers, showering the causeway with color and scent. Bak felt a tightness in his throat, the same awe he had felt as a child when his father had brought him to a long-ago procession, holding him high on his shoulders so he could see his sovereign and his god.

Farther along the processional way were more priests with censers and lustration vessels, followed by the gilded barques of the lady Mut and the lord Khonsu, both smaller than the barque of the lord Amon, but impressive nonetheless.

Musicians followed the magnificent glittering vessels, playing drums, clappers, sistra, and lutes. Singers clapped their hands and chanted. Dancers and acrobats, their gestures often much alike, swirled around, turned somersaults, arched their backs to touch the path behind them.

The standard-bearers—noblemen chosen especially for the task—approached the sanctuary. Bak raised his baton of office in salute and heard the soft rustle of movement indicating the Medjays behind him were shifting into a fighting stance, right leg forward, shields in front of their chests, spears tilted forward at a diagonal.

"Sir!" Bak heard off to his side where Amonked stood. "A priest has been found dead inside the sacred precinct. Murdered. Will you come, sir?" Bak looked half around and saw the messenger, a youth of twelve or so years, glance at the procession. "If you can," he added in a thin, hesitant voice.

Amonked looked appalled. "Not inside the god's mansion, I pray!"

"Oh, no, sir. In a storehouse." Looking apologetic, the boy added, "I tried first to find User, Overseer of Overseers of all the storehouses, but I had no luck. When I saw you and you weren't in the procession . . . Well, I thought . . ."

Amonked glanced toward his royal cousin, uncertainty on his face. The musicians were turning toward the sanctuary, followed by priests preparing to usher the two sovereigns and the lord Amon to their first place of rest. His mouth tightened in a decisive manner and he waved off the youth's bumbling words. "Very well." He turned to Bak. "You must come with me, Lieutenant."

"Sir?" Bak eyed Maatkare Hatshepsut and Menkheperre Thutmose walking in lofty splendor not twenty paces away. "What of your cousin? Will she not miss you?"

Amonked flung another quick glance her way. "With luck and the help of the gods, we'll find that the dead man was truly murdered and of sufficient importance to warrant our leaving."

Bak stepped aside, beckoned Imsiba to stand in his place, and hurried after Amonked and the messenger. He might never get another chance to stand before his men on so auspicious an occasion, and was sorry he had to leave. He would have to be content with catching up with the procession later, hopefully in time to watch the dual rulers make offerings to the gods before they entered the southern mansion of Ipet-resyt.

They hastened northward, passing behind the almost deserted booths and the crowds watching the procession with much oohing and ahing, clapping and shouting. Nearing the unfinished gate out of which the procession was filing, the boy led them down a lane between the westernmost construction ramp and a residential sector off to the left, avoiding the building materials piled well out of the way of paraders and celebrants. They turned to hurry along the base of the massive mudbrick wall that enclosed the sacred precinct of the lord Amon, passing its alternating concave and convex sections, gradually leaving behind the shouts of rejoicing.

"Through here, sir," the boy said, turning into a small, unimposing doorway.

They stumbled along a dark passage that took them through the thick wall. Beyond, bathed in sunlight, lay the sacred precinct, an expanse of white-plastered buildings. Crowded around Ipet-isut, which was painted white with brightly colored inscriptions and decoration, were shrines and chapels, housing, office buildings, and row upon row of storehouses. Unlike the great warehouses built outside the enclosure walls and closer to the river, most of which contained bulk items such as grain, hides, and copper ingots, too heavy and ungainly to carry far, these held smaller items of higher value.

The youth ushered them down a lane between two rows of long, narrow, interconnected mudbrick buildings whose elongated barrel-vaulted roofs formed a series of adjoining ridges. Doors, most closed and sealed but a few standing open, faced each other all along the lane. Near the far end, a dozen men hovered around the open portal of a storehouse in the storage block to the right. Included among them were shaven-headed priests, scribes wearing long kilts, and three guards carrying shiclds and spears. A guard spotted them, and they pulled back from the door, making way for the new arrivals. Drawing near, Bak noticed the smell of burning and saw smudges of soot on most of the men.

Amonked's eyes darted around the group. "A man is dead, the boy told us. Murdered."

All eyes turned toward a priest, a tall, fine-boned man no more than twenty years of age. His kilt was as dirty as all the rest. Clearly distraught, he clutched the bright blue faience amulet of a seated baboon, the lord Thoth, hanging from a chain around his neck and rubbed it between his thumb and forefinger.

"Yes, sir. Of that there's no doubt." He gulped air and clung to the amulet as if to life itself. "I was finishing a task before going out to watch the procession. I smelled smoke and came to look. When I opened the door, I saw him lying on the floor, the flames around him."

"The rest of you came to put out the fire?" Bak asked.

"We all had a hand in it, yes." One of the guards, an older man, pointed at the young priest. "Meryamon called for help and we came running. Thanks to the lord Amon, it hadn't yet gotten out of control and was confined to the one small room. On the floor mostly, burning some scrolls and . . ." The words tailed off and he licked his lips, uneasy with the memory. "We dared not let it reach the roof for fear it would spread to the adjoining storage magazines. We keep aromatic oils in this block and if they were to catch fire . . ." He had no need to explain further. A major conflagration might have resulted, sweeping through, at the very least, this sector of the sacred precinct.

"You did well," Amonked said, letting his gaze touch every man among them. "You're to be commended for such swift action."

Bak peered through the door. A small room had been walled off from the rest of the storehouse. Illuminated only by the natural light falling through the door, it was too dark to see well. The body lay in shadow, the floor around it cluttered with charred papyrus scrolls and the reddish shards of broken pottery storage jars. The dead man's clothing was wet, as were the documents lying in the puddle around him. The smell was stronger here.

"We need light," he said, "a torch."

The boy sped down the lane and vanished. In no time at all, he hurried back with a short-handled torch, its flame irregular but free of smoke.

Bak took the light and stepped into the room. He tried not to breathe, but the stench of blood, fire, body waste, burned oil, and charred flesh caught in his throat. As accustomed as he was to death, he felt ill. Swallowing bile, hardening his heart, he walked deeper inside. Careful not to disturb anything on the floor, he knelt beside the dead man. Amonked entered the room, gasped.

The body was that of a sharp-faced man of about thirty-five years, small and wiry. The fire, which had burned many of the scrolls lying around him, had consumed one side of his kilt and had darkened and blistered the right side of his body. A blackened oil lamp, a possible source of the fire, lay broken at his feet. His throat had been cut, the gaping wound dark and ugly. The pool of blood around his head and shoulders had been diluted by water, making it difficult to tell ex-

actly how much the man had lost, but quite a lot. Bak
guessed he had been lifeless when the fire started. He prayed
such had been the case.

"Do you know him?" he asked Amonked.

"Woserhet." Amonked cleared his throat, swallowed. "He
was a ranking scribe, but was to serve throughout the Opet
festival as a priest. He'd been given the responsibility for
this year's reversion of offerings."

The daily ceremony was one in which food offerings were
distributed as extra rations to personnel who toiled in the
god's mansion and to others who petitioned for a share. Why
would a man who held such an important but transitory and
innocuous task be slain?

"I'd guess the slayer stood behind him, reached around
him knife in hand, and slashed his throat with a single deep
and firm stroke." With an absentminded smile, Bak accepted
a jar of beer from the boy who had brought them from the
barque sanctuary over an hour earlier. "He was slain in much
the same way as the Hittite merchant we found dead last
week."

The boy, wide-eyed with curiosity and thrilled at being allowed to help, handed a jar to Amonked and another to
Meryamon. Taking the remaining jar for himself, he plopped
down on the hard-packed earthen floor of the portico that
shaded three sides of the open courtyard. After the dead man
had been carried off to the house of death, he had brought
them to this peaceful haven in one of several buildings that
housed the offices of the priests and scribes responsible for
the storehouses.

"You believe Maruwa and Woserhet were slain by the
same man?" Frowning his disbelief, Amonked pushed a low
stool into the shade and dropped onto it. "What would they
have in common?"

"Both men's lives were taken in a similar manner, that's
all I'm saying." Bak gave the Storekeeper of Amon a fleeting

smile. "To tie the two together would be stretching credibility. Unless there was a link between them that we know nothing about."

"One man was burned and the other wasn't," Amonked pointed out. "Would not that suggest two different slayers?"

"Probably." Bak rested a shoulder against a wooden column carved to resemble a tied bundle of papyri. "What task do you have, Meryamon, that delayed you in leaving the sacred precinct?"

The young priest sat on the ground near Amonked. His eyes darted frequently toward the portal and the men hurrying along the lane outside on their way to the gate, eager to watch the procession. Whether intentional or not, his desire to follow was apparent. "I distribute to the officiating priests items used in the sacred rituals: censers, lustration vessels, aromatic oils and incense, and whatever else they need." Pride blossomed on his face. "I perform the task throughout the Beautiful Feast of Opet, yes, but also for the regular daily rituals and the various other festivals."

"A position of responsibility," Amonked said.

Meryamon flashed a smile. "I daily thank the lord Thoth that I was diligent in my studies and learned to read and write with ease and at a young age." Thoth was the patron god of scribes.

The leaves rustled in the tall sycamore tree in the center of the court, and Bak spotted a small gray monkey swinging through the upper branches. "So you're not a man who serves the lord Amon periodically. You earn your bread within the sacred precinct."

"Yes, sir. And I dwell here as well. I share quarters with several other priests who, like me, have yet to take a spouse."

Bak glanced at Amonked, thinking to defer to him, but the Storekeeper of Amon urged him to continue with a nod of the head. "Tell me of the men who helped put out the fire. Why did they remain behind?"

"Most were passersby, heading out to watch the procession. The three guards, I assume, were ordered to stay, to keep an eye on the gates and patrol this sector of the sacred precinct." Meryamon smiled ruefully. "Bad luck for them, having to stay while their mates were given leave to play."

Bak felt as if he were fishing in a muddy backwater, poking his harpoon at random in a place he couldn't see. "The room where Woserhet was found. What was its purpose?"

"It's a records storage room, sir, a place where we keep scrolls on which are recorded activities conducted in that particular block of storage magazines. Each object is tracked from delivery to disposal. Like other men with similar tasks, I make a note of each and every object I remove and return, and many of my own transactions are stored there." A shadow passed across the priest's face. "Or were."

"The room received a moderate amount of damage, but a considerable number of scrolls lay on the floor. Do you have any idea how many records might've been lost?"

"I noticed a number of empty spaces—fifteen or twenty, I'd guess—on the shelves along the walls and quite a few broken storage pots on the floor. So many jars would've contained a significant number of scrolls, but the vast majority, I thank the lord Amon, were saved."

Amonked broke his silence. "How well did you know Woserhet, Meryamon?"

"Not at all, sir. I've seen him now and again and I knew his name, but I didn't know he was responsible for the reversion of offerings."

Amonked looked skeptical. "Are you not the man who'll supply ritual implements and incense to that ceremony?"

"Yes, sir," Meryamon said, looking uncomfortable, "but I must deal with Ptahmes, the chief priest's aide, not the man who performs the ritual. I had no need to know who he was."

"There goes a singularly uninquisitive man," Amonked said later as they watched the priest hurry away.

*   *   *

Bak and Amonked strolled into the lovely limestone court in front of the imposing pylon gate that rose before the mansion of the lord Amon. The last of the procession had moved on, leaving the enclosure empty and quiet. The banners fluttered lazily atop the tall flagpoles clamped to the front of the pylon. Birds twittered in a clump of trees outside the court, and a yellow kitten chased a leaf blown over the wall by the breeze. A faint floral aroma rose from a slick of oil someone had spilled on the floor.

Built fifteen or so years earlier by Akheperenre Thutmose, Maatkare Hatshepsut's deceased spouse and Menkheperre Thutmose's father, the court contained two small limestone chapels. In each, a central stone base supported a statue of the lord Min, a fertility god identified closely with the lord Amon. One structure was of an ancient date, built many generations ago by Kheperkare Senwosret, and the other more recent, erected just fifty years earlier by Djeserkare Amonhotep, grandfather to Maatkare Hatshepsut.

"Were the scrolls set on fire deliberately to burn the body?" Bak asked, thinking aloud, "or to get rid of information the slayer wished to destroy? Or did the slayer—or Woserhet himself—accidentally tip over an oil lamp and set them on fire?" He did not expect an answer and he got none.

"Woserhet was a senior scribe who reported directly to the chief priest." Amonked's face was grave. "I never met the man, merely saw him several times at a distance, but according to Hapuseneb, the chief priest, he was extremely competent and adept at dealing with difficult situations."

"Not adept enough, it seems."

Ignoring the mild sarcasm, Amonked rested his backside against the balustrade wall that rose up the outer edge of a broad but shallow stairway giving access to the older of the two chapels. "I fear I wasn't entirely forthright when I stopped to chat with you earlier today. I'd received a disturbing message from Woserhet and thought to have you go with me when I met him. Unfortunately, with the procession up-

permost in my thoughts—and in everyone else's, I assumed—I saw no need for haste."

Bak gave him a sharp look. "You'd never met him and yet
he wrote to you?"

"Hapuseneb must shoulder many tasks through the length
of the Beautiful Feast of Opet. As a result, he'll be unavail-
able much of the time. He told me he'd given Woserhet a
special assignment and asked me to be available should he
need me. He said Woserhet would explain if necessary."
Amonked glanced at the kitten, his expression troubled. "I
agreed and thought no more of it. Much to my regret now
that we've found him dead."

Bak leaned against the low outer wall of the beautifully
symmetrical building, indifferent to its rich reliefs of the ancient king and the lord Min. The colors, though no longer as
vibrant as they once had been, were still lively enough to
please the eye and lighten the heart of a man far less preoc-
cupied than he. "Can you tell me what the message said?"

Amonked released a long, unhappy sigh. "It was short and
direct, and I fear it deepens the mystery surrounding his
death. He said he'd learned something quite shocking and
requested a private meeting before nightfall this day."

"That's all?"

"Yes." Amonked stood erect and signaled that they must
leave. "I feel I've let Hapuseneb down, and I don't like to
think of myself as a man who fails to live up to his promises." He paused, obviously reluctant to speak out. "I hesi-
tate to ask you, as you must be looking forward to the
festival as much as everyone else. But I wish you to discover
what the message refers to and to snare Woserhet's slayer.
Hopefully before the end of the festival when the lord Amon
returns to Ipet-isut and you must travel on to Mennufer."

Chapter Three

"Like the priest said, most were headed out of the sacred precinct. They were all in a hurry; didn't want to miss the start of the procession." The older guard, Tetynefer, glanced at his two companions, who nodded agreement. "Like us, they heard him yell and came running. None of us wasted any time talking. That fire had to be put out."

"The well is close, I see." Bak looked over the waist-high wall that protected the broad, round mouth of the well. Inside, a spiraling stairway led down to a platform that encircled the top of a narrower shaft up which water was drawn. "Still, it takes a lot of water to put out a fire—and it must be delivered fast."

"You see the problem," Tetynefer said, eyeing the officer with respect. "Water alone would never have done the task."

A tall, sturdy young guard whose accent marked him as a man of the north grinned. "Tetynefer sent me off in search of something to smother it. The lord Amon smiled on me, and right away I found a heavy woolen cloak."

"I led the rest off to the well." Tetynefer looked upon the young man with considerable pride. "By the time I got back with a jar of water, he'd shoved well out of the way all the scrolls that weren't burning and had quenched the fire licking the ends of others." He motioned toward the young man's sandals, which were black and charred. An angry red burn ran up the side of his right ankle. "Look at his feet. No common sense at all but the courage of a lion."

Trying without success to look modest, the young guard said, "As soon as they brought the water, it was all over."

"We didn't get a good look at the dead man until the fire was out." The third guard, a shorter and stouter man, stood his shield against the wall and knelt beside it. "We saw the wound in his neck and sent the boy for the Overseer of Overseers. Instead he brought you and the Storekeeper of Amon."

Bak turned away from the well and sat on a mudbrick bench shaded by a half-dozen date palms. Fronds rustled above his head, stirred by the light breeze, and the sweet song of a hoopoe filled the air.

"Since most men would give their best kilts to see the procession, I assume you were ordered to stay," he said.

"Yes, sir." Tetynefer hunkered down in the scruffy grass in front of him. "I've seen enough processions to satisfy me through eternity, and these two," he nodded toward his companions, "grew to manhood in Waset. Our sergeant thought to give men new to the capital the opportunity to watch."

The sturdy guard looked up from the dirt in which he was drawing stick men. "He's vowed to assign us to the courtyard in front of Ipet-isut when the lord Amon returns from his southern mansion. We'll get to see him close up, closer than we ever would standing alongside the processional way. And the other gods and our sovereigns, too."

A fair exchange of duties, Bak agreed. "Amonked and I saw no sentry when we came through the gate, and unless I'm mistaken, no one's on duty there now. Aren't the gates guarded?"

"Yes, sir. At least in a manner of speaking." The tall guard leaned back against the wall of the well, raised his spear, and shoved it hard into the ground, making it stand erect. "Our task is to keep an eye on the gate and at the same time patrol the streets and lanes within this sector of the sacred precinct, making sure no one roams around who has no right to be here."

His shorter companion nodded. "With so many people come to Waset from afar, you never know who might allow his curiosity to lead him inside to explore."

"Or to take something of value," Tetynefer added.

Bak was not especially surprised at so casual an attitude toward guarding the sacred precinct. Few people would risk offending the greatest of the gods. "Did any of you happen to see Woserhet arrive?"

"I did," Tetynefer said. "He came from the north, as if from the god's mansion. I wouldn't have noticed him—there were too many others hustling and bustling around, performing tasks related to the festival—but he was so deep within his thoughts that he stumbled over a blind dog that lays in the lane every morning, warming his tired old bones. He felt so bad he gave me a food token, telling me to get meat for the cur. After that he went into the storage magazine where Meryamon found him."

"Did you go then to get the meat?" Bak asked.

"I didn't have time." Tetynefer's eyes narrowed, fearing Bak might be questioning his honesty rather than his whereabouts. "Never fear, sir. I'll not take food from a dog's mouth."

Bak reassured him with a smile. "The three of you never left this sector after Woserhet came?"

"No, sir," they said as one.

"After he entered the storehouse, how much time passed before Meryamon smelled smoke?"

"A half hour." Tetynefer's eyes darted toward the younger guards. "I told you right away about the token. Would a half hour be a fair guess?"

The stout one nodded; the other looked doubtful. "Closer to an hour, I'd say."

"Did you notice any strangers wandering around after he came?"

The three guards laughed.

"One man in three, maybe one in four, was a stranger," the

taller guard explained. "During this busy time, the regular priests need all the help they can get."

Bak listened to the chatter of birds in the otherwise silent sacred precinct and imagined how full of life it must have been so short a time ago. The mansion of the god and the many buildings crowded around it, literally a city within the city of Waset, had been alive with people and activity. Then almost everyone had gone, leaving the streets and lanes deserted, the buildings empty, the scrolls and sacred vessels abandoned. The slayer could have struck at any time, but the most opportune time would have been those last few confusing moments when everyone was preparing to leave, too busy to notice and too eager to get away.

"He's not dead! He can't be!"

"I'm sorry, mistress Ashayet, but you must believe me. His ka has flown to the netherworld." Of all Bak's many and varied duties as a police officer, the one he disliked the most was informing the family of a loved one's death.

The small, fragile woman knelt, wrapped her arms around the three young children clinging to her skirt, and hugged them close. "We're waiting for him. He'll come at any instant to take us to Ipet-resyt to see the end of the procession."

"Mistress Ashayet . . ."

She released the children, stepped back, and sent them toward the rear of the house with a fond slap on the oldest one's bare behind. She smiled brightly at Bak. "What can I be thinking, leaving you standing in the doorway like this? Come in, sir. You may as well await my husband in comfort."

Wishing he could flee, Bak followed her through the front room, which was cluttered with hay for the family donkey, large water and storage jars, spindles and an upright loom, and four ducks nesting in large flattish bowls. She led him into the next room, the primary family living space, whose high ceiling was supported by a single tall red pillar and pierced by windows that allowed inside a generous amount of light. A couple of stools, a woven reed chest, and a tiny table shared the space with the low mudbrick platform on which the family sat and the adults slept.

"Take my husband's stool, sir. Would you like a beer while you wait?"

"Mistress Ashayet." He caught her by the upper arms, making her face him. "I regret I must be so harsh, but you leave me no choice. Someone took your husband's life. He was slain early this morning. In a storehouse in the sacred precinct of the lord Amon."

"No!" Her eyes met his, a plea formed on her face. "No," she said again with less assurance, a faltering conviction.

"Your husband is dead, mistress." He held her tight, forcing her to give him her full attention. "You must believe me. You alone shoulder the responsibility for your household, your children. You must be strong for them."

A look of horror, of unimaginable pain fell over her face like a cloud. She jerked away, stumbled through the next room and into the kitchen, a small area lightly roofed with branches and straw, where she dropped to the hard-packed earthen floor and began to sob. The children gathered around her, lost and forlorn. Bak shifted a stool to a place where he could watch, making sure she did no harm to herself, and sat down to wait.

After what seemed to him an eternity and no doubt longer to a child, the youngest of the three, a girl less than two years of age, began to whimper. The oldest, a boy of no more than four years, looked hopefully at his mother. When she failed to notice, he went to the little girl, put his arms around her, and tried to soothe her. Left alone, the middle child, another boy, hurried to his mother and prodded her, trying to attract her attention.

She lifted her face from her hands, saw the youngsters' unhappiness and confusion. Gathering her courage, she wiped away the tears with the back of her hand and spoke to them in a soft and comforting voice. Not until they returned to their play did she give a long, ragged sigh and look at Bak. Rising from the floor, she plucked two beer jars from a basket, broke the plugs from both, and entered the room in which he sat.

"Who slew my husband?" she asked.

"We don't yet know." Bak saw anger forming, a substitute for sorrow. "I made a vow to Amonked, the Storekeeper of Amon, that I'd snare the vile criminal—and I will."

She handed a jar to him and sat on the platform. Her eyes were puffy and red, her face pale. Her expression grew hard and determined. "Woserhet was a good man, Lieutenant, a good father to our children. Whoever took his life must be made to pay with his own life."

"Do you know anyone who might've wished him dead?"

"I told you, he was a good man. He had no enemies."

Bak took a sip of beer, which was milder and smoother than most kitchen brews. The woman erred, thinking her husband had no foes. Woserhet's death had been no accident. "I've been told he reported directly to the chief priest. Can you tell me what his duties were?"

"He seldom spoke of his task. Each time he did, he had me vow that I'd not repeat his words. You must ask Hapuseneb."

"Hapuseneb is presently walking to Ipet-resyt in today's procession. He'll be leading rituals of one kind or another for the remainder of the day and for ten days more. As much as I'd like to speak with him, I can't."

She stared at her fingers, wound tightly around the beer jar.

"If I'm to find Woserhet's slayer, I must begin without delay. Not in eleven days' time."

"I promised . . ."

He leaned toward her, willing her to help. "Mistress Ashayet, your husband was responsible for the reversion of offerings for the Beautiful Feast of Opet. To be given so important a task, to dole out foodstuffs for such a momentous occasion, he must've held some position of responsibility."

The silence stretched, then suddenly, "He was an auditor."

"An auditor?" he echoed.

She nodded. "Hapuseneb, the chief priest, sent him to the lord Amon's storehouses here and throughout the land of Kemet. He gave him a scribe and four other men, all servants indentured to the god. His task and that of Tati, the scribe, was to make sure the records matched the stored items. The other four lifted and fetched, ran errands and, when the need arose, saw that no one impeded them while they went about their task."

Bak whistled softly. "A heavy responsibility." A task where a man might well make enemies.

"Yes, sir." She spoke so softly he could barely hear.

"His most recent audits have been conducted here, I gather, in the southern capital."

She nodded. "He's been in Waset for about a month. We were so happy to have him home." She swallowed hard, flashed a smile much too animated to be real.

"Had his behavior changed recently in any way? As if he might've quarreled with a priest or scribe who resented his intrusion? Or as if he'd come upon a dishonesty?"

"He's been troubled for the past few days, yes." She could not help but see the expectancy leaping into his heart. "He wouldn't speak of it, but he was distracted much of the time. When I tried to draw him out, he grew irritable. Impatient with the children. Quarrelsome even. He wasn't like that usually." She bit her lip, her voice trembled. "He was a good, kind man, Lieutenant. Decent. Who would want to slay him?"

Bak knew he must soon leave, allowing her the privacy to mourn. "Did he ever bring home any records?"

"No, sir." Tears spilled from her eyes. She hastily wiped them away and glanced around the room. "As you can see, we have little enough space. To add anything more would've made us too crowded by far."

"Where would he have kept them?"

"The chief priest assigned him a small building not far from the mansion of the lord Amon, somewhere outside the walls of the sacred precinct. Hapuseneb wished to separate him and his servants from all who might wish to influence them. Ptahmes, Hapuseneb's aide, can tell you how to find it."

"They've all gone, sir." The guard, a man of advanced years with a huge mane of white hair, looked at Bak as at a man befuddled. His task was to watch over the spacious building, built around the open courtyard in which they stood, where the chief priest and his staff carried out their administrative duties. "Surely you know that not a man within the sacred precinct would miss the procession if he didn't have to."

"I know that a large number of priests escort the lord Amon to his southern mansion," Bak said, smothering his irritation, "and I'm also aware that many men must stand well behind them, making sure they're properly cleansed, clothed, and equipped. I assume much of the preparation is done here, after which they're free to go."

"I fear, Lieutenant, that you suffer from the common illusion that priests are an idle lot. Most toil from dawn till dusk, their tasks never ending."

The old man was so haughty Bak wondered if he had been a priest. "What of Ptahmes? Is he equally industrious or might I find him watching the procession?"

The guard pursed his lips in disapproval. "He certainly can't speak with you today. He's at Ipet-resyt, preparing for the lord Amon's arrival and the rituals that will be conducted through the next ten days."

Bak gave up. With no one available to help, he had no choice but to forget the dead man for the remainder of the day and give himself over to the festivities.

Bak stood on the processional way in front of the barque sanctuary where last he had seen his Medjays. As expected, the structure was empty, his men gone. Gods and royalty had long ago marched on, accompanied by the priests and dignitaries, the dancers and acrobats and singers. The spectators had drifted away, many following their sovereigns and gods to Ipet-resyt. Those few satisfied they had seen enough were making their way home, while a large number had gone off in search of beer and a good time. The booths had been dismantled to be carried farther along the route and set up again. The soldiers had broken ranks to join the rest in whatever endeavor most appealed to them.

He had forgotten how utterly deserted the processional way could be after everyone moved on. Sparrows twittered undisturbed in a sycamore whose limbs brushed the sanctuary. Leaves rustled along the crushed limestone path, blown by the desultory breeze. Crows marched across trampled grasses and weeds, searching for bits of food dropped and forgotten. A dog gnawing a bone growled each time one of the large black and gray birds came close, threatening to steal his prize.

Bak glanced at the lord Re, already three-quarters of the way across the vault of heaven. No wonder he was hungry. The food vendors would, by this time, have all moved to the far end of the processional way, near Ipet-resyt. More than a quarter hour's fast walk.

He hastened southward. At first he had the path to himself, but the farther he strode, the more people he came upon. Many walked toward Ipet-resyt, while a few strode in the opposite direction. Some in a rush and others ambling along as if they had all the time in the world. People alone or in groups, chatting and laughing. Persons with the serious demeanors of the awe-struck or devout. Revelers who had watched the sacred barques and their sovereigns pass by and now saw fit to make merry. The few remaining police and soldiers turned a blind eye to all but the worst offenses.

About halfway between Ipet-isut and Ipet-resyt, Bak spotted two familiar figures approaching from the south: his scribe Hori and Kasaya, the youngest of his Medjays. He waved. Smiling with pleasure, they hastened to meet him.

"What are you two doing here?" he asked. "Have you grown weary of the pageantry?"

"We were looking for you, sir," Hori said, falling in beside him. Delighted with the festival, the chubby young scribe practically skipped along the path.

"Where are the rest of our men?"

Kasaya took his place on Bak's opposite side and they strode southward. "As soon as the procession was well away from the first barque sanctuary, Imsiba went off with his wife, leaving Pashenuro in command." The tall, hulking young Medjay shifted his shield to a more comfortable position and slung his spear over his shoulder in a very unsoldierly fashion. "He suggested we all stay together and keep up with the procession. So we did, hoping you'd rejoin us."

"When the lord Amon rested at the fourth barque sanctuary, we saw Amonked slip in among the noblemen, but you weren't with him." Hori eyed a pretty young woman standing in the shade of a sycamore with what had to be her parents and siblings. "For the longest time, he was surrounded by people of wealth and position, and we couldn't get near him."

The young Medjay noticed Hori's wandering attention and winked at Bak. "At the seventh barque sanctuary, Pashenuro finally managed to speak with him. To ask him where you were."

The girl turned her head to look at the three of them and Hori glanced quickly away, his face flaming. "He told us of the dead man and said you'd stayed behind to investigate. We could probably find you in the sacred precinct."

"So we decided to look," Kasaya said.

Half facing Bak, the scribe danced sideways up the processional way, his feet scuffling the limestone chips, the girl forgotten. "Will you tell us about the dead man, sir? Who was he? What was he doing in the sacred precinct? Was he . . . ?"

Laughing, Bak raised a hand for silence. While he spoke of all he had seen and heard, they hurried on. The crowds walking along with them grew thicker, the talking and laughter louder, more anticipatory. Seldom did anyone have the opportunity to see their sovereigns down on their knees before the lord Amon, adoring the deity with incense and food offerings. But here and now, at the beginning of the Beautiful Feast of Opet, all who could get close enough could witness their rulers' public subjugation to their divine father.

Bak vividly remembered the first time he had seen the offering ritual, the disappointment he had felt. The festival had been much less grand during the reign of Akheperenre Thutmose, the ritual not so formalized. Bak had been a child of ten or so years, grown too large to sit on his father's shoulders. The older man had knelt so his son could stand on his knee and look around the heads of the multitudes. The lord Amon had been concealed within his golden shrine, their sovereign kneeling, hidden by the crowd. He had seen nothing.

"Who do you think slew him, sir?" Hori asked.

Kasaya laughed. "How would Lieutenant Bak know that? He hasn't met anyone worthy of suspicion."

"He met Woserhet's wife."

"Why would she slay him in the sacred precinct when she could much easier have slain him at home?"

Bak spotted Meryamon ahead, standing in the shade of a grove of date palms that towered over the sixth barque sanctuary. The young priest was looking one way and then another, studying the people walking along the processional way, and peering down the lanes that ended near the sanctuary. He had been in such a hurry to leave the sacred precinct, yet here he was, apparently waiting for someone. A woman perhaps?

Hori flung a contemptuous look at the young Medjay. "She wouldn't want to point a finger at herself. Which she'd be doing if she cut his throat while he lay sleeping."

"Cut his throat!" Kasaya shook his head in disgust. "A woman cut a man's throat? No!"

Bak groaned inwardly. The pair's squabbling seemed never to end. Fortunately neither took the other seriously and their friendship remained firm.

"If she was angry enough . . ." Hori turned to Bak. "Is Woserhet's wife a large woman, sir?"

"She's small and slight. I suppose she could've slain him in the heat of anger, but I doubt it." Bak felt a trickle of sweat working its way down his breastbone, his mouth felt as dry as the desert, and his stomach as empty as the barren wastes. Tearing his thoughts from himself, he thought over his conversation with Ashayet. "She was very upset when I told her of his death, and I saw no pretense in her sobbing. After she collected herself, she became angry, and that, too, was no sham." He shook his head. "No, she did not slay her husband, of that I'm convinced."

"What of the priest Meryamon?" Hori asked, unaware of the fact that they were approaching the man of whom he spoke.

Bak's eyes leaped forward to the young priest, who had left the palm grove and was striding up the processional way toward Ipet-resyt. He was not hurrying, but he was walking with purpose. "I suppose he could've slain him, but what reason would he have? He does nothing day after day but care for, hand out, and take back the special items used in the rituals."

"What reason would anyone have?" Kasaya asked.

"Woserhet was an auditor," Hori said scornfully. "Auditors make enemies."

Kasaya matched derision with derision. "Within the sacred precinct?"

"Priests are no different than anyone else. They can be

tempted by wealth. They can be seduced by a beautiful woman. They can get frustrated and angry. Since he was an auditor . . ." The young scribe stubbed his toe on a rock and stumbled. "Well, I'd sure be unhappy if I found someone prying in my records."

Ahead, Meryamon veered around a large family group and Bak lost sight of him.

"Was he slain in anger, sir?" the young Medjay asked.

Bak raised his baton of office, responding to the salute of four soldiers walking in the opposite direction. "An inspection of the partly burned documents might give us an idea of what he was doing. If we can find a reason among them for slaying a man, we may conclude that anger was not a factor."

Hori did not have to be told who would go through the documents. "When am I to start, sir?"

"At break of day tomorrow. I've sealed the room, but have told the guards to allow you inside." Bak veered to the edge of the crushed limestone path. The scribe and Medjay fell in line behind him and they walked around the family group. When they were once again close enough to talk, he said, "I wish you to sort the scrolls that were scattered around the body into three groups: those too burned to read, those partly burned, and those you find undamaged."

Meryamon, again in view, had increased his speed and was catching up with another loose group of people. Bak, his curiosity aroused, also walked faster.

"How can I help, sir?" Kasaya asked.

Noting the expectant look on the Medjay's face, the hope that he could be of use, Bak gave him the only assignment he could think of. "You can stand guard, making sure no one enters the room and disturbs Hori."

Kasaya nodded, satisfied with a task he must have known was unnecessary. "Yes, sir."

"While you sort the documents . . ." Bak saw Meryamon closing on the people ahead. ". . . I'll be searching out

Woserhet's scribe. With luck and the help of the lord Amon, he'll know what the auditor was looking for, and he may even point us toward the slayer."

Meryamon moved up close to a man with fuzzy red hair. Briefly the two walked side by side. Whether they spoke to each other, Bak was unable to tell. He could not say exactly why, but he thought they did—and he could have sworn the priest passed something to the other man before quickly moving on.

"What are we to do today?" Hori asked.

"We can't do anything," Bak said. "The sacred precinct is deserted except for a few guards, and all who aren't making merry must by this time be watching the ritual outside Ipet-resyt. You're free to enjoy the festival."

The two young men exchanged a glance that told Bak they were not disappointed at their release from duty.

"And you, sir?" Kasaya asked.

"I hope to find Amonked at Ipet-resyt. He'll want a report."

Meryamon merged into the crowd ahead. The red-haired man turned off the processional way into a side lane. He stopped in the shadow of a white-plastered mudbrick building and looked at something in his hand. Dropping it to the ground, he stepped on it, hurried on down the lane, and vanished among the small, decrepit houses that lined this portion of the processional way.

Bak, more curious than ever, plunged off the thoroughfare and into the lane where the redhead had been. On the ground he found the crushed pieces of a gray pottery shard. Kneeling, he picked up a few of the larger fragments and studied them. He saw signs of writing, a message destroyed.

"Is something wrong, sir?" Hori asked, eyeing the grayish bits with curiosity.

Bak shrugged. "I thought I saw the priest Meryamon pass something to another man. I wondered what it was, that's all."

"A note?"

Bak slipped out of the lane and looked up the processional way. Meryamon had vanished in the crowd ahead. "I'll ask him when next I see him."

Chapter Four

Bak, Hori, and Kasaya passed the final barque sanctuary and stopped at the southern end of the processional way to look upon the crowd ahead. After dwelling three years on the southern frontier, where man could eke out a living only on a narrow strip of land along the river, keeping the population low, the vast number of individuals gathered in this one place was staggering.

"I grew to manhood across the river and often came to the festival," Hori said, "but I've never seen anything like this. Each year more people come from afar and each year the procession is grander."

"And more wonders are offered to tickle the senses," Kasaya said. "The food, the acrobats, the musicians . . ." He chopped off the rest of the thought, distracted by a sultry young woman passing by.

Bak smiled. "Are you as hungry as I am?"

Hori shook his head. "We ate not an hour ago."

Clearing his thoughts of death and duty, Bak led the way in among the crowd that filled the large walled court in front of Ipet-resyt. At the back of the court rose the main gate through the high mudbrick wall that enclosed the lord Amon's southern mansion and its support buildings. The procession had earlier passed into the sacred precinct, leaving the court swarming with people. They milled around the flimsy booths amid a buzz of talk and laughter, purchasing what struck their fancy or pausing to watch performances designed to please the eye and excite the senses: acrobats, dancers, and musicians; trained animals and mischievous monkeys; archery contests, pole fights and wrestling matches. Men and women from the land of Kemet shared their joy in the greatest of the gods with dark, smiling strangers from far to the south and bearded and mysterious foreigners from the north. The poor gaped at the wealthy, at their fine jewelry and elaborate, bejeweled wigs. The affluent inspected one another's garb and hairstyles more furtively, but with an equally avid interest. Sharp-eyed policemen and soldiers walked among them, seeking out thieves and mischief makers.

Attracted by the smell of roasting meat, Bak wove his way to its source, where a man squatted beside an open and very smoky hearth over which was suspended the well-cooked carcass of a lamb. He traded garrison tokens for several pieces, a loaf of bread and, at another booth, three jars of beer. Rejoining Hori and Kasaya, he found a section of wall near the rear of the court on which they could sit while they ate. The two young men consumed the food as greedily as he.

From where they sat, they watched the activity around them. Children played tag or hide and seek among the booths and in the crowd, shrieking their delight. Cats and monkeys poked through garbage thrown behind the booths and outside the wall, sniffing out bits of food before it could rot in the heat. Dogs walked among the people, ready to pounce on any edible scrap. Grooms led finely matched teams of horses pulling empty chariots out of the sacred precinct and through the multitude to vanish down a side street.

Their meal finished, Bak climbed atop the wall to scan the court in search of Amonked. He spotted his Medjays scattered around, watching a variety of performances, but could not find Maatkare Hatshepsut's cousin. He must have gone with the procession into the sacred precinct.

The number of revelers was increasing dramatically, with people approaching from all directions. The crowd was spilling out of the court and north along the processional way. Additional booths offering innumerable delicacies and temptations were being set up to accommodate the swelling throng. Fresh dancers and musicians and acrobats, wrestlers, stick fighters and boxers streamed into the melee. The sounds of merrymaking must have carried to the far edges of the city.

Bak sent the two young men on their way and set out to find Amonked. At the gate to the sacred precinct, a member of the royal guard noted his baton of office and allowed him to pass through. Inside, a large open court lay between the gate and the deep, columned portico that stood in front of the god's mansion. The crush of people was intense. The fine clothing worn by most marked them as men and women of wealth and position. The rest were soldiers, priests, and envoys representing the kings of far-off lands.

Booths lined the walls, these containing offerings to the gods: huge mounds of fruits and vegetables; fowl and beef; jars of wine, beer, honey, aromatic oils; vessels of gold and bronze; masses of flowers. Bak could not recall ever seeing such a magnificent display of plenty.

Seven fine steers crowded into a corner, bawling, terrified by the smell of fresh blood. Nearby, butchers were killing, bleeding, and cutting up the animals' brethren, more gifts to the gods. The air was heavy with the smells of manure, incense, blood, perfume, and sweat.

He looked the length of the long court toward the southern mansion of the lord Amon and relived for an instant the first time he had been brought to the ritual, a four-year-old child sitting high on his father's shoulders. Then as now, he had glimpsed gold—the barques of the gods—over the many heads, but, as before, he could not see his sovereigns. In spite of himself, in spite of the fact that Maatkare Hatshepsut had exiled him to the southern frontier and the youthful Menkheperre Thutmose held little power, he felt a pang of disappointment.

He spotted Amonked standing not far from the main gate with the chief treasurer Djehuty and Pentu, the governor of Tjeny. With them were Pentu's wife and her sister, a man with the shaven head of a priest, and one with white hair who stood as rigid as a soldier. Except for the priest and the older man, all wore sumptuous wigs and jewelry befitting their lofty status.

Amonked saw Bak, spoke a few words to his companions, and parted from them to join the policeman. "You've news."

"Nothing of note, I regret to say." Bak went on to report what he had seen and learned. "Perhaps tomorrow I'll unearth more, but any further effort today will be futile."

"Considering the circumstances, you've done well." Amonked clapped him on the shoulder, smiled. "Now come with me. I understand you met Pentu and Djehuty a few days ago. You must get to know them better."

Before Bak could offer an objection, Amonked took his arm and ushered him toward the small group. Certain such lofty individuals as the chief treasurer of Kemet and a provincial governor would have no more than a vague memory of him standing on the ship with Commandant Thuty, he was surprised by the friendly manner in which the two men greeted him.

"You remember my wife, Taharet, of course." Pentu took the tall young woman's hand and gave her an adoring smile.

She bowed her head briefly, acknowledging Bak, and eyed him with an open curiosity that made him feel like a beetle crossing the sand beneath the sharp eye of a curious boy with an empty jar in his hand.

The governor glanced at his wife, passing along a secret thought, and smiled at the other woman. "This is her younger sister Meret, if you recall."

"Yes, sir," Bak said, choosing not to point out that he had never met either woman, merely seen them at a distance.

Meret's eyes twinkled with good humor, as if she recognized the situation in which he found himself. "We'd newly arrived in Waset and you were on the ship moored behind ours. You were with a garrison commander from the south, I believe."

"Commandant Thuty, yes."

"This is Sitepehu, Lieutenant." Pentu laid his hand on the priest's shoulder. "He's high priest of the lord Inheret and a trusted adviser, a friend as close to me as a brother."

Well formed in body and face, Sitepehu looked to be about forty years of age. An ugly puckered scar on his left shoulder testified to an early career in the army. Inheret was the divine huntsman, an ancient god identified with the lord Shu, son of the lord Re. Tjeny was his primary seat of worship.

The priest smiled, but before he could respond to the introduction, Pentu beckoned to his side the older man with military bearing. "This is my longtime aide Netermose, a man of infinite patience, whose willingness to assist me in all my endeavors knows no bounds."

Bak looked upon the aide with interest. The man's deeply lined and unattractive features seemed not to fit his slight build and softly curling white hair. Most men in his position were much younger, men who would readily accept menial tasks and adapt themselves to their master's whims in the hope of bettering themselves later in life.

"Can we not leave this place, my love?" Taharet asked. "The heat is suffocating and the stench is making me ill."

Looking shamefaced at her gentle but definite reminder that he was neglecting his duty toward her, the governor glanced around as if he had forgotten the brilliant sunlight, the milling crowd, the bawling cattle, and the competing smells. "Forgive me, dearest. Of course we must leave."

"I'd hoped we could get closer to Ipet-resyt, where we could watch Maatkare Hatshepsut and Menkheperre Thutmose make offerings to the lord Amon. We're so far away now . . ." The words tailed off and she looked hopefully at Amonked.

"I've done my best, my love." Pentu took her arm and walked her toward the gate.

"I sometimes wish your best would be more effective."

Amonked and Djehuty exchanged a look of clear disapproval. Meret's face was expressionless, her feelings about the exchange closed to the world. Sitepehu and Netermose carefully avoided each other's eyes as if embarrassed by the governor's show of weakness.

Outside the sacred precinct, the aide led them across the crowded court to a half circle of shade cast by a sycamore whose limbs reached over the wall. The people occupying the space, farm servants if their appearance told true, took one look at the lofty intruders and hastened away, leaving them in relative peace and quiet.

Taharet took a square of linen from beneath a bracelet and patted the moisture from her forehead. Smiling at Amonked, she said, "We have a dwelling near here, sir." She pointed gracefully toward several blocks of large interconnected multistory houses built to the east of Ipet-resyt. "You can see it from where we stand. The three-story building with trees growing from pots beneath the pavilion on the roof."

"How nice," Amonked said.

Bak smothered a smile. Amonked's voice had been as neutral as Meret's expression had been. Since a babe, he had walked the corridors of the royal house. When the need arose for tact or dissimulation, he had no master. As in this case, where he disapproved of the woman, but preferred not to alienate her doting husband.

"Ah, here comes Pahure." Pentu smiled at a man hurrying out of a shadowy lane separating two of the building blocks. "He's my steward. Thanks to him, our temporary move to Waset has gone so smoothly I've barely noticed the change of residence."

Several male and female servants followed the steward. Upon entering the court through a side entrance, Pahure strode toward Pentu and his party, while the others veered into the throng, intent on merrymaking. The belt of his calf-length kilt was snug across the beginnings of a paunch. His broad beaded collar accented heavily muscled shoulders and upper arms. Bak guessed him to be close on thirty-five years.

Pentu introduced him, as generous with his praise as he had been with Netermose and Sitepehu. The moment he paused for breath, Taharet began firing questions at Pahure about several household tasks.

Sitepehu bestowed upon the pair a bland, unrevealing look and turned his back to them. "Before you joined us in the sacred precinct, Lieutenant, Amonked was singing your praises. You must've led quite a life on the southern frontier. I've heard those desert tribesmen can be fierce."

"Bak was a police officer, a most successful one." Amonked spoke with considerable pride, as an uncle might speak of his most favored nephew. "Understandably, a frontier policeman must first and foremost be a soldier."

"It appears that you've seen battle, sir," Bak said, thinking to deflect attention from himself.

Sitepehu touched the scar on his shoulder, shrugged. "A skirmish, nothing more. It occurred in the land of Retenu. You know how those petty rulers of city states can be. Every king affects the sensitivity of a newborn lamb. The slightest insult from another king and he sets out to right what he claims is a wrong, with the further acquisition of wealth and power his real goal. My infantry company found itself between two such kings." Suddenly he laughed. "So here I stand, marked for life."

Bak laughed with him. He, too, had scars, but none so dramatic. "We fought few real battles in Wawat. Our enemies were usually smugglers or a few ragged bandits out to steal from a helpless village."

Amonked, who knew from personal experience how bitter

the fighting could get on the frontier, frowned his disapproval.

Pahure slipped away from Taharet to join them. "I long ago served on a ship that more often than not sailed the Great Green Sea. We fought pirates mostly." He gave his companions a wry smile. "The battles I'd rather remember occurred in foreign ports, where we drank and made merry and fought for the pleasure of doing so."

Netermose's smile was rueful. "I fear my finest battles have been in Tjeny, convincing the landholders to pay all the taxes due my master and the royal house." He directed the smile at Pentu. "Unlike your contests, sir, where tact and diplomacy have won the day."

"Not always, Netermose, as you well know. I've . . ."

Taharet laid her hand on her husband's arm, interrupting with the indifference of a woman utterly secure in her position. "We're having guests tomorrow," she said to Amonked. "We'd like you and your worthy spouse to honor us with your presence."

"I regret that my wife cannot come. She's a chantress of the lord Amon. A noteworthy honor, certainly, but a task requiring time and dedication throughout the festival. She'll be fully occupied for the next ten days."

Taharet looked appropriately impressed and at the same time disappointed. "Will you not come alone?"

"I don't usually . . ." Amonked hesitated, glanced at Bak, smiled. "If you'll allow me to bring my young friend here, I'd be glad to drop by."

Taharet beamed at him, at her husband, and at Bak. "You will come, won't you, Lieutenant?"

Bak had a feeling something was going on that had passed over his head. He queried Amonked with a glance. The Storekeeper of Amon nodded and formed a smile that could have meant anything. Bak accepted.

"I'm delighted." Taharet flung a smile at her sister. "And so is Meret. You'll find her a most pleasing companion."

Not until the small group had broken up and he and
Amonked were strolling through the crowded, festive court
did it occur to him that Amonked and maybe Djehuty or
Pentu were trying to make a match of him and Meret. She
was a lovely young woman, but if she was anything like her
sister, he wanted no part of her.

"Reminds me of you, sir, when you use your baton of office to good purpose. Remember the time when . . ." Never
taking his eyes off the two men who were stick fighting,
Sergeant Pashenuro related a tale Bak had long ago forgotten.

He listened with half an ear while he, too, enjoyed the battle. The two fighters, one representing western Waset and the
other the village of Madu, swung their long wooden sticks
hard and fast, pressing each other back and forth across the
small space allotted them. Each series of swings and parries
was broken by one man or the other leaping free and dancing out of the way. Each brief respite ended when one or the
other imagined his opponent losing his vigilance—or when
the yelling onlookers grew impatient and began to boo and
hiss. Sweat poured down their oiled bodies, dust rose from
beneath their feet. The onlookers shouted out wagers, yelled
encouragement, groaned at each perceived loss.

"You'd do well, sir," Pashenuro said, caught up in the battle. "Better than either of them. Why don't you challenge the
winner?"

Laughing, Bak moved on. He spotted three of his Medjays watching male acrobats doing backward handsprings to
the rhythm of a drummer and clapping, chanting onlookers.
He looked on with admiration, wondering if he had ever
been so agile. His eye caught a touch of color beyond their
leaping bodies, the fuzzy red hair of the man to whom
Meryamon had passed the message. The redhead scanned
the crowd—looking for someone, Bak felt sure. He doubted
the man would recognize him or had even seen him walking

along the processional way, but he breathed a sigh of relief when the searching eyes slid over him as if he were not there.

The drummer changed his cadence, a servant brought out and distributed several poles. While two of the acrobats raised one of the poles ever higher, the remainder used theirs to vault over it. The red-haired man glanced to his right and his face lit up. Bak spotted a swarthy foreign-looking man shouldering his way through the onlookers. The redhead sidled toward him, the movement inconspicuous but definite.

Soon the two men were standing together, talking. Bak had no way of knowing what they were saying and could not approach lest he draw attention to himself. Their conversation was short and, if appearance did not deceive, quickly grew heated, with the swarthy stranger often shaking his head in denial. The redhead's face grew florid from anger, he snapped out a final remark and hurried away.

Bak hesitated, wondering if he should follow, seeking a reason to do so. Other than the furtiveness of Meryamon's behavior, none of these men's actions were suspect, nor could he tie their activities in any way to Woserhet's death. Still, he was curious.

Bidding farewell to his Medjays, he followed the redhead to a circle of men and women urging on two wrestlers and from there to an archery contest. Nothing of note occurred at either match, and he was sorely tempted to drop the pursuit. Except his quarry continually looked around as if he expected—or at least hoped—to meet someone else. Then again, he might simply be enjoying the festivities.

The lord Re was sinking toward the western horizon and the red-haired man weaving a path through the throng, heading back toward Ipet-resyt, when Bak spotted Amonked standing in a small circle of spectators, watching a dozen desert dwellers perform a synchronized leaping dance to the hard, fast beat of a drum. The redhead stopped to watch a nearby group of female dancers, so Bak slipped up beside the Storekeeper of Amon.

"I've never seen such a wondrous crowd," Amonked said. "If my cousin could see the abundance of people, the joy on their faces, she'd be most pleased."

"I thank the gods that I'm a mere servant, not the child of a deity. I can well imagine what she and Menkheperre Thutmose will endure inside the god's mansion. The near darkness. The air stifling hot and reeking of incense, burning oil, and food offerings. A never-ending murmur of prayers. Bruised knees and an aching back from bending low before the lord Amon for hours at a time."

"The lord Amon is a most beneficent god, my young friend. Serving him can get tedious, but one must put aside one's physical discomforts and let piety enter one's heart."

Bak gave him a sharp look, but found neither censure in his demeanor nor cynicism.

The red-haired man strolled away from the dancers. Bak felt compelled to follow, and Amonked, he had learned some months earlier, could ofttimes be torn from his staid existence. "I've been following a man for no good purpose. Would you care to join me?"

"I don't think . . ." Amonked eyed askance the many people circulating around them. "Well, yes. Yes I would. But in this crowd? How is that possible?"

"Come. I'll show you." Bak pointed at the redhead, who was sauntering past a row of booths offering bright amulets and trinkets, mementos of the festival. "You see the man with fuzzy red hair? Not one in a thousand has hair so conspicuous. He's not tall, so it's easy to lose sight of him, but a diligent search will never fail to reward you with another glimpse."

"Let's hurry," Amonked said, leaping into the spirit of the chase. "We don't want to lose him."

Grinning, Bak motioned the older man to precede him. Amonked took the game seriously, seldom taking his eyes off the man ahead. Of equal import, he was not one to draw attention to himself and, in spite of the fine jewelry and wig he wore, readily merged into the crowd.

Their quarry led them into a smaller, more festive version of Waset's foreign quarter. Here, the food offered for sale looked and smelled and tasted different from the usual fare of Kemet. The entertainers wore unfamiliar costumes; the music was more strident with an unusual beat and timbre. The games and sports were similar, but differed in rules and manner of play. Many of the people strolling through the area were foreigners, men and women from far to the north and south, the east and west, strangely garbed, often odd in appearance, speaking words impossible to understand.

The red-haired man stopped behind a semicircle of people watching a troupe of Hittite acrobats performing to the beat of a single drum. One man was climbing a pyramid of standing men to take his position at the top. The redhead studied the spectators, then headed purposefully in among them to stop beside a short, dumpy man wearing the long kilt of a scribe.

"Do you know the man beside him?" The question was foolish, Bak knew. Hundreds of scribes daily walked the streets of Waset, and hundreds more had come from throughout the land of Kemet to participate in the festival. However, Amonked had surprised him before and would again with the vast amount of knowledge stored within his heart.

The beat of the drum swelled to a climax. The acrobat reached the top of the human pyramid and stood erect. The crowd roared approval.

"He's called Nebamon," Amonked said. "He's overseer of a block of storehouses in the sacred precinct of Ipet-isut, including the storage magazine in which Woserhet was slain. He's responsible for many of the valuable supplies and objects used during the rituals: aromatic oils, fine linens, bronze and gold vessels."

"The same items handed over to the priests by Meryamon."

"Those and many more." Amonked poked a stray lock of his own hair back beneath his wig. "Nebamon's task is more wide-ranging and on a higher level of authority. He receives items shipped to Waset from throughout the land of Kemet and oversees their distribution." Amonked stared hard at the redhead and the scribe. "Are they talking, or did our red-haired friend just happen to stand beside him?"

Bak shrugged. "I can't tell. Men who speak together usually make gestures, and I haven't seen any." Nor had he seen a message being passed from hand to hand.

The acrobats broke formation. A servant approached with a tall, wide-mouthed jar containing an efflorescence of lit torches. Each of the performers grabbed two. Holding them high, they began to dance, whirling round and round to the ever faster beat of the drum in a frenzy of flying braids and sparks.

Bak's eyes drifted over the watching men and women, paused on a man standing slightly off to the right. "Speaking of Meryamon, there he is."

The priest stood at the end of the semicircle, watching the acrobats, seemingly indifferent to any other person or activity. From where he stood, he might or might not have spotted Bak and Amonked, but he could not have failed to see Nebamon and the red-haired man. Yet his face revealed no hint of recognition.

Was this another furtive act? Or had the young priest seen the other men when first they had joined the spectators and dismissed them from his thoughts? Had following the red-haired man been an exercise and no more? Or had some important act occurred that Bak had failed to recognize for what it was?

Fresh hordes of spectators flowed in among the onlookers and around the nearby booths and performers. The ceremony inside the sacred precinct had ended. Offering ritual completed, the lord Amon and his mortal daughter and son would have entered Ipet-resyt, leaving the spectators free to eat and play through the remainder of the day and far into the night.

Amonked grabbed Bak's arm to draw him close and shouted in his ear that his wife would soon be free to return home and he had promised to meet her there. Bak bade him good-bye. When he turned around, the flood of humanity had swept away the men he had been watching.

"I don't like it." Commandant Thuty scowled at the hot, red coals lying in the mudbrick hearth Bak's Medjays had built in the courtyard.

"The dead auditor?" Nebwa asked. "Seems simple enough. He learned something to someone's discredit and that someone slew him."

No longer hungry, but tantalized by the rich smell of fowl and onions and herbs, Bak reached into the large pot setting on the coals and withdrew a piece of well-cooked goose, a feast bestowed upon them by the lord Amon to celebrate the opening day of the Beautiful Feast of Opet. This and other foods richer and more luxurious than their usual fare had been given them during the reversion of offerings, the task Woserhet would have performed if he had been allowed to live.

"Someone must lay hands on his slayer," he said, "and Amonked trusts me to do the best I can."

Thuty transferred his frown from the fire to Bak. "Amonked knows, Lieutenant, that you never fail to accept the challenge when faced with a crime and an unknown criminal. And he likes you. He provides you with murdered men as a shepherd provides his flock with grass."

"Bak's probably the one man he knows who hasn't befriended him because he's cousin to our sovereign." Nebwa spat on the hard-packed earthen floor, showing his contempt for men who hoped to gain through another man's position.

Knucklebones rattled across the floor. The Medjay who had thrown snarled a curse and the three men playing with him burst into laughter. A man called out a bet. Another responded and another. Bak looked their way, smiled. The torch mounted on the wall flickered in the light breeze, making their features appear ill-formed and indistinct, but he knew each as well as he would know a brother.

From the day his men had set foot in Buhen, until the day they left, throughout the voyage north he had been told, and here in their temporary quarters, the game had never ceased. Their bets were small, their enjoyment large, so he refused to interfere. Two had been assigned to guard the dwelling and their belongings, but why the other two remained when they could be out making merry, he could not imagine.

Imsiba laid a hand on the thick neck of the large, floppy-eared white dog curled up against his thigh, a cur Hori had long ago adopted. "Do you fear Amonked will steal Bak from us, sir?"

Growling an affirmative, Thuty picked up his beer jar, took a deep drink, set it down with a thud. "This is the second murder he's asked him to investigate since he arrived in the capital. Waset has plenty of police officers. Surely one of them would serve equally well."

"Bak has a talent few men have." Nebwa tore a chunk from a thin round loaf of bread, dipped it in the stew. "But that's of no import. We can't let him stay here when we journey on to Mennufer."

"Would you two stop speaking of me as if I'm that dog . . ." Irritated, he glanced at Hori's pet. ". . . unable to understand a word you're saying. I *will* snare the man who slew Woserhet, and I *will* go with you to Mennufer." To close the subject, he plucked another piece of goose from the pot and took a bite off the bone.

"Can I help you search for the slayer, my friend?" Imsiba asked.

"How can you? Your wife has yet to find a new ship."

"You know very well that the captain of the vessel we left behind in Abu is here with us. As he expects to command her new one, he has much to gain by offering sound advice. I go with them to the harbor only because she wishes me to."

"As much as I'd like your help, you must stand by her side until she finds a suitable vessel. Pashenuro and Psuro can take temporary charge of our men."

"You must promise to summon me should you need me."

"Never fear, Imsiba, but as of now I can see no purpose in dragging you along with me. Today the murder seems impossible to solve, but tomorrow, when I talk to men who knew of Woserhet's mission, the reason for his death may be revealed and the name of the slayer as well."

Chapter Five

"Hapuseneb has been told of Woserhet's death." Ptahmes, the chief priest's aide, a young man as free of hair as a melon, wore across his chest the sash of a lector priest. "He's very upset, Lieutenant. I can't tell you how strongly he feels that the man who slew him must be snared and punished as quickly as possible."

The priest, with Bak at his side, walked slowly down the narrow lane toward the multitude of buildings that formed the house of life, the primary center of priestly learning in the land of Kemet. The lord Khepre reached into the lane, turning the plastered walls a blinding white and heating the earth upon which they trod. The second day of the festival promised to be as hot as the first. Soft voices could sometimes be heard beyond the doorways to either side, but in general, silence and peace reigned.

Bak tried not to show his annoyance. The last thing he needed was the chief priest adding to the burden Amonked had already placed on his shoulders. "To do so, I need to know more of his activities."

"Ask what you will." The young priest stepped over a yellow dog sunning itself in front of a door. "I can't promise to give you the answers you need, for I've been told close to nothing. I'll do the best I can."

"Mistress Ashayet, Woserhet's wife, had no idea what he's been doing—evidently he seldom spoke of his task—

but she said he'd been troubled for several days. Can you tell me why?"

"All I know is what he told Hapuseneb: he'd found some discrepancies in the records of the storehouses of the lord Amon. What they were, he didn't say, evidently wishing to be more certain before he pointed a finger."

Bak grimaced. He had hoped for more. "Were the storehouses here in Waset or in some other city?"

"Here, I believe, but of that I'm not certain. You must speak to his scribe, a man named Tati."

"Can you tell me where to find him?"

Bak made his slow way down the narrow, meandering lane, counting the open doorways as he stepped over a crying baby, sidled around donkeys and several women barring the path while they argued, and stopped to allow a pack of snarling dogs to race around him. Crowding in to either side were the walls of small, single-story interconnected houses from which grimy white plaster flaked. The lane, untouched by the early morning sun, smelled of manure, rancid oil, unwashed humanity, and, strangely enough, of flowers. The poor of the city loved the delicate beauty of the blooming plants they had neither the space nor the leisure to grow and, during the reversion of offerings, would ofttimes choose blossoms over food.

This and several neighboring building blocks, though less than two hundred paces from the sacred precinct of Ipet-isut, seemed a world away. According to the chief priest's aide, Woserhet and his scribe and workmen had been given a house here for that very reason. In this private place, with no one the wiser, the lord Amon's servants could dwell on the premises, the auditor could study untroubled the documents they had taken from the storehouses, and they could keep their records.

Bak reached the twelfth doorway on his right and walked inside. The main room was fairly large, an irregular rectan-

gle with the wall to the right longer than the opposing wall.
Two rooms opened off to the left. Light and fresh air entered
through high windows at the back. A quick glance told him
this was the dwelling he sought. Rather than a loom or signs
of other household industry, he saw sleeping pallets rolled
up along one wall and several small woven reed chests and
baskets containing personal belongings.

Footsteps sounded, drawing his eyes to a short, squat, and
muscular man descending the mudbrick stairway built
against the rear wall. "Who are you?" the man demanded.

Bak gave his name and title, saying he represented
Amonked. "And you are . . . ?"

"You'll be looking for Tati." The man dropped off the bottom step and pointed upward. "He's on the roof, sir. He's expecting you. Or someone like you."

He looked no different from any other workman in the
land of Kemet and wore the same skimpy kilt, but he spoke
with the accent of the people of the western desert and carried the brand of a prisoner on his right shoulder. Bak
guessed he had been taken in a border skirmish and offered
by Maatkare Hatshepsut to the lord Amon in gratitude for
the victory. "You've been told of Woserhet's death?"

"We have," the workman nodded. "May the gods take him
unto themselves and may the one who slew him burn
through eternity."

Bak was not quite sure what family of gods had given
birth to the words, but he could see the sentiment was heartfelt. "You liked him, I see." He smiled, hoping to draw the
man out.

"He could be as sour as an unripe persimmon, but he was
always fair and made no unreasonable demands." The workman hesitated, then blurted, "What'll happen to us now, sir?
Has anyone said?"

"With so many men in authority participating in the Beautiful Feast of Opet, I doubt if a decision has been made."

The workman nodded in mute and unhappy understanding.

Bak headed up the stairs. He sympathized with this man and the others. As servants of the lord Amon, their fate rested in other men's hands. The scribe would probably be kept at Ipet-isut or be sent to another god's mansion, but the odds were weighted heavily that the four workmen would be taken to one of the lord Amon's many estates to toil in the fields.

At the top of the stairs, a long expanse of white rooftop baked in the morning sun, with no line marking where one dwelling ended and another began. A half-dozen spindly pavilions had been erected to expand the living and work space of the houses below. North-facing airshafts projected here and there, and stairways led downward to each home. Lines had been strung from which dangled strips of drying meat or newly dyed thread or yarn. Fish lay spread out to dry. Sun-baked dung had been piled in neat mounds for use as fuel; hay was spread in loose piles; baskets, tools, and pottery lay where they had been dropped.

Beneath a rough pavilion roofed with palm fronds, he found a small, elderly man seated cross-legged on the rooftop. His upper back was so stooped his head projected from between his shoulders like a turtle peering out from its shell. His brand, different from that of the workman, had faded, speaking of many long years as a servant.

"You must be Tati," Bak said.

"Yes, sir."

The scribe motioned him to sit in the shade. While Bak explained who he was and why he had come, Tati made a tiny mark on the scroll spread across his lap and another on the limestone flake on the roof beside him. Noting the curiosity on Bak's face, he explained, "The scroll contains the official list of all the faience statuettes and dishes thought to be in a storage magazine we inspected last week. The shard shows all we found."

"Do the two match?" Bak had expected an accent, but could detect none.

"Well enough." Tati sat up as straight as he could and for an instant a cloud of pain passed over his face. "We rarely find a perfect match when the items are small. Woserhet never failed to insist that we count each and every one, while the men who originally store them are always far too impatient to take care."

Bak shifted forward and brushed away a small stone digging into his backside. "The workman in the dwelling below said you were expecting me."

"Our task was one of great import, given to us by the chief priest, Hapuseneb himself. We doubted Woserhet's death would be allowed to go unnoticed. Or unpunished."

Again Bak noted the lack of an accent. "You're a man of Kemet, an educated man, and yet you carry a brand?"

"I was born far to the north in the land of Hatti." The scribe smiled at Bak's surprise. "I left as a callow youth, apprenticed to my uncle to become a trader. While traveling through Amurru, Maatkare Hatshepsut's father Akheperkare Thutmose marched through the land with his army. I was taken prisoner and brought here."

"You speak our tongue very well."

"I learn with ease the words of other lands. For many years I served as a translator, journeying with our sovereign's envoys to distant cities. A most satisfying and happy time that was." His smile was sad, regretful. "But alas. The years have caught up with me. With this deformity . . ." He touched his shoulder. ". . . and the pain that sometimes besets me, I can no longer travel. So our sovereign gave me as an offering to the lord Amon."

"And you were loaned to Woserhet."

"A good man. I shall miss him."

"We all will." The workman who had greeted Bak had come up the stairway unheard. He brought several jars of beer, two of which he handed to Bak and Tati. The rest he placed in a basket before going back downstairs.

Bak broke the dried mud plug out of his jar. "Evidently he told Hapuseneb he'd found some discrepancies in the records of the storehouses of the lord Amon. Other than that vague statement, no one seems to know what he was doing."

"That was our task, sir. To search out discrepancies. Not the small ones like those I've found here . . ." Tati tapped the document on his lap. ". . . but significant differences."

"Woserhet surely wouldn't have troubled the chief priest with talk of something insignificant."

"No, he was not a man to worry others needlessly." Tati let the scroll curl up and set it on the rooftop beside the shard. "He seemed to think he'd found some irregularities, but he wouldn't tell me what or where they were." He sipped from his beer jar, frowned. "He often left me puzzled like that, saying if I couldn't find anything wrong, he might well be mistaken. I appreciated his reasoning, but found the practice most annoying."

"As would I." Bak glanced at a woman who had come onto the roof at the far end of the block. She got down on her knees and began to turn over the fish drying in the sun. "You've found nothing thus far?"

"No, sir." Tati smiled ruefully. "I'll continue to search until the chief priest or one of his aides remembers us. After that . . . Well, who knows what the lord Amon has planned for us?"

Bak had no way of setting the scribe's anxiety to rest, so he made no comment. "Woserhet's wife, mistress Ashayet, said he'd been troubled for the past few days."

"Yes, sir." Tati looked thoughtfully across the cluttered rooftop. "Something bothered him, but what it was I've no idea."

"The irregularities he'd mentioned?"

"Perhaps, but I don't think so." Seeing the puzzlement on

Bak's face, the scribe hastened to explain. "When he initially suggested I look for discrepancies, he didn't seem unduly disturbed, so why would he become upset later? Also, why would he not mention the irregularities we'd previously discussed?"

Good questions, both. "Didn't you ask what the trouble was?"

Sadness clouded Tati's expression. "Normally, he explained what he was thinking, but this time . . . Well, as he offered no explanation, I assumed the matter personal and let it drop."

Bak sipped his beer, thinking over what he had learned. Practically nothing. Many men confided in their servants, but Woserhet had been a man of limited means, one unaccustomed to retainers and no doubt unwilling to share his thoughts with them. "You must let me know if you find any discrepancy of significance, or anything else unusual. One of your workmen can deliver the message to my Medjays' quarters."

While the scribe wrote the location on a shard, Bak said, "The workman who brought this beer obviously liked Woserhet, but indicated he could be sour at times. So much so that he made enemies?"

"Sour. Not a word I'd use." Tati set the shard aside and laid down his pen. "He was honest to a fault, sir, and blunt in all he said. He angered many people, especially the various storehouse overseers when he pointed out problems that, with proper supervision, could've been avoided. But I can't honestly see a man slaying him, offending the lady Maat in the most dire manner possible, for so small a thing."

Bak had known men to slay for less, but usually in the heat of anger and after too much beer. He doubted such had been the case with Woserhet's death.

"Many of the scrolls are like this one, sir."

Hori, seated in the lane outside the small room in which

Woserhet had died, carefully unrolled the partially burned document. In spite of the care he took, the charred outer end flaked off onto his lap. Deeper inside the roll, only the lower and upper edges had burned and were dropping away. Most of the words and numbers remained, but the more exposed surfaces were difficult to decipher because of soot and water stains. Farther in, the stains were fewer, the document easier to read.

Bak, kneeling beside the youth, eyed the three piles of scrolls. The largest by far was the one from which Hori had plucked the open document. Another was made up of scrolls slightly damaged or not burned at all. The third was a mass of badly burned documents that looked impossible to salvage.

"Can we take these to our quarters, sir?" Kasaya asked. "We'd be a lot more comfortable on the roof, have more room to spread out, and nobody would bother us."

Bak looked into the fire-damaged room. Most of the broken pottery had been shoved off to the side, out of the way. A black splotch on the now-dry floor identified the spot where the oil had burned, and a larger brownish patch had to be dried blood. The smell of burning remained, but not as strong as before.

"All right, but you must reseal this room before you go, and warn the guards to let no one inside. You may need to look at other records, and we don't want them to walk away while your back is turned."

"If Woserhet was fretful, I have no idea why." User, the Overseer of Overseers of the storehouses of Amon, gave Bak an irritated look. "All I know is that Hapuseneb summoned me one day and told me to expect him and those servants of his. He said I was to cooperate with them in every way and give them free access to all the storehouses. I repeated his instructions to the men who report to me, and that was that."

Bak stepped into the shade cast by the long portico in

front of the squarish treasury building. User was seated on a low chair about ten paces from the gaping doorway. His writing implements lay on a small, square table beside him. He looked the perfect example of the successful bureaucrat: his spine was stiff, his demeanor august, with an expansive stomach that brought the waistband of his long kilt almost up to his plump breasts.

"You were never curious about what he was doing?"

"I knew what he was doing." User sniffed disdainfully. "He was an auditor, wasn't he?"

Bak smothered a smile. He had asked for that. "How close was he to the end of his task?"

"As far as I know, he'd almost finished." User looked out into the courtyard, where four royal guards idled in the shade of a sycamore tree. Their officer had gone inside the building with two treasury guards and a priest. "Most of the overseers had come to whisper in my ear, ofttimes to complain that he exceeded his authority. I quickly set them straight, repeating Hapuseneb's order that we give him every assistance."

"You never looked into what he was doing?"

"Why should I? He had his task and I have mine."

"Were you not worried that he might find irregularities in the records?"

"Irregularities, Lieutenant? Someone counted wrong or transposed a number? Someone omitted a line when transferring amounts from a shard to the final scroll?" User snorted. "Everyone makes a mistake at one time or another."

The Overseer of Overseers, equal in rank to Amonked but with not a shred of the common sense, was too self-satisfied for his own good. Bak was beginning to understand why Amonked took such a strong interest in the large warehouses of the lord Amon outside the walls of the sacred precinct, those that housed the real wealth of the god: grain, hides, copper ingots. His title of Storekeeper of Amon had undoubtedly been intended as a sinecure, yet he toiled daily at the task, as would any conscientious man. If he, like User, had been responsible for the day-to-day operations of the storehouses, Bak had no doubt he would have known exactly what the auditor did.

"Could Woserhet have uncovered a theft?"

"Who would steal from the greatest of the gods?" User scoffed. "Such an offense is unthinkable. No man would be so bold."

"Given sufficient temptation . . ."

"Yes, yes, I know." User waved off Bak's objection. "But not here. Not in the sacred precinct of Ipet-isut."

The man was insufferable. Offering a silent prayer to the lord Amon to give him patience, Bak glanced at the royal guards, who had begun to play with three fuzzy kittens whose mother watched from a safe distance. "Did Woserhet audit the treasury?"

"He began here. I assured him that I take personal responsibility for the god's most valuable possessions and can list from memory all the items stored here." User scowled. "Nonetheless, he insisted."

Bak had never been inside this particular treasury, but its size alone told him no man could remember each and every object it contained. "How long ago was that?"

"A month, no more. The very day Hapuseneb told me to open all doors to him and his men."

Too long ago, Bak suspected, to have anything to do with Woserhet's most recent worry. Unless fresh evidence had been found leading back to the treasury. "This building must contain more items of significant value than all the other storehouses added together. Would it not be logical for a thief to look here for the most worthy prize?"

"How many times must I repeat myself, Lieutenant?" User pursed his lips in irritation. "I take considerable pride in the fact that the treasury falls within my realm of responsibility, and I daily walk through its rooms. I frankly admit to being obsessed with beautiful objects, and where else can one find so many in so confined a location?"

"I understand the storage magazines in the block where Woserhet died also contain objects of value."

User laughed, disdainful. "Nothing worthy of offending the lord Amon, believe me."

"Aromatic oils, ritual instruments made of precious metals, fine linen, and . . ." Bak broke off abruptly. The Overseer of Overseers was not listening.

User was staring hard at the royal guards, frowning. When he spoke, it was more to himself than to Bak. "That officer has been inside a long time." He rose from his chair and took up his baton of office, which had been leaning against a column. "I must see what the matter is."

Bak stepped in front of him, halting him. "I must ask questions within the sacred precinct, sir, and many of the men with whom I speak will be overseers of the storehouses for which you are responsible."

"Question anyone you like. Ask what you will." User stepped sideways and raised his baton, barring Bak from his path. "You'll find everything in order. You'll see."

Bak stopped with Amonked just inside the door and studied the bejeweled, bewigged men and women circulating around Governor Pentu's spacious reception hall. The odors of beer and wine, roast duck and beef, onions and herbs competed with the aromas of sweet-smelling perfume and luxurious bouquets of flowers. Voices rose and fell; laughter rang out. The late afternoon breeze flowing in through high windows failed to compete with the heat of bodies and human energy. A rivulet of sweat trickled down Bak's breastbone, and he thanked the lord Amon that he had had the good sense to wear no wig. Amonked had groused all the way to Pentu's dwelling about the need to wear the finery of a nobleman.

He leaned close to Bak, muttered, "We'll stay an hour, no more."

Bak, who saw not a single face he recognized, feared that hour might seem an eternity.

Pentu's aide Netermose hastened to meet them. He ushered them through the crowd to the slightly raised dais the governor shared with his spouse and Chief Treasurer Djehuty, and slipped away. Bak and Amonked bowed low to the trio, who were seated on chairs surrounded by bowls of fragrant white lilies floating on water. They murmured the customary greetings and were welcomed in turn. After Pentu extended to them all the good things his household had to offer, they moved aside, allowing other newly arrived guests to take their place.

A female servant gave them stemmed bowls filled with a flower-scented, deep red wine and asked if they wished anything else, relating a long list of food, drink, flowers, and perfumes. From what they could see on the heavily laden flat dishes carried through the hall by servants and on the low tables scattered along the walls, occupied mostly by women who chose to sit and gossip while they ate, her description could in no way prepare them for the sumptuous reality. Bak helped himself to the honeyed dates while Amonked sampled a variety of spiced meats.

"Good afternoon, sir." The priest Sitepehu bowed his head to Amonked and smiled at Bak. "Lieutenant."

"Pentu has truly outdone himself," Amonked said.

"We owe much of this bounty to Pahure, his steward. He traveled to Waset a few days ahead of us to prepare the dwelling for our arrival and to see that we had plentiful fresh food, drink and flowers."

"Not an easy task at this time of year, with most of the fields flooded, the best cropland under water."

Sitepehu chuckled. "Pahure is not a man to let a slight difficulty get in his way."

"Do you not share some of the acclaim?" Amonked asked, smiling. "Did you not pray to the lord Inheret that he'd be successful?"

The chuckle turned into a wholehearted laugh, drawing the attention of the people around them. "Frankly, sir, I saw no need. If Pahure stumbles, it'll not be over something as small as preparing for guests." The priest glanced beyond them, smiled. "Ah, Netermose. Meret."

The young woman welcomed the two of them to the governor's dwelling. Amonked hurried through the appropriate compliments, then immediately spotted an elderly priest he said Sitepehu should meet. He and Netermose rushed the priest off through the crowd.

Turning to Bak, flushing slightly, Meret smiled. "Your friend isn't very subtle, is he, Lieutenant?"

He laughed. "Amonked seems to think I need a wife."

"Do you?"

The question was so arch that for the briefest of moments he was struck dumb. "I've always thought myself capable of seeking out the woman with whom I wish to spend the rest of my life."

"Seeking out? Are you trying to tell me you need no matchmaker? Or that you know of someone you plan someday to approach?"

Her thoughts were difficult to read, but he suspected the latter question was prompted by mixed emotions, a touch of concern that he might not be available mixed with relief that he might be committed.

"I found a woman I wished to wed, but I lost her."

"To death?"

"To a lost life, yes, but not her own."

When he failed to explain, she said, "I sorrow for you, Lieutenant." A woman's laughter drew her glance to the people milling around them, and she lowered her voice. "I, too, once shared my heart with another."

He beckoned a servant, who exchanged their empty wine bowls for fresh ones. Taking her elbow, he steered her toward one of four tall, brightly painted wooden columns supporting the high ceiling. With the pillar at their backs and a large potted acacia to their right, they could speak with some privacy. "What tore the two of you apart?"

She stared at the noisy crowd. "He left me one day and never returned."

Bak could guess how she must feel. He had heard nothing of his lost love since she had left Buhen. Like him, he assumed, Meret had no idea whether her beloved lived or died, whether he had wed another or remained alone. "I assume Pentu shared with Amonked the wish that you and I become friends. More than friends. Does he know of your loss?"

"My sister told him. Together they decided I must forget. I must find someone new and wed. When Amonked suggested to Djehuty that you needed a wife, the four of them thought to bring us together." She looked up at Bak, a sudden smile playing across her face. "Now here we are . . ."

He eyed her over the rim of his drinking bowl and grinned. "Thrown at each other like a boy and girl of twelve or thirteen years."

They laughed together.

"Mistress Meret." Pahure stood beside the potted tree, looking annoyed. "A servant tripped while carrying a large storage jar filled with wine. When it broke, it splashed most of the other servants. The few whose clothing remains unstained can't possibly serve so many guests. You must come with me and see that those with soiled clothing change as quickly as possible."

"Tripped!" Meret looked dismayed. "The floor in the servants' quarters is perfectly smooth, and all obstacles were placed against the walls. What could he have stumbled over?"

"His feet, I suspect."

She shot an apologetic glance at Bak. "I fear I must leave you, Lieutenant. I may not return before you go, but do come again. We have more to talk about than I ever thought possible."

He gave her his most charming smile. "I'll see you another time, that I vow."

*   *   *

"You like her, I see." Bak's father, the physician Ptah-hotep, leaned against the mudbrick wall of the paddock and looked with interest upon his son.

Bak poured two heavy jars of water into the trough and stepped back. Victory and Defender, the fine black chariot horses he had been unwilling to part with when he had been exiled to the southern frontier, paid no heed. They had drunk their fill from the first jarful he had carried from the over-flowing irrigation channel outside the paddock.

"She seems not at all like her sister. I thank the lord Amon. If I'd found her to be manipulative, I'd have greeted her and no more."

"Amonked wouldn't do that to you." Ptahhotep's features were much like those of his son and he was of a similar height and breadth. The years had softened his muscles and turned the brown of his eyes to a deep gold, but no one could have thought him other than the younger man's sire. "Would you make a match with her?"

Bak knew Ptahhotep hoped to see him settle down with wife and family. "How can I say? I must spend more time with her, get to know her. But first, I must lay hands on the man who slew Woserhet."

Chapter Six

"Were you aware that Woserhet was an auditor?" Bak dropped onto the single free stool in the workshop, a rough-cut rectangular affair made for straddling.

"Yes, sir." On the floor beside his leg, Meryamon laid the long, delicate censer, shaped like an arm with an open hand at the end, that he had been inspecting. Newly polished, the gold it was made from glistened in the light like the flesh of the lord Re.

"Why didn't you say?"

Meryamon flushed, then glanced surreptitiously at the half-dozen men scattered along the lean-to that shaded two sides of the open court. A warm breeze rustled the palm fronds spread atop the shelter. Surrounded by ritual implements, they were cleaning and buffing bronze and gold and precious inlays for use during this and the eight remaining days of the Opet festival. Unseen craftsmen in another part of the building could be heard hammering metal. The young priest sat cross-legged on a reed mat, surrounded by objects given him for inspection. Many were outstanding examples of the metalsmith's craft.

"I guess I was too surprised to hear he'd been given the responsibility for the reversion of offerings. I had no idea he was so highly thought of."

"Were you not told that he reported to no less a man than the chief priest?"

"I knew Hapuseneb sent him, but I thought the audit routine."

Had it been routine? Bak did not know. Nor had Ptahmes been able to tell him. The aide had assumed so, at least at the beginning, but when Bak had found him in the house of life not an hour ago, before the long arm of the lord Khepre could reach into the sacred precinct, he had said, "Hapuseneb is a wily old bird; he may've sensed a transgression within the storehouses and brought Woserhet here without telling even him of his suspicions."

Unfortunately, Woserhet had repeated the same mistake with his scribe Tati, telling him nothing, letting him search with his eyes blinded by lack of knowledge.

Irked at the thought, Bak asked Meryamon, "How often did you have occasion to speak with him?"

The priest shrugged. "Two or three times at most. A greeting usually and not much else."

"What was your impression of him?"

Another shrug, and the closed expression of a man unwilling to commit himself.

Sighing inwardly, Bak wiped a film of sweat from his forehead. "Surely you thought something about him."

The priest studied his foot, refusing to meet Bak's eyes. "The sacred precinct is like a village, sir. People talk and you can't help listening. Listening and being influenced."

Bak felt as if he were pulling an arrow driven deep within a wooden target. The man would offer nothing without it being dragged from him. "From what you heard, Meryamon, what did you conclude about him?"

"They said he was a plodder, a man who searched out minor errors like a bee eater seeks a hive, and he wouldn't let rest the least significant matter until someone wasted the time it took to resolve the problem."

"Is that what you saw the few times you spoke with him?"

The priest's eyes darted toward Bak and away. A reddish

stain washed up his face. "I thought it best to have as little to do with him as possible."

Bak muttered an oath beneath his breath. Meryamon had no spine whatsoever—or so he appeared. He had managed to convince someone in authority that he was responsible enough to see that the priests were provided with the proper supplies and equipment for the various rituals. A demanding task he must be performing well or he would not be here.

Bak picked up a tall, thin, spouted libation jar. Made of gold and polished to a high sheen, it surpassed in beauty all the other objects scattered around the priest. "This was kept in the storehouse where Woserhet was found?"

Meryamon eyed the jar as if he feared the officer would drop it, marring its perfection. "Behind the records room, yes."

"So if the building had burned, this and all the other ritual objects except those being used in the procession would've burned with it." Thanking the lord Amon that such had not been the case, Bak returned the jar to the spot from which he had taken it. Such a loss would have been an abomination.

"All that remained inside would've been destroyed, yes, but these were safe. As is the custom, I'd gone to the storehouse the day before and removed everything the priests will use throughout the festival." Meryamon gestured toward the men toiling beneath the lean-to. "The ritual implements will be used time and time again until the lord Amon returns to his northern mansion. They're cleaned after each use."

Bak looked at the men and the precious objects scattered around them. Many had been crafted of gold, a few of the much rarer metal silver, others of bronze or faience or glass. Each a work of art. Objects considered by User to be of insignificant value when compared to those stored in the treasury.

"Where do you keep them when they're not in the storehouse?"

"Here. In this building. It's safer than carrying them back and forth." Meryamon smiled. "Never fear, sir. They're well cared for."

A short, fleshy servant seated beneath the lean-to spat out an oath and scrambled to his feet, swatting at something too small to see, a flying insect of some kind. His fellows laughed—until the tiny assailant moved on to fly around their heads. Spitting curses, a few men waved the creature off while the remainder covered their heads with their arms. Finally, an older, thinner man slapped the back of his neck and chortled success. Laughing at themselves, the men returned to their task.

Bak stood up, prepared to leave. As if an afterthought, he said, "Oh yes, I meant to ask you. The day the lord Amon traveled to Ipet-resyt, I saw you walking south along the processional way. You were with a red-haired man. I thought to join you, but lost you in the crowd. I once knew a man of similar appearance, but don't remember his name. I wonder if your friend is the one I knew."

A frown so slight Bak almost missed it touched Meryamon's face; he paused an instant to think. His eyes met Bak's and he spoke with the candor of an honest man. "I may've talked with such an individual, but I don't recall doing so."

Bak left the workshop, convinced Meryamon had lied. Why tell a falsehood over a trivial matter? Or was it trivial? What message had the shard contained? Had it in some way related to Woserhet's death?

He thought of the beautiful and valuable objects he had seen in the workshop. User might not believe them worthy of stealing, but to him—and no doubt to Meryamon as well—they were of greater value than anything he could hope to attain in a lifetime. Even when melted down and impossible to identify, as the objects would have to be in order to be disposed of in the land of Kemet, their value would be awesome.

Another telling fact to Bak's way of thinking: Meryamon had been the first man at the scene of the murder. He had raised the alarm in plenty of time to save the storage magazine and the valuable objects that had remained within, but had not summoned help until after many of the scrolls strewn around the body had burned. If he had been stealing from the storehouse, he would certainly know which documents might incriminate him.

"I didn't hear of Woserhet's death until yesterday morning." Nebamon, overseer of the block of storehouses in which Woserhet had died, glared blame at the elderly scribe at his side. "Before I could come to Ipet-isut to look into the matter, one of the scribal overseers at Ipet-resyt fell ill and I was pressed into taking his place. There went the day."

Bak broke the seal and swung open the door of the small room where Woserhet had been slain. "Stay near the entrance. I'm not satisfied I've learned all I can from this place."

The overseer grunted acknowledgment and stepped across the threshold. His scribe followed, holding aloft a flaming short-handled torch to illuminate as much of the room as possible. Bak remained outside but watched them closely to be sure they disturbed nothing.

"Hmmm." In the wavering light of the torch, Nebamon studied the chamber. Some men might have considered his appearance amusing, men who failed to notice how serious his demeanor was. He had a short and pudgy body, a three-quarter circle of curly white hair, and bushy white eyebrows. "The floor will need to be cleaned and the walls and ceiling repainted to cover the soot, but the damage appears to be minimal."

"The guards were quick to act. They feared the roof would catch fire and it would spread to other magazines."

"I'll see their swift action is rewarded. I'm convinced they averted a catastrophe." Nebamon shuddered. "With so few men nearby to fight a conflagration, it could've spread all through the sacred precinct."

Bak thought of the multitudes standing outside the enclosure wall, watching the procession. He was certain every man among them would have come running. "You knew of Woserhet's task, I've been told."

"User told us." The overseer turned to leave the building, and his scribe followed.

"Did you keep a close watch on what he was doing?"

"Close enough." Nebamon stepped up to a ladder leaning against the front of the building and placed a foot on the lowest rung. "From what I saw inside, I doubt the roof suffered damage, but I must look nonetheless. Will you come with me, Lieutenant?"

Bak followed him upward, while the scribe remained behind. A large flock of pigeons, caught sunning themselves in the warm glow of the lord Khepre, took flight as the men climbed onto the roof. The vaults of the long row of interconnected storage magazines formed a series of half cylinders butted together side by side. The smooth white plaster surface was mottled by bird droppings, and windblown dirt and sand filled the depressions between the ridges.

"You followed his progress from one storage magazine to another?" Bak asked.

"As long as he was examining this storage block, yes." Nebamon knelt on the ridge at a spot Bak judged to be directly above the area where the fire had been the hottest. The overseer drew a knife from the sheath at his belt and began to dig a hole in the plaster and the mudbrick beneath. "He finished with us over a week ago, apparently satisfied, and went on to another block. I was surprised to hear he'd come back. What was he doing here, Lieutenant? Do you know?"

"I was hoping you could tell me."

The overseer gave him a startled look. "Are you saying he told no one?"

"Not as far as I know."

"It never pays to be too secretive. Never."

Shaking his head to reinforce the thought, Nebamon dug deeper. He studied the hole as he excavated, searching for signs that the fire had crept through the straw mixed into the mud when the bricks were made. "You know, of course, that these storehouses are filled with valuables. Not merely ritual vessels but cult statues, amulets carved or molded of precious stones and metals, aromatic oils, incense, objects brought from far-off lands to adorn the god, the sacred shrine, the sacred barque."

"Meryamon mentioned only objects used in the rituals. Does he know of the other items?"

"He should. He comes here daily."

Kneeling beside the overseer, Bak picked up a small chunk dug from the rooftop and crumbled it with his fingers. The straw was brittle and dry but unburned. The dried mud was brown, not the red of burned brick. "Would he have an opportunity to steal?"

Nebamon's eyes narrowed. "Meryamon? What gave you that idea?"

"I'm asking, that's all."

"I suppose he could steal an item or two, but why would he? He has a position few men attain at such a young age. A man would have to've lost his wits to risk so much." The overseer moved to the hollow between the ridges and again dropped to his knees. "If anything had been missing, I'm confident Woserhet would've discovered the loss. He and his servants were very thorough. I watched them. They counted every object."

"You respected him, I see."

"He could be irksome at times." Nebamon, brushing the sand from the hollow, looked up and smiled. "As are all auditors." Sobering, he said. "He had a task to do and he did it well. He was slow and careful and precise, as wary of making a wrong accusation as he was of overlooking an offense against the lord Amon. I can't fault him for that, now can I?"

"I've heard he wasn't well liked."

"I suppose a few men resented him, feeling he was prying—and he was. But we're all men of experience. He's not the first auditor we've met, nor will he be the last."

Bak appreciated the overseer's attitude, a man who accepted the bad with the good, making no special fuss. "What can you tell me of Meryamon?"

"We're back to him, uh?" Nebamon grinned at Bak, then began to dig another hole. "He seems a likable enough young man."

"I seek something more specific," Bak said, returning the smile. "Where, for example, did he come from?"

"Somewhere to the north. Gebtu? Abedju? Ipu? That general area."

Some distance away, several days' journey at best. No easy way of narrowing that down without asking Meryamon himself. "His task requires a man of trust and dependability. To attain such a post, he must've come from a family of position and wealth. Or some man of influence befriended him."

Nebamon took a cloth from his belt and wiped the sweat from his face. "I've heard a provincial governor spoke up for him, but who that worthy man was, I don't recall. If ever I was told his name."

Vowing to dig deeper into Meryamon's past, Bak watched the pigeons circle around and settle on the far side of the roof, their soft cooing carrying on the air. "I saw you two days ago after the procession entered Ipet-resyt, watching a troupe of Hittite acrobats. Standing beside you was a red-haired man." He disliked deceiving so likable and industrious an individual, but the ploy had satisfied Meryamon, so why not use it again? "Many years ago, I knew someone who looked very much like him, but I don't recall his name. I wonder if he could be the man I knew?"

The overseer looked up from his small excavation. "I talked to dozens of people that day: friends, acquaintances, strangers." He broke apart a lump of dried mud and studied the straw embedded inside. Nodding his satisfaction, he rose to his feet. "The roof appears undamaged. I'll send a man up here to fill the holes and replaster, and it'll be as good as new."

As they walked together to the ladder, Bak asked, "Do you by chance remember the redhead? If I bump into him during the festival, I'd like to be able to call him by name."

"I've no idea who you're talking about. How can I recall one of so many?"

Was he telling the truth? Bak liked the overseer and thought him honest—at least he hoped he was. However, he could not deceive himself. As overseer of the storage block, Nebamon had unrestrained access and was less likely to be watched closely by those in attendance than was Meryamon. Also, he was responsible not only for storing the items, but for receiving them from far and wide and distributing them elsewhere. To where? Bak wondered. Amonked had not explained.

Bak left the lovely limestone court in front of Ipet-isut and walked south to the partially completed gate. The sun-struck pavement was so hot he could feel the warmth through the soles of his sandals. Striding through the gate, he paused at the low end of the construction ramps and looked south along the processional way toward the first barque sanctuary. There, just two days earlier, he had stood with his men, awaiting their dual sovereigns and the sacred triad.

The unfinished gate towers stood sadly neglected, the workmen released to enjoy the festival. A dozen boys, none more than ten years of age, were towing a large empty sledge up the ramp built against the east tower. One shouted out commands, pretending to be an overseer slapping his thigh with a stick, a make-believe baton of authority. The rest struggled mightily to pull the heavy vehicle. What they meant to do with the sledge when they reached the top, Bak dared not imagine.

On an impulse, he decided to climb the west ramp, bare and unoccupied except for a sledge laden with facing stones. With no foreman to complain that he would get in the workmen's way, he could ascend unimpeded to the top. From there he would have a panoramic view of the southern portion of the city.

The slope was not steep and soon he reached the upper end. As he had expected, the scene laid out before him was lovely. After passing the first barque sanctuary, the processional way swung west around the small walled mansion of the lady Mut, then cut a wide swath south to Ipet-resyt. Along much of the way, buildings pressed against the strips of trampled grass lining both sides of the broad thoroughfare. The sea of white rooftops was dotted at times with the dark brown of unpainted dwellings and islands of dusty green trees standing alone or clustered in groves. A sizable crowd had gathered beyond the mansion of the lady Mut to watch a procession of some kind.

He waved to the boys, who had stopped to rest, and moved to the western edge of the ramp, where he looked down into the housing area outside the small gate he and Amonked had used to reach the storehouse where Woserhet was slain. Few people walked the lanes; the day was too hot. Donkeys stood close to the dwellings in narrow slices of shade, and dogs lay well back in open doorways. A movement caught his eye. A man, a redhead, coming out of the sacred precinct. Turning toward the unfinished gate and the ramp on which Bak stood, the man walked along the lane at the base of the enclosure wall.

Bak could not see his face clearly, but the fuzzy hair was the color he remembered. He raced down the ramp, entered the lane running alongside, and ran back toward the enclosure wall. The redhead rounded the corner. He saw Bak, pivoted, and retreated the way he had come. Bak turned the corner and spotted him ahead, veering into a lane that led in among the housing blocks.

Bak raced to the point where the man had vanished, saw him turn into an intersecting lane. He sped after him. The man ducked into a narrower passage and another and another, zigging and zagging between building blocks that all looked much alike. Each time Bak lost sight of him, the sound of running footsteps and at times the barking of an agitated dog drew him on.

The red-haired man was fast and knew this part of the city well. He maintained his distance, twisting and turning without a pause. How far they ran, Bak had no idea, but he had begun to gasp for air and sweat was pouring from him when his quarry dashed out from among the building blocks and onto the grassy verge lining the processional way. A short burst of speed took him into the crowd Bak had seen from atop the ramp.

He was so focused on the redhead that he was slow to realize the procession was made up of men leading exotic animals imported from afar. Though not nearly as long as the procession of two days earlier, the number of spectators was large, with a multitude of wide-eyed and noisy children among equally enthralled adults. The redhead used the crowd to his advantage, letting his bright hair blend in among the many colorful banners carried by the youthful spectators. Bak lost him within moments.

Stopping to catch his breath, he paused at a booth to buy a jar of beer. He drank the thick, acrid liquid while he walked the length of the procession, searching for his quarry. His eyes strayed often to the creatures parading along the thoroughfare. He assumed they were the more manageable of the animals Maatkare Hatshepsut kept in a zoo within the walls surrounding the royal house. Except for a few special occasions, they were never seen by any but a privileged few. Why she had chosen to show them now, he had no idea.

An elderly black-maned lion held pride of place. Behind him, carried by porters wearing the bright garb of southern Kush, came a caged lioness and a leopard, both of which

Bak might well have seen in Buhen, being transported from far to the south on their way to Kemet. A leashed and muzzled hyena led a parade of baboons and monkeys, antelopes and gazelles, each creature with its own keeper. Men carried a few caged birds that had somehow survived the long journey from distant lands. Last in line, occupying another place of honor, lumbered a bear from lands to the north, led by a man of Mitanni.

The red-haired man, Bak concluded, had eluded him. Not one to give up easily, he turned back toward the sacred precinct.

"No, sir." The thin elderly scribe, whose dull white hair hung lank around his ears, dipped the end of his writing brush into a small bowl of water and swished it around, cleaning the black ink from it. "At least I don't think I know him. Your description lacks . . ." His voice tailed off, the silence saying more emphatically than words that his interrogator could have been describing almost anyone with red hair.

Bak was painfully aware of the deficiency of his spoken portrayal. The red-haired man had been too far away to describe properly. Bak would know him when he saw him, but to create a recognizable verbal image was close to impossible.

"Do you know all the redheads who toil within the sacred precinct?"

The scribe touched the tip of his wet brush to an ink cake and dabbed up a slick of red ink, letting Bak know he was a busy man and must get on with his task. "Not all, but I can tell you where to find one or two."

Bak walked into a large room whose ceiling was supported by tall columns. Light flooded the space from high windows, shining down on twenty or more men seated cross-legged on reed mats, writing beneath the sharp eye of their overseer. Near the front sat a youth with flame red hair. Curly but not fuzzy. A closer look revealed a body pale from spending most of the time indoors. The man Bak was looking for had the ruddy skin of one accustomed to the sun.

"Try Djeserseneb," the youth said after Bak had explained his mission. "His hair is red, about the color of a pomegranate. You'll find him at the goldsmith's workshop."

Had the man he chased had hair the color of the succulent fruit? Bak wondered. He would not have called it so, but different men saw things in different ways.

"Roy might be the man you've described."

The metalsmith, a muscular man whose hair was truly the color of a pomegranate and as straight as the thin gold wire his neighbor was forming, paused to adjust the tongs clamped around a small spouted bowl. Satisfied he would not drop the container, he poured a thin rivulet of molten gold into a mold on the floor in front of him. Bak could not tell what the finished image would be.

"He's a guard, one who watches over the sacred geese." The craftsman glanced upward to see the sun's position in the sky. "About this time of day, they open the tunnel and let the birds out for a swim. You'll find him awaiting them at the sacred lake."

A guard. A promising occupation. The red-haired man he had followed through the lanes had looked well-developed of body and had certainly been fast on his feet.

The guard's hair was bleached by the sun, strawlike and dry. Unlike the man Bak had chased, it had no spark of life and could be mistaken for brown from ten paces away.

"Sounds like Dedu," Roy said. "He's a sandalmaker. You'll find him in a workshop behind the house of life."

"And so my search went." Bak sat on a stool beneath the newly erected pavilion on the roof of the building where his men were housed. Hori had needed a shaded place to unroll and read the scrolls, so the Medjays had built the light structure before leaving to partake of the day's festivities. "I'm confident I met every red-haired man who toils within the sacred precinct. The man Meryamon denied knowing was not among them."

"If he's not there, where can he be found?" Kasaya asked.

· The ensuing silence was filled with birdsong, children's laughter and adult voices, the barking of dogs and the bray of a donkey.

Hori glanced ruefully at the scrolls spread across the rooftop, unrolled and held in place with stones. "Our day's been more productive, but I can't say we've learned anything."

Bak left the pavilion to look at the documents, making his way down one narrow aisle after another. The lord Re hovered above the peak beyond western Waset, offering plenty of light to see by. Many of the scrolls were in the condition he would have expected after Hori's initial sort: wholly intact or damaged at the edges with the ends burned away. The remainder, those he would never have guessed could be unrolled, were in various stages of destruction. Large segments remained of a few. Of the rest, patches of decreasing size had been salvaged, some little more than a few charred scraps.

He whistled. "I'm amazed you recovered so much."

"We've Kasaya to thank, sir." Hori grinned at the young Medjay. "He has the patience of a jackal sniffing out a grave. He'd sit there for an hour, bent over a charred scroll, unrolling it a bit at a time. You'd think the whole document a total loss, but sooner or later he'd find something inside I could read."

Bak smiled his appreciation at the hulking young Medjay, whose hands looked too large to manage any kind of delicate effort. "You've done very well, both of you. I couldn't have asked for more."

Hori and Kasaya exchanged a pleased smile. "We decided

that if the slayer took Woserhet's life to hide the fact that he's been stealing from the lord Amon, he'd probably have thrown any documents that might point a finger at him into the fire. If that was the case, the worst burned would be the most useful."

"I guess you know what you must do next," Bak said, his eyes sliding over the display.

"See if we can learn what the culprit was stealing."

"Should we concentrate on items Meryamon would've handled?" Kasaya asked.

Bak thought over the idea and shook his head. "No. Let the throwsticks fall where they will. If he's been stealing, signs of his activity should appear naturally, without making an effort to find them."

"But, sir," Hori said, clearly puzzled, "you told us the red-haired man ran when he saw you. Wouldn't that indicate guilt?"

"Guilt, yes, but for what reason we don't know. Also, I chased him, not Meryamon. One man's guilt is not necessarily that of another, and Meryamon's lie about knowing him doesn't make either man a thief."

"Can we help in any way, sir?" Sergeant Pashenuro reached into the pot of lamb stew and withdrew a chunk containing several ribs. "None of us can read, and it sounds to me as if that's what you need, but we'd like to be of some use."

"Never fear, Sergeant. When I require help, I'll summon you." Bak tore a piece of bread from a round, pointed loaf so recently taken from the heated pot in which it had been baked that it stung his fingers. "Until I do, let the men play. The festival won't last forever, and when it ends we'll set off for Mennufer. The lord Amon only knows when next they'll have time to relax."

Sergeant Psuro, a thickset Medjay whose face had been scarred by a childhood disease, swallowed a bite of green onion. "You don't seem too worried about laying hands on Woserhet's slayer."

"The more I learn, the more straightforward his death appears. He was probably slain because of a problem he unearthed in the lord Amon's storehouses. The trick is to learn exactly what that problem is—theft, no doubt—and to search out the man responsible."

Pashenuro looked across the courtyard, illuminated by a single torch mounted on the wall. The two men assigned to remain on watch were playing knucklebones with a marked lack of enthusiasm, both having returned after a long, hard day of revelry. Deep shadows fell around them, and around Bak and the sergeants, accenting the sporadic reddish glow beneath the cooking pot, dying embers stirred to life by the light breeze. Hori's dog lay with his back against a row of tall porous water jars, snoring and twitching.

A small boy came through the portal from the street. "Lieutenant Bak?"

"I'm Bak."

"I've come with a message, sir." The child spoke rapidly, running his sentences together in his eagerness to pass on what he had to say. "A man named Amonked wishes to see you, sir. He asks you to meet him at a grain warehouse near the harbor. Right away, he said. I'm to take you there."

The three men looked at one another, their curiosity aroused.

"Shall we go with you, sir?" Psuro asked.

"What did this man look like?" Bak asked the boy.

The child shrugged. "Like a scribe, sir."

"You could be describing any one of a thousand men," Pashenuro said, disgusted.

"Wouldn't Amonked send a note, sir?" Psuro asked.

"He may not have had the time or the means." Bak scooped up his baton and rose to his feet. "I suspect we're making too much of a simple summons. Lest I err, I'll send the boy back after we reach the warehouse. If I don't return by moonrise, he can lead you to me."

The building they approached looked like all the other warehouses strung along the river, especially in the dark, and the slightly ajar door before which they stopped opened into one of countless similar storage magazines in the area. A strong smell of grain greeted them, making Bak sneeze. He shoved the door wider and peered inside, expecting a light, finding nothing but darkness and an empty silence.

Amonked was not there. Disappointed, Bak turned to speak to the boy. The child was halfway down the lane, running as fast as his legs could carry him. Something was wrong!

Bak sensed movement behind him, started to turn. A hard object struck him on the head, his legs buckled, and his world turned black.

Chapter Seven

A pounding head brought Bak to his senses. He lay still and quiet, reluctant to move. Time passed, how much he did not know. He opened his eyes. At least he thought he did. But he could see nothing. What had happened? Where was he? He tried to rise, but pain shot through his head, intense and agonizing, centered somewhere over his right ear.

He had no choice but to lay motionless, allowing the pain to lessen to a fierce, persistent throbbing. He felt himself lying on . . . On what? He tried to think, to remember. He had been summoned by Amonked. A boy had led him to a warehouse near the river. He recalled standing outside, watching the child run away, and then . . . Yes, he had heard a movement behind him. After that . . . Nothing.

He could see no stars overhead, nor could he hear the creaking and groaning of ships moored along the river's edge or feel the light breeze. His assailant must have moved him. The air was hot, heavy, and dead silent. It carried the musty smell of grain and another odor he could not quite identify. A food smell. He was inside a building. A warehouse. Probably the one to which Amonked had summoned him.

No. Not Amonked. Someone else. Someone who wished to slay him? Or get him out of the way for a while?

He slid a foot back, raising his knee, and crooked an arm, thinking to prop himself up. The realization struck: his assailant had left him untied. Offering a heartfelt prayer of thanks to the lord Amon, he explored with his fingers the rough bed beneath him. He felt fabric, the heavy weave of storage bags, and a layer of dust. Touching a finger to his tongue, he tasted ashes, used to protect grain from insects and worms.

The sacks were full, plump with grain. A few kernels had escaped to lay among the ashes. As he had guessed, he was in a warehouse, most likely the same one he had approached without a qualm, thinking to meet Amonked. A block of buildings near the river, the lanes around it untraveled at night. In the unlikely event that his cries for help would carry through the thick mudbrick walls, no one would be outside to hear.

Why, in a warehouse, could he smell food? He frowned, trying to think. Not food, but what? Something scorched, burning. A thought, the sudden certain knowledge, sent a chill down his spine. The grain was on fire.

He sat up abruptly. The world spun around him and his head felt ready to burst. He thought he might be sick. He swallowed hard, reached up and gently probed the painful spot. A lump beneath his hair came alive to his touch and he felt a small patch of something wet. Blood.

Not enough to fret about, he told himself.

Twisting his upper body, taking care how he moved his head so as not to arouse the evil genie inside, he looked all around. He could see no bright, writhing inferno. The fire, he assumed, was smoldering in a bag or two of grain. The bags too tightly packed, too close together, to allow air to fuel the flame. Maybe the heart of the grain still lived, slightly green and moist. How long the fire would smolder, he could not begin to guess.

One thing he knew for a fact: he had to get out of the warehouse. He had heard tales of grain fires, of the very dust in the air bursting into flame. Even if untrue, the air would fill with a suffocating smoke as deadly as a conflagration.

This warehouse, like most others, would have a single

door and no windows. It might be vented in some manner, but the interior was blacker than night, making any small opening impossible to find. Therefore he must either excavate a hole in the mudbrick wall or find a way out the door. He needed a tool of some sort. Automatically he reached for the leather sheath hanging from his waist, felt the dagger inside. He laughed aloud; his assailant had been careless. The laugh was cut short by a cough, which jarred his splitting head.

He thought of Nebamon, the way the overseer had dug into the mudbrick of the storehouse in the sacred precinct. The arched roof had to have been at least four palm-widths thick. The walls supporting the heavy arch might be thicker. He would need a hole almost a cubit in diameter to crawl through. He felt certain the smell of burning was growing stronger. Could he dig himself out in time?

Better try the door. How hard was the wood? he wondered. How thick? Two fingers? Three? No matter. He could delay no longer.

He had not the vaguest idea where the door was, so first he had to find it. The bags beneath his feet were at a slightly lower level than those he sat on, which might mean some had been removed at one time or another. No man assigned to carry the heavy bags would collect them from deeper inside than necessary; he would take those nearest the door. Also, assuming Bak's assailant had been eager to get away, he would not have taken the time to drag him deep within the tunnellike chamber.

Satisfied with his reasoning, Bak faced the slope and rose to his feet like a sick, old man, holding his head straight and stiff. He took off a sandal and eased his foot forward, feeling the roundness of the bags and the slight hollows where they touched. The last thing he wanted was to fall—or to step into the fire he could not see. If the man had left him near the door, the odds were good that he had started the fire close by.

A second short, careful step. A third and a fourth. Without

warning, his forehead struck the ceiling. The pain in his head exploded. He stood motionless, letting the pounding dwindle to a painful but tolerable throb. He reached into the darkness ahead, found he had struck the downward curve of the vaulted arch. Ducking low, he stepped forward to the wall. A side wall, not the one at the end of the building that held the door.

Again he used the slope of the filled bags as a guide. Those to his right were piled lower than those to the left. He turned in that direction. After two cautious steps, he found himself half stumbling downward on the none-too-stable slope formed by the bags. He stepped onto the hard-packed earthen floor with a jolt. Congratulating himself for having guessed right thus far, he walked along the wall a half-dozen paces to the intersecting wall. Less than three paces away, if his assumptions were correct, he would find the door, the sole exit. He laughed aloud, coughed, felt sure his head would split.

Trying not to breathe, trying to ease the tickle in his throat, he realized that the smell of smoke was more noticeable than before. He must waste no more time.

Using the wall as a guide, he walked forward and quickly found the door. Well aware of how futile the effort was, he gave it a good hard shove. In this case, his assailant had taken due care. The door had been barred shut. He slipped his dagger from its sheath and, squashing all thought, set to work. He started at a crack between boards and at a point slightly above waist height, where the bars were usually placed on doors. His dagger was sharp, the bronze well hardened. The wood of the door was softer than he expected but with knots as hard as granite.

He put all his strength behind the effort, shaving away the wood along the edges of the adjoining boards, cutting ever deeper and widening the hollow. The sweat poured from him and thirst plagued him. His aching arms and wrists felt heavy and wooden. The smoke thickened and he coughed hard and often. The pain in his head seemed less intense, less nagging. Maybe because he was too distracted to give it attention. Maybe because he was getting used to it, or his senses were too numbed to feel.

He stopped to wipe the sweat from his face. A fit of coughing reminded him again to hurry. Before the warehouse filled with smoke. Before the fire burst into life.

With grim determination, he gouged another chunk of wood loose, shoved the blade hard, and burst through the last fragile sliver between him and the outside world. He knelt, tried to see through the hole. It was too small, the night outside too dark. He bared his teeth in a sardonic smile. Now all he had to do was make the hole big enough to reach through to the bar and lift it. An endless task, that promised to be. Or to call for help in the unlikely event that anyone passed by.

He blanked out so discouraging a thought and began to enlarge the hole. The smoke made his eyes sting and tears spilled from them. He had to stop often to wipe them. Sudden, violent attacks of coughing beset him. He needed air. Good, clean air. Like the air seeping in from outside, caressing his hand while he enlarged the hole.

Chiding himself for his failure to think of so obvious a relief, he knelt before the opening, which had grown to roughly the size of a goose egg, and took several deep breaths. After an initial spate of coughing, his breathing became less labored. How long he knelt there, his forehead resting on the door, taking in the sweet cool air, he had no idea. When he set to work again, he felt considerably better—and more optimistic.

The feeling was short-lived. The blade of his dagger began to lose its edge, and he struck a small knot so hard the pointed tip broke off. Spitting out a string of oaths, resentful of every moment it took, he cut the softer wood from around the harder. In the end, with just a small segment holding the knot in place, he turned his dagger around and, with the handle, broke the stubborn thing away, leaving a greatly enlarged, odd shaped hole that he could almost get his hand through. Anger turned to exultation.

He rewarded himself with another brief respite, wiping his streaming eyes and gulping in air. Somewhat restored, he poked his fingers through the hole and felt around for the bar holding the door closed. He could not reach far enough.

He toiled on, trying not to think or feel. Trying not to see how slowly the hole was expanding and how dull the blade was getting. Trying not to notice how light-headed he was beginning to feel. A long fit of coughing stopped him, forced him to put mouth and nose to the hole and breathe in the clean outside air. When the dizziness passed, he slipped his hand into the hole. It went all the way through and his wrist followed. Offering a quick prayer to the lord Amon, he felt for the bar, found it above the hole, forced it upward with the tips of his fingers. It tilted slightly to one side, but he could not raise it above the supports holding it in place.

Snarling an oath, he shoved his arm painfully far into the opening and raised the bar as high as he could. It fell away, striking the ground outside with a thud. Feeling immeasurable relief, he shouldered the door open and staggered out. Falling to his knees, he took a deep breath, coughed, sucked in air, and coughed again. He offered a hasty but fervent prayer of thanks, struggled to his feet and ran on unsteady legs toward the harbor and help. The god's warehouse and the grain within must be saved.

"I thank the lord Amon the fire had no chance to flare." Bak bit into a chunk of lamb left over from the previous evening. "If it had, the entire block would've burned and the god would've lost enough grain to feed a small city."

He sat with Pashenuro and Psuro in the courtyard of his Medjays' temporary quarters, savoring the cold stew after an exhausting night and not enough sleep. The bump on his head was no smaller, but it hurt only when touched. The sound of snoring came from inside the building, where many of his men had collapsed on their sleeping pallets after a long night of revelry. A pigeon drank from a bowl of water left for Hori's dog, and a mouse sneaked a bit of stale bread thrown out for birds.

Pashenuro used a chunk of bread to spoon up the stew. "The gods truly smiled upon you, sir, placing nearby a cargo ship and its crew."

"I'm grateful they were on board. They might well have been away, celebrating the festival as our men were." Bak took a sip of beer, thinking to wash the huskiness from his voice, the soreness from his throat. The brew was too bland to serve the purpose. "The captain sent a man off to get more help, and the fire was out in less than an hour."

Psuro toyed with his beer jar, his brow wrinkled with worry. "That was a deliberate attempt to slay you, sir."

"So it would seem."

"Who was responsible? The man who slew Woserhet?"

"Fire was used in both cases." Bak's grim expression changed to one of puzzlement. "Yet if both vile deeds were the acts of a single man, why did he not slash my throat as he did the auditor's? He had every opportunity."

"He felt certain you'd perish in the fire," Pashenuro said.

"He must soon be snared. To start a fire in such a place was an abomination, proving he has no regard for man or beast. There are housing blocks nearby, other warehouses, ships moored along the waterfront. The lord Amon only knows how many might've died if the fire had not been quenched."

"Are you sure you're all right, sir?" Hori, seated on the rooftop in the shade of the pavilion, flung a worried look across a large round basket containing several rolled scrolls.

Bak waved off the youth's concern. "Other than this cough, a raw throat, a headache, and the stench of smoke lingering in my nostrils, I feel well enough." Dropping onto the stool, he eyed the scrolls in the basket, most undamaged, a few singed, and a pile of five or six lying flat beside the container and held down by stones. The latter documents' edges were blackened and irregular; the writing tailed off at the burned ends. "Tell me what you've learned so far."

"The morning's young, and I haven't had much time."

"When a man tries to slay me, I wish to learn his name as quickly as possible." Bak formed a smile, thinking to soften the sting of words all too true.

Flushing, Hori wasted no time in prologue. "I wanted first to get a general impression of the scrolls' contents, so I started by reading an undamaged document and writing down all the items it mentioned." He gestured toward the basket—which held the scrolls he had read so far, Bak assumed—and a white-plastered board on the rooftop beside him, containing several columns of the youth's small, neat symbols. "I went on to a partly burned document and did the same." He pointed to the pile of scrolls spread flat on the roof. "After that, I tried to read a badly burned one." He nodded toward the charred scraps laid out where Bak had last seen them. "Those were so fragile I thought it best not to move them."

Kasaya came bounding up the stairs with Hori's dog at his heels. He ducked beneath the shelter, overturned a large pot, and sat down. The dog settled beside him and eyed his young master with sad brown eyes. He knew better than to disturb the scribe when he was surrounded by scrolls.

"You've come back empty-handed," Bak said to the Medjay. "Where's Tati?"

"I couldn't find him." Kasaya kicked off a sandal and bent to scratch a foot. "The one workman watching the house where they dwell didn't know where he was, and when I asked if we could come and look at the records, he refused. Tati had told him they belong to the lord Amon, and no less a man than the chief priest can see them." He noted Bak's scowl and spread his hands wide, absolving himself of all responsibility.

Bak closed his eyes and began to count, seeking patience. His inability to speak with Hapuseneb during the Beautiful Feast of Opet was becoming more burdensome each day. The records, he felt sure, would shorten his path to the auditor's slayer, and he needed Tati's help. "Go on, Hori. Tell me what you did next."

"I continued as before, moving from one group to another. I have a long way to go, but I think I've found a pattern. Perhaps more than one."

"For example." Bak's words came out like the croak of a frog.

"Each scroll lists many objects, all of a similar type," Hori said. "More than half the undamaged documents I've read so far are for the various kinds of grain stored here in Waset. They give the date a shipment was received and the quantity placed in the warehouse and, later, the date and number of bags removed, either for use here at Ipet-isut or for shipment to one of the lord Amon's estates."

"I assume the other items that turn up regularly are hides and metal ingots."

"Yes, sir."

"Like the grain, items too heavy and bulky to move with ease." Bak cleared his throat, smothering a cough.

Hori flung a concerned look his way, but had the good sense to make no comment. "Of the partly burned scrolls I've read so far, most list items manufactured in the god's workshops and on the various estates and sent here for storage and use. Lengths of linen, pottery, sandals, wine, and so on. As for the scraps Kasaya managed to save, they're really hard to read and take a lot of guesswork, but I saw the symbols for bronze and gold. Aromatic oils. Something that might've been ivory."

"Interesting," Bak said thoughtfully. "The items listed are many and varied. The documents obviously came from more than one storage block."

"Yes, sir. I think Woserhet himself took them into that

room, at least some of them. Or someone else did. There's
certainly no grain in that storehouse."

"He couldn't have carried very many without a basket."
Bak's eyes darted toward the Medjay. "I saw no burned remains. Did you, Kasaya?"

"I didn't notice, sir. Should I take a closer look?"

"Yes." Bak looked across the roof at the scraps of burned
scrolls the young policeman had so painstakingly saved.
"Do you think you could glue some of those broken storage
pots back together? I'd like to know where they came
from."

The Medjay thought over the idea, smiled like a child facing a new challenge, and stood up. "I must find a basket first,
then I'll bring the pieces back here."

"You were right about a pattern." Bak stood up and arched
his back, stretching muscles made stiff from hunching over
the blackened scraps of papyrus Kasaya had saved. He
walked to the pavilion, pleased with the morning's effort.
"With few exceptions, the documents not damaged by fire
list grain or some other product valuable in itself but not
easy to move."

Hori shoved aside the large basket, now filled with the intact scrolls they had read. "You'd think the slayer would've
thrown them into the fire, too. If for no other reason than to
confuse."

"He was probably in a hurry, afraid of being seen."

The scribe pulled over a small basket containing, if the
smell told true, fish wrapped in wilting leaves. A flat, round
loaf of bread lay on top with a spray of green onions and a
bundle of radishes. "As I guessed earlier, most of the partly
burned scrolls list products made for the lord Amon and
brought from afar."

Bak dragged the stool into the shade, sat down, and accepted a leaf-wrapped packet. "User told me the storage
magazines in that block contain not only vessels and prod-

ucts used during the rituals, but other objects made to adorn
the god, his shrine and the sacred barque."

The scribe broke off a chunk of bread and handed it over.
"The same items listed on the worst burned scrolls. Those
few scraps we could read with certainty, at any rate."

Kasaya laid aside the third storage jar whose inscribed
shoulder he had roughly pieced together and scooted closer
to the food basket. "In other words, the man who slew him
threw onto the fire the documents that might point a finger
at himself, calling him a thief, and added a few others as
fuel."

"We've not yet confirmed that Woserhet was searching for
a thief," Bak reminded him.

"I can think of no more logical an assumption," Hori said.

"Nor can I," Bak admitted. He opened the packet and
sniffed the slab of fish laying inside, boiled so long the flesh
was flaking apart. "Kasaya, how many storage pots do you
think were broken?"

"I'm not sure. More than a dozen, I'd guess."

"Meryamon said there were fifteen or twenty empty
spaces on the shelves."

Kasaya eyed the three jars whose shoulders he had reconstructed. "You've read the inscriptions I've pieced together
so far. They say the jars belonged in the room where we
found them."

"Both Nebamon and Meryamon have easy access to that
storehouse." Hori thought a moment, added, "But Meryamon lied about knowing the red-haired man." He turned to
Bak, his eyes glittering with a growing conviction. "You
saw with your own eyes the one pass a message to the
other."

"I admit he looks guilty, but . . ."

"He has a secret he doesn't want aired," Kasaya said. "A
secret of some import. What could be more loathsome than
the theft of ritual equipment?"

"Sir!" Psuro poked his head up through the opening at the top of the stairs. "A messenger has come from Amonked. He wishes you to meet him right away. A man has been found slain. A second death in the sacred precinct."

Chapter Eight

Bak let out a long, stunned breath. "It's Meryamon."

"Yes." Amonked stared down at the body, his face bleak. "Another death much like that of Woserhet."

Taking care where he placed his feet, Bak stepped closer to the dead man through tall, thick weeds and grasses that had sprung up on the moist earth behind Ipet-isut. "No attempt was made to burn him."

"No, but his throat . . ." Amonked's voice tailed off and he looked away.

Bak bent low to study the body, bringing to life the dull ache in his head. The young priest lay on his back, his shoulders raised slightly on a thick clump of grass, his head hanging back to reveal a long cut across his throat. Flies swarmed around the wound and over reddish smudges on his body. He had not been slain where he lay. The vegetation beneath and around him was smeared with dried blood, as was a trail of bruised foliage about four paces long leading out to a path that ran along the base of the god's mansion. An attempt had been made to make the bloody trail look normal. The weeds had been pushed roughly back into place and dirt had been thrown over them, probably while the blood was wet, so no one would notice. Several whose stems had broken were wilting, an anomaly that had caught the attention of the young man who had found the body. Visibly upset, he stood on the path with Amonked, Psuro, and two Medjays from Bak's company of policemen.

Bak waded through the weeds beside the track along which Meryamon had been dragged. As was to be expected from such a long and deep incision, the priest had bled freely. The dirt and sand thrown over the foliage in no way covered the stains, but would have concealed them from casual passersby.

As he neared the edge of the vegetation, he snapped from a bush a twig thickly covered with small leaves. Kneeling beside the path, he studied the dirt, which looked as if it had been disturbed by the passage of perhaps a half-dozen people coming and going. Not nearly enough, to his way of thinking, for a path in constant use day in and day out, as this one was.

The footprints ended not far away, at the center back of the mansion of the lord Amon, in a jumble of smudged tracks left by individuals who had come to offer prayers at the chapel of the hearing ear. A length of white linen, stained by age, dust, and burning sunlight, covered the opening to a shallow booth that sheltered what he knew to be a deep relief of the deity carved into the wall directly behind the sanctuary. There, he reasoned, was the most likely place to slay a man, catching him unawares while he conversed with the god.

He carefully brushed away the upper surface of dirt about a pacc to the right of the spot where the body had been dragged into the weeds. He found blood. Here, too, the slayer had thrown dirt, thinking to hide all signs of the murder—and his own footprints as well.

Bak swept away more dirt, following the trail of blood. Although trampled by those who had come since the murder, the track was clear enough, and soon he reached a spot directly in front of the chapel. A small brownish stain at the lower edge of the cloth told him he had guessed right. He brushed away more dirt and found a much disturbed puddle of dried blood that had flowed beneath the cloth and into the shelter. Pushing aside the cover, he revealed the relief in a niche. On both sides of the windowlike frame were the large, deeply carved ears of the lord Amon. Here, any man or woman great or small could come in times of need to pray to the god or to seek aid.

Visited by many through the course of a day, this would have been a risky place to slay a man. It was, however, isolated and hidden from the general view, making it an ideal place to commit so heinous a crime at sunset when people were eating their evening meal and preparing for the night, or early in the morning before they began to stir.

He let the cloth fall into place and joined the others. "Bring him out to the path. I need a better, closer look."

Psuro nodded to the two Medjays, who carried a litter into the weeds. While they rolled the body onto it and brought it back, Bak questioned the young man who had found Meryamon. He had seen a woman and child bending a knee before the shrine and no one else. The wilted vegetation had caught his attention and the many flies had drawn his eyes to the body. He had realized right away that the blood was dry, that Meryamon had been dead for some time. He had sent the woman for help and that's all he knew.

Bak allowed him to leave and turned to the body. He ran his fingers through Meryamon's hair and detected no bump or blood. He rolled him one way and then the other and found no bruises or cuts. The priest must have been down on his knees, praying to the god, when his assailant came up behind him and slit his throat. It had probably happened so fast that he had felt nothing, simply toppled over. Not wanting him found too quickly, the slayer had pulled him into the weeds and hastily thrown dirt around, hiding him temporarily from all but the most inquisitive.

Glancing at the chapel, Bak imagined the deeply carved image of the lord Amon, listening to Meryamon speak, possibly plead for . . . For what? What had the priest needed or desired? Had he known Woserhet's slayer and asked for advice or absolution? Had he feared his life would be taken by the same hand? Whatever his need, the god had failed him.

Bak whisked the flies away from the wound with the twig. The insects swarmed upward. Swallowing his distaste, he took a closer look at the dead man's neck. He muttered an oath. He had seen a similar cut before, not once but twice.

"Take him away," he told Psuro. "To the house of death."

"Yes, sir."

"And I must speak with Hori."

"I'll send a man for him."

The sergeant, followed by the Medjays carrying the litter, hastened down the path and vanished around the corner of Ipet-isut. Bak and Amonked followed at a slower pace.

Bak flung his makeshift brush into the weeds and wiped his hands together as if ridding them of the feel of death. "The Hittite merchant Maruwa was slain in the same way as Meryamon and Woserhet, and by the same man."

"Are you certain?" Amonked asked, caught by surprise.

"I'd wager my iron dagger that they were." Iron was a metal more rare than silver and more valuable than gold, and the dagger had been a gift from the only woman Bak had ever loved. To him, it was priceless, as Amonked knew. "Two men slain in a similar manner over a short period of time might be a coincidence. Three such occurrences are more likely than not related."

"I can easily see a connection between Woserhet's death and that of Meryamon. Each man toiled for the lord Amon and dealt daily with the valuable objects in his storage magazines. But what of the Hittite?"

"I have no idea," Bak admitted. "Importing horses for the royal stables is a world removed from the storehouses within the sacred precinct."

"Meryamon had no family in Waset, so he shared these quarters with several men of similar circumstances who toil here in the sacred precinct." Bak crossed the threshold, leaving the small dwelling in which the priest had lived.

Hori stood outside, trying to catch his breath after his speedy journey from the Medjays' quarters. "How will I know which records were his, sir?"

"They keep no records here." Bak led the way down the narrow, dusty lane. "Such a thing is frowned upon by the Overseer of Overseers, who insists that all records remain in the storage blocks or be taken to the central storehouse archives. Also, the house is too small, with no space for anything but the most personal of items. In Meryamon's case, clothing, scribal equipment, and a few short letters from his father, a public scribe in Abedju."

The path they trod was hugged on both sides by small interconnected buildings that housed servants of the lord Amon and their families: craftsmen, scribes, bakers and brewers, and innumerable others who performed duties related to the well-being of the deity and the priests and scribes who tended to the god's needs.

Hori half ran to keep up. "Since many of the records Meryamon kept in the storage block now lie on the roof of our quarters, practically impossible to read, I'll go to the archives. How far back should I begin?"

"The day he was given his present task. About three years ago, according to the men who shared his dwelling place."

"I thank the lord Amon he was a young man." Hori dropped back to follow Bak around a donkey tethered in front of an open doorway. Inside they heard a woman berating her husband. "By the time I finish this task, I'll know the comings and goings of the ritual equipment as well as he did. Maybe better."

Bak ignored the mild complaint. "While you're there, ask the scribes if they have any records of dealings between the Hittite merchant Maruwa and any scribe or priest within the sacred precinct."

"Why would the lord Amon have need of horses? They're

much too valuable to be used as beasts of burden or for food or to be sacrificed. I know couriers sometimes ride them, but all they're really good for is to pull a chariot."

"I'll not lay down a bet that you'll find him named," Bak admitted, "but you must look anyway. And don't forget the workshop where the objects are cleaned and repaired. They'll have records, too."

"I know no more now than I did the day Maruwa died." Lieutenant Karoya eyed the busy market, his expression glum. "I've had scant time to give the matter the attention it deserves. My duties during the Beautiful Feast of Opet are many and varied, and the offenses my men detect each day are multiplied ten times ten over those of any ordinary day." He raised a hand as if to stave off comment. "I know, sir. I'm making excuses where none should be made."

Bak ducked out of the way of two men carrying a large rectangular wooden box that looked much like an unadorned coffin. "I can see for myself how many ships lie along the waterfront and how busy this market has become."

His elbow bumped a wooden support, making the rickety stall beside them rock. Strung beads hanging from a cross-beam rattled, earning Bak a scowl from the proprietor, a wrinkled old man who sat on the ground surrounded by his wares: beads and amulets, bracelets and anklets, combs, perfume bottles, and the sticks and brushes used for painting the eyes and lips.

"I wish I had more time. From what little I've learned, Maruwa was a decent man and deserves better." Karoya's attention was focused on three harbor patrolmen standing in the middle of the broad pathway between the rows of stalls, questioning a man caught substituting false weights for true. The miscreant was on his knees, with two patrolmen holding him and one applying a stick to his back and legs. A crowd had begun to form around them, blocking the pathway, forcing others to watch whether or not they wanted to. The onlookers talked among themselves, some curious, some complaining, some thrilled by the small spectacle. A few offered wagers as to exactly how long the scoundrel could hold out before admitting his offense.

Bak queried Karoya with a glance, and the young Medjay officer nodded. Together, they stepped into the open, making themselves visible. Men of authority keeping an eye out for trouble. The crowd seemed mild enough, but like all spontaneous and uncontrolled gatherings, could quickly go out of control.

"Have you learned anything about his activities here in Waset?" Bak asked.

"Not much."

"Was he not a regular visitor to the city?"

"He came often enough, once or twice a year. But merchants come and go. They seldom establish long or deep friendships. Not here at the harbor, at any rate." Karoya paused, letting a braying donkey have its say. "I wish I could be of more help, sir, but you see how it is." He swung his arm in an arc encompassing the growing crowd and the noisy activity around them.

Bak sympathized. The waterfront was lined with ships four or five deep and the market was three or four times larger and busier than when last he had seen it. "I'd suggest you go to the garrison for help, but by the time you've trained more men, the festival will be over."

"I'm sorely tempted nonetheless."

Karoya studied the gathering crowd, the increased betting. A resolute look settled on his face and he whistled a signal to his men. They jerked their prisoner to his feet and lowered their spears to a diagonal, the points slightly above head level should they need to force their way through the crowd. Onlookers stepped aside, opening a path, and they half walked, half dragged the rogue to the side lane that led to their building.

The Medjay officer visibly relaxed. "The men I've talked

with—both sailors and other merchants—all agreed that Maruwa was good-natured, easy to be with, and was utterly honest in his dealings. As far as they know, he had no woman troubles, no debts, no bad habits."

"What of Captain Antef's suggestion that he might've been involved in Hittite politics?"

Karoya stepped away from the booth and led the way into the rapidly dispersing crowd. "If he was, either no one knew or no one will speak of it."

"I assume you've talked with Hittites dwelling in Waset?"

"Yes, sir. Well, with one, at any rate. I spoke with a man named Hantawiya, who's a kind of informal leader among them. He seemed not to like Maruwa very much. I guess the merchant had taken a woman of Kemet as his concubine and it didn't set well with Hantawiya, but he could find nothing bad to say about him." Karoya smiled, remembering. "I could see he wanted to."

Bak stepped hastily around a woman carrying a large basket of coarsely ground flour. She reeked of sweat and a harsh perfume. He was not convinced one man's opinion of another was in any way satisfactory. "He made no connection between Maruwa and the sacred precinct of the lord Amon?"

"The subject never arose, and I'm certain it would've if Hantawiya had suspected such a thing. He's the kind of man who seeks reasons for disapproval, and he'd certainly not condone one of his countrymen getting involved with a god of any land but that of Hatti."

"He sounds a disagreeable sort."

"He is." Karoya sidled past a mound of greenish melons displayed on the ground. "I can't believe Maruwa's murder is connected to those in the sacred precinct, yet your description of the men's throats . . ." He shook his head, obviously mystified. "What in the name of the lord Amon can the connection be?"

* * *

"I can't say I knew Maruwa well, but I enjoyed his company, respected him. I suppose I thought of him as a friend." Commander Minnakht, master of the royal stables, walked beneath the portico that shaded a long line of open doorways, from which came the strong smell of horses. The thud of hooves, the rustle of hay, an animal's soft nickering could be heard within. "He seemed a fine man, and I mourn his death."

"Did he speak of other men he provided with horses?" Bak asked. Each time he inhaled the rich smell of the stable, a twinge of homesickness touched his heart. Most of the time he did not regret his exile to the southern frontier and his life as a policeman, but now and again—here and now— he yearned to return to the past and resume the life of the chariotry officer he had once been.

"He told me more than once how proud he was that we thought all his horses worthy of the royal stables. From that, I assumed we were his sole customers. We and Menkheperre Thutmose, of course. Maruwa also delivered horses to the royal house in Mennufer on a regular basis."

"Who exactly do you mean by 'we'? You and . . ."

"Those of us who looked at the animals he brought and made the decision to keep them. I speak of myself and the men who see to the animals' training."

The commander was a large man in every respect. He was tall and heavy, his legs solid and muscular. His neck was so thick it seemed a part of his head. He had the largest hands Bak had ever seen, and the thickest wrists. His voice was deep and strong, his manner self-assured.

A hefty young man emerged from the large walled circle surrounding the well in front of the portico. Two heavy water jars were suspended from a yoke across his shoulders. The acrid smell of sweat wafted from him as he walked past and entered the nearest doorway.

Bak peeked inside. Beyond a high mound of straw mixed with manure, he saw a narrow room, somewhat like a storehouse but longer, with openings all along the roof to let in light and air. No horses were there, but several men were laying fresh straw, while others were filling the water and grain troughs that lined one wall. Each animal's position was marked by a stone fixed into the floor, with a hole in the center for tying the creature.

He thought of the many long days his own team had spent in an identical stable, and could not help but wonder if they missed the companionship of others of their kind. Smiling at such a flight of fancy—the two horses were more than content, gamboling around the large paddock at his father's small farm—he turned his thoughts to more productive exercise.

Captain Antef had suggested Maruwa might have been involved in Hittite politics, but could he have assumed Hittite when in reality the merchant had been embroiled in the politics of Kemet? He would not have dealt directly with either Maatkare Hatshepsut or Menkheperre Thutmose, but might well have favored one over the other.

"Did he ever express a preference between our sovereign and her nephew?" The young man who shares the throne but not the power, Bak added to himself. A young man wise enough to come to Waset and participate with his aunt in the all-important Opet rituals, thereby reminding those who should one day bow before him that he was the offspring of the lord Amon. Best not to air those thoughts while within the confines of the royal residence.

"He didn't seem to care which of the two ruled our land. He told me once he thought them both capable, a high compliment from a man as able as he was." The commander laughed. "Oh, he was puzzled by the fact that Maatkare Hatshepsut allows Thutmose to live. Which is understandable. Any man who assumes the throne in Hatti slays everyone who might have the least excuse to wrest the power from him. A man born and reared there would expect the same of us."

Bak chose not to mention that he had heard men of Kemet, especially soldiers on the southern frontier, express the same puzzlement. "Did he ever give any indication that he might've been involved in the politics of his homeland?"

"None whatsoever." A horse screamed somewhere beyond a block of storage magazines. Minnakht raised his head, listening. When no further sound was heard, he smiled ruefully. "A couple of young stallions have been fighting. We decided to geld them."

Bak returned a sympathetic smile. Increasing a herd of fine horses through breeding was as important, if not more so, than importing animals from other lands to enhance the royal herd. "So you believe Maruwa held no interest in politics."

"He was a sensible man, Lieutenant. He'd not have been allowed to export horses from Hatti or import them here if anyone in power had had the least suspicion he dabbled in politics, theirs or ours. I'd wager our sovereign's favorite chariot team that he stayed well clear."

Far too rash a wager to dismiss lightly the commander's conviction, Bak thought.

Minnakht eyed him speculatively. "Have you heard otherwise?"

"One man suggested the possibility. I suspect he threw it out because it was the first reason he could think of for the slaying."

"A loose tongue," the commander said scornfully. "Bah!"

"Did Maruwa ever mention knowing anyone who lives or toils in the sacred precinct of the lord Amon?"

Minnakht laughed. "What would a Hittite merchant dealing in horses have to do with piety and priests?" He noticed the look on Bak's face; the laughter faded to a wry smile. "I see my question is not new to you."

"I've asked it of myself, yes. More than once." Realizing an explanation was in order, Bak told the commander of Woserhet's death and of Meryamon's. "You see why I've come today."

"I've been wondering. I'd been told the harbor patrol was investigating Maruwa's death and now here you are. Amonked's friend. The man from Buhen who laid hands on the malign spirit at Djeser Djeseru. A considerable step up from a simple harbor patrol officer."

"Lieutenant Karoya is a good man, sir."

"I'm certain he is." Minnakht glanced at the man with the yoke, returning to the well with empty jars. "Maruwa had a woman here in Waset. Has anyone told you of her?"

"Someone mentioned a concubine, but I wasn't sure she'd remained a part of his life."

"I believe he was very fond of her. He may've confided in her."

Several men came out the door, carrying baskets of manure-laced straw, and passed through a gate at the far end of the portico. The waste, Bak assumed, would be saved for use as fertilizer in the gardens within the royal compound.

"Can you tell me where I can find her?" he asked.

The commander shook his head. "I don't know her name or where she dwells, but Sergeant Khereuf may. He oversees the training of all our horses. He and Maruwa became quite friendly."

"I was proud to count Maruwa among my friends." Sergeant Khereuf, a tall, sturdy man of middle years, clutched the rope halter of a young white stallion and ran his hand down its long nose. The animal trembled at his touch, but made no attempt to break away. "I doubt I'll ever meet another man who knows horses like he did."

Bak walked around the stallion, examining its slender legs, sturdy neck, and muscular body. Its coat was damp from a long, hard run, and it needed to be cooled down and dried off. "Who'll bring horses to Kemet now?"

"The lord Amon only knows!" Startled by the vehemence in the sergeant's voice, the horse jerked backward. Other than tightening his hold on the halter, Khereuf gave no sign that he noticed.

"Should you not walk that stallion?" Bak asked.

A look of approval touched the sergeant's face, a hint of surprise that a police officer would recognize the animal's need. As he led the horse to a well-worn path shaded by date palms that lined the rear wall of the royal compound, he asked, "You've spent time with horses, sir?"

"I once was a chariotry officer, a lieutenant in the regiment of Amon."

Khereuf was openly impressed, and any reticence he might have had about speaking to a police officer vanished. "What do you wish to know, sir? I'll help you all I can. I liked Maruwa. I want to see his slayer punished."

"Other than horses, what did the two of you talk about?"

The sergeant shrugged. "Not much of anything, I guess."

Bak smothered an oath. He had met men like Khereuf in the garrison stables, men who could converse better with horses than with their fellows. But since Maruwa had come from a far-off land, perhaps he had given birth to a wider interest. "Did he speak of the land of Hatti?"

"Oh. Well, yes. He told me of the mountains, the vast plains, and hills covered with trees." Khereuf's step faltered, he gave Bak an amazed look. "Can you imagine, sir? Trees everywhere you look?" Shaking his head in wonder, he walked on.

"What else did he speak of?"

Khereuf said nothing, gathering his thoughts, then the words overflowed. "He told me of the village where he was born and the city where he made his home. He told me of his travels and the many wondrous things he'd seen. Rivers that flow in the wrong direction, from north to south, and mountains reaching high into the clouds. Frequent rainstorms where the gods throw fire and shake the earth with noise, where in the cold months, rain turns solid and white and covers the land."

Bak did not smile at the sergeant's awe, for he, too, had trouble imagining such wonders. From the first time he had heard of them, he had hoped one day he would see them for himself. "Did he dwell in the capital? In Hattusa?"

Spotting a man ahead approaching with a big bay gelding, Khereuf led the stallion off the path, onto the damp earth between the trees. "No, sir. He kept his wife and family in a place called Nesa. Many days' walk from the capital, he told me."

"Did he go often to Hattusa?"

"Not unless he had to. He disliked the endless quest for power he found there, preferring instead a simpler life."

Bak fervently wished the sergeant was more garrulous. "Why did he go to the capital? To get passes and other documents allowing him to travel and trade?" He paused, giving Khereuf time to nod. "I suppose he met men of wealth there, men who felt the need to be close to the seat of power."

"Yes, sir. Those who had horses fine enough to bring to Kemet, at any rate."

The gelding neared them and whinnied a greeting to the stallion, which danced nervously in response. The man nodded to Khereuf, eyed Bak with open curiosity, and led his charge on by.

"You said hc disliked the endless quest for power in Hattusa," Bak said, returning to the path. "Does that mean he stayed well clear of Hittite politics?"

The sergeant thought over the question and nodded. "He once told me he valued his life and the lives of his family far too much to play with fire, and he'd toiled too long and hard to allow all he'd earned through the years to fall into the coffers of the king."

Bak continued to press, approaching the same subject from different directions, but Khereuf's answers never varied. The sergeant was convinced the merchant had had no political dealings, and Bak himself began to believe that the suggestion had been a figment of Captain Antef's imagination.

He thought it time he ventured further afield. "Commander Minnakht mentioned that Maruwa had a woman here in Waset. Did he ever speak of her?"

"Irenena," the sergeant said. "He went to her for many years. She was to him like a wife."

"Did you ever meet her?"

"Oh, no, sir!" The sergeant looked shocked. "He would never have asked me to his home."

Bak could well imagine how a woman might feel about the prospect of listening to endless talk of horses. "Did you never see him away from these stables?"

"We sometimes went together to houses of pleasure, yes."

"What did you speak of there? Other than horses, I mean." Bak thought the sergeant a good, honest man, but his taciturnity was driving him mad.

Khereuf seemed puzzled as to why Bak wished to know. "We often played knucklebones or throwsticks and wagered on the games. We talked of hunting the wild beasts, or of wrestling or some other sport. Or of the women we saw around us, those who toiled in the houses of pleasure, whose bodies we took and then left behind."

Soldier talk. The talk of men away from their families. No different than the thousands of conversations Bak had heard in houses of pleasure along the Belly of Stones. "Did he ever say where Irenena lives?"

Khereuf shrugged. "Somewhere near the foreign quarter, I think. He spoke with pride of the house he had provided her. Three rooms, he said, and from the roof she can look down upon a well and a small grove of date palms."

With that, Bak had to be satisfied. How many wells could there be in or near the foreign quarter?

"Lieutenant Bak!" Commander Minnakht stepped out of the walled yard that lay between the well and the building which held offices and storage magazines. "I trust Sergeant Khereuf was helpful?"

"Yes, sir. He feels even more strongly than you that Maruwa had no interest in politics. I'm beginning to believe the reason for his death lies elsewhere."

"After we parted, I thought of something Maruwa once told me. The tale may have nothing to do with his death, but I'd be remiss in not repeating it."

"Sir!" A sergeant came through a solid wooden gate in a wall beyond the office building. "We're getting ready to smoke out the rats. Do you want to see?"

Minnakht glanced at Bak and groaned. "I guess I'd better. Come, Lieutenant. We can talk while the men get on with the task."

Bak could understand Minnakht's reluctance. As a chariotry officer, he also had been obliged to watch while the granaries were cleansed of vermin. A necessary task some men enjoyed, but he for one did not. They followed the sergeant into a walled area containing ten conical granaries. Three men stood off to the side, each holding two large, thick-chested dogs by their collars. Another man carrying an unlighted torch stood at the top of a stairway on a long, narrow mudbrick platform that ran along the back of the granaries, connecting them and providing a platform from which to fill the structures.

"All right," the sergeant yelled, "let's get started."

"A miserable chore," Minnakht said, "but we can't allow the rats to multiply. In spite of all the precautions we take, they get into everything, leaving their filth behind and consuming far more than their share of grain."

Bak watched the man at the top of the steps set the torch afire. Rather than bursting into flame, a cloud of thick, dark smoke rose in the air. "You have something to tell me, sir?"

The commander drew Bak off to the side, out of the way. "Maruwa told me a tale some time ago. Three years, maybe more. A friend who toiled in the royal house at Hattusa, the stablemaster, wished him to relate the story to me so I could pass it on. According to him, someone in the household of the envoy from Kemet was interfering in the politics of Hatti, fomenting trouble."

Bak whistled. "A most dangerous endeavor if true."

"So perilous I wasn't sure I believed it. Nonetheless, I thought the possibility so grave that I passed the message on to Commander Maiherperi, who stands at the head of our royal guards."

The man on the platform shoved the torch through an opening at the top of the granary, held it there, and spread a heavy cloth over the hole so no smoke could escape. The sergeant opened a small, square door at the bottom of the structure. Not much grain spilled out, which meant the granary was close to empty.

Bak thought over the tale and frowned. "Would not so serious a matter have come through official channels?"

"I know what you're thinking, and so did I. Maruwa, who'd had many more days than I to think it over, had concluded that someone in authority in Hattusa wanted to pass the word on in an informal manner, hoping Maatkare Hatshepsut would act before the Hittite king was forced to. After hearing him out, I was inclined to agree. For some time, our sovereign has looked upon the king of Hatti in friendship. If the traitor had been caught in Hattusa, he would've lost his life, which would've strained that relationship."

Bak nodded his understanding. Whispers in the background were often more effective than blustering on the surface.

A rat raced out of the granary, setting the dogs to barking. Eight or ten other rats followed, adults and their half-grown young streaking off in all directions. The handlers released the dogs, who sped across the sand, growling, barking. The rats, frantic to escape, sought shelter, but the best they could find were the long shadows of evening. They had no chance. Within moments they were dead and the handlers were racing around, catching the dogs before they could gobble their prizes and lose their ardor for the game.

"Did Maiherperi think the tale true?" Bak asked.

"He must've. He told me later that the envoy had been recalled to the land of Kemet."

"I'll need that envoy's name, sir."

"I never knew it. You must ask elsewhere."

Amonked would know or, if not, would be able to find out. "Was the identity of the traitor ever established?"

"Maiherperi never said."

A connection between the incident in Hattusa and the slayings in the sacred precinct was even harder to imagine than tying those two murders to Maruwa's death.

Chapter Nine

"I agree with Lieutenant Bak, sir." Lieutenant Karoya stood as stiff as the long spear he held in his hand. "The priest Meryamon was slain in exactly the same manner as the Hittite merchant Maruwa."

"You went to the house of death this morning?" Amonked asked.

"Late yesterday."

A dozen or more priests hurried down the wide stone path joining the sacred precinct to the quay at the edge of the artificial lake that provided waterfront access to Ipet-isut. Chattering like swallows, they walked around the raised limestone platform on which Amonked, Karoya, and Bak stood. Hastening down the shallow stairway, the priests boarded a small traveling ship that would carry them to wherever the day's rituals required they go, probably Ipet-resyt.

Amonked spoke no more until they were too far away to hear. "What of Woserhet?"

"It was difficult to tell, sir."

"The priests who prepare the dead for eternity had already removed his internal organs and covered him with natron," Bak explained. "Between the fire, which had blackened and blistered his skin, and the salts that had entered the wound, its shape was lost to us, but I'll not soon forget how it looked the day he died. Much the same as the other two."

Karoya may have been awed by such lofty company as Amonked, his sovereign's cousin, but he was not so impressed that he could not speak up. "I'd wager he was slain exactly like them. Come upon from behind, his head jerked back, and his throat slashed."

"I see." Amonked turned away from them, placed his hands on the parapet surrounding the platform, and stared westward toward the broad canal that connected the lake to the river. Bak doubted he noticed the traveling ship pulling away from the quay or heard the beat of the drummer who kept the rowers' movements in harmony.

Swinging around, Amonked raised his hand to shade his eyes from the bright early morning sun and gave the pair a speculative look. "The two of you have come to me with a purpose. Tell me."

"As the three murders appear to be related . . . No! As we're convinced they are, we feel they should be treated as one." Without thinking, Bak slapped a mosquito on his arm. "Many people have come from afar to participate in the festival, making merry and giving no thought to right behavior. The harbor and market are much more difficult to control than usual, leaving Lieutenant Karoya with insufficient time to seek a slayer."

"And since you're involved with the other deaths, you wish also to look into Maruwa's murder."

"To combine all three would make sense, sir."

Loud laughter rang out from among the trees and brush abutting the slightly raised path that surrounded the lake and lined both sides of the canal. A scantily clad man appeared, splashing through water left behind by the receding flood. Though he was some distance away, they could see he carried a harpoon, and a long string of fish dangled from his shoulder. Another man, cursing soundly, sidled through the morass, thrusting his harpoon time and time again. Water splashed, a fish trying to save itself in the too shallow backwater.

"Should not Mai, the harbormaster, have some say in the matter?" Amonked asked.

"We spoke with him earlier." Karoya ignored a rivulet of sweat working its way down his breastbone. "He feels as we do."

Amonked stared at the pair of them, thinking, then gave a quick nod of his head. "All right. You've convinced me. The three crimes we'll now count as one, and Bak will investigate them all." He looked pointedly at Karoya. "I trust you'll be available to aid him, should he need your help?"

"Yes, sir.

"Do you have anything else to report, Lieutenant?" Amonked asked Bak.

Bak told him of his conversation with the stablemaster, concluding with Maruwa's account that had led to the recall of an envoy. "Are you familiar with the incident, sir? If not, would you look into the matter for me? Commander Minnakht didn't know the name of the envoy and he was never told what happened to the one who involved himself in Hittite politics. I believe the knowledge would be most helpful."

A long silence, a certain sign that this was not the first time Amonked had heard the tale. "In what way can that affair possibly be connected to the three murders?"

From the unhappy scowl on Amonked's face, Bak guessed the story had been sealed away in a jar and forgotten. Now here it was, thanks to him, rearing its ugly head anew. "It may not be, but how can I eliminate it if I don't know the facts?"

Amonked clasped his hands behind him and paced back and forth. "What to do?" he muttered to himself.

"You surely know you can trust me, sir," Bak said.

"I can leave, if you wish," Karoya offered.

"No, no. It's just that . . ." Amonked stopped in front of the two of them and eyed Bak. "You know the parties involved, Lieutenant. Thus you place me in an awkward position."

Bak was mystified. "I do?"

A triumphant yell rang out from the edge of the canal, and the fisherman raised his harpoon from the backwater. Caught on the barbs was a small, limp fish, its silvery scales glistening in the sunlight. A gray and black projectile plummeted out of a nearby tree, a cry of alarm burst from the second man, and a crow grabbed the fish and streaked away. The trio on the platform failed to notice.

"Maatkare Hatshepsut appointed Pentu as envoy to the Hittite court at Hattusa," Amonked said. "He served her well for close on two years—or so she believed."

Bak rapidly overcame his surprise. He recalled the several times he had met the governor, each time with the chief treasurer, and the many lofty guests who had been at his home. No wonder the incident in Hattusa had been kept quiet. To Karoya, he said, "Pentu is governor of the province of Tjeny."

The young officer's soft laugh held not a shred of humor.

"When word reached my cousin," Amonked said, his tone ponderous, "she was inclined to ignore it, thinking Pentu a man of too much integrity to involve himself in the politics of another land. Her advisers, however—and I among them—convinced her he must be recalled. No one believed him to be the guilty party, but someone close to him was. He was compromised, so much so that he could no longer serve her needs."

"Thus he was brought back to Kemet and someone else was sent to Hattusa in his place." Bak rubbed the spot on his arm where the mosquito had been, rousing the itch. "Was the traitor ever identified?"

"As the activity stopped upon Pentu's recall, the investigation was dropped."

"Perhaps it shouldn't have been." Bak flung a wry smile at Karoya. "Pentu and the members of his household arrived in Waset a few hours before Maruwa was slain. They're still here and will remain throughout the festival."

Amonked's mouth tightened. "Pentu may be overly trusting, but he'd not involve himself in the politics of another land. Nor would he kill, not even to silence a man capable of spreading a tale that would besmirch his character."

"My hands are tied, sir, because men who might help me are fully occupied with the Opet rituals. Must I also be blinded because I dare not approach a man as lofty as Pentu?" Bak knew he should have exercised more tact, but he thought Amonked a good enough friend to overlook the impertinence.

Amonked glared at the sentry kneeling in front of the main gate to the sacred precinct, scratching the belly of a black puppy. "I'll speak with the vizier." Forgiving Bak with a humorless smile, he grumbled, "He may wish you to reexamine the incident."

So saying, he strode across the platform and up the path toward Ipet-isut. Bak, praying he had not leaped into waters too deep and swift to navigate, followed with Karoya. The young Medjay officer looked vastly relieved that he was not the man who might have to tread on such noble and lofty toes as those of a provincial governor.

"Is the ship on which Maruwa was slain still moored at the harbor?" Bak asked.

"It is, but not for long. Captain Antef came to me yesterday, saying he wishes to set sail tomorrow. I saw no reason to hold him."

"Tomorrow? Midway through the Beautiful Feast of Opet?"

"Since unloading the horses, he's taken on a new cargo. He has a long voyage ahead of him, all the way to Ugarit, and carries objects that must be transported overland before winter falls."

"What difference would five or six days make when the length of the voyage can vary greatly, depending upon the weather?" Bak raised his baton of office, saluting the sentry, who had shot to his feet the instant he noticed their approach. The puppy sat on its haunches, looking up at the man, crying. Bak followed his companions through the gate that opened into the limestone court in front of Ipet-isut.

"Sir," he said to Amonked, "will you send an official order to the harbormaster? I wish Captain Antef's ship to be detained, its cargo guarded so nothing can be moved."

"I resent being held here, Lieutenant." Antef, standing in front of the forecastle of his ship, glared at Bak. "Must I be made to suffer merely because I had the misfortune of having a man murdered on my vessel?"

"I'd think you'd look upon Maruwa as the unfortunate one."

"I do. Of course I do." The captain's breast swelled with indignation. "Nonetheless, I should not be required to remain in Waset. I know nothing of his death except what I saw the day you found him."

Bak stood with his back against the angle of the prow, looking the length of the deck, which appeared much different from the last time he had been aboard. The mat walls of the deckhouse had been raised, allowing him to see all the way to the stern. The stalls had been removed, the piles of hay and bags of grain had been carried off, and the wooden flooring was so clean it glowed. Baskets and bundles and chests were stowed everywhere, not a large cargo, but enough, he assumed, to make an extended voyage worthwhile. Most of the crew had gone ashore. The two who remained were toiling near the mast, talking together with the amity of men who have shared their tasks for months. When they believed themselves unobserved, they sneaked glances at Bak.

"You said at the time he may've been involved in Hittite politics. Do you know for a fact that he was?"

"A guess, that's all." Antef glanced around as if looking for something to sit on. Evidently the mounds of cargo lashed to the deck did not appeal, for he remained standing. "A logical assumption. During all my voyages north, I've never seen a more bloodthirsty nation."

"How often have you traveled in the land of Hatti?"

"Well . . . Never," Antef admitted reluctantly. "But I've met many a man from there, and they're all alike."

Bak kept his expression bland, concealing his irritation with such generalities. "I've been told Maruwa was a fine man. Good-natured, hardworking, honest to a fault."

Antef flushed. "He was different from the rest. A bit secretive, but otherwise a good, cheerful companion on a long voyage. He cared for those horses he shipped as if they were beloved children. I know they were valuable, but still . . ."

The ship rocked beneath their feet, making the fittings creak, and the hull bumped hard against the mudbank beside which it was moored. One of the sailors, climbing up the mast, clung for his life and snapped out a chain of filthy oaths. The man seated on the deck below, unsnarling a tangle of ropes, laughed heartily.

"Had you known him long?" Bak asked.

"Five years, maybe six."

"Did he always transport the horses on your ship? Or did he use other vessels when this one wasn't available?"

"Not many cargo ships are stable enough or have enough deck space to carry the numbers of animals he brought regularly to Kemet. He knew of us all, and he used whichever vessel he found in Ugarit when he arrived. Or whichever was the first to reach that port if we all happened to be at sea."

"What of his return journeys?"

"I'm quick to set sail—as are all of us who earn our bread on the water—and he usually stayed longer. Traveling alone, with no horses to transport, the size of the ship was of no import. He could leave at any time on any vessel that happened to be sailing northward."

Bak left the prow and walked slowly down the deck, looking at baskets and bundles as he passed them by, reading labels on the closed containers. Antef hurried after him like a mother goose concerned for her goslings. The cargo was diverse: the roughest of pottery and earthenware of a mediocre quality, leather goods, sheep skins, rough linen and fabric of a slightly higher quality, wine from a vineyard he had never heard of, strings of beads and other bright jewelry of small value. Scattered among these very ordinary trade items were bundles and baskets identified by their labels as containing finer goods. They appeared to have come from provincial estates, although some had labels with ink so smeared they were illegible. Luxury items made within the household to be traded for a profit. Or so they seemed.

"Did you know Maruwa kept a woman in Waset?" Bak asked.

On a woven reed chest, he spotted a label he could not read: a flat chunk of dried mud tied to the handle, the symbols scrawled and indecipherable. He knelt before the container, broke the seal, and released the cord securing the lid. Ignoring Antef's shocked gasp, he looked inside. The chest was filled to the brim with fine linen.

"Damaged goods," Antef hastened to tell him. "Or so I've been told."

Bak read the tags on the surrounding containers and words inked on the shoulders of pottery jars. He found nothing unusual or suspicious. Except the captain standing beside him, shifting from foot to foot, clearly uncomfortable with the silence—or with Bak's interest in his cargo.

"I knew he had a woman," Antef said. "He never spoke of her, but the members of my crew would see them together in the market here or in the foreign quarter."

Bak walked a few paces farther along the deck. Amid a stack of baskets, he spotted one labeled as having come from a provincial estate located considerably closer to Mennufer than to Waset. The nobleman might have brought the items south to trade in the teeming festival market, but the large port and market at Mennufer offered infinitely more possibilities for exchange.

Breaking the seal, he snapped the cord securing the lid and peered inside.

"Sir!" Antef exclaimed. "You can't do that! The merchant who entrusted me with these items will hold me personally responsible."

The basket held a dozen or more bronze cups and pitchers. The linen might truly have been damaged goods, but these small, fine objects clearly were not. They had to be destined for the home of a wealthy nobleman or for the royal house of some far-off king.

"Send him to me or to Lieutenant Karoya. We'd be glad to explain our authority."

Antef opened his mouth to object, but Bak's cold stare silenced him. They walked on, passing the sailor at the base of the mast. The man was toying with the ropes, acting busy, but the tangle had been unsnarled. Bak glanced upward, caught the man above leaning out from the masthead, staring. The sailor pulled back and busied himself with a fitting.

Wondering how much the crew knew about the goods the vessel carried, Bak peered beneath the roof of the deckhouse. Inside were the captain's rolled sleeping pallet, a basket of personal items, and a few baskets of foodstuffs gathered for the coming voyage. One basket, so the label said, contained small bronze tools: harpoon heads, knives, needles, and so on. These were no doubt for daily shipboard use. Another, larger basket had no label at all. He broke the seal and cord, glanced at Antef. The captain was sweating profusely.

Bak lifted the lid and found ten or twelve small jars. They were unmarked, but he had seen enough during the several years he had conducted inspections at Buhen to guess that they held aromatic oils. Definitely not an ordinary trade item. A product much coveted by the wives and concubines of foreign kings. "This is your property, Captain?"

"No, sir." Antef wiped the moisture from his forehead with the back of his hand. "It belongs to the merchant whose goods I'm to deliver to Ugarit. He asked me to keep that basket out of the sun. Other than in the hold, where else could I stow it but here?"

"Are you transporting goods for only the one merchant, or for other men as well?"

"Just Zuwapi."

Bak was not surprised by the captain's easy revelation of the merchant's identity. The name would be on the ship's manifest and registered in the customs office. "A Hittite, if his name tells true."

"Yes, sir. A highly respectable man, so I've been told."

"Was he acquainted with Maruwa?"

"That I can't say. He's not as amiable as Maruwa was, so I'd guess not."

Bak was skeptical. The number of Hittites in Waset was small. "I must speak with him. Where can I find him?"

"He dwells in Mennufer and journeys often to Ugarit." Antef bared his teeth in a tenuous smile. "Where he is now, I can't tell you."

Bak muttered an oath. "If he's not here in Waset, who sees that his cargo is properly loaded?"

"I do, sir. He sends me a list of what I'm to transport, and I check off the items as they're delivered to me."

"He must be a trusting soul."

"I've carried his trade goods for years, and I've never once failed to deliver each and every object to the port of his choice." Antef stepped into Bak's path so he could walk no farther along the deck. "Sir! You must speak up for me to the harbormaster. He must release my ship. I've goods on board that I must deliver to Ugarit for shipment by donkey train to cities farther inland."

"I'll do what I can."

The promise was empty. Bak had no intention of letting the ship leave the harbor. The more valuable of the goods he had seen might well have come from a storehouse of the lord Amon.

The lord Re was hovering above the western horizon when Bak walked into yet another open plot of ground containing a well and a grove of date palms. This was the fifth well he had found in his thus far vain search for Maruwa's concubine. The smell of burning fuel and the odors of foods being cooked for the evening meal wafted through the air, reminding him that another treat awaited him at his Medjays' quarters, food gleaned by Pashenuro from the daily reversion of offerings.

At the apex of the irregular triangle of scruffy grass was a well encircled by a wall, while a healthy grove of date palms filled the opposite end. Several acacias grew in a clump near the well, shading a mudbrick bench. Two women sat there, chatting with five others. One of those who stood balanced a large water jar on her head, while the others supported similar jars on their hips. Two jars stood at the feet of the women occupying the bench.

The woman holding the jar on her head noticed Bak, murmured something to her friends, and they stopped talking to stare as he approached them.

"I'm Lieutenant Bak. I'm looking for a woman who may dwell nearby." He kept his expression grave, hoping to discourage light conversation and questions. "I must speak with her of a matter of note. A very serious matter."

A young woman holding a jar on her hip flashed bold eyes at him. "Her name, sir?"

"Irenena."

"The Hittite's woman," she said, exchanging a look with the others.

"What do you need of her?" a seated woman asked.

"Has she not had enough unhappiness?" the woman with the jar on her head asked. "Must you give her more?"

"Leave her be," another woman said. "Let her mourn her loss in peace."

He raised a hand, silencing them. "I'm seeking the man who took the Hittite's life. With luck she can help me lay hands on him."

Again the women looked at one another, sharing a thought. The oldest in the crowd spoke for them all:

"She'd want to see his slayer punished. I'll take you to her."

"They've been very kind to me." Irenena stood beneath the pavilion on the rooftop outside her small home, looking down at the well and the women disappearing into several lanes leading to their dwellings. "I feared when I learned of his death they would turn their backs, thinking me the whore of a vile foreigner, left alone and helpless. But no. They knew I loved him and he loved me, and they respect that."

"You've dwelt here long?" Bak asked.

"Maruwa brought me here almost ten years ago."

The view below was most attractive, one few city dwellings offered. The dusty green of the trees, the white-plastered wall around the well, and the white dwellings enclosing the open area were softened by the late evening light. A yellow cat lapped water from a bowl left by some anonymous donor, while her kittens played hide and seek in the grass. A woman on the rooftop across the way crooned a song of love to her baby.

"May I offer you a jar of beer, Lieutenant?"

He accepted and followed her into the home she had made for herself and Maruwa. Her dwelling, in reality the second story of the building, consisted of a large room for living and sleeping, a tiny room for storage, and a kitchen with an open roof covered by loosely spread dry brush that would provide some shade and let out the smoke. The furnishings were sparse but of considerable value, many of the pillow covers,

floor mats, and wall hangings imported from the northern
lands through which Maruwa had traveled.

While she placed sweetcakes on a flat dish, he studied the
comfortable room and the woman herself. Small and sturdy,
she had dark hair sprinkled with white, and her round face
was no longer youthful. Maruwa must surely have loved her
as a wife, a woman to share his time with through eternity,
not one to take and throw away.

"Shall we sit on the roof?" she asked. "The breeze is always lovely at this time of day."

Following her outside, he said, "Before you came here,
where did you dwell?"

She raised her chin and her voice took on a note of defiance. "I was not what you think, sir. I was a respectable
woman, a widow. A burden to my eldest brother, a servant to
his wife. When Maruwa said he wanted me, I accepted his
offer gladly. A rash move, perhaps, a situation that could
have ended as rapidly as it began, with me impoverished and
alone. Instead our love grew and now here I am, a widow in
my heart if not in reality. Unlike before, Maruwa left me sufficient means to take care of myself."

"I meant no offense, mistress. I've been told he usually remained in Waset long after he delivered his horses to the
royal stables." Bak allowed a smile to touch his lips. "I
doubted he stayed behind for the animals' sake, nor would
he have been long detained by a plaything."

The rigidity went out of her stance, and she mirrored his
smile. "Will you sit with me, sir?" she asked, nodding toward a reed mat spread out beneath the pavilion.

After he complied, she set the cakes beside him and offered a jar of beer. The breeze, as she had predicted, wafted
gently across the rooftop, bringing with it the scent of flowers.

"How can I help you?" she asked, seating herself on the
opposite side of the bowl. "I wish justice done, punishment

for my beloved's slayer while still he lives as well as in the netherworld."

Bak took a drink of beer, savoring the warm, rather thick but tasty brew. "Was Maruwa involved in Hittite politics?" He no longer believed the merchant would have become so foolishly embroiled, but of all the people he had talked to, she would know best.

"What on earth gave you that idea? He was the least political man I've ever met."

"Did he ever speak of the politics of Kemet, of our two sovereigns, one seated on the throne at Waset and the other occupying the royal house in Mennufer?"

"He thought the situation odd, but who doesn't? Especially men and women from other lands, places where life is harsher and kingship more precarious." She must have realized he wished her to be more specific and shook her head. "No, sir, he showed no more concern with the affairs of Kemet than with those of his homeland."

"On the day he died, I've been told, he never left the vessel on which he brought the horses. Most of the sailors disembarked, as did the captain, but he chose to remain on board with the animals."

"He would have." Rather than taking into her mouth the morsel of sweetcake she held, she dropped her hand to her lap as if she had lost her taste for the delicacy. "They were his responsibility. He'd have stayed with them until they were safely delivered to the royal stables."

"You didn't see him at all that day?"

"No, sir." The words caught in her throat; she paused, regaining control. "I never knew exactly when to expect him. Sometimes upon his arrival he'd summon me, but not often. He preferred that I wait here in the comfort of our home rather than wander around the market while he cared for the horses. If only . . ." She bit her lip, cutting short whatever she had intended to say, acknowledging the futility of regrets.

Bak took a sweetcake, more for politeness sake than because he wanted it. "Did he ever speak to you of a scribe named Woserhet or a priest named Meryamon? Both men toiled in the sacred precinct of the lord Amon."

"I don't remember those names." Irenena frowned at the cake crumbled in her hand. "He was not of a religious nature, and he was certainly not interested in our gods. On the rare occasion when he felt the need for prayer, he spoke to the gods of his own land."

"Did he mention a man named Pentu? He served our sovereign as an envoy in Hattusa."

"Pentu." She threw the crumbs onto the open rooftop. Several sparrows darted from the date palms to the low parapet, then hopped down for the treat. "I've no memory of the name."

"He was and is now governor of Tjeny."

Her eyes widened with surprise. "How could I have forgotten? Yes, Maruwa did speak of him. He said the man had a viper within his household."

Bak could barely believe his good luck. "When was this?"

"During his last visit to Kemet seven or eight months ago."

"Did he explain himself?"

"No. I thought the words curious and pressed for details, but he said . . ." Suddenly her hand shot to her mouth and she looked stricken. "Oh, my!"

He leaned forward, laid his hand on her wrist. "What is it, mistress Irenena? What's the matter?"

"He said he thought he knew the name, but wanted to make doubly sure before passing it on to Commander Minnakht when next he came to Waset. Why did I not insist he do so at that time? Why?"

Bak regretted the storm of tears that followed and prayed the release would be as valuable to her as was the information she had given him. The odds were good that Maruwa had verified the name and had planned to give it to the stablemaster the day he was slain.

*   *   *

Bak walked back to his men's quarters along rapidly darkening lanes filled with merrymakers. He had not been able to console Irenena, but had managed to convince her that she was in no way responsible for Maruwa's death. The decision to remain mute had been his alone.

Besides, Bak was not convinced the so-called viper had slain the merchant. Maruwa had been in Waset for less than two hours when his life was taken. How would that vile creature have learned of his knowledge in so short a time? True, Pentu's traveling ship had reached the harbor not long before the cargo ship, but even if Maruwa had bumped into the man, he would not have been so foolish as to reveal what he knew.

Another thought nagged. What could stirring up trouble in the land of Hatti possibly have to do with the storehouses of Amon? Had he erred in thinking the three deaths were related? If someone was stealing from the god and smuggling the items to a foreign land, as he suspected, would it not be wiser for that individual to do nothing that might attract official attention?

Bak stumbled over a mallet someone had left in the lane. Cursing himself for not watching his step, he walked on. Again his thoughts wandered. The hours he had spent in the foreign quarter, the many men and women he had walked among and talked to, some of them Hittites, had brought back memories of the one woman among many that he had never forgotten. A Hittite woman. He could see her smile, hear her voice, feel her courage and strength of will. No one had ever taken her place. No one ever would.

Had he been unfair to Meret, Pentu's wife's sister? Had he inadvertently led her to believe a relationship might develop between them?

Chapter Ten

"I've just come from the vizier." Amonked glanced around the courtyard, empty so early in the morning except for Bak and a couple of sleepy-eyed Medjays seated at the cold hearth, eating pigeon left over from the previous evening's meal and dunking hard bread into milk. Hori's dog was standing over a bowl of water, lapping loud and fast. The majority of Bak's men were sleeping off another night of merrymaking.

"I convinced him Maruwa's death and those in the sacred precinct might well have been committed by the same man." Amonked pulled close a low stool and sat down. "When I told him one of the trails you've been following has led you to Pentu, he agreed that you must now look at the members of the governor's household."

Bak stifled a yawn. Unable to further his investigation after speaking with Irenena, he had taken advantage of the unexpected but welcome freedom from duty to go with Psuro in search of a good time. They had found what they sought. Amonked had not quite caught him on his sleeping pallet, but had come close. "Am I to actively search for the man who brought about Pentu's recall or can I only look for a potential slayer among them?"

A hint of a smile touched Amonked's lips. "Discovery of the traitor would be an added bonus, so the vizier said."

Bak frowned. "He gave no definite instructions to seek the snake?"

146

"He merely inferred, but I see no need to burden Pentu with that small bit of information."

"Nothing was ever proven." Pentu ran his fingers through his thick white hair, betraying his distress. "I felt cruelly used and still do. To accuse a man in such a way, to tear him from a task he knows he's doing well . . . It was unconscionable. Utterly unconscionable."

Amonked exchanged a quick glance with Bak, who stood in a thin rectangle of early morning sunlight, facing the dais on which the Storekeeper of Amon had been invited to sit with the governor of Tjeny. "You yourself were not accused, surely."

"Not as such, no. But to lay blame on anyone in my household is to blacken my good name."

Letting pass a statement so clearly true, Amonked scooted his armchair half around so he could see Pentu without always turning his head. The dais occupied the end of the reception hall, the room Bak had seen four days before bright with laughter, good food and drink, and beaming guests. A servant had placed a camp stool in front of the dais for his use, but he had opted to stand rather than lower himself to the level of the two noblemen's knees.

"What were you told when you were recalled?" Amonked asked.

"No reason was offered." Bitterness crept into Pentu's voice. "Not until I reported to the royal house was I given an explanation. And then a poor one."

Amonked's tone turned hard, brutal almost. "Someone in your household had taken an active interest in the politics of Hatti. Was that not sufficient reason to withdraw you?"

A stubborn look came over the governor's face. "I refuse to believe any man close to me guilty of so foul a deed."

"Word was brought to our sovereign in an unofficial manner, carried by the Hittite merchant Maruwa. Later, after you were withdrawn, your successor verified the accusation at the highest levels of power in Hattusa."

Pentu's mouth tightened, sealing inside a rebuttal.

"Forgive me, sir," Bak said, "but did you ever seek the truth? Did you question those who accompanied you to the Hittite capital?"

"I spoke with them, yes. Each and every one denied his guilt."

"You believed them."

"They are honorable men, Lieutenant."

Bak wondered at the governor's apparent blindness. Was he really so trusting? Or did he know they were innocent because he was the man who had dipped a finger into Hatti's politics? Amonked appeared to take for granted Pentu's innocence, but perhaps he erred.

"Exactly who accompanied you?" Amonked asked, for Bak's benefit rather than his own, Bak suspected.

The governor spoke with reluctance, though he must have known the names were readily available to all who chose to inquire. "My aide Netermose. My steward Pahure. My friend Sitepehu, who served at the time as my chief scribe."

A fat black dog carrying a bone in its mouth waddled around the nearest brightly painted pillar. It scrambled onto the camp stool and settled down to gnaw its prize. The dubious treat smelled as strong as the animal did, overwhelming the stringent scent emanating from a huge bowl of flowers beside the dais.

"Your wife accompanied you, did she not?" Bak asked.

Pentu released a long, annoyed sigh. "As did her sister Meret. Also with us were a dozen or so servants, men and women important to our comfort while we dwelt in that land of strange customs and abominable food." His head swiveled around and he gave Amonked a long, hard look. "What's this all about? Why bring up a subject long dead and most distasteful to me?"

Amonked rose from his chair and stepped off the dais. Ignoring the dog, he stood beside Bak, lending the weight of his authority to the younger man. "Maruwa has been slain."

Pentu expelled a humorless laugh. "Have you come to ask that I mourn him, Amonked?"

"Some months before his death, while preparing to travel to Hattusa, he told a friend he expected to bring back to Waset the name of the traitor in your household. Upon his return, he had not yet set foot on the good black earth of this city when he was slain. I think it unlikely that the two events are unconnected. The vizier agrees and has ordered Lieutenant Bak to investigate the charge that brought about your recall, beginning with the members of your household."

"Is the identity of the traitor—if one ever existed—now so important? A matter thought at the time to be worth dismissing?"

"That individual's interference in the politics of Hatti was perceived as posing a threat to the king and might well have caused a breach between him and our sovereign. A serious matter should he have decided to march south and attack our allies, thereby bringing about a war."

"Nothing of the sort happened."

"Solely because the Hittite king, being a reasonable man, chose not to suspect Maatkare Hatshepsut of being a party to the problem and passed the word along informally, and because she acted without delay."

Amonked glared at Pentu, daring him to rebut the charge. The governor remained mute.

"Lieutenant Bak is to report directly to me and I to the vizier." The implication was clear: the matter had the attention of the second most powerful individual in the land, and Pentu had no choice but to cooperate, to treat Bak with the same deference he would show Amonked.

The governor slumped back in his chair, scowled at Bak. "What do you wish, Lieutenant?"

"I wish to speak to the members of your household, first

to Netermose, Pahure, and Sitepehu, each man alone. Before I see them, you must tell them of my purpose and urge their cooperation."

Bak watched the servant slip through the doorway to go in search of the three men who had accompanied Pentu to Hattusa. Amonked had previously taken his leave. "Did you know Maruwa, sir?"

Pentu's expression darkened at the very mention of the trader's name. "I'd never heard of him until I learned, upon reporting back to Waset, that he'd carried the message that brought about my recall."

"Did he never come to you in Hattusa? Was he not required to obtain from you, as envoy to the land of Hatti, a pass each time he wished to travel within the land of Kemet?"

"Sitepehu dealt with such routine matters."

Bak had no reason to doubt the governor, or to believe him, either. "Do you have many dealings with the priests and scribes who toil in the sacred precinct of the lord Amon?"

"On the rare occasions when I come to Waset, I usually meet the chief priest and a few acolytes at various social occasions. Not during the Beautiful Feast of Opet, when they're fully occupied, but at other times throughout the year." Pentu eyed Bak, visibly puzzled. "What does my social life have to do with the death of that wretched Hittite merchant?"

"Have you ever met the scribe Woserhet or the priest Meryamon?"

"Aren't they the two men who were slain in the sacred precinct?"

Bak was not surprised the governor had heard of the murders. Word of one death in the sacred precinct would not have gone unnoticed. News of a second killing would have spread throughout Waset at the speed of a falcon diving to earth to catch a rodent.

Pentu glared at Bak. "Why would I know them? Do you think I'm acquainted with every man who's been slain in this city since we disembarked from our ship at the harbor?"

"This terrace should offer ample privacy, sir."

Pahure, looking very much the efficient functionary, stepped through the doorway. He led Bak along a portico that shaded the roof of a narrow two-story extension added sometime in the past to the north side of the three-story dwelling. The outer edge of the shelter, lined with small potted trees and flowering plants, was a riot of color. Bees buzzed around blossoms whose sweet fragrance perfumed the air. A very young female servant hurried after them, carrying a basket containing several jars of beer and a lumpy package wrapped in clean white linen.

Bak dropped onto one of several low stools scattered along the portico and the steward sat beside him. The girl drew close a small table, deposited the basket on it, and spread wide the linen to reveal small, round loaves of bread so fresh out of the oven they smelled of yeast.

"You understand my purpose," Bak said after the servant departed.

"Pentu left no doubt."

Bak helped himself to a warm loaf, which had bits of date erupting through its golden crust. "Did you know the merchant Maruwa?"

Pahure shrugged. "I may have met him, but if so I don't recall." He broke the plug from a jar and handed the brew to Bak. His demeanor was serious, reflecting the gravity of the question. "You must understand, sir. I met a multitude of people during the course of my duties in Hattusa. As several years have passed since our return, I've forgotten many, especially those individuals I met in passing." He took a bite of bread and washed it down with a sizable drink. "Also, Sitepehu handled official affairs, while my tasks were related solely to household matters. I normally dealt with local merchants, obtaining food, clothing, furniture, everything required for our day-to-day living."

Bak studied the man seated before him. Pahure's shoulders were broad and muscular, giving an impression of strength that contrasted with his gently rounded stomach. His manner was pleasant, ever so slightly subservient, yet Sitepehu had once inferred that the steward was a man who usually got what he wanted. Certainly the latter trait would be useful to one who had attained the lofty position of steward to a provincial governor or envoy.

"Let me describe Maruwa," Bak said, and he did so.

Pahure looked down his substantial nose at the officer. "I saw many such men while in Hatti, sir."

Bak ignored what he assumed was a subtle attempt to put him in his place, an unexpected fracture in the steward's facade of respect and deference. "Do you spend much time in the sacred precinct of the lord Amon?"

A wry smile flitted across Pahure's face. "I can't remember when last I was inside its walls. I seldom come to this city and when I do, I've other, more pressing business."

"Have you ever met a scribe named Woserhet or a young priest, Meryamon?"

"Aren't they the men who were slain in the sacred precinct?"

Bak described them as best he could, asked again, "Have you ever met them, Pahure?"

"I've met many such men, Lieutenant. They come through Tjeny, pay their respects to Pentu and Sitepehu, sometimes even stay the night. I seldom can tell one from another and never can recall their names."

Doggedly Bak pressed on, asking another question for which he expected to receive an equally unsatisfactory answer. "Did you ever meet a Hittite trader named Zuwapi?"

"Zuwapi?" Pahure drew the basket close, sorted through the loaves of bread, finally selected one with sesame seeds dotting the crust. "One would think I'd recall a name that rolls so harshly off the tongue."

Was that a yes or a no? Bak wondered. "Among other things, he deals in luxury items: fine linen, bronze vessels, aromatic oils. Goods exported from Kemet for trade in northern lands. Objects one would sorely miss when dwelling in a strange and distant city."

"Ah, yes," the steward smiled. "Small items for the ladies. I several times purchased from him linens and perfumes for mistresses Taharet and Meret. Items not easy to find in Hattusa. He was a godsend, I tell you."

Gratified at having finally received an answer, and a positive one at that, Bak asked, "Can you describe him?"

Pahure seemed surprised by the question. "He's very ordinary, very much a Hittite."

"Is he tall or short?" Bak asked, trying not to show his irritation with so vague a response. "Does he have any special features that would make him stand out from all other men?"

"None that I remember."

Bak felt like a man trying to knock a hole in granite with a wedge of cheese. "Did anything happen when you dealt with him, or have you heard anything about him, that might lead you to believe he's less than honest?"

"He was a sharp trader, one who demanded full value and more." Pahure's laugh exuded self-satisfaction. "But so am I. I always came out ahead in our dealings."

Bak allowed the steward a stingy smile. "Do you believe the charge true that someone in your household became embroiled in the affairs of the land of Hatti?"

"I can't imagine any of us—or anyone else, for that matter—trying to cause dissension in that wretched land. Their royalty and nobility make enough trouble for themselves." Pahure's expression turned scornful. "One would have to be completely witless to interfere in the politics of a nation where punishment by death is commonplace and where a man's family and close friends more likely than not die with him."

Bak found Netermose on the roof of the original dwelling, seated in the shade of a sturdy pavilion. Bushy trees growing in pots formed a screen of sorts, partly concealing several small granaries and a far less elegant shelter containing a loom, grindstones, brazier, and water jars. Additional potted trees lined the edge of the roof facing the river. Reed mats covered the floor beneath the pavilion, and thick pillows had been strewn around for seating. The aide sat on one, studying rows of columns on a long roll of papyrus. Four slick-haired brindle puppies played around him.

"I knew Maruwa well," Netermose said, motioning Bak to a pillow. "When Pentu told us of his death . . . Well, suffice it to say, I felt as if I'd lost a friend."

Bak was not surprised by the admission. He had noticed the dismay on the aide's face when the governor had broken the news.

"I'm not much of a man of action, Lieutenant, but should you need help in snaring his slayer, I'll do what I can."

"At the moment, I need nothing but information." Bak was again struck by the man's advanced age and wondered what had placed him at Pentu's beck and call. "How long ago did you meet him?"

"When first we went to Hattusa. He came for a travel pass." Netermose rolled up the scroll, laid it beside the pillow on which he sat, and handed Bak a jar of beer. "When he learned I was reared on Pentu's family's country estate and that I sorely missed the company of animals, he invited me to go to his stable and look at the horses he meant to bring to Kemet. The invitation was open, so I went often. I saw him almost daily each time he came through Hattusa."

Netermose, then, had probably come from a long line of servants of Pentu's family. He and the governor had undoubtedly played together as children, learned to read and write together as they grew to manhood, but always one the servant, the other the master. "He kept the horses in the capital and not at his home in Nesa?"

A puppy whimpered, trying to escape from a more sturdy brother, who had caught its ear in his mouth and was tugging at it. Netermose gently separated the two. "Has no one told you how he handled his business?"

"I assumed he collected horses from all over the land of Hatti and stabled them where he dwelt, where men he trusted could care for them while he went off to trade for others."

"He preferred to limit the distances the animals had to travel, so he kept four stables along the route between the capital and the Great Green Sea. Those horses he got from the north, he kept at Hattusa, those from farther south at Nesa. He had another stable midway between there and the port city of Ugarit, where he kept a fourth stable. As for men he could trust, his wife had four brothers. Each managed a stable, tending to the animals and assuring their safety."

A sensible arrangement, Bak thought. "Did you ever meet him after your return to Kemet?"

"I'd hoped I would, but our paths took different directions. He knew we dwelt in Tjeny, and the cargo ships carrying his horses had to have passed us by, but he never stopped." Netermose scratched the head of one of the puppies. "I guess he couldn't convince the ship's master to take the time."

"Or he believed he'd be unwelcome. After all, he was the man who brought word to Kemet that someone in Pentu's household was causing trouble in the land of Hatti."

Looking unhappy, Netermose gave the puppy a gentle shove, pushing it toward its brothers, and folded his hands in his lap. "So Pentu told us when he learned of the reason for our recall."

"Did Maruwa ever hint that something was amiss?"

"Would that he had!"

"What would you have done?"

"I'd have warned Pentu, of course."

A futile effort that would have been, Bak thought. "Who do you believe the traitor was?"

"The tale was untrue, I'm convinced."

The resolute look on Netermose's face told Bak that no less a being than the lord Amon himself would alter the aide's conviction. Whether such certainty had come from deep within himself or had been born as a result of Pentu's denials, he could not begin to guess.

Having followed that path to its end, he asked a question he had neglected to ask Pahure. "Pentu, like all provincial governors, must share the bounties of the land with our sovereign and divert a portion to the lord Amon. Products gathered yearly from his own estate and the fields of all who dwell in the province. Does he also send to the sacred precinct a share of the excess items made by the women of his household and the craftsmen who live on his personal estate? Luxury items, to be specific."

Netermose looked puzzled, as if unable to find the connection between the governor's obligation to the lord Amon and the murder of Maruwa. "We expect all who reside in the province to do so, so we can do no less."

"Have you ever had occasion to meet any of the priests and scribes responsible for storing such items?"

"A senior priest comes each year to this house to thank Pentu for his generosity, and other men at times come with him, but I've taken no interest in their exact duties."

"I speak specifically of Woserhet, a senior scribe who toiled for the lord Amon, and of the young priest Meryamon, who dwelt and toiled in the sacred precinct." Again he described the two men.

"They may've come at one time or another, but I'm not especially observant. To me, one man with a pious demeanor looks much like all the others." Netermose flung Bak another perplexed look. "Why do you ask, sir?"

Bak glanced up at the lord Re, whose solar barque had journeyed at least two-thirds of the way across the brilliant blue sky. He had become so involved in what was beginning to seem a futile exercise that he had missed the midday meal. "What of a Hittite trader named Zuwapi? Do you know him?"

The aide frowned, further deepening the wrinkles on his brow and at the corners of his eyes and mouth. "I may've heard the name, but in what context I can't say."

"While you dwelt in Hattusa, Pahure obtained items from him for the women of your household. Objects imported from Kemet, difficult to find in the land of Hatti."

Shrugging, Netermose pulled another puppy close and tickled its belly. "I knew he satisfied their needs for costly and what were, in Hattusa, rare items, but I've no memory of the man who supplied them."

"The political situation in the land of Hatti is always precarious." Sitepehu waved a small bee away from a bowl of plump purple grapes sitting on the low table beside him. "Kings come and go in regular succession, with fathers and brothers being murdered for the crown. Only the most adept in the art of survival cling to power."

"Not a pleasant nation in which to dwell," Bak said.

After convincing the cook to give him a loaf of bread and a bowl of cold mutton stew, he had sought out the priest. They had settled themselves beneath the portico atop the dwelling's extension, thinking the breeze would make it the coolest place to be in the burning heat of midafternoon.

"The land itself is most agreeable much of the year." The priest smiled. "Oh, it's not easy to accustom oneself to the cold season, especially when snow blankets the land, but the other seasons are most pleasant. The mountains are tall and impressive. The plain southeast of Hattusa goes on forever, far beyond the distant horizon and not a sand dune in sight. Water is plentiful, falling from the skies in sufficient quantity to make the land bountiful. Magnificent trees, glorious flowers, people of kindness and good humor who strive mightily to survive cruel laws, harsh gods, and weak kings."

Breaking off a crust of bread, Bak dipped it in the stew, which tasted strongly of onions, celery, and pepper. "Your praises outweigh your criticisms, Sitepehu."

"I was sorry we had to leave." The priest's expression grew bleak. "I wanted very much to help those good-hearted and generous people, yet I could do nothing for them."

Bak eyed the priest with sudden interest, the well-muscled body, the scar on his shoulder. A man who felt as he did might, with the best of intentions, have become involved in the politics of the land. "Were you surprised to learn of Pentu's recall?"

"I was dismayed when I was told we were to return to Kemet, shocked when I learned the reason, and mystified by the charge."

After licking the stew from his fingers, Bak reached for his beer jar. "You had no idea you dwelt side by side with someone who had more than a passing interest in the land of Hatti?"

"None." Sitepehu gave Bak a cynical smile. "If I dwelt there with a traitor, I do so to this day. Every man and woman who went with Pentu to Hattusa lives with him still."

"You included?" Bak asked, surprised.

Sitepehu bowed his head in acknowledgment. "The lord Inheret is a modest god, with few properties to support him, none of which include a house, and my duties for him are not demanding. Pentu provides a place where I and my son—my wife died of a fever two years ago—can live in comfort, and in exchange I help with his accounts."

Bak nodded his understanding. While offerings flowed in vast quantities to the lord Amon and other major deities, the lesser gods were not so fortunate. Few of their priests were able to survive solely on the generosity of their followers.

"Who among you would be the most likely to dabble in the politics of Hatti?"

"I've asked myself that question time and time again. The present king, like those before him, occupies an unstable throne, but to side with anyone—the king or a contender—would be foolhardy. Any of them could vanish overnight and another take his place."

Bak thanked the gods of the land of Kemet that he had not been born into the uncertain and dangerous world of the Hittites. "Did you know the slain merchant, Maruwa?"

"I knew of him." Sitepehu absentmindedly rubbed the scar on his shoulder. "Netermose befriended him, so he always dealt with him, passing the necessary scrolls back and forth when need be."

A gust of warm air swept along the portico, carrying the scent of flowers. Fallen petals chased one another across the rooftop.

Bak took a sip of beer, savored its slightly bitter taste. "Did you ever meet the trader Zuwapi? He exports items from Kemet and transports them to Hatti. The usual trade goods: pottery, rough linen, small tools, and so on. He also deals in luxury items such as aromatic oils and fine linen."

"He'd have to have come to me for a pass, allowing him to travel freely in Kemet, but the document is so routine I'd not remember. As for the items he exported from Kemet, they'd have been listed on the manifest of the ship on which he transported them, prepared and approved at the point of origin."

Vowing to take a look at Antef's manifest, Bak fished around in the stew for a chunk of mutton. "As high priest of the lord Inheret, you must often have dealings with those who toil in the sacred precinct of the lord Amon."

"Not as often as you'd think." Sitepehu smiled. "I pay my respects when I come to Waset, and Pentu provides food and a sleeping pallet on the rare occasions when a priest or scribe comes through Tjeny, but that's about all."

"Do you recall any who stopped within the past few months?"

"A ranking scribe stayed overnight five or six weeks ago. He had a document from Hapuseneb himself, demanding that I show him the records of the lord Inheret's meager estate. He asked also for a list of Pentu's personal offerings to the lord Amon."

His interest quickening, Bak hastily swallowed a bite of meat. "His name was . . . ?"

"User? Woser? Woserhet. Yes, that was the name."

Bak felt like shouting for joy. At last he had come upon a man who had tied the auditor to . . . Well, not directly to Maruwa, but indirectly through Pentu's household. "What was he looking for?"

"He never said." The priest must have noticed Bak's growing excitement for he eyed him with open curiosity. "He seemed disappointed when he left, as if he'd been unable to find what he hoped to."

"Did Hapuseneb's letter demand that you specifically show Woserhet your records, or was it more general, asking all to whom he spoke to open their files to him?"

Sitepehu had no trouble remembering a request he obviously took as being of some note, which indeed it had been: a demand made by the chief priest himself. "My name was not upon it, nor was that of Pentu. Woserhet was far from being a garrulous man, but I gathered he'd traveled throughout the land, speaking with many priests and officials along the way."

"Did Pentu know of his visit?"

"He wasn't home at the time, though someone may've told him later." The priest plucked a grape from the cluster. "A nobleman had come south from Mennufer to visit the tomb of the lord Osiris in Abedju. His rank was such that no less a man than the governor could accompany him."

"No, sir, you cannot speak with either mistress Taharet or mistress Meret." The elderly servant looked sincerely regretful. "They left well before midday, saying they meant to call on a friend whom they seldom see. I believe they'll be away for the remainder of the day."

Bak had hoped to question the two women before nightfall. Still he felt a sense of relief at not having to speak with Meret. He wanted to believe her an intelligent woman who had looked upon him as a friend, a man who had shared a similar loss to hers, but he feared she might have misunderstood, thinking him more interested in her as a woman alone than he actually was.

"Did you go to Hattusa with your master when he served as envoy to the Hittite kingdom?"

"I did, sir."

"Then I must ask a few questions."

The lord Re had vanished beyond the western horizon when Bak finally left Pentu's dwelling. Long shadows lay across the city, darkening the narrow streets and lanes. Torches lit up the court in front of the sacred precinct of Ipetresyt and the nearby stretch of the processional way, illuminating the booths erected on the opening day of the Beautiful Feast of Opet. The crowd, colorful and ever-changing, was gathering for a night of entertainment, food, and drink. Men and women sauntered from booth to booth, from athletic to acrobatic performance, from tricksters in the magic arts to scribes writing letters to the dead, asking for good health or love or to place a curse on an enemy. Children and animals ran free. Laughter and shouting, music and singing, the braying of donkeys and barking of dogs filled the air with gaiety.

Bak worked his way through the multitude, stopping briefly to watch one performance and another, looking at rich and exotic products few men could afford and the more common items made by and for the poor. He spotted several of his Medjays but stayed well clear, not wanting to inhibit their play.

Reluctantly he left the crowd to walk north along the processional way, heading toward his men's quarters. While he strode through ever deepening darkness, he mulled over his day. He had learned nothing from Pentu's servants except that they had disliked Hattusa, had felt imprisoned within the massive stone walls that surrounded the city. As for the governor and his staff, no man looked more guilty than another. If one had told him a falsehood, he had been unable to detect the lie.

Why would any of them—why would any resident of the land of Kemet, for that matter—wish to cause trouble in Hatti? To unseat the king seemed likely. But why? What would be the goal? Personal gain? Political gain? He was mystified.

He regretted the need to return to Pentu's dwelling, to speak with mistresses Taharet and Meret, but experience had taught him that he must not overlook the women of the household.

He turned into the dark, narrow lane that would take him to his Medjays' quarters. A nightbird whistled behind him. Ahead, three men staggered out of an intersecting lane, carrying a torch to light their way, singing loud, their voices raucous. Men besotted. As they drew near, he glanced to either side, seeking a doorway so he could step out of their way. He wanted no confrontation with men too befuddled to think clearly.

A stone rattled behind him. He glanced around, saw two men running toward him in the dark, each carrying a short, thick staff. He looked forward, muttered a curse. The three ahead had grown silent, their staggering gait had been thrown aside. They, too, carried weapons. One held a staff; his two mates carried scimitars.

He remembered the nightbird, heard in a place where no trees grew. The sound had been a signal, letting the men in front know he was coming.

The pack must have followed him from Ipet-resyt—or

from Pentu's dwelling. When he had entered the residential area, with its cramped lanes and building blocks that looked all alike, two had raced on ahead to block his way.

He had walked into their trap.

Chapter Eleven

Snapping out a curse, Bak pivoted and raced back along the lane toward the two men who had come up behind him. The pair paused, confused by his sudden approach. His eyes darted along the windowless, doorless wall to his right, searching for a narrow passage he vaguely remembered seeing as he passed it by, a slice of black opening onto the gray-black lane. An escape route, he prayed. He carried his baton of office and his dagger hung from his belt, but in the hands of a single individual, they would be no match against five armed men.

There! he thought, spotting the cleft a half-dozen paces ahead, midway between him and the pair. He leaped toward it.

"Stop him!" yelled one, lunging forward.

Bak felt the man's groping hands just as he ducked into the passage. Blackness closed around him, with not a speck of light above—or at the far end.

What had he gotten himself into?

A quick glance back revealed a man at the mouth of the passage, peering inside. A rude reminder that retreat was impossible. Whatever lay ahead, he must face.

"It's blacker than night in there," the man said.

"Go in and get him, you louts." A second voice, gravelly, irritable.

Bak took several cautious steps deeper into the passage. It

164

was as wide as his shoulders with no room to spare, its walls rough and uneven—bare mudbrick, he realized. The hard-packed earthen floor was slick, and he smelled manure. Shuddering at the very thought of what he might be walking through—and into—he pressed forward.

The men outside had begun to argue about who would enter the passage first. The gravel-voiced leader barked out a name. A man cursed and shifted his feet, sending a pebble skittering across the lane. Bak glanced back, saw someone standing in the mouth of the passage, blocking what little light there was.

"I can't see a thing."

"Then neither can he!" the man in charge snapped. "Go on."

"But, sir!"

"Get a torch, one of you," the leader commanded.

"Where?" another man whined. "The houses are all dark."

"Go find a sentry."

"But . . ."

"If you come up behind him, he'll never know who or what hit him." The gravel voice paused, growled, "Now hurry up. We can't let that accursed lieutenant get away." He spat out the words, as venomous as a horned viper.

Bak's blood ran cold. If they had set their trap, meaning to snare a man at random, the first to come along, they would not have known his rank. They had planned to catch him and, if their weapons were any indication of intent, they meant to slay him.

He walked on, trying not to rush, placing his feet with care. The last thing he wanted was to slip and fall. He moved through the darkness, his hands against the walls, thinking to find a gap, a door. He could not be sure, but he thought the lane was curving gradually to his right, which might explain his failure to see light ahead. He prayed such was the case, that he would soon find a way out.

Something skittered across the floor. It ran over his foot,

its tiny claws sending chills down his spine, and raced away toward the mouth of the passage. A rat, he thought. A yell sounded behind him, the thud of a man falling. Angry curses from gravel voice, nervous laughter from the others. As dire as his situation was, Bak could not help but smile.

His foot bumped into something hairy. If the faint smell of decaying flesh was any indication, an animal had some time ago crawled into the passage to die. Carefully he stepped over it. His foot came down on something wet and soft that squished between his toes. He closed his thoughts to the possibilities.

"He did it!" Bak heard behind him, the shout muted by the rough walls between him and the lane. "Look! He got the torch."

Bak had no idea how far he had come, probably not a great distance. One thing he knew for a fact: the light would give his pursuers a distinct advantage.

Would this vile passage never end?

He moved forward, two paces, four, eight. Far ahead, the walls had taken on a kind of texture, as if he could distinguish one mudbrick from another. He squeezed his eyes shut, opened them. Was the world around him growing lighter? Or was his heart so filled with hopeful thinking that he imagined an end to this nightmare journey? Flinging caution aside, he hurried on into a darkness that seemed not quite so black.

Without warning he bumped into a low barrier, and at the same time the wall to his right came to an end. The barrier was a gate, he discovered, made of the thin branches of a tree. He scrambled over, and the space around him opened up. In the lesser darkness, he saw sheaves of hay stacked along a wall and a water trough built against a second wall. A pile of straw lay nearby. He was in an animal shelter. Four paces farther and he stood in a courtyard lit by the moon and a sky sprinkled with stars. Seven or eight donkeys lay on a bed of straw strewn around an acacia. One made a blowing sound, the rest were content to stare.

Relieved beyond measure, Bak thanked the lord Amon for freeing him from the passage. Before he could form another prayer, this one asking for a way out, he spotted, beyond the tree, a door closed by a sturdy mat.

Light flashed into the shelter, he heard voices approaching along the passage. His pursuers were closing on him. He raced around the tree, struck the mat with his shoulder, tearing it down, and stepped into a room as black as the passage had been. He walked forward, sliding his feet along the earthen floor, hoping not to blunder into anything.

A man with a torch rushed through the door behind him.

In the flickering light, Bak spotted an open doorway three paces ahead and a stairway only a pace away. Lunging toward the stairs, he raced upward and burst out onto the moonlit roof. He swerved aside, narrowly avoiding stumbling over a family sleeping there, taking advantage of the cool night air. The man, jerked rudely from his slumber, sat up and yelled. A baby began to howl. All across the roofs of the interconnected houses, men and women and children sat up and looked around, trying to understand what had awakened them.

Bak sped across the open expanse, racing around flimsy pavilions and people aroused from sleep, leaping over braziers, baked clay pots and dishes, tools, animals and domestic fowl. His pursuers formed a ragged line behind him, the nearest no more than three paces back. The man carrying the torch was second in line, careless of the light, letting the sparks fly where they would. Dogs barked, men cursed, women screamed threats or demanded their men act, small children whimpered while their older brothers shouted out in excitement.

Bak angled toward the low parapet that marked the edge of the building block and looked into the lane below. The roof was so far above the ground that he would more likely than not break a leg if he jumped. The gap between the buildings was too wide.

"Got him!" a man shouted and raised his staff to swing. His expression was hard and mean, revealing his deadly intent.

Bak danced sideways, slammed his baton across the man's shoulder. As his would-be assailant cried out in agony and fell to his knees, Bak dodged another man's grasp. Breathing hard, he swung his baton at a third man, forcing him back against a flimsy pavilion. The structure collapsed, the dry brush atop the shelter tumbled around the nearest pair. One support, a rough pole, broke free and rolled across the rooftop.

Praying it was a good, solid piece of wood, Bak scooped it up, raced toward the parapet, and vaulted into space. He heard the wood crack beneath his weight, but momentum carried him safely over the gap between the buildings.

Later, sitting in the courtyard of his Medjays' quarters, watching the two men on duty playing knucklebones, Bak let his thoughts return to his near entrapment and narrow escape. He was following two paths, that of Pentu and the traitor in his household and that of the possible thefts in the sacred precinct. Which was the one causing the cobra to rear its ugly head? Or were the two paths converging?

Bak went to Pentu's house the following morning with a renewed determination to lay hands on the man he sought. He doubted his questions of the previous day had led to the attempt on his life, but one way or another he meant to find out.

The governor was most unhappy when he learned Bak had come to speak with his wife and her sister. He made it clear that the sooner the police officer finished with his household, the happier he would be. After agreeing to tell the women they must cooperate, he summoned a servant to usher his unwanted guest outside the house to a small walled garden, rare in a crowded neighborhood such as this. There

Bak had to wait for more than an hour, sometimes sitting, sometimes pacing along neat paths that meandered through an oasis of pruned, shaped, and trained plants and shrubs, none allowed to flourish in their natural form. He thought of leaving more than once, but he, too, wanted the interviews over and done with.

"I know nothing of that Hittite's death," Taharet said, sitting down on a shaded bench beside a small fish pool. "I can't imagine what gave you the idea that I could help."

"You were in Hattusa with your husband." Bak, irritated by the long wait, spoke like a teacher enumerating important points to a callow youth. "Someone who dwelt with you in the envoy's residence became involved in the politics of the land of Hatti. As a result, Pentu and all his household were recalled to Kemet. Maruwa's death may well be related to that recall."

"We returned three years ago. If a connection exists, why was he not slain before now?"

Bak knelt on the opposite side of the pool so he could see her face, which was cool, composed, a picture of studied refinement. Like the garden and the pond, where not a leaf marred the water's surface, her appearance was faultless. He eyed a small green frog sunning itself on a lily pad and wondered how it dared invade a place of such perfection. "Do you have any idea who in your household might've wished to foment trouble in Hatti, and for what reason?"

"My husband is a man of integrity, Lieutenant. I suspect he made the Hittite king look and feel small. I think that king accused someone in our household, offering no name or proof of wrongdoing because none existed, and had us withdrawn so he wouldn't have to be reminded day after day of his own petty nature."

"An interesting theory."

"You sound skeptical, Lieutenant."

Bak thought her idea absurd. "Did you ever meet Maruwa?"

"I did not." Her voice was firm, the statement absolute.

Rising to his feet, he said, "While you dwelt in Hattusa, mistress, Pahuré obtained for you and your sister several small but desirable items imported into Hatti from the land of Kemet. Did you ever meet the merchant he purchased them from? Zuwapi is his name."

"What reason would I have to talk to a Hittite merchant? Or a merchant in Kemet, for that matter. That's Pahure's task, one he performs well enough."

Bak walked a few paces along a path he had trod many times over the past hour. He had to admire the steward, who must surely have the patience of a deity to put up with this woman. Was she the daughter of a nobleman, reared to look down upon all others? Or did she come from baser stock and thought to prove her superiority by belittling all who drew near?

"Do you ever meet priests or scribes who toil in the sacred precinct of the lord Amon?" Walking back to the pool, he made a silent guess as to her answer. She did not disappoint him.

"I've met the chief priest and a few of his closest advisers on social occasions." She flashed a bright smile. "Hapuseneb is such a wonderful man. I'm sorry we won't see him during the Beautiful Feast of Opet, but as you may or may not know, he's much too involved with official rituals to celebrate with good and companionable friends, as the rest of us do."

Before he could congratulate himself on his perspicacity, she added, "You're not interested in Hapuseneb, are you? You want to know if I was acquainted with the men who were slain in the sacred precinct."

"Your husband told you I'd ask," Bak said, trying not to sound annoyed. Of course Pentu would have warned her; carrying the tale might have earned him a pat on the head.

"We keep few secrets from each other, Lieutenant."

"And you keep no secrets from your sister, I'd wager."

She smiled, bowed her head in acknowledgment. "We're very close, yes."

Bak snapped a large yellowish blossom from a vine that climbed the wall of the one-story dwelling that abutted the garden. The flower gave off a heavy, slightly musty scent. "Did you know either the priest Meryamon or the scribe Woserhet?"

"No, Lieutenant, I didn't. Neither was of sufficient rank to accompany Hapuseneb."

Bak dropped the blossom into the pool, earning a scowl from Taharet. "I've no further questions, mistress, at least not at the moment. Perhaps later my quest will take me down a different path and I'll have a need to make additional inquiries."

She rose gracefully to her feet, formed a gracious but not especially sincere smile. "I'll have a servant see you to the door."

"Before I go," he said, his smile matching hers, "I must speak with your sister."

She paused, raised an eyebrow. "Oh, didn't I tell you? She's ill, unable to talk with anyone."

"When will she be well enough to see me?"

"I'm not a physician, Lieutenant. How can I predict the course of an illness?"

Walking away from the dwelling, thoroughly annoyed, Bak thought over his interview with the woman. Her attitude, once warm and friendly, had changed completely. Why? he wondered. Did she feel his investigation threatened her husband and therefore her comfortable existence? Meret's illness, he felt sure, was a lie. Had Taharet decided to hold him and her sister apart, fearing they might grow fond of each other?

"I'm sorry, sir, but they've all gone." The haggard-looking woman stood with one thrust-out hip straddled by a naked child about two years of age. The boy, his thumb in his mouth, stared wide-eyed at Bak.

"Do you have any idea where they went?" Bak stepped out of the house where the scribe Tati and the four workmen had dwelt and toiled for Woserhet. He had found the building empty of furnishings and life.

"They came without a word, and that's the way they left."

Bak muttered an oath. Why had he not sent Kasaya back another time? He needed to speak with the man, needed to look through the auditor's records. "Did the scribe leave with the others?"

She snorted. "Do you think they'd make a move without him?"

"My Medjay came three days ago, searching for him. When he didn't find him, he left a message that I wanted to see him." Bitterness tinged Bak's voice. "Now I find he's been here all along."

"No, sir. He's been gone." She grabbed the child by its bare bottom and heaved it higher on her hip. "I hadn't seen him for several days, then he returned this morning and in less than an hour they'd all moved out."

Why such a hasty departure? Bak wondered. Was Tati afraid for his life for some reason? Were they all frightened? Or had they merely been given another assignment? Where had Woserhet's files been taken?

"They're not here, sir."

Bak frowned at the mat covering the door of the house where Ashayet dwelt with her children. "Have they gone for an hour or a day?"

The girl, roughly eight years of age, the tallest of the six children barring Bak's path, kept her expression grave. He guessed she was an older sister, caretaker of her smaller siblings. "Mistress Ashayet's husband, Woserhet, has been slain, sir. He's in the house of death. As he'll be there for some time, she thought to go away, to stay with her mother and father until she must place him in his eternal resting place."

Recalling the modest way in which Woserhet had dwelt, Bak doubted the widow had sufficient wealth to have his body preserved in the most elaborate and lengthy manner. What little she had, she must use to care for her children. "When does she plan to return?"

"Not for a long time, sir."

"They'll be gone for at least a week," said a small boy in a chirpy voice.

"Shush!" the girl commanded. "He doesn't know what he's talking about, sir. They went to Abu. They'll be gone close to two months."

A voyage to Abu? An extended stay? "Woserhet will remain in the house of death that long?"

"Oh, yes, sir." A bright, excited smile lit up the girl's face. "A priest named Ptahmes came and he spoke for no less a man than the chief priest Hapuseneb. He told mistress Ashayet how highly regarded her husband had been and said the lord Amon himself would see that he received the best of care in the house of death. He'll also be given a resting place befitting his upstanding character."

Bak whistled. The smaller children nudged each other and giggled, delighted their sister had impressed him so.

"If the chief priest can take the time to provide Woserhet with more in death than he had in life, why can't he spare a half hour or so to tell us of the auditor's mission?"

Bak had to smile at Hori's disgruntled expression. "I suspect Ptahmes took upon himself the task of rewarding Woserhet without a word from Hapuseneb. Which tells me that, though he might not know what Woserhet was doing, he had no doubt of the auditor's importance to the chief priest and the lord Amon."

The young scribe laid the last fragment of charred scroll on top of all the others, carried them into the shade beneath the pavilion, placed them on top of the rolled scrolls in the basket, and weighted them down with a rock. "What a waste of time this task was! I didn't find a thing that would lead us to Woserhet's slayer."

"I doubt your search was all in vain." Bak told him of the auditor's visit to Tjeny and his request to see Pentu's files. "Evidently Woserhet wasn't interested in any of the governor's records except those that list the items he sent as offerings to the lord Amon. Which leads me to believe he was tracking objects from their point of origin to the god's storehouses and maybe on until they were consumed or shipped elsewhere or reverted back to the priests or the people for ordinary use."

"We can't very well follow in his footsteps." With a clatter, Kasaya dropped a handful of baked clay shards and chips onto a pile of similar fragments for which he had no use. "We've no authority to inspect all the governors' records, and even if we had, we'd have to travel the length of the river from the Great Green Sea to Abu. To visit so many provinces would take several months."

Bak knelt to examine Kasaya's handiwork. The Medjay had glued together only the shoulders of the broken storage jars, where the contents of each had been written. The odd-shaped remnants were lined up like soldiers two abreast at the edge of the shadow cast by the pavilion. "Have you learned anything at all from these vessels?"

The Medjay, who could not read, looked to Hori to answer.

"We went to the room where Woserhet was slain. From the empty spaces on the shelves, we concluded that fourteen jars had been removed." Hori plopped down before the reconstructions. "Kasaya has pieced twenty-one back together and he's found enough shards with symbols on them for at least two more."

"Twenty-three all told." The young Medjay eyed the jars with more satisfaction than the potters who created them must have felt.

"Leaving nine jars that came from storehouses containing grain, hides, and metal ingots," Bak said.

"No, sir." Kasaya sat down beside the scribe. "When we separated out the jars listing bulk items, we came up with two extra jars, two too many for the available space in the room where Woserhet was found."

"These two." Hori pointed to two vessels' shoulders, both painstakingly reconstructed using a multitude of small fragments. Riddled with holes, left empty when the pieces could not be found, they both were lopsided and bulged in places. "The labels are hard to read because so many symbols are missing, but we both think they came from somewhere else, another storehouse that contained valuables probably."

Bak knelt beside him, gingerly lifted one of the two reconstructions, and compared it to several others. "What gave you that idea?"

"These two were much more badly damaged. I think someone removed the documents and threw them on the fire." Hori pointed toward the charred scrolls in the basket. "When the jars were empty, he flung them down, breaking them, and stomped on the fragments."

"I found a lot of crushed pieces on the floor close to where Woserhet fell," Kasaya said. "The slayer was determined to destroy those pots."

Bak stared at the label, but could make nothing of the few legible symbols. "Have you gone yet to the main storehouse archives, Hori?"

"Yes, sir." The scribe took the piece and set it with the others. "Woserhet audited the records there about four months ago, and he came back several times during the past month. The chief archivist knew him fairly well, and he's convinced the auditor would've drawn his attention to anything he found amiss."

"Did Woserhet concentrate his effort in any special part of the archives?"

"If so, the archivist took no notice."

"Perhaps another scribe paid more heed." Bak rose to his feet. "You must go back and ask. Then you must look through all the records anyone remembers Woserhet examining. When you finish with that, you must look at past records for the storage block in which his body was found, going back five years or so. You must also ask if any storage jars are missing."

"A huge effort, sir, too big for a man alone."

Bak smiled at the scribe's lack of enthusiasm. "I'll find someone to help. In the meantime, I've another task you may find more to your liking. This at the customs records center."

Kasaya, useless for any task requiring the ability to read, looked glum. "Is there nothing I can do, sir?"

"You must find Woserhet's servant Tati. We could use his help, and we need the files that have disappeared with him."

"I don't understand, sir." Hori veered around the gangplank of a large, graceful traveling ship moored against the bank of the river. Two sailors sat on board, paying more attention to the comings and goings in the market than to the ropes they were mending. "Why are we going to the customs office?"

"I saw objects on Captain Antef's cargo ship that looked very much like those used in the sacred rituals. I think someone is stealing from the storehouses of the lord Amon and the Hittite merchant Zuwapi is shipping the objects to Hatti, and probably to other lands to the north of Kemet as well."

Hori shook his head, unable to understand. "Who would dare steal from the lord Amon? Or any lesser deity, for that matter?"

"With luck and if the gods choose to smile upon us, an examination of the shipping records may point to the thief."

"What specifically am I to look for?"

Bak veered around a mooring post sunk deep into the riverbank. The line snugged around the post squeaked each time a swell lifted the small cargo ship, whose deck was mounded high with rough chunks of golden sandstone. A lone sailor sat on the rocks, his head bowed over his fishing pole, snoring.

"Keep your eyes open for anything suspicious, but basically ask yourself these questions: Does Zuwapi always ship his trade goods on Antef's vessel? Did Maruwa ever make his return journey to Hatti on Antef's ship when it was laden with Zuwapi's cargo? Focus also on Zuwapi's export items and look for objects of value. I suspect the destination shown on the manifests is always Ugarit, but if any other port is listed, take note, paying heed to exactly what was delivered where."

Hori nodded, understanding. "If Zuwapi is transporting stolen goods out of Kemet, Maruwa may have noticed."

"A strong possibility. And if he did, he would've reported the fact." Bak ducked around a man seated on the moist earth with a small, chirping monkey. The man was examining a handful of bright beads and amulets thrown to him as a reward for the animal's performance. Or stolen by the monkey from a market stall.

"Do you think Zuwapi slew Maruwa?"

"I've been told he dwells in Mennufer when he comes to the land of Kemet. If we should discover he's here in Waset, we must take a long, hard look at him." Bak caught Hori's arm and eased him around a half dozen sailors, hurrying off their ship in search of fun and games. "I've no trouble thinking he'd slay Maruwa, but why would he take the lives of Meryamon and Woserhet?"

"I'll wager Meryamon was the thief, a man who could point a finger at him."

"Woserhet was slain first. With the auditor dead, Zuwapi would've had no need to slay Meryamon. The man who may've been providing him with stolen goods. Goods sold in cities to the north at a substantial profit."

Hori gave Bak a sheepish smile. "Put that way, my theory seems a bit thin."

*   *   *

After leaving Hori at the customs records center, Bak purchased from a market stall a chunk of boiled fish wrapped in leaves. Eating as he walked, he strode along the waterfront toward Antef's ship, thinking to check the men who were guarding the cargo. As he approached the vessel, he saw in the distance several men coming toward him. Taking them for sailors, he paid no heed.

He reached the gangplank and headed upward. Captain Antef stood at the bow, watching him with an obvious lack of enthusiasm, understandable since he rightly blamed Bak for the harbormaster's decision to hold his ship in Waset.

At the top of the gangplank, Bak ate the last bite of fish and threw the leaves overboard. He caught another glimpse of the sailors, paused, looked at them harder. The three in front were walking side by side, while the fourth was slightly behind. It took but an instant to register the laggard's appearance, his swarthy complexion. He was the foreign looking man who had argued with the red-haired man to whom Meryamon had passed a message.

Bak hurried down the gangplank and walked at a good fast pace toward the approaching men. The swarthy man abruptly veered aside and strode swiftly into the nearest lane, vanishing between two building blocks. Bak broke into a run, sped past the sailors, and darted into the mouth of the lane. He spotted the swarthy man at the far end, running full out. The man vanished into an intersecting street. By the time Bak reached the corner, he had disappeared. He searched the nearby lanes, but the man had gone.

The exercise, though futile, had been informative. The swarthy man knew who he was and did not wish to be questioned. Could he be Zuwapi? A man supposed to be in Mennufer?

Chapter Twelve

"I'm beginning to worry, Imsiba." Bak leaned against the rail of the cargo ship, a broad, sturdy vessel spotlessly clean but badly in need of overall maintenance, and shook a pebble from his sandal. "The day Woserhet lost his life, Amonked said he hoped I'd find the slayer before the festival ends."

The Medjay sergeant whistled. "You've only four and a half days, my friend. Not a lot of time."

"Soon after—two or three days, I'd guess—we're to sail to Mennufer with Commandant Thuty." Bak's voice turned grim. "I'd not like to leave behind a vile criminal unaccountable to the lady Maat."

The two men walked up the deck. Imsiba's eyes darted here and there and everywhere, seeking faults in the ship his wife might purchase. A northerly breeze made bearable the heat of the harsh midafternoon sun. The vessel rocked gently on the swells. Fittings creaked, ropes thunked against the mast, a crow perched on the masthead called to two others on a nearby rooftop. Sitamon, as delicate as a flower, stood at the forecastle with the vessel's grizzled owner and the tall, rangy man who had served as master of the cargo ship she had owned while in Buhen. As he would captain the vessel she ultimately chose, his questions were sharp and perceptive, designed to reveal the craft's good points as well as its flaws.

Imsiba knelt to examine a large coil of graying rope lying on the deck. "Do you have any idea who the slayer might be?"

"If valuable objects are being stolen from the storehouses of Amon, as I believe, practically anyone who toils within the sacred precinct might be guilty of taking Woserhet's life and that of Meryamon. If governor Pentu's withdrawal from Hattusa was the reason for their deaths, someone in his household is probably the slayer."

"Do I detect uncertainty, my friend, a lack of confidence?"

Bak grinned. "Simple confusion. I've too many loose ends, making me mistrust both theories. And neither meshes well with the other."

Imsiba lifted the coils, one or two at a time, and looked closely at the rope. About midway through, he revealed a long segment that was so frayed and worn it looked ready to pull apart under the least bit of strain. Scowling, he laid the coil so the worn part was visible and continued the task. "How can I help?"

Though sorely tempted, Bak shook his head. "No, Imsiba. Sitamon needs you more than I do." He saw doubt on the Medjay's face, smiled. "Look at the large number of ships moored here in Waset and likely to remain throughout the festival. Seldom does such an opportunity arise. She needs you by her side."

Bak thought to go to the sacred precinct, but decided instead to speak with Netermose, a man who would know well those who dwelt in Pentu's household and the one he felt would more readily divulge that knowledge.

The aide was not an easy man to find, but thanks to a servant who had toiled for Pentu's family for a lifetime and knew her betters as well as she knew herself, Bak found him at the river's edge. He was carrying a basket from which he threw kitchen leavings, a handful at a time, into the river.

Twenty or more ducks bobbed on the swells, competing for fish heads, wilted lettuce, and melon rinds.

Finding Netermose away from the house was a gift of the gods. Here he might speak more freely than when under the roof of the man to whom he owed his livelihood.

"It's hard to believe the festival is almost over," the aide said, eyeing a dozen or so men adding fresh white limestone chips to the short length of processional way along which the lord Amon would travel from Ipet-resyt to the river for his homeward bound voyage to Ipet-isut.

"Other than the first day and one night, I've had no opportunity to take part in the revelry," Bak admitted.

"Have you found the man who slew Maruwa?" Looking embarrassed, Netermose laughed. "Of course you haven't. You'd not have searched me out if you had."

Bak reached out, palm up, signaling that they should walk south along the river. The ducks swam along beside them, squawking for another handout. "When I asked you yesterday which member of Pentu's household might've hoped to cause trouble in the land of Hatti, you said the tale was untrue. You spoke with utter conviction, yet you surely know that an envoy is not lightly recalled. And you must've been told that Pentu's successor, when he arrived in Hattusa, verified the charge."

"Your presence has brought back much that I'd hoped to forget."

They strolled past a mooring post sunk deep into the moist, grassy bank and swerved around an acacia hanging out over the river, bowing toward the lord Hapi and his beneficent floodwaters.

"Three men have died, Netermose. The incident in Hattusa may or may not be linked to their deaths. If it is, any information you offer may help snare the slayer." Bak saw a denial forming on the aide's face and raised his hand for silence. "If those who dwell in Pentu's household prove innocent, the sooner I learn the truth and put aside my suspicions, the sooner I'll turn down a more fruitful path."

A long silence, an unhappy sigh. "I was appalled at the very thought that someone in our household had been involved with Hittite politics." Netermose, his face gray and strained, shook his head as if denying a thing he knew to be true. "According to Hittite law, if a man is caught plotting against the king, he and everyone in his family are slaughtered. That might also have held true if a member of an envoy's household were found guilty of plotting against the throne. I consider myself and all who served Pentu in Hattusa to be lucky that we were withdrawn before the traitor was identified."

"Who do you think would take such a risk? You must've given the matter some thought."

Netermose looked truly puzzled. "I never reached a conclusion. Each and every one of us is a man or woman of Kemet, loyal to our sovereign and the land she governs. Why any one of us would do such a thing is beyond me."

To stir up trouble in the land of Hatti—or any other land, for that matter—did not necessarily mean a man was not loyal to his homeland. The true test of loyalty depended on whom he was backing and how that individual meant to deal with Kemet. "You grew to manhood on Pentu's estate, I believe you once said." Or inferred.

The aide did not blink an eye at the more personal question. "Yes, sir."

"Have you always toiled for the governor and his family? Or did you leave Tjeny for a time?"

"Why would I leave? Pentu and his father before him have always been good to me. Through his father's generosity, I learned to read and write. I studied with Pentu as a child, played with him. I'm pleased to count him among my friends. Of equal import, he raised me up to my present position. If not for him, I'd be toiling in the fields with my brothers."

Bak noted the pride on the aide's face, the devotion of a servant for a longtime master. "Did Pentu not go to Waset as a child to study in the royal house, as other noble youths do?"

"Yes, sir, but he didn't remain for long. His father died when he was twelve years of age and he had to return to Tjeny to assume his duties as landowner and to learn from his uncle the duties of a governor."

"He never served in the army?"

"No, sir."

Bak wondered if any man who had spent his life so close to his provincial birthplace would become involved in the politics of another land. Netermose's very innocence might allow him to stumble into a predicament that was beyond his understanding, but to venture into a situation he understood would be unlikely. Pentu must have been almost as sheltered, so the same would most likely be true for him. Why, in the name of the lord Amon, had Maatkare Hatshepsut named him her envoy to a distant and alien land like Hatti?

"Tell me of Sitepehu. He was a soldier in Retenu, he said, but I know little else about him."

Netermose turned away to throw a handful of kitchen leavings into the river. The ducks fluttered across the water to grab what they could. Quacks blended in a single ear-splitting racket. "I don't like speaking of a man behind his back, Lieutenant."

"Better to speak of him now than to find him one morning with his throat cut. As Maruwa's was. Or to find him cutting someone else's throat, possibly yours."

The aide flushed, then spoke with a reluctance that gradually diminished. "He served in the infantry from the age of fourteen and rose to the lofty position of lieutenant, learning to read and write along the way. He likes to say he climbed through the ranks with the tenacity of a hyena stalking its prey. He was wounded, came close to dying. You saw the scar on his shoulder. He went to his sister, who dwelt in Tjeny, to recover.

"Pentu met him, liked him, and took him into his household as a scribe." The aide's smile was rueful. "I sometimes resent his success in Tjeny, in our household, but I'm the first to admit he never shirks his duty. He rapidly attained the position of chief scribe, and thus he went with us to Hattusa. When we returned, Pentu appointed him chief priest of the lord Inheret."

"While a soldier, did he ever travel beyond Retenu to the land of Hatti?"

"If so, he never said."

They walked on, each man immersed in his own thoughts. Bak had no doubt that Sitepehu could steal up behind a man and slay him with a single slash of a blade. He had been trained in the art of death, and his heavily muscled shoulders and arms would ease the act. But Bak liked the priest, enjoyed his wry sense of humor, preferred not to think of him as a heartless killer.

Ahead, the grassy verge narrowed, squeezed between the riverbank and the massive enclosure wall around Ipet-resyt. A dozen small boats nudged the bank below an unimpressive gate. Accompanied by the clinking of fittings and the chatter of men who knew each other well, fishermen and farmers hurried across boards spanning the narrow gap between boats and shore, balancing on their shoulders baskets of fruits and vegetables and fish. They passed through the gate, delivering offerings perhaps. Or simply food to be consumed by hungry priests and scribes.

Bak and his companion turned around to walk back the way they had come.

"I recall Pahure saying he was once a sailor," Bak said.

Netermose nodded. "He's quite proud of the fact that as a young man he sailed the Great Green Sea."

"Is he, too, a man of Tjeny?"

"You might call him a neighbor. He came from Abedju. His sister dwells there yet."

The two cities were about a half day's walk apart. "Pentu

dwells in Tjeny. It's the provincial capital, I know, but would it not be to his advantage to make his home in Abedju instead? It's a larger city and far more sacred, with many significant tombs and shrines, and pilgrims constantly coming from afar. I'd think his presence would be required almost daily."

"His estate lies between the two—closer to Tjeny, I must admit. He'd rather live there than in his town house in Abedju. The dwelling is far lighter and more spacious, and mistress Taharet prefers it to the smaller, less comfortable home."

What mistress Taharet desires, Bak thought, mistress Taharet receives. "With so many priests needed for the sacred rituals, as well as the men and women who support them, does he not have many responsibilities in Abedju?"

"He goes weekly, staying several days each time. He doesn't shirk his duty, sir."

It must be a relief to hurry off to Abedju and wield the power he cannot exercise at home, Bak thought. "Tell me more of Pahure."

Netermose hesitated, as he had when asked about Sitepehu, but Bak's grim expression urged him on. "He and his sister had no father and their mother toiled in a house of pleasure. Often besotted, she beat them. One day Pahure ran away. He slipped aboard a cargo ship and sailed to Mennufer, where he joined the crew of a merchant vessel bound for Ugarit. After a few years sailing the Great Green Sea, he jumped ship in Tyre, where he became a guard in the residence of our envoy to that city-state."

The aide reached into the basket and threw another handful into the river. Birds collided in a mass of feathers and quacking. "Like Sitepehu, Pahure is a man of infinite determination. He taught himself to read and write and after a few years became the envoy's steward. When he thought to return to the land of his birth, he sought a similar position in our household."

"What do you think of him?" Bak asked, wondering if the aide resented the steward as he did Sitepehu.

Netermose's smile was sheepish. "I don't much like him, but he performs his task in an exemplary manner."

"Sitepehu inferred that Pahure is a man who knows exactly what he wants and always attains his goal."

"In that respect, the two of them are much alike." The aide's smile broadened. "Pentu has more than once told me I should be more aggressive. Not only am I not inclined that way, but I'm convinced that to have three such men in one household would be disastrous."

Bak laughed, but quickly sobered. He hesitated to ask his next question, but could think of no way around it, no better approach than the most direct. "Tell me of the mistresses Taharet and Meret."

Netermose threw him a startled look. "You can't think one of them slew Maruwa!"

"I have no idea who slew the Hittite, but I learned some time ago that women are as capable of committing vile crimes as are men."

"Mistress Meret is the kindest woman I've ever met," Netermose said, indignant, "and as for mistress Taharet, it's true she's strong-willed, but she'd never knowingly hurt anyone."

Bak noted how carefully the aide worded his defense of Taharet, his use of the word "knowingly." "Would you rather tell me about them or would you prefer I ask someone else, someone who might not be as generous about Taharet's sharp tongue?"

Looking miserable, cornered, Netermose raised the basket and flung the remaining contents far out into the water, causing another eruption of feathers and racket. "She's not the most tactful woman in Kemet," he admitted, "but she doesn't mean to be heartless."

"Were she and Meret also children of Tjeny?"

"Their father was a merchant in Sile, and there they grew

to womanhood." The aide glanced into the basket, found a piece of melon rind, and flung it at the squabbling birds. "Mistress Meret wed a traveling merchant, but he was slain within months by bandits, leaving her childless and alone. Mistress Taharet convinced their father that their lives would be wasted in so remote a town, so he sent them here to Waset, where they dwelt with an elderly aunt. Soon after, Pentu came to pay homage to our sovereign. He met Mistress Taharet and in a short time they wed."

Sile was a town on the eastern frontier of Kemet. Located on a major trade route, it had grown prosperous by providing weary men and donkeys with a place to stop and rest and to replenish supplies. As for Meret, he was surprised to learn she was a widow. When she had talked of a lost love, he must have jumped to the conclusion that she, like him, had never wed the individual to whom she had given her heart.

"Since Mistress Meret was a widow with no one to care for her, Pentu also brought her into his household." Netermose allowed himself a humorless smile. "The two sisters are very close. I'd not be opposed to taking Meret as my wife, but mistress Taharet guards her like a falcon and I stay well clear."

Bak gave him a sympathetic smile. "I've a feeling mistress Taharet wishes her to wed a man of means." He thought of the woman's previous interest in him, added, "Or one she believes has future prospects." He would not have been so blunt, but the knowledge was clear on the aide's face.

Later, as he hurried back along the processional way, he mulled over all Netermose had told him. Dig as deep as he would, twisting words and seeking hidden meanings, he could not sort one individual out from another as being more likely to have slain a man—or to become involved in the politics of Hatti. Was he wasting his time, looking at Pentu's household? Would he be wiser to focus his attention on the sacred precinct?

* * *

Bak was not surprised at finding the Overseer of Overseers of the storehouses of Amon at the treasury, where he had found him before. Where else would a man be who was as obsessed with the wealth of the deity as User was?

"You've come to tell me all is well, I take it." User, summoned by an elderly scribe, stood in the doorway, a hand on either jamb as if to prevent Bak from entering. "I knew you'd find no irregularities in our records, no missing objects in our storehouses."

"Many records were destroyed by the fire when Woserhet was slain, sir. I'm convinced they were burned deliberately so no one would know their contents."

"Bah! You're imagining a crime where none exists."

"Woserhet informed the chief priest, Hapuseneb himself, that he'd found some discrepancies in the records of the storehouses of the lord Amon."

Dismissing the charge with a wave of his hand, User walked to his armchair, plumped up the pillow, and dropped onto it. "To an auditor, a transposed symbol is a discrepancy."

"Hapuseneb held him in sufficiently high regard to allow him to look deeper into the matter, and I've found no reason why anyone would slay him outside of his task as an auditor." Bak paused, stressed his next words. "An auditor of the lord Amon's storehouses where he'd found discrepancies."

Frowning, User adjusted the pillow, fussed with the band of the kilt riding high on his ample stomach. "To steal objects from the lord Amon would be sacrilege, Lieutenant."

True, Bak thought, but more than one man had been so tempted by wealth while living that he had set aside all thoughts of death and the weighing of his heart on the scale of justice before the lord Osiris. "The priest Meryamon—also slain, if you recall—handled the same objects that were held in the storehouse where Woserhet died. That's too much of a coincidence to take lightly."

"Humph."

Bak leaned a shoulder against a brightly painted wooden column, jarring the roof. A sparrow let out a startled chirp and flitted into the sky. "As a man who regularly removed and replaced items kept in the storehouse, Meryamon could easily have held back a number of objects and altered the records."

"No priest would do such a thing."

"Priests suffer from the same fallibilities as other men, sir."

"Steal from a god? The greatest of the gods? No."

Bak could not begin to guess if the overseer's denials were heartfelt or if he was merely defending his territory. "The entire storage block, I understand, is filled with objects used in the sacred rituals."

"I believe I told you so the last time we spoke."

"I know that many items offered to the lord Amon are consumed, such as aromatic oils, perfumes, the linens used to clothe his image, and so on. On the other hand, ritual implements, such as libation vessels and censers, are reused time and time again. Are they kept forever or, when the storehouses become too crowded, are some of them disposed of?"

User stared past Bak, watching the scribe latch and seal the treasury door, securing the wondrous riches of the lord Amon. The old man looked toward the overseer, who dismissed him with a wave of his hand, and shuffled across the lane to enter a smaller building.

"You were saying?" User's eyes focused on Bak and he nodded. "Oh, yes. Each year when we take inventory, we separate out items no longer of use. We distribute a few to the lord Amon's small mansion in Mennufer and to his various shrines. The rest go to the royal house, where they're stored if deemed worth keeping, either for use there or to be given as gifts to some wretched foreign king or princeling. If unworthy, the objects are destroyed. The pottery items are broken up, while those made of metal are melted down and recast."

Bak cursed to himself. Another path to explore. "Does this happen often?"

"No, Lieutenant, it doesn't. To give away anything of value is to drain the life from the lord Amon."

Gold was the flesh of the god, but to think of the lesser metals and other materials as the blood of the deity was stretching the imagery too far. "Are linens or perishable items such as aromatic oils ever sent to the royal house?"

"We sometimes send small gifts to our sovereign, items for her personal use."

"And each transaction, from beginning to end, is documented."

"Of course."

Bak scowled. He had traveled full circle and was back where he started. Items intended as offerings and objects used in the rituals had been taken from the storehouses of Amon. By Meryamon? Could the young priest have stolen undetected the large quantities hinted at by the many valuable objects placed among the cargo on the deck of Antef's ship?

User stared at Bak for a long time, thinking thoughts he could not begin to guess. Slowly the overseer's look of stubborn resistance turned to one of alarm. "You don't think Woserhet found discrepancies in the treasury!"

Where that idea came from, Bak had no idea. "I suppose it's possible, but I doubt the thief dared aim so high. I think the thefts occurred in the storage block where he was slain."

"If there's the slightest chance . . ." User bit a lip, nodded to himself. "Yes, a criminal so vile might well begin to think himself untouchable and look toward the treasury as a source of greater wealth." His eyes darted toward Bak, he said, "Can I help you in any way, Lieutenant?"

Bak was surprised by the man's change of heart, but not so much so that he failed to leap at the offer. "I need to bring in another auditor, one unconnected to the sacred precinct. A senior man, as Woserhet was."

User stood up, the movement abrupt, decisive. "I suggest you speak with Sobekhotep. He's my counterpart in the royal house. Tell him we'd like to borrow the best man he has."

Chapter Thirteen

A distant trumpet blared, followed by the slow beat of a drum and the clamor of sistra and clappers. Swallowing a chunk of cold fish, Bak walked swiftly to the end of the narrow, deeply shadowed lane and looked out upon the processional way. To the south, the thoroughfare was blocked by large numbers of spectators looking toward the mansion of the lord Amon-Kamutef, one aspect of the lord Amon, called the bull of his mother. The building, located across the processional way from the first barque sanctuary, where he and his Medjays had awaited the lord Amon seven days earlier—a lifetime ago, it seemed—was enclosed by scaffolds and construction ramps. Another of the many public examples of Maatkare Hatshepsut's devotion to the gods.

He had had no time to think of the progression of the festival, to pause and watch the various processions to the gods that marked the week's advance to the finale, the lord Amon's return voyage from Ipet-resyt to Ipet-isut. The gentle early morning breeze, the temperate air, the smell of incense and the rhythmic beat of drums were tempting, seductive. He glanced eastward toward the lord Khepre, still too low in the sky to burn away the blue haze hanging over the swollen river and flooded fields. Yes, he could stay for a short while.

Tossing the last of the fish to a skinny cat and flinging away the leaves in which it had been wrapped, he hurried

along the processional way. Reaching the throng, he veered
onto the trampled grass verge and wove a path through the
spectators, about half the number who had watched the inau-
gural procession on the opening day of the festival. He was
surprised to see so large a crowd so early in the morning, but
the majority, he guessed, had come from afar and wished to
make the most of their journey, seeing as much as possible
during the eleven days of festivity.

He made his way to the barque sanctuary and climbed the
ramp to stand in the portico, already occupied by a half
dozen priests and four infantry officers. The raised platform
proved an excellent vantage point, for he could look over the
heads of the spectators and watch the procession come out
of the god's mansion.

The trumpet sounded again. The inconsequential chatter
of the onlookers dropped to a murmur. A buzz of expectation
filled the air. Men, women, and children eased forward,
crowding the soldiers standing along the procession's route.

Men beating drums and women with sistra and clappers
strode out of a passage through the center of the scaffolding,
their backs to the newly risen sun. A contingent of priests
came next, a dozen or more men draped in white robes,
holding colorful banners and the standards of god and sovereign. Other priests followed, each shaven bald and wrapped
in a long white robe that covered him from neck to ankles.
Half of these oddly garbed men purified the air with incense,
while the remainder sprinkled milk and water on the ground
over which the deity would be carried.

The lord Amon-Kamutef followed, his golden shrine held
high on the shoulders of priests. Voices, Bak's among them,
rose in adulation. The sides of the shrine were open, revealing a golden god, his penis erect, standing stiff and straight.
Beneath him, two rows of priests held the long poles supporting the shrine. Shrouded in white, with nothing showing
but their shaven heads and bare feet, they looked like a walking platform for the god. Perhaps in the distant past they had

been intended to represent a snake. Another aspect of the
lord Amon was Amon-Kematef, a primeval creator god who
could resurrect himself by taking the form of a snake shed-
ding its skin.

On either side of the deity walked Maatkare Hatshepsut
and Menkheperre Thutmose, each touching a leg of the image as if steadying it. They were too far away to see clearly,
but Bak thought they were bedecked much as they had been
in the opening procession of the festival. He could well
imagine how hot the royal regalia would become as the sun
rose higher and the day grew hotter.

Following along behind were musicians playing handheld
harps and oboes and drums. Dancers performed intricate
steps; singers chanted the words to a song so aged and ob-
scure that none but the god's priests could understand. Shaking off the temptation to stay, to watch the procession from
beginning to end, Bak left the sanctuary. He had to get help
for Hori.

With the beat of drums throbbing in his ears, he left the
crowd behind and hurried north along the processional way,
his feet crunching gravel no longer blindingly white, made
dingy by the passage of many feet. Passing a company of
soldiers, a family, and several men and women walking
alone and in pairs, he rapidly approached the half-finished
gate opening into the sacred precinct of Ipet-isut. The most
direct route to the royal house, which lay north of the mansion of the lord Amon, was to walk through the sacred
precinct.

"Sobekhotep told me of Woserhet's death and explained
your need." Thanuny, the auditor Bak had borrowed from
the royal house, had thinning gray hair and a worn face, but
looked like a man who could wrestle a bull and come out the
winner. "I knew him and liked him. I'll gladly help you
snare his slayer."

Bak slowed at the intersection and looked both ways before crossing. He had vowed, after the second attempt on his life, to take greater care, but had immediately forgotten. Now, remembering the pledge, he found himself being overly cautious. "When did you last speak with him?"

"A month or so ago. Upon his return to Waset after his latest trip downriver."

"He was inspecting the accounts of the gods' mansions and also those of the provincial governors, I've been told." Bak sidled around a laden donkey, the baskets hanging on either side filled with golden grain. "Can you guess the reason in light of what you now know?"

Thanuny dropped behind him to pass the sturdy creature. "If, as you believe, he wished to trace offerings made to the lord Amon from production to disposal, the provinces would be the place to start. He'd learn what items were sent to Waset, follow their path to the storehouses, and find out if they were there. If not, he'd try to discover where they went.

"The only objects he wouldn't be able to trace from the source are imports from foreign lands: gifts and tribute given to our sovereign by kings from afar who wish her continued good will, items wrested from far-off lands in times of conflict, and objects obtained for the royal house through trade. All are the property of our sovereign, who offers a portion to the gods, the lord Amon among them, as a demonstration of her generosity and devotion."

Another intersecting street, another pause to look for trouble, a silent curse at the need. "User, the Overseer of Overseers of the storehouses of the lord Amon, told me that a few objects no longer of use in the sacred precinct are given to the god's small mansion in Mennufer and to his shrines, while the rest revert to the royal house. I'm speaking specifically of the smaller, more valuable objects like those contained in the storage block in which Woserhet's body was found."

"We receive items from the lord Amon, yes. Often in surprisingly small quantities." The auditor flung Bak a cynical smile. "Between you and me, Lieutenant, User is a stingy caretaker. Those storehouses in the sacred precinct must be filled to bursting, yet he doles out the excess as if each object was more precious than life itself."

"If someone is systematically stealing from the god, perhaps User truly doesn't have the objects to give away. Maybe he's blind, not miserly."

They approached a major street. Bak felt the need to pause, to peek around the corner. He resisted the urge. If he was to snare the slayer before the festival ended, he had no time to slink around the city like a feral dog.

They turned the corner and strode toward the building that housed the central archives for the storehouses of Amon. "You'll find my scribe Hori to be young and, in many ways, an innocent, but he knows records and he knows how to search through them. He's done an exceptional job so far, but he's one man alone. To do by himself what must be done would take him half a lifetime."

"As I said before, Lieutenant, I'm happy to help. I'd not like to see Woserhet's slayer go free and unpunished."

The auditor seemed a competent and congenial man. Bak had an idea he and Hori would get along well.

"The task will be a pleasant break from counting spears and shields and pairs of sandals in the storehouses of the royal guards." Thanuny's smile vanished as quickly as it had formed. "But I must admit I'd not like to end my life as Woserhet did."

"You'll find two Medjays with Hori. They're well armed and well trained and exceedingly loyal. A man would have to slay them both to reach either of you."

"You were right, sir. Zuwapi always ships his trade goods to Ugarit on Captain Antef's ship."

Hori glanced uncertainly at the auditor, standing at Bak's side beneath the sycamore tree that shaded much of the

courtyard in the center of the archives building. Two Medjays stood with their backs against the trunk, chatting in
their own tongue, looking very much at ease. Sharp, alert
eyes belied the picture of relaxed disinterest.

"Say what you will," Bak said. "I've told Thanuny of my
suspicions. You must fill in later any details he needs to
know."

Hori gave the auditor a tentative smile, then went on with
his report. "Maruwa seldom traveled north on Antef's vessel, but twice he did in the past three years. Once—the first
time—when the ship was delayed in Waset to recaulk the
seams. The second time about a year later. He received a
message from his family, saying bandits had raided one of
his stables. He had to return without delay."

Bak's smile was grim. Two long voyages to Ugarit. Many
days of boredom, with nothing to do but look at the coastline
they were following. Plenty of time to notice something
amiss with the cargo. "What items does Antef usually list on
his manifest when he sails from Kemet to the port cities at
the eastern end of the Great Green Sea?"

Referring to the limestone shard on which he had made
notes, the young scribe said, "Much of his cargo—nineteen
items out of twenty—is almost always rough pottery, bulk
wine, coarse linen, sheep skins and cowhides, bronze items
such as fishhooks and harpoon points, sometimes papyrus
stalks. Three years ago, he hauled several shiploads of wheat
to Retenu when famine struck that foul land."

"Other than the grain, all the items are made for trade and
not of the best quality."

"Yes, sir."

"What of the more valuable items? I saw them on deck.
Not placed where they were easily seen, but not hidden either. An inspector wouldn't miss them. They'd have to be on
the manifest."

"That's the rest of the cargo, the one item in twenty." Hori
referred again to the shard. "Aromatic oils, perfumes, fine

linen, bronze vessels of one kind or another, faience amulets, multicolored bead jewelry."

The breeze rustled the leaves, which rained down from the tree. Bak brushed one from his hair. "Are all the goods, both ordinary and special, shown as belonging to the trader Zuwapi?"

"Usually. But sometimes, when Antef has the space, he accepts the goods of smaller traders or takes on board the household items of a family moving north."

"Do any of those people include valuable objects among their belongings?"

"Nothing but personal items, and those of modest worth."

Bak turned to the auditor. "As you may or may not know, Thanuny, a manifest lists the items on board the ship, the man who's shipping them, their port of departure, and the port where they're to be off-loaded. No mention is made of where they initially came from or where they're to go after they leave the ship."

Thanuny peered at the shard in Hori's hand. "Captain Antef's ship is still in Waset?"

"It is," Bak said, "and the harbor patrol is guarding it so nothing can be removed."

"You've not arrested him, confiscated his vessel and cargo, questioned him?"

"I wanted more information, and now I'm glad I waited. I've begun to think Zuwapi is in Waset. He has to be worried, but I don't want to frighten him, forcing him to flee the city."

Thanuny agreed the decision was wise, then said to Hori, "I suggest we begin our task, young man." Noting the reluctance on the youth's face, he smiled. "We need go back two years at most, I think. After we finish, we'll go calling."

Bak smiled at the scribe's mystified look. "More provincial governors come to Waset for the Beautiful Feast of Opet than at any other time of the year. If the lord Amon chooses to smile upon us, they'll remember most of the items they've sent as offerings to Ipet-isut, especially those of value. The

thefts might well occur during the voyage to Waset or at the
harbor when they reach this city."

Confident Hori and the auditor would find anything that
could be found, Bak left the archives to return to Pentu's
house. The governor would not be happy to see him, but so
be it. He was approaching the outer court in front of Ipet-
resyt, tempted by the milling crowd, the mingled aromas of
a dozen different types of food, the laughter and chatter of
merrymaking, when he saw Amonked walking out of the
lane leading to Pentu's house.

The Storekeeper of Amon spotted him, signaled that he
should remain where he was, and hurried toward him. "Bak!
I was on my way to search you out."

Bak saw no urgency on Amonked's face, just the set look
of a man none too happy. "You've news, sir?"

Shaking his head, Amonked drew him into the scattering
of people around the nearest booths, where they would not
easily be seen from afar. "Merely a word of warning."

Bak glanced toward the top of Pentu's dwelling, visible
over the nearer roofs. He could see no one standing among
the potted trees, but that did not mean no one was watching.
"Am I to be barred from the governor's house?"

"I squelched that idea, but he's very upset with you."

"Because I talked with mistress Taharet, I'll wager. He
wouldn't have liked that."

"He thinks the woman a goddess, unapproachable."
Amonked scowled, his disapproval plain. "I made it clear
that you were to do what you must and if that meant talking
to the women of his household, he had no recourse but to
agree."

Bak's frown matched Amonked's. "She told me mistress
Meret was ill and could see no one. I'd not be surprised to
learn that today she's come down with the same malady as
her sister."

*   *   *

"No one in my household fomented trouble in Hatti."
Pentu's chin jutted out, his face flamed. He looked like a
man ready to burst. "Instead of trying to lay blame where no
blame can be laid, I demand you prove I was withdrawn for
no good reason."

"Sir, our sovereign recalled you with great reluctance, and
only because her advisers heard all the evidence and agreed
the charge was true."

Pentu, seated in his armchair on the dais in his reception
hall, the fat black dog sleeping at his feet, glared at his tor-
mentor. "I'm a man of Kemet, Lieutenant. I'd do nothing,
absolutely nothing, that would bring about the least problem
for my sovereign or her people."

"No one accused you, sir, but certainly someone in your
household posed a threat to the king of Hatti."

"I refuse to believe it!" The dog leaped up, startled by the
harshness in its master's voice.

Pentu was so angry Bak feared for him. "Sir, if you let
me, if you place no obstructions in my path, I may within the
next few days lay hands on the man who brought about your
recall. Would you not be happier to know his name and put
an end to the matter for all time?"

Pentu shrank back in his chair, his expression sulky. "I
spoke with Amonked not an hour ago. He left no doubt as to
the vizier's wishes." The look he threw Bak was virulent.
"Do what you must, Lieutenant. Then leave my home and
never again cross my threshold."

Bak eyed the man seated before him. He could not imagine Pentu, whom Amonked was convinced held Kemet foremost in his heart, dabbling in the politics of any foreign land
unless ordered to do so by his sovereign. Yet if he had betrayed her trust, what might have impelled such behavior?
Bak could think of but one reason: if he thought he would be
aiding the cause of his homeland.

*   *   *

When he asked for Sitepehu, a servant directed Bak to a small chapel at the back of the garden behind Pentu's dwelling. What he guessed had once been a gatekeeper's shelter had been cleared out and freshly whitewashed, and a shrine to the lord Inheret had been built into the wall at the back of the room. Jambs and lintel around the niche were painted yellow, and a small bronze image of the deity, a bearded man carrying a spear and wearing four tall feathers on his head, stood in front of a red background. Lying on the gray granite offering table in front of the shrine were a cooked goose and a bouquet of flowers. Sitepehu was on his knees before the block of stone, blowing gently at a dollop of very pungent incense, urging it to burn. Thick smoke wafted toward the god, thanks to the hot breeze entering through the open door.

"Back again, Lieutenant?" Sitepehu asked, rising to his feet.

"I don't mean to disturb your ritual."

"You didn't. I found the incense no longer burning and had to relight it."

Bak glanced around the chapel, which was far from large but more than adequate for a provincial deity visiting the capital. "Pentu treats you and your god very well, I see."

"He's a good man, Lieutenant, one I fear you've thoroughly misjudged. He may've been in a position to cause trouble in Hatti, but let me assure you, he didn't. I should know. I helped him daily with official documents, and I accompanied him to all state affairs."

"I don't say he's the guilty man, but someone in this household is." Bak looked thoughtfully at the priest. "He took you with him when he went to the palace in Hattusa? Was that not unusual?"

Sitepehu scowled at the smoking incense, so thick it was more apt to smother the god than sweeten his nostrils with its heavy scent. "He didn't entirely trust the translators, and though I speak the language with difficulty, I can understand it well enough to spot a poor or erroneous rendering of the words."

"You're a man of many talents, Sitepehu. You know the arts of war, you're a gifted scribe, and you can understand a foreign tongue. Perhaps you were the man who wished to cause trouble in Hatti." Bak smiled, trying to make light the accusation.

Sitepehu flung him a startled look, then laughed. "I value my life far too much to poke around in the politics of Hatti."

The breeze faltered, letting the smoke travel where it would. A spiral of black twisted and turned like an unkind spirit seeking them out. Bak stepped backward, hoping it would not find him. "Have you ever met Captain Antef, master of a cargo ship that plies the waters between here and Ugarit?"

"I've never seen incense burn so poorly. I must've bought an inferior product." Sitepehu waved away a coil of smoke and motioned Bak to precede him out the door. "I'll let it smolder for a while. With luck, whatever is making it misbehave will burn away."

"Captain Antef?" Bak prompted.

"Hmmm." Sitepehu led him to the bench by the pool. "Wasn't that the name of one of the seamen who came to the dwelling we were using in Ugarit? Pahure brought several men to see Pentu when we were searching for a ship big enough to hold all our personal and household belongings."

"Can you describe him?"

The priest sat down, plucked a spear of grass from a nearby clump, and bit off the tip. "A man of medium height, going to fat. One whose appearance in the past must've drawn women like flies to honey."

Bak spotted the small green frog he had seen before, sunning itself on a lily pad. Its long tongue shot out, catching a tiny flying insect. "Sounds like him." He eyed the priest with interest. "Did you select his ship for your move?"

"Pahure made the decision. Not I. And he chose another vessel." The priest scratched his elbow. "As I recall, the cargo already on board was large, leaving the deck with insufficient space to accommodate our belongings."

"What did you think of Antef?"

"A scoundrel, like most men of the sea. A bit too effusive. Likable in his own way, I suppose."

"Did you ever see him anywhere else? In Hattusa, for example?"

Sitepehu chuckled. "The Hittite capital, Lieutenant, is many days' journey inland by donkey, not a trip a seaman would be likely to make."

Chapter Fourteen

Pahure was not at Pentu's dwelling but, thanks to yet another servant, Bak learned he had gone to a nearby market. As he walked along a narrow lane that would take him to the river's edge and the place where fishermen and farmers tied up their small vessels, he thought of the ease with which he had obtained the steward's location. Servants normally were not so helpful to an outsider, especially one prying into the lives of those to whom they owed their daily bread. Did that particular servant hold a grudge against Pahure, or was there a general discontent in the household? The latter seemed to be the case, since a different servant had as easily helped him find Sitepehu and another had directed him to Netermose the day before.

He walked out of the mouth of the lane and swerved aside, making way for several women laden with fresh fish and string bags and baskets filled with the bounty of the fields. He was always amazed, when so much of the land lay beneath the floodwaters, to see fresh fruit and vegetables in the markets, yet he should not have been. He had grown to manhood in this valley and knew the ways of the land and its tenants. Farmers whose fields lay higher than most, those who suffered dearly in times of a stingy flood, reaped an abundant harvest when the flood was normal, while their fellows waited for the lord Hapi to withdraw his gift of water.

He walked along the river's edge, eyeing the fish laid out

on the grass; crisp lettuce, radishes, and melons; ducks and geese slaughtered and dressed for use or caged to be sold alive; fresh bread; jars of honey, local wine, and beer; flowers. Along with the many mistresses of the house and female servants doing their daily shopping, a few well-appointed men were walking along as he was, looking at the produce, comparing one offering with another, haggling for the best price. Most had servants in tow. They were like Pahure, Bak assumed, men responsible for provisioning the households of provincial noblemen come to Waset for the festival.

He spotted Pahure standing before a fisherman whose years in the sun had burned his skin to the texture of leather. The old man squatted on the grass behind a display of silvery fish, most the size of a hand, but one a perch as long as Bak's arm. A younger man identical in size and shape and with similar features sat in the small, unpainted fishing boat drawn up against the riverbank, mending a net while his father sold the day's catch.

A plump, ruddy-faced female servant knelt before the display, examining the perch. The creature's scales glistened in the sunlight; it smelled as fresh as the water from which it had been pulled. Two youths stood beside Pahure, one carrying a string bag bulging with produce, the other holding an empty basket.

"That fish has been lying in the sun a long time," Pahure said, acknowledging Bak's presence with a nod. "I'll give you . . ." He made an offer, slightly below the customary half of the initial asking price.

The old man's expression darkened. "I pulled it from the water at dawn, sir."

The steward raised his offer slightly and the fisherman lowered his demand by a similar amount. And so the haggling went until buyer and seller were close.

"I can offer no more." Pahure rested a well-groomed hand on the slight bulge of his stomach. "That's all the perch is worth to me."

"I can't give away so fine a catch. I've a family to feed."

Pahure shrugged. "The morning's almost over. Soon this market will close. Do you wish to return home with a fish this size?"

The old man looked at Bak. "This fish is fresh, sir, I swear by the lord Hapi. Surely you can see this man's not offering fair value."

Bak, well aware that the offer was equitable, creased his brow as if giving the matter serious thought. "The perch is indeed a worthy creature, a thing of exceptional beauty, but by nightfall its value will drop to nothing and by tomorrow you'll have to bury it to escape the smell. Are you willing to lose everything in a vain effort to gain an insignificant amount?"

Pahure's mouth twitched slightly. "How many other fish are you taking home, old man? Will they go bad along with this one because of your greed?" Before the fisherman could answer, he signaled his servants that they should leave. The young woman rose to her feet and turned away, as did the youths.

The old man adopted a look of utter dejection. "All right, sir. All right. You can have the fish for the pittance you've offered. I can only hope my children . . ."

The steward gave him a sharp look, silencing what was no doubt a pathetic lie, and handed over several small items in exchange for the fish. The youth with the string bag took the creature in his arms and hurried off in the direction of Pentu's house. Pahure, with Bak at his side, walked slowly along the riverbank, keeping pace with the two remaining servants, who stopped at irregular intervals to inspect an item they might wish to purchase.

"Have you come to help us with our marketing, Lieutenant, or do you have a more sinister purpose?"

Bak smiled at what he chose to take as a jest. "Do you usually accompany the servants when they select food for your household?"

The steward laughed, perhaps at Bak's evasion. Or maybe his own: "This morning I wished to get some fresh air."

Bak thought back to his visit to Pentu's dwelling, the servants scurrying here and there, the governor in a foul humor. "I spoke with Pentu earlier. He's not a happy man."

"The Beautiful Feast of Opet is meant to be a time of renewal and rejoicing, Lieutenant. Instead, for those of us who dwell in that household . . ." Pahure shook his head, suggesting emotions he could not begin to describe. "You've been probing an unhealed wound. Your constant presence, your endless questions have upset everyone."

"Therefore your decision to come to the market."

"This isn't a frivolous errand, I assure you." Pahure nodded toward the plump female servant, who had stopped to look at two large mounds of onions and cucumbers. "Benbu is new to our household. I thought today a good day to teach her to pick out the best of the available foods and to negotiate to our household's advantage. To let her know my expectations. Upon our return to Tjeny, she must market alone, and I don't wish her to disappoint me."

Bak noted how seriously the steward took himself and a task most men in his position would hand off to someone else. Any man or woman who toiled in the kitchen could train this woman as well as he. "Your task must be easier on Pentu's country estate, where life seldom varies and the servants can do what they must with a minimum of guidance."

Kneeling before a man seated on the ground behind a half-dozen large bowls, Pahure summoned Benbu. He pulled aside the cloth covering one of the containers and examined the white goat cheese inside, impressing upon her what to look for if she wished to please him. The young woman did not understand. With forced patience, he showed her again what he expected and a third time to be sure she understood.

Standing up, he muttered through gritted teeth. "You'd

think her a woman of the city for all she knows, not one who grew to womanhood in a country village."

"She probably knows no more than the cheese her mother made and her mother's mother before her."

Pahure snorted his contempt. "One day, if the gods choose to smile upon me, I'll dwell here in Waset—or in the northern capital of Mennufer. I'll have a multitude of bright and willing servants and a steward of my own, one who'll train those servants for me."

Bak squelched the urge to raise an eyebrow. The steward had taken upon himself a task he had no need to do; now he was complaining. Or was today's schooling a means of looking after his own interests? "It can't be easy to live up to mistress Taharet's high standards."

Pahure said nothing, nor did his face betray his thoughts. A good steward never discussed his master and mistress, and Bak felt certain that this man performed his duties in an exemplary manner.

While the steward showed Benbu the finer points of selecting a plump duck, Bak wondered how the man intended to make so great a leap in status. Was he so filled with ambition that he believed he could reach whatever goal he set himself? Or had he merely been airing a distant dream?

The thought was still fresh when two dressed ducks, covered with leaves to keep away the flies, were safely stowed away in the basket. "As steward to an envoy in Hattusa, you must've been considered a man of influence."

"No more so than in Tjeny." Pahure chuckled. "There Pentu can be likened to a minor king and I to his vizier."

Bak acknowledged the jest with a smile. "Did you like the land of Hatti?"

"Not at all." The steward's face took on a look of distaste. "It's a foul land. Cold in the winter, hot in the summer, peopled with men and women thick of body and slow in thought."

An impression of the people at odds with those of Sitepehu and Netermose, Bak noted. "How'd you happen to contact Captain Antef when you were looking for a suitable ship on which to return to Kemet?"

Pahure queried Bak with a glance, as if wondering where that question had come from. "I saw his vessel in the port of Ugarit. It was large enough for our needs, so I asked him to speak with Pentu. A wasted effort, it turned out. He'd already made arrangements to take on another man's goods and hadn't sufficient room for all of us, the animals we wished to bring back, and our household belongings."

"He failed to tell you when first you spoke with him?"

The steward scowled. "I think he felt Pentu might be of use to him, so he saved the truth until after they'd met."

"Has Pentu been of help to him?"

Pahure flashed Bak a satisfied and none too kind smile. "Pentu forgot he existed the moment he left the reception hall."

Unable to think of further questions, Bak left Pahure to his task and hurried to Ipet-resyt for a much belated midday meal. The outer court teemed with pleasure seekers, men, women, and children indulging themselves with food and drink and the multitude of entertainments. Music and laughter filled the air. The heady aromas of flowers and perfumes competed with the equally tantalizing odors of cooked meats and fresh breads. The long arms of the lord Re reached into the court, filling it with intense light and enveloping everyone in heat. Sweat ran freely down men's and children's naked backs and legs, while women's shifts were stained and damp.

Each day the multitude of booths, the acrobats and singers and musicians, the various processions that ended at Ipet-resyt, drew larger crowds at an earlier hour. The merrymaking daily grew louder and more raucous, the nights of revelry longer. As if everyone wished to make the most of a festival shortly to end.

While standing with a dozen other people before one of the many crowded food stalls, waiting for the vendor to serve him, Bak evaluated what he had learned through the morning. Nothing, as far as he could see.

He accepted a round loaf of crusty bread, its center cavity filled with fresh braised lamb, and found a shady place on the surrounding wall where he could sit and eat. The thought nagged: Had he been wasting time much better spent in the sacred precinct? Or should he see Antef imprisoned and the cudgel applied? Would the captain know the name of the man stealing from the lord Amon? If not and if the seaman's arrest set Zuwapi to flight—providing, of course, that the merchant was in Waset, as Bak believed—he would have completely severed his link to the thief. No, better to wait. Better to see what Hori and Thanuny would discover. Better to go back again to Pentu's dwelling and question mistress Meret. The very thought sent his spirits plummeting.

"Did I not tell you my sister is ill?"

Bak formed a smile that was none too genial. "A servant told me she's quite well. I understand she spent the morning on this terrace, overseeing women who were dyeing thread to be used to embroider designs on clothing and bright pillows."

Taharet had the grace to blush; nonetheless, she flung her head high, added a chill to her voice. "If you wish to see her as a policeman, Lieutenant, she can't help you. If you've come to court her, you're wasting your time. You have nothing to offer a woman of refinement."

Untouched by her attempt to demean him, he shifted to a more relaxed stance and eyed her speculatively. The same servant who had betrayed her lie had directed him to the portico atop the extension to Pentu's dwelling. There he had found her by herself. Two stemmed drinking bowls partially filled with a deep red wine stood on a low table between the

stool on which she sat and another stool, telling him she had
not been alone for long.

Her open dislike was a total reversal from her warmth of a
few days earlier. Why had her attitude changed so completely? Why was she so reluctant to let him speak to mistress Meret? She must have known of his background from
the beginning: the son of a physician, neither a man of
means nor impoverished. She would, without doubt, have
asked before setting in motion any kind of matchmaking,
and Amonked would not have painted an untrue picture.

"I've heard that you and your sister, daughters of a merchant, grew to womanhood in Sile." He did not mean to infer
that she was no better than he—although such was the case,
he felt sure—but he could see by the fresh spots of red on
her cheeks that she thought he did.

"Just because Sile is on the frontier, you mustn't assume it
offers no culture or knowledge. My sister is far more accomplished than many women who dwell in this city."

"I'm not in the habit of underestimating anyone."

Taharet gave him a look that would have silenced a herald
trumpeting the call to battle. "She has all the skills required
of a mistress of the house and is accomplished in other areas
as well. She can direct a servant to cook to perfection, and
can make sure a house is cared for in a superlative fashion.
She can spin and weave and sew. She can play the lute and
the harp, and she's served as a chantress to the lady Hathor.
She speaks several tongues common to the lands north of
Kemet, and she often helped my father in his business by
translating the words of passing traders. Does that surprise
you, Lieutenant?"

"Not at all." He reached uninvited for a date in a bowl on
the table beside her, earning a frown for his impertinence.
She had done nothing to encourage him to remain, neither
inviting him to sit nor asking him to share the fruit. "I've
known children on the southern frontier who can understand

the tongues of every village along the Belly of Stones and every tribe in the surrounding desert. I would assume those who dwell in Sile, on a busy trade route joining Kemet with lands farther north, would be equally adept."

"What of you? Can you talk to people whose tongues are different from those of Kemet?"

Bak chose to ignore a question he would have had to answer in the negative. "Do you share in equal measure your sister's attributes, mistress Taharet?"

"Certainly." She lifted a drinking bowl from the table and sipped the last of the wine from it. "The sole advantage I have over her is that I have a greater determination than she does. She sometimes allows people to use her." She gave him a pointed look across the rim of the bowl, as if he, too, would make use of her sister.

Concealing his irritation, he asked, "Do you and Mistress Meret speak the tongue of Hatti?"

"Of course."

The words held an undercurrent of bitterness, and Bak suspected he knew why. "Did either of you serve as interpreters for your husband while he served in Hattusa?"

Her nostrils flared with contained anger. "At times, yes."

"Sitepehu said he sometimes accompanied Pentu to affairs of state. He admitted his knowledge of the tongue of Hatti was faulty, but he said he knew enough to ensure that the translators were honest. Did you help your husband in equally weighty matters?"

She let out a most unseemly snort. "You know nothing of the Hittites, lieutenant, or you wouldn't have asked so ridiculous a question. Both my sister and I speak the tongue far better than Sitepehu, but my husband refused to let either of us interpret for him when he most needed a good translation. He said our ability to speak the Hittite tongue when he himself had no such knowledge would make him look small in the eyes of the king."

"Was that not the truth?"

"Unfortunately, yes."

Bak reached for another date and nibbled the soft, sweet meat from the seed. He could see that the slight, though not intentional, still grated after all this time. Had she been so embittered by being left behind, dealing with trivial household matters while her husband spoke to a king of important state affairs, that she had chosen to stir the ingredient of discord into the politics of Hatti?

By speaking the language, she—and her sister—would have been able to associate with many Hittites. Not at such a lofty level as Pentu and Sitepehu, but definitely at occasions where noblemen were present. No one was more likely to cause dissension with the goal of overthrowing the king than members of the nobility. Would she, would anyone, be so petty as to foment trouble for so small a reason?

"Good afternoon, Lieutenant," a soft, musical voice said.

Bak's eyes leaped toward the doorway. Meret stood on the threshold, a jar of wine and a stemmed bowl in one hand, a flattish bowl of sweetcakes in the other. The smile she directed his way was tentative, as if she was not quite sure how he would receive her. A sharp indrawn breath drew his attention to Taharet, whose scowl of disapproval would have set a servant to sobbing.

Meret was not a servant.

Smiling, she walked out onto the terrace. Setting the wine and bowl of cakes on the table, she gestured toward a nearby stool. "Please join us, sir. We've plenty of food and drink, and the remainder of the day in which to enjoy it." Ignoring her sister's thin-lipped glare, she shifted the stool that was close to the table, making room for another. "I understand you've been asking questions about Pentu's recall from Hattusa."

"I'm trying to lay the matter to rest, yes." He pulled close the proffered stool and sat down.

She broke the plug from the wine jar, filled his glass and Taharet's, and added more to the third one. "I can assure you that he's completely innocent of any charge that might've been made against him. He has far too much integrity to speak to a king with a smile on his face one day and try to overthrow him that night."

She spoke softly, her tone gentle yet firm. Bak could not help but compare her with her sharp-tongued sister. "Pentu was never seriously suspected of duplicity. A member of his household was thought to be the guilty party."

"The servants are all talking . . ."

"Meret!" Taharet spoke sharply, her anger held on a tight rein. "What our servants speak of is of no concern to the lieutenant. They chatter like sparrows, gossiping about anything and everything, saying nothing of consequence."

Meret squeezed her sister's hand, smiled at Bak. "They're saying you're seeking the slayer of three men, two who died in the sacred precinct. Search as I might within my heart, I can see no link between our household and the deaths of two servants of the lord Amon."

"The third man who was slain was a merchant named Maruwa, a Hittite, the one who initially reported the traitor in your household. Did you ever meet him?"

"He was a merchant?" Meret looked at her sister. "We now and again accompanied our servants to the market in Hattusa, but I don't recall . . ." Her eyes opened wide. She turned to Bak and smiled. "Oh, you speak of the merchants who came to our residence, hoping to obtain travel passes to Kemet. Sitepehu dealt with those people. Taharet and I might've seen them in passing, but would have no reason to remember any specific individual."

"Maruwa spoke more often to Netermose, so I understand."

"He, too, dealt frequently with men of Hatti. Pentu could in no way receive the large numbers of men who sought his favor or that of our sovereign. Netermose was most effective in sifting out those unworthy of an audience."

Bak pressed no further. In a busy residence such as that of an envoy, men came and went in large numbers. One would have to stand out above all others to attract notice.

He took a sip of the tart red wine, smiled his appreciation. Meret's answers and demeanor were calm and sensible. Unlike Taharet, so intent on keeping her sister away from him that she made no pretense at the most basic of courtesies. "Your sister was telling me that the two of you came from Sile. Don't you miss the excitement of dwelling in a border city, one situated on a major trade route?" The question was prompted more by his own sorrow over leaving Buhen than by his quest to find a slayer.

"Waset has far more to offer than that wretched town," Taharet snapped.

"You've a fine dwelling here in the capital," Bak said, "but you spend much of the year on a country estate near Tjeny. A far quieter place than Sile, I'd think."

Meret smiled at her sister, silencing what looked to be an angry retort. "I miss Sile, yes. I miss the many opportunities to speak with people from other lands, to see the beautiful objects they bring to trade in the land of Kemet, to get to know . . ."

"Mistress Meret." Pahure's voice.

Both sisters started. Their heads snapped around, their eyes leaped toward the doorway.

"Pahure!" Meret flung an angry look his way. "Must you skulk around like a common thief?"

Pahure crossed the threshold and walked along the row of colorful blooming potted plants lining the terrace. His mouth was tight with annoyance. "You must come immediately, mistress. Two of the servants have quarreled. One has been hurt. Your presence is required in the kitchen." He paused, added emphatically, "Right away, mistress."

An odd look passed over her face, and with visible reluctance she rose to her feet. "Very well." Forming a smile for

Bak's benefit, adding warmth to the chill in her voice, she said, "I'm delighted you came, Lieutenant. I hope you'll visit us here again before we return to Tjeny."

"I must go, too." Taharet stood up, smiled at Bak with an insincerity born of dislike. "I assume you can find your way out. You've been here often enough."

Leaving the dwelling, Bak hurried along the processional way toward the sacred precinct of Ipet-isut, hoping to catch Hori and Thanuny before they left the storehouse archives. Meret's invitation was uppermost in his thoughts. He liked her, appreciated her candor, her quiet and straightforward manner, a total absence of the anger boiling within her sister. Given the chance, could Meret fill the void in his heart left by the woman he had thought never to forget?

Thanks to the lord Amon, Bak found the scribe and auditor where he had hoped they would be. A young apprentice ushered him into the main room of the storehouse archives, vacated so late in the day by the men who normally toiled there. The room was long and narrow, its ceiling supported by tall columns, with high windows lighting a space large enough to accommodate at least twenty seated scribes.

The two Medjays welcomed Bak with the broad smiles of men expecting an early release from an onerous task. He guessed they wanted very much to join the hordes of merry-makers filling the city.

"You were right, sir." Hori scrambled to his feet and stretched his weary muscles. "With two of us searching the records, one far wiser than the other in the ways of vile criminals . . ." He grinned at Thanuny, seated cross-legged on the linen pallet normally occupied by the chief scribe. ". . . it didn't take long to find a discrepancy."

Thanuny swished a writing brush around in a small bowl of water, cleaning red ink from it, and slipped it into the slot in his scribal pallet. A reflected shaft of late evening sunlight brightened the water to the color of blood. "It took over a half hour, Lieutenant, but once we found that initial discrepancy, it told us what to look for. After that, the rest leaped out like gazelles startled by a pack of hunting dogs."

"They weren't that obvious," Hori said. "If they had been, Woserhet and Tati would've found them."

"I'd bet my wife's best cooking bowl that Woserhet hadn't yet inspected the records we looked through today." Thanuny eyed the twenty or more baskets scattered around him, each containing a half-dozen reddish storage jars filled with scrolls. "He was too competent and thorough a man to have missed all we found. And surely he'd have told his scribe if he'd verified his suspicions."

Taking in the large number of jars, Bak's expression turned grim. "Exactly how serious is this crime which has been perpetrated against the lord Amon?"

"Very serious indeed." The auditor's expression was grave. "I know theft is commonplace in the markets and the fields, on shipboard and on caravans. Even within the royal house, men steal. Who can resist taking some small object should the opportunity arise? But here in the sacred precinct? Stealing from the lord Amon himself? On such a large scale?" Thanuny shook his head as if unable to believe such greed, such audacity.

Bak dropped onto the woven reed mat beside the auditor. "Tell me what you found."

Thanuny withdrew a scroll protruding from the mouth of one of the storage jars. "We've marked the documents that contain erroneous entries," he said, pointing to a conspicuous red dot near the edge. "They'll have to be corrected, or a note made on each of which items have vanished. Have been stolen," he added sadly.

As he untied the knot in the cord binding the scroll, Hori sat down on the floor beside him. The two Medjays exchanged a dejected look and hunkered against the wall to wait.

"We began by picking out a few specific examples of valuable items commonly used during the sacred rituals," Thanuny said. "Aromatic oils, incense, lustration vessels and censers, amulets, and the like. We tracked them on the appropriate documents from the time they were received in Waset and stored in the sacred precinct until they were either consumed or were sent to another of the god's holdings or to the storehouses of our sovereign."

"You'll never believe what first drew our attention." Hori's eyes danced with excitement. "An amulet. A simple stone scarab. Dark green, mounted on gold."

Bak whistled. "Not at all simple, I'd think."

Thanuny smiled at his young colleague. "Fortunately for us, it was offered to the lord Amon far enough in the past that all the records had been turned into the archives. It should have been recorded on a continuous string of documents from arrival to disposal."

"But it wasn't," Hori broke in. "According to the records, it was delivered by ship from Mennufer, dropped off at the harbor here in Waset, and sent on its way to the storehouse where Woserhet was slain. However, the record of the storehouse contents failed to mention it. It either vanished somewhere between the harbor and the sacred precinct, or was never recorded when it arrived at the storehouse, or was stolen from there and the record altered."

"Altogether, thirty amulets were listed as having been brought from Mennufer at the same time." Thanuny pulled a brush from his writing pallet and, using the top end, reached around to scratch his back. "We found that four others of somewhat lesser value had also vanished—on papyrus at any rate. We sent that young apprentice who brought you to us out to the storehouse to look for the missing items. He didn't find them, of course."

"What other types of items have vanished?" Bak asked.

"Anything of value," Hori said.

"I fear our young friend isn't exaggerating," Thanuny said. "Several methods were used to conceal the thefts, depending upon the items taken and how they were recorded. The shorter records were copied, we believe, omitting whatever was taken. As for the longer lists too time-consuming to copy, we found signs of erasure, with other objects inserted in the spaces."

"I must see some specific cases. Amonked will wish to know."

A long-suffering sigh burst forth from one of the Medjays. Bak ignored the hint. Their task as guards would be over by sunset, when the inside of the building grew too dark to read. The men would have plenty of time to play after escorting Thanuny home. Hori, he assumed, would remain with them.

Bak, having decided to spend the night across the river with his father, bade good-bye to the two scribes and their Medjay guards and left the storehouse archives with his head reeling. So many numbers, so much of value stolen over the past two years. And for how many years before?

Passing through the gate that took him outside the sacred precinct, he looked to right and left to be sure no one lay in wait, thinking to attack him. The lord Re had passed over the western horizon, leaving behind a reddish glow in the sky and deep shadows in the narrow lane, making it hard to see. He heard sounds of revelry to the west, where merrymakers would be seeking out food, drink, and entertainment along the broader, lighter streets closer to the river, but the lane was empty, the block of interconnected houses quiet. He turned to the right and hurried along the base of the wall enclosing the sacred precinct, choosing the shortest path to the busier streets and the ferry that would carry him to western Waset.

Again he turned his thoughts to the stolen items. Someone was rapidly becoming a man of vast wealth, but who? Not a man or woman among his suspects displayed an affluence beyond his or her station. For that matter, Meryamon, the man most likely to have stolen the objects, had given no indication of having had any wealth at all. With his daily bread supplied by the lord Amon, he had most assuredly not lived a life of want, but neither had he given any sign of prosperity. True, Pahure had set high goals for himself, but he gave no more sign of being a man of wealth than did Netermose or Sitepehu.

As he neared the corner of the housing block, two men suddenly stepped into the lane ahead of him. In the dim light, he could see that one carried a mace, the other a dagger. He muttered a curse, swung around to run back the way he had come. Three men, all brandishing weapons, raced out of the gate that pierced the wall of the sacred precinct. He snapped out another oath. These had to be the same men who had tried to slay him before. If he had had the time, he would have cursed himself roundly. He could not believe he had walked into a trap almost identical to the one he had earlier evaded.

Very much aware that his options were limited, he pivoted and raced toward the two men at the end of the housing block. The warren of lanes offered his sole chance of escape. If he could overcome the pair, he could slip into the lane they had come out of and vanish in the gathering darkness.

He closed on the two men, aiming toward the one with the mace. At the last moment, he veered toward the other man, grabbed the hand wielding the scimitar, and shoved it hard against the wall of the sacred precinct. The man yelped and dropped the weapon. Bak kicked him high between the legs, immobilizing him, and turned to face the man with the mace. The running footsteps of the trio behind drew closer. He grappled for the mace, with he and his opponent doing an odd little dance while they struggled for possession.

A man leaped on his back, knocking him to the ground. In an instant, they were all upon him, holding him face-down with the weight of numbers.

"We've got him this time," the man with the gravelly voice said with a satisfied laugh.

Bak managed to raise his head, to take a look at the men who had caught him. One bent double, clutching his manhood; three other hard-faced men held him against the dirt. Standing over him, mace raised to strike, he glimpsed the swarthy man he thought was Zuwapi.

The man's arm came down and he saw no more.

Chapter Fifteen

The world was dark, hurtful. A throbbing place where low voices came and went. A place where the air smelled of dirt and sweat and stale beer. Where the surface on which he lay was sometimes hard and dusty, sometimes not there at all. Or was it he who was not there?

He lay in the black space, sensing the world around him come and go, offering snatches of itself. A man gulping from a jar, a belch, the stench of foul breath. Something small and whiskered—a mouse, he imagined—sniffing his cheek. The crisp sound of a man chewing a radish with his mouth open. A harsh "Shhh." The mouse again, or something bigger, exploring his leg. A man cursing and a short scuffle.

He opened his eyes, but could see nothing. The throbbing in his head was intense and he felt disoriented. He tried to move, but the pain sharpened, forcing him to be still. He lay motionless, barely daring to breathe, praying the agony would lessen.

"How much longer?" a man whispered.

"An hour, maybe more," a gravelly voice murmured. "After the revelers have gone to their sleeping pallets and the streets and lanes are empty."

A third man groaned. "I'd hoped to have some fun to-

night. There's a game of knucklebones in a house of pleasure north of the royal house, the one the lame Hurrian runs.
It started the day the festival began." He kept his voice low,
as if he feared someone nearby would hear. "I'd like to sit in
just once. They say it's the best game in Waset."

The first man laughed softly. "The way your luck's been
going lately, you'd do better to find yourself a woman, one
with udders as big as a cow and . . ."

The description went on, a buzz of words running together, sometimes audible, sometimes fading away.

Feeling ill, he clamped his eyes shut, swallowed, and let
his head roll to the right. The place above his ear, the spot
where he had been hit, struck the hard-packed earthen floor.
Pain exploded and he felt no more.

He knew he was going to die, prayed it would happen
sooner rather than later. His wrists were tied together and so
were his ankles. His body, limp and helpless, was slung
from a stout pole like the carcass of a dead deer. His head
hung close to the ground, swinging free, a mass of agony too
intense to endure.

Each time the pole jiggled, each time one or the other of
the two men carrying him made an abrupt movement, the
torture worsened. The searing pain inside his head took his
breath away, clouded his vision. He prayed for relief, for the
darkness of oblivion, yet he never lost sight of the man near
his head, the sturdy legs pumping, large callused bare feet.

"Shhh. We're close," gravel voice said.

The two men lowered the pole, letting him drop roughly
to the ground. His head seemed to split apart, and blessed
darkness set in.

He came back to life slowly, in bits and pieces. Once he
heard a man's shout, a reassurance that all was well. Another
time he glimpsed two men carrying him, walking rapidly
along a narrow lane, his body swinging from the pole be-

tween them. He saw a dog nipping at the heels of a stranger, who threw a rock to frighten it away. He saw the swarthy man standing on the deck of a ship, ordering its mooring ropes released. He felt himself lying on the ground, the pole on top of him, hearing the loud laughter of a dozen or more revelers passing by. He saw his father, standing with Hori and Commandant Thuty on a ship bound for Mennufer. He saw a woman's back, knew she was the one he had vowed to love forever, but when she turned around to smile, her face was that of mistress Meret.

The visions ended and for a while he must have slept. Or perhaps he fell into a deeper unconsciousness.

When Bak came to, or awakened—he knew not which—he felt better. He lay motionless in the dark, letting his thoughts pull themselves together. His head throbbed, but no longer felt as if it would burst. His side ached as if he had been kicked, but a cautious intake of breath did not bring about the sharp pain of a broken rib. He was groggy and confused. His tongue felt thick and was so dry he could not moisten his lips.

He sensed he was alone. Knew it for a fact when he heard the tiny noises vermin make when they seek out sustenance undisturbed. He was lying on a sloping wooden bed of some kind. He tried to move his arms from behind his back, but was unable to do so. Burning wrists awakened a hazy memory of being bound hand and foot.

He wondered where his captors had left him. The darkness was total. The world around him felt unstable, as if it might be moving, swaying. Or were his thoughts playing tricks on him? He could smell stagnant water and rotting wood, the leavings of small creatures. He tasted grit between his teeth and something else. Blood. His own, he felt sure. He heard the soft whisper of . . . Of what? Running water. He was very close to the river. Or on a ship.

Yes, a ship. His feet were in a shallow pool, his body on a

slightly curving incline. Not a breath of air stirred around him. As muddled as his thoughts were, he knew exactly what those facts signified. He had been dropped down the hatch of a ship and lay in the hull beneath the deck in the space normally filled with ballast. The water bathing his feet was sloshing back and forth, probably along the center-board, while he must be reclining between two ribs. Thanks to the lord Amon, he had fallen with his head well out of the water.

He could hear no voices, no sound of rowing, no flapping sails, nothing but the tired, sporadic groan of the wooden hull. The vessel had to be moored against the riverbank. Most likely in Waset or not far from the city. Had his captors meant to leave him alive, thinking he would be found and rescued? Or were they planning to come back and slay him? Was there something about his situation that he had not yet begun to understand?

Water inside a hull was normal, common to all ships. Only time would tell how much was seeping inside. The musty smell of rotting wood was strong, indicating that the vessel was old, its condition questionable. As far as he could tell, the rats had left him alone, but that did not mean they were not skulking somewhere in the dark, waiting for him to die. Or waiting to abandon ship, should it begin to sink.

He sat up abruptly, awakening the demon in his head. He had to get off the vessel. Fast.

The pain, the dizziness, a hint of nausea forced him to wait, to sit quietly until the throbbing eased and the world around him stopped spinning. When at last he could think clearly, he realized he had a decision to make. Should he try to find a hatch and attempt to climb out, bound as he was? Or should he first rid himself of the ropes?

To release his hands would be time-consuming, but with luck and the help of the gods he could untie his ankles, which would allow him greater freedom of movement. He lay down on his side, drew his legs back as far as possible, and tried to reach the rope around his ankles. He managed to touch the wet cord with his fingertips, but could get no closer. Cursing his body for being so inflexible, he sat up and scooted down the incline into the puddle. Better to look for a hatch than waste further time.

The water tempted him, but it smelled of rot and fish and the lord Amon only knew what else. Promising himself a drink from the river the instant he got out of this wretched ship, he cautiously rose to his feet. He could not believe how frail he felt, how wobbly his knees were.

The hull was so shallow, he could not stand erect. The vessel was not large. Shoulders hunched, head down, he tried to raise his hands high enough behind him to search for the way out. He could reach the beams that supported the deck, but was not limber enough to raise them all the way to the underside of the deck planks. Unable to think of a better solution, he decided to run his battered head along the boards. With luck, he would find the hatch through which he had been thrown almost directly above him.

He shuffled forward, moving less than a hand's breadth with each step. As expected, he promptly found the hatch. It was a rudimentary affair, a square hole cut into the deck with a flat wooden cover on top. Hunching his shoulders beneath it, he pushed upward as hard as he could. Whether he was not quite tall enough to gather the force necessary to raise it or whether he was too weak or whether it had been fastened down, he had no idea.

Cursing his failure, more determined than ever to escape his vile prison, he shuffled along the centerboard, water sloshing around his ankles, in search of another hatch. Moving at so slow a pace had an advantage: he did not have to worry that he might stumble over a ballast stone or trip over a loose board or step on some disgusting creature alive or dead. Nor did he have to worry about bumping his injured head too hard.

Within a half-dozen paces—or what would have been

paces if he had been able to walk normally—the centerboard began to rise and the space between it and the deck gradually narrowed, forcing him to squat. He could not be sure, but he thought he was in the stern. Turning around, he shuffled back the way he had come. Was the water getting deeper? he wondered. Had he been on his feet long enough to tell?

He passed the underpinnings of the mast and, not long after, found a second hatch. He stood directly beneath the cover and shoved upward with his shoulders. He managed to push it up a distance of two fingers' width, allowing the fresh, cool night air to seep inside, but he could raise it no farther. He had to get rid of the ropes around his wrists and ankles. Freed from his bounds, he should be able to raise one or the other of the hatches high enough to climb through. He refused to think that both might be impossible to open.

On the incline near the hatch, he sat down, placed his back to a rib and, feeling a moderate amount of roughness on the wood, began to rub the rope up and down. Time dragged. His hands, already swelling, grew thick and clumsy. His wrists bled where the rope chafed them. He seldom stopped, but when he did he heard the skittering of rats, felt them coming closer, drawn by the smell of blood. Anger filled his heart, as much at himself for walking into the trap as at the men who had snared him.

After he knew not how long, something struck the boat. It shuddered and water splashed onto his kilt. He glanced up, saw pinpoints of light showing through the hull across from him. Night had turned to day.

Realizing how stiff he was, he stretched his arms and legs, flexed his tired muscles. His feet splashed into water noticeably higher than before. He stopped breathing, focused on the world around him. The vessel was rocking more, as if the river outside had grown rougher. He looked again at the spots of light showing through the hull. They were well above the waterline, but for how long? How long ago had the boat last been caulked. How many similar holes, lower in the hull, were allowing water inside.

He had to get out.

He twisted his hands around as best he could and reached with numb fingers toward the rope, praying he would feel some sign of fraying. He felt a few loose fibers, nothing more. With sagging spirits he ran his fingers along the wooden rib. He should have sought out a board far rougher, with more jagged edges that would tear the fibers apart.

Scooting on his rear toward the bow, he ran his swollen hands up one rib and down another, finding most of them worn from years of use and the wood in a few crumbling from age and rot. He wondered how the boat stayed afloat.

Once again something struck the vessel, this time with a crash so strong it jarred his teeth. It slewed around. What he thought was the bow took the place of the stern. How could that be? Again the vessel was struck, a solid blow that tipped it half onto its side, covering him with roiling, filthy water. His heart leaped into his throat and he prayed frantically to the lord Amon.

Moments seemed like hours. Fear held him captive, paralyzing all thought and action. He clung to the nearest wooden rib as if it alone could save his life. Then the vessel slowly righted itself and even more sluggishly turned the rest of the way around. When his fear abated, when he no longer lay witless, he realized the boat was not moored and secure against the riverbank. It was running free on the floodwaters, with no one on board to guide it.

Memory rushed in, words he had heard and forgotten, words he could suddenly recall as if he could hear them yet:

"This should do it," gravel voice said.

"I say we slay him here and now." A second voice.

"He's supposed to vanish somewhere far away, and we don't have time to take him."

A third man: "He got out of that burning storehouse. Who's to say he won't get out of this?"

"We didn't tie him then."

"Weren't we supposed to make his death look like an accident?" the second man asked.

Gravel voice snorted. "Who cares how he dies? When his body's found, if it ever is, he'll be at least a day's walk north of Waset. Maybe farther. There'll be nothing on him to identify him, no way of guessing who he is. He'll be just another man set upon by robbers, tied up and thrown into this old hulk to die."

Remembering that promise of death, Bak was consumed with anger. He would get himself out of this foul vessel, and he would hunt down the men who had put him here. He would see the lesser men sent to the desert mines and the one who had ordered his death executed in the vilest manner possible.

Bak found a wooden rib that was not simply rough and splintery, but had a prominent knot with a sharp edge. It was high up in the bow, well above the growing pool of water. Here, the boat was narrow and the deck close to the hull, which gave him no room to stretch out or make himself comfortable. He had to smile at the thought. Comfort was far from being his greatest priority.

He lay curled up in the confined space, located the sharp knot behind him, and began to saw away at the rope. His hands were so swollen, his fingers so numb, that he could barely feel them. He hoped he would be able to untie the rope around his ankles. He chided himself for thinking so far ahead. First get the hands free and go on from there.

The prow of the boat hit something solid. Unlike before, the jolt was easy, gentle almost, and he heard a grating noise somewhere beneath him. The familiar sound of wood being dragged across sand, as if he were helping his father draw

his skiff onto a sandy shore. The vessel in which he was
trapped must have gone aground. Praying such was the case,
he doggedly went on with his task.

After a while, how long he had no idea, he stopped to see
if the rope was beginning to fray. The effort failed. He could
not bend his wrists, could barely feel his hands, and his
swollen fingers were stiff and helpless. More disappointed
than he thought possible, he located the sharp edge of the
knot and began again to rub the rope over it.

Sweat poured from him as the day grew hotter. The water
sloshing around in the hull made the air damp and sticky.
The moist heat, the intense effort, the confined space sapped
his energy. His head ached, his muscles cramped from ex-
haustion, and thirst besieged him. His stomach was empty,
but the sour taste in his mouth drove away all thoughts of
food.

Several times he felt the boat swing as if the bow was on a
pivot. Each time he started, his heart leaping upward, and he
offered a prayer to the lord Amon that the craft would not
lose its precarious hold on the land.

He had no idea how long he had been trapped or how far
the lord Re had traveled across the sky. Time was impossible
to measure inside the dark hull, and his life had become an
endless sequence of small movements. How deep was the
water inside the boat? he wondered. How deep would it be if
the bow broke loose from the land that held it and the vessel
sank lower?

He became obsessed with the knot on the wooden rib.
When he could no longer feel it, how could he be sure he
was rubbing the rope across it? How could he . . . ? He
squashed all thought, gritted his teeth, and kept on dragging
his weary arms up and down, up and down.

Bak licked his dry and cracked lips, but no moisture
reached them. What could possibly happen if he took a tiny
sip of water? He squelched the moment of weakness, re-

minded himself of the vermin, the sailors who urinated wherever they happened to be, the insects, reptiles, and rodents that had died among the ballast stones.

No. He would wait. The rope had to break apart soon. It had to.

The boat swung. The bow grated on sand and Bak felt its sudden buoyancy, the freedom he wished for himself. The vessel had pulled away from the shore. Then it bumped the land, wood grated over sand, and it came to rest.

Bak toiled on, rubbing the rope over the knot, or what he hoped was the knot. How much longer would he have the strength to continue? How long before the boat sank? So much water had seeped in that each time he straightened his legs, it touched his feet. From the angle of the centerboard, from the number of rats he heard scampering about in the bow, trying to find a way out, he suspected the stern was by now filled with water.

The rope snapped. Bak lay quite still, unable to believe. Afraid he might be imagining that it had parted. He pulled an arm forward, shook off the frayed rope, and touched his face. The fingers were numb, but he felt pressure on his cheek.

He was free! Or almost free.

He felt like sobbing.

Wasting no time, he backed out of the cramped space, slipped into the water, and shuffled down the centerboard. He had lost all sense of distance, but the hatch could not be far. Raising an arm, hoping he had enough feeling left to locate the cover, he ran his hand along the underside of the deck and crept forward. The water level rose rapidly from knees to thighs to waist.

Relieved of his weight, the bow broke free of the shore. The current carried the boat a short distance, it bumped against land and was caught once again.

He waded on, praying with all his heart that he would reach the hatch before water covered his head, praying he

could get the cover off. Again the bow lifted, grated across
sand, came to an abrupt halt. He was thrown forward and at
the same time a wave that formed inside the vessel struck
him hard. He lost his balance. Frantic to save himself, he
pushed his numb hands hard against the boards above him.
He felt them raise up. Not much, but enough to know he had
found the hatch.

When the frantic sloshing of water subsided, he shoved
the cover upward. As before, he could raise it no more than
the width of two fingers. Something was holding it in place.
Summoning every bit of strength that remained in his body,
he pushed as hard as he could. Something began to slide
across the cover. It flew open and whatever had been holding
it down fell with a thud onto the deck.

With a vast sense of relief, he hauled himself through the
hatch. Rats erupted with him, some so brazen as to use him
as a ladder. He did not care. He was too happy to be out of
that obscene prison.

Hoisting himself to his feet, he glanced at the lord Re,
dropping toward a western horizon totally different than the
familiar skyline above western Waset. About two hours of
daylight remained. He shuffled to the bow, thinking to see an
island or a rise of land on which the boat had gone aground.
He saw nothing but a solid sheet of water, its surface ruffled
by a stiff wind. The land holding the vessel was submerged
beneath the floodwaters.

What through most of the year was a broad, placid river
had grown into a gigantic lake. Its silvery waters appeared to
cover the land as far as he could see from the desert on the
eastern side of the valley to the foot of the cliffs to the west.
He knew better. The flood was ebbing, the water no longer at
its greatest depth. Fields on higher patches of land were
draining, almost ready for the farmers to turn the soil over in
preparation for planting.

Still, he would have to swim and wade across long

stretches of water. He could swim with bound ankles, although the effort would be considerable. But creeping across the flooded landscape in increments of less than a palm's width was another story. One he could not imagine.

His hands were too numb to untie a knot, so he scanned the deck, searching for a sharp object to cut through the rope binding his ankles. The stern half of the vessel was under water and swells were threatening to overturn the small shabby deckhouse. Soon the vessel would be submerged. Ropes darkened by time snaked across the bow, and parts of wooden fittings were strewn about. Somewhere in all that trash he should be able to find what he sought.

He shuffled to the deckhouse, a flimsy construction of poles and worn reed mats. Inside, a thin, filthy sleeping pallet lay spread out on the floor. A brazier had been tipped over and its spilled charcoal was melting into the water washing beneath the walls. Several empty beer jars rolled back and forth in the narrow space between wall and pallet. A man of no means had evidently used the boat as a sleeping place. Bak wondered what had happened to him. Had he been chased away by gravel voice and his helpers or had he been thrown overboard?

One of the jars bumped against something hard at the edge of the pallet. Bak knelt, pulled the soaked fabric farther from the wall, spotted a harpoon. With his hands nearly useless, he did not know how he could hold it, but somehow he would.

Chapter Sixteen

"The boat sank?" Hori asked.

"It must've." Bak wrinkled his nose at the sour-smelling brownish poultice the scribe had spread on a strip of linen and was wrapping around his lacerated wrist. The knot on his head was tender to the touch and throbbed each time he bent over, his wrists felt as if they were on fire, and his bruised ribs ached; nonetheless, he felt lucky to have escaped so lightly. "Can you imagine how the farmer will feel when the water recedes and he finds a boat that large lying in his field?"

He sat with Hori and Sergeants Psuro and Pashenuro beside the hearth in the courtyard of his men's quarters, a place he had doubted he would ever see again. His entire company of Medjays knelt and stood around them, hanging on every word. The image of the stranded boat drew their laughter, momentarily wiping away the gravity of his imprisonment.

Even Psuro, who took Bak's capture very seriously indeed, had to smile. "After you left the vessel, you must've been in the water for hours."

"I set foot on dry ground at dusk and there I collapsed, too weary to stand. Dogs came running and their barking summoned the villagers. They cleaned my wounds and fed me, and the headman led me to a sleeping pallet. I awakened at sunrise, and thanks to the fisherman who brought me to Waset, here I am."

A nearly empty bowl of cold duck stew smelling strongly of onions was nestled among the dormant coals. Hori's dog was crouched before a hole in the wall into which he had chased a mouse. Each time the tiny whiskered face peeked out, he growled softly in his throat. The quiet courtyard, the food, the dog, and especially the concern on his men's faces warmed Bak's heart.

Psuro's expression turned remorseful. "I'll never live down the shame, sir. We didn't even miss you."

Bak laid a reassuring hand on his shoulder. "I told Hori I meant to spend the night with my father, and he told you. How could you know I never reached western Waset?"

"You didn't once contact us. Yesterday or last night. We should've guessed something was wrong."

"If you had, you wouldn't have been able to find me."

Hori took both Bak's hands in his and turned them one way and the other, squeezing the fingers gently. "Your hands are swollen, sir, but nothing like they must've been yesterday."

"They're stiff, but at least I can use them." To demonstrate, he tore a triangle of bread from a flattish loaf, dipped it into the bowl, and lifted out small chunks of duck, onions, and beans. He took a bite, savoring the flavor.

"If you couldn't hold the harpoon, sir, how did you cut through the rope around your ankles?" Kasaya asked.

Bak glanced at the weapon on the ground beside him. "I laid the pole on the hatch cover and sat on it to hold it steady. Then I propped the point on a broken cleat and pulled my feet back and forth, rubbing the rope across the barbs. I thank the lord Amon that they were sharp."

"What of the men who snared you?" Pashenuro asked. "You recognized one of them, you said."

"A swarthy man with a gravelly voice. I'm fairly certain he's Zuwapi. The others may well be crewmen on Antef's ship, but they could as easily be ne'er-do-wells who linger at the harbor."

The sergeant, his expression forbidding, looked around the circle of Medjays. "Captain Antef has much to answer for, and Zuwapi far more."

A murmur of agreement swept across the courtyard.

"We must all be patient a bit longer." Bak tore another chunk from the bread and dipped it into the stew. "While wading across all those flooded fields, I had plenty of time to think. I have an idea Zuwapi can be found somewhere along the waterfront. We've no authority there. The harbor patrol must seek him out."

"Lieutenant Karoya seems a reasonable man," Psuro said. "Will he not let us help?"

Bak picked up the remaining piece of bread and wiped the last of the stew from the bowl. Swallowing a bite, he glanced toward the sun, midway up the morning sky. The tenth morning of the Beautiful Feast of Opet, with just one day remaining.

"Come with me and we'll ask," he said, rising to his feet.

He had proof of the thefts within the storehouses of Amon and would soon lay hands not only on the thieves, but on the men who had been smuggling the objects out of Kemet. He thought he knew who within Pentu's household had attempted to stir up trouble in the land of Hatti, but the conclusion was based on logical thinking rather than proof, and the reason behind the act eluded him. With luck and the help of the lord Amon, he would find a way to bring about a speedy resolution.

In spite of all he had learned, the many conclusions he had reached, he was still unsure who had slain Maruwa, Woserhet and Meryamon. He might well be able to resolve the two other crimes, yet fail to satisfy Amonked's wish that the slayer be snared by the end of the festival.

"Captain Antef." Mai, who had been staring out at the waterfront through the large opening in the wall of his office, turned to face his visitors. "I've never been fond of him, but

I thought him no less honest than any other man who plies the waters of the Great Green Sea. It takes a certain amount of guile to remain untrammeled in the ports along its shores."

"My scribe has taken an auditor from the royal house to the customs archive to examine old records of Antef's voyages." Bak, standing before the harbormaster with Psuro and Lieutenant Karoya, wished he could look down upon Antef's ship, but it was too far north to be seen from this central location. "Thanuny's eyes are as sharp as those of a falcon, and he thinks like the thieves he seeks out. I'm confident he'll find proof of wrongdoing over and above the objects stowed on Antef's deck."

Looking grave, Mai asked, "The trader you suspect is called Zuwapi? A Hittite?"

"Yes, sir."

Mai's eyes darted toward Karoya. "How long will it take you to find him, Lieutenant?"

"If he's staying somewhere along the waterfront, as Lieutenant Bak believes, an hour, no more." The young Medjay officer noticed Bak's raised eyebrow, smiled. "I've plenty of informers in the area, sir, a few who've been victimized by besotted Hittite sailors. They'll have noticed Zuwapi, that I promise you."

Bak acknowledged the pledge with a smile. Karoya and his men toiled at the harbor day after day. They knew its denizens far better than he. "Antef and his crew must also be taken. Is your station large enough for so many men?"

"We'll take them to a building we sometimes use to detain men who've committed no heinous crime but must not be allowed to go free unpunished. Few people know of it and none use it but us."

"Will you allow my Medjays to participate?"

Karoya glanced at Mai for approval. The harbormaster eyed the two officers, undecided.

"Sir." Psuro stepped forward. "Lieutenant Bak has asked

nothing of me or of the other men in our company since the festival began. He's given us leave to make merry for the past ten days. In return, we let those men snare him . . ."

"You had no way of knowing I'd walk into a trap," Bak insisted.

"Nonetheless, while you were made to suffer, we played." To Mai, Psuro said, "Now we'd like to help, to see with our own eyes that they pay for their foul deeds."

Mai tried without much success to hide a smile. "I'd hate to think territory is more important than justice. Your men may participate with those of Lieutenant Karoya."

The building used by the harbor patrol had once been the residence of a prosperous craftsman, taken over by the royal house for some unexplained reason. Inside the high walls were an uninhabited house of modest proportions with quarters for lesser help tacked onto the back. Auxiliary structures included a well encircled by a thigh-high mudbrick wall, an empty stable and poultry yard, and a lean-to built against the outer wall. Other than the latter shelter, nothing relieved the harsh midday heat. Not a blade of grass or a weed grew in the yard; no trees or brush shaded the bare earth. Not a breath of air stirred.

That the craftsman had been a potter was apparent. A shallow pit in which the moist clay could be trampled had been dug near the edge of the lean-to, where space had been provided for at least four men to toil over potter's wheels. Nearby stood a neatly stacked mound of grayish pots of various sizes, many cracked and broken, left to dry after being formed but never fired. Several kilns stood out in the open, placed to benefit from the prevailing north breeze. Their lower ends where fires had once roared were partially underground, while the chimneylike section in which the pots had been fired rose upward at a right angle. A small pile of kindling and scavenged wood lay against the house, awaiting a potter who would never return. A pile of failures lay where they had been thrown against the wall near the main gate: bowls and pots of all sizes and shapes, their walls cracked or broken, their fabric bubbled, their forms misshapen.

"Ideal for our purpose," Bak said, looking around. "Do you use this place often?"

"Several times a year, the most recent being two days before the festival began." Karoya watched one of his sergeants and Psuro climb onto the roof of the house. Three of Bak's Medjays were posted near the main gate and at two smaller exits, while the remainder and a few members of the harbor patrol were hunkered down in the shade of the lean-to. "A ship's crew, besotted and mean, staggered through the market, knocking over stalls and destroying merchandise. They spent five days here while the master of their vessel gathered together the goods to replace the loss and more. Needless to say, they're now indentured to him for many years to come."

Bak's eyes came to rest on the kilns. "I suggest we heat up a furnace. I can think of no better an incentive than fire to set men's tongues to wagging."

Karoya's men outdid themselves. Four harbor patrolmen hustled their prisoner through the gate in less than an hour. Wooden manacles pinned his hands behind his back and a swath of linen had been wound around his head and shoulders, hiding his identity from all who walked the busy streets and lanes. His clothing was disheveled and specks of red dotted the front of his shift. A patch of color on the shroud around his head spoke of a bloody nose. Evidently he had not come willingly.

"Here he is, sir," one of the patrolmen said, and shoved his prisoner toward the officers.

The man stumbled, lost his balance, fell to his knees. With his head covered, Bak could not tell if he was the gravel-voiced swarthy man he believed to be Zuwapi.

"Well done," Karoya said, "and the others?"

"As soon as we tamed this one, Sergeant Mose and his men went after them."

"Excellent." Karoya smiled at Bak. "Shall we see what we've snared?"

So saying, he signaled the patrolmen to unwrap the man's head. Two men moved in. One, taking no trouble to be gentle, unwound the linen and snatched it away. The second man grabbed an arm and jerked the prisoner to his feet.

His eyes darted toward Bak. He gaped. "You! No!"

The gravelly voice set Bak's blood to boiling. He formed his most menacing smile. "Zuwapi. At last we meet in the light of the lord Re."

The Hittite jerked away from the man gripping his arm and ran toward the main gate. The other patrolman leaped after him, the length of linen trailing in the dirt. Made clumsy by his shackled hands, the prisoner's gait was awkward, not fast enough. His pursuer rapidly gained on him, caught the loose end of the linen in his free hand, and flung it over his quarry's head, catching him by the neck and pulling him backward until he fell to the ground in a puff of dust. He sat up and spewed out invective in his own tongue, a string of curses filled with hate. The patrolman cuffed him hard across the side of the head, silencing him.

Bak crossed the yard to where the prisoner sat and stood before him, legs spread wide, tapping his baton of office against his calf. "You are the Hittite trader Zuwapi, are you not?"

"My name is of no concern to you," the man growled.

"You've tried three times to slay me." Bak's tender head and ribs, the fire in his wrists, added menace to his voice. "Do I not have the right to know who wants me dead, and for what reason?"

The man looked up at Bak with the scorn he might reserve for an insect. "I'm a guest in the land of Kemet. You've no authority to demand anything of me."

Bak eyed the prisoner's shift, made of the finest of fabrics, and the broad gold bracelets he wore. His dress and jewelry, his arrogance, said he was a man of substance in Hatti. But Hatti was not Kemet. Bak placed the tip of his baton on the man's breastbone and shoved hard. The prisoner sprawled in the dust, half on his side. Fury suffused his face and he spat at Bak's feet. Muttering an oath, the patrolman placed a foot against the nape of his neck and shoved him downward.

"You must speak your name," Bak demanded. "Now!"

The prisoner wiggled to get free. The patrolman pressed harder, forcing his face into the dirt.

"I am Zuwapi!" The Hittite's voice pulsed with anger. "I'm from Hattusa, where I'm a highly regarded merchant. You can't treat me like this!"

The main gate swung open and the patrol sergeant Mose came through. Behind him, two patrolmen held Captain Antef, red-faced and sputtering, between them. The rest of the unit guarded a long line of bound prisoners, the crew of Antef's ship. A rope tied around each man's neck fastened them together like widely spaced amulets on a cord.

"Let him rise," Bak told the patrolman holding Zuwapi down. "He must see his fellow prisoners and they must see him."

Captain Antef looked their way. His face paled and he paused, as if unable to take the next step. A guard urged him on with the butt of his spear.

At the same time, one of the sailors spotted Bak and barked a startled oath. The next in line cried out in horror, swung around and tried to run, nearly strangling himself and the prisoners ahead of and behind him. A third began to whimper and a fourth covered terrified eyes with his bound hands. Their guards prodded them forward. Fear added speed to their pace and the ragged line filed into the stable.

The sailors' fright at seeing Bak alive and well, their obvious conviction that they were looking at a spirit from the netherworld, was better than a confession as far as he was concerned. His enjoyment of the moment was torn asunder by another long stream of curses from Zuwapi.

"Take him into the house," he said. "We'll talk next to Captain Antef."

"I'm not a smuggler, I tell you." Sweat poured from Antef's face, whether from fear, his close proximity to the kiln, or the hot breath of the lord Re reaching into the unshaded yard, Bak could not tell.

He pointed his baton at the prisoner, made his tone hard and cold. "The cargo stowed on the deck of your ship includes fine linen, ritual vessels, aromatic oils and any number of other items stolen from the storehouses of the lord Amon. That you cannot deny."

"You've been sailing the Great Green Sea for a long time, sir," Karoya said in a softer, kinder tone. "I find it difficult to believe you'd take such a risk."

"I know nothing about anything stolen from the sacred precinct. Or from anywhere else, for that matter."

"I've had an auditor from the royal house look at past records of your voyages," Bak said, taking his turn. "Each and every time you've sailed to Ugarit over the past three years, you've hauled items few noblemen and certainly no ordinary men could legitimately lay their hands on so often and in such large quantities."

No one had ever noticed, Thanuny had explained, because no single inspector had examined Antef's cargo time after time. As a result, the consistency had escaped detection.

"I'm the master of a ship, not a customs inspector." The captain wiped the sweat from his brow and edged away from the kiln. "You can't expect me to examine every object brought on board. And if I did, how would I know if something was stolen?"

"You wouldn't know," Karoya said sympathetically, "but did you not wonder about the many valuable items you saw?"

Instead of taking advantage of the opening the officer had given him, Antef merely shrugged. "Why should I? Cargo is cargo, nothing more."

Bak stepped closer to the captain, forcing him back toward the kiln. The heat was making his head ache and his raw wrists burn. The game he and Karoya were playing did not sit well with him, but intimidation, he felt, was far more apt to get a true answer than a beating with the cudgel. "I've been told that Zuwapi collects his goods in a storehouse near the waterfront and waits until you arrive to ship them. Why would he do that if he didn't trust you to keep your mouth shut?"

"Why shouldn't he trust me? I've never lost a cargo, his or anyone else's."

"You're an excellent seaman," Karoya said. "Your reputation in that respect is impeccable."

"Stop treating him as if he were related to our sovereign, Lieutenant," Bak snarled, feigning anger. "A thief is a thief." He grabbed the captain by the shoulders, turned him roughly around to face the kiln, and made him kneel before the furnace. "His right hand," he said to Kasaya, whose large, muscular form and stolid demeanor would bring fear to any man's heart.

"No!" Antef screamed.

Karoya intervened. "Captain Antef, you must tell us the truth. I'd hate to see you suffer mutilation when all you have to do is speak out."

Kasaya grabbed the seaman's hand and jerked it toward the mouth of the furnace.

"No!" Antef screamed again. "I beg of you! I'll tell you what you wish to know!"

Bak exchanged a quick look with Kasaya, who continued to hold the captain's hand at the edge of the heat radiating from the red-hot coals within the kiln. He suspected the Medjay was as relieved as he that the seaman had broken so easily.

Antef's voice shook as much as his body did. "I never talked to Zuwapi about the goods he shipped to Ugarit. He was too good a customer, too faithful in bringing his cargo to me. And he always allowed me a fair return. He saw that I had a good mooring place in that distant port. He even helped me replace crewmen lost to other vessels there, or to houses of pleasure."

"You're not a stupid man, Antef," Bak said. "You knew exactly what you were hauling."

"No!" Antef wiped his brow and dried his free hand on his damp-stained kilt. "I suspected some of the objects were stolen, yes, but I closed my eyes to what my heart told me. I never once thought they'd come from the sacred precinct, from the lord Amon himself. Never!"

Suspecting the admission was partially true at best, Bak pressed on relentlessly. "Did Maruwa guess what you were doing, forcing you to slay him?"

Antef looked truly horrified. "No!"

"If he saw valuable objects on board and guessed they were stolen, you most certainly would've done what you thought necessary to save yourself."

"I didn't slay him, I tell you. Would I be so stupid as to murder a man on my own vessel? Especially when it was loaded with horses. Flighty creatures they are, easily panicked. They could've torn my ship apart."

Bak was inclined to believe him, and from the thoughtful look on Karoya's face, he also believed he was hearing the truth. "If not you, who did take his life?"

"Zuwapi. The slayer could've been no one else." Antef's words, his demeanor were firm, containing not a hint of reluctance at accusing his partner in crime of so heinous a deed.

"No!" Zuwapi flung the word out like an angry and fearful child throws a denial at a parent. "I didn't slay Maruwa. He knew nothing of the smuggling. He wouldn't have recognized a sacred vessel if a priest had held one in front of his eyes."

"You knew him well?" Karoya asked.

"We weren't friends, if that's what you mean, but we greeted each other when we met." Zuwapi eyed the kiln and the heat waves reaching up from the opening at the top. The sand around the furnace was scuffed, indicating the earlier struggle. With luck and the generosity of the gods, he had heard Antef's fearful cries. "I'm a businessman—a good one—and he cared for nothing but horses."

"I say you took his life," Bak said, "and you took the lives of two men in the sacred precinct. Men who could've pointed a finger at you."

"I did not. Other than once during a battle at sea, I've never slain anyone."

"You tried three times to slay me."

"Would that I had," the Hittite mumbled beneath his breath.

As before when they had questioned Antef, Karoya's manner was more sympathetic. "You can't mean that, sir. If you'd wanted Lieutenant Bak dead, you'd have slit his throat."

Zuwapi grew sullen. "I've no stomach for blood. How was I to know he's as slippery as an eel?"

Bak signaled Kasaya, who forced the Hittite to get down on his knees in front of the kiln. "If you didn't slay Maruwa and the others, why try to slay me?"

"I was told . . ." Zuwapi's eyes flitted toward the bandages on Bak's wrists, and he sneered, "Why should I tell you anything?"

"Someone ordered you to slay me?"

"No one orders me about. No one."

Bak nodded to Kasaya, who eased the Hittite's hand closer to the heat. "Who wanted me dead, Zuwapi?"

Staring at the burning coals in the gaping furnace, Zuwapi growled, "I don't know!"

"You have heard of the murders in the sacred precinct, have you not?" Karoya asked.

"Who hasn't?"

"Did you know the two men slain there?" Bak demanded.

Zuwapi licked his lips. "I did not."

"Do you always lie when the truth would serve you better? You knew Meryamon. He stole the objects you placed on board Antef's ship."

Zuwapi's mouth tightened, holding inside his answer.

"What of the red-haired man?" Bak asked. "Will you try to tell me he, too, is a stranger to you?"

Surprise flitted across Zuwapi's face, but was quickly wiped away with a sneer. "I don't know who you're talking about."

"I saw Meryamon pass a message to a red-haired man, and he, in turn, spoke to you. You were in front of Ipet-resyt during the opening ceremonies of the festival."

Zuwapi's attitude changed once again, this time to a sly defiance. "If you saw me talk to a red-haired man, I don't doubt that you did. I've exchanged words with many men since the festival began. Strangers mostly. How can I recall one over another?"

"You were not strangers to one another." Bak gave the Hittite a long, speculative look. "I believe Meryamon passed word to the red-haired man that the auditor Woserhet had been slain. He most likely mentioned that I'd noticed a similarity between Woserhet's death and that of Maruwa. The redhead, in turn, passed the word to you. Who did you pass it to, Zuwapi? Captain Antef?"

"Antef was a man in a hurry," Karoya said, "pressing me to allow him to sail away from Waset. At the very least, you warned him to take care."

Bak formed a scornful smile. "Does the red-haired man pull your strings, Zuwapi, as a child would pull a toy with movable parts?"

The Hittite's laugh failed to conceal his resentment at being called a puppet. "Have you ever thought to become a teller of tall tales, Lieutenant?"

"Somehow I can't imagine any of you—neither you nor Meryamon nor Antef—thinking of a way to safely steal from the sacred precinct. The priest was young, too unworldly to create a plan that would go on successfully for several years. Captain Antef has no direct connection with the sacred precinct and wouldn't know how to go about it. You're a foreigner who knows not the ways of the lord Amon and the men who toil for him. Which means someone else planned the thefts. Who, Zuwapi?"

"I don't know what you're talking about."

Irritated with the game the Hittite was playing, Bak signaled Kasaya, who jerked Zuwapi's right hand toward the furnace. "Did you take the lives of Maruwa, Meryamon, and Woserhet?"

Zuwapi flung a contemptuous look at him. "You wouldn't dare burn me. I've friends in the royal house in Hattusa. Do harm to me and your sovereign would hear of their objections in the strongest possible terms."

"Answer my question, Zuwapi."

"I've no answer to give you. Sir!" he added in a mocking manner.

Bak nodded to Kasaya, who jerked the Hittite forward, propelling his hand into the mouth of the furnace. Sweat popped out on Zuwapi's brow, his expression grew pained. Whether the intense heat of the coals had reached his hand or he simply feared being burned, his interrogators could not tell.

"Did you slay Maruwa, Woserhet, and Meryamon?" Bak demanded.

Zuwapi's voice rose in pitch, losing its roughness. "How many times must I tell you? I've slain no one."

"If you didn't, you surely suspected their deaths were related to the thefts in the sacred precinct."

"Not at first. Not until Meryamon was slain. Then . . ." He hesitated, appeared to reach a decision, said, "I didn't know what to think."

Bak did not believe him for an instant. "If you didn't slay them, you must know who did."

Karoya, equally skeptical, dropped his role as mediator. He signaled Kasaya, who shoved Zuwapi's hand closer to the burning coals.

"Don't!" Sweat reeking of fear poured from the Hittite.

"We don't wish to maim you," Karoya said, "but we must if you don't tell us who took those men's lives."

Kasaya shifted forward as if readying himself to shove the Hittite's hand onto the coals.

"Nehi." Zuwapi stared into the furnace and swallowed hard. "He's the man you saw, the one with red hair. He said he didn't slay them, but he must've." The Hittite's eyes darted toward Bak. "He's the man who told me I must get rid of you."

"Where can we find him?" Karoya asked.

"He toils at the harbor. He's overseer of the men who carry newly arrived offerings from the ships to the storehouses of Amon."

At a nod from Bak, Kasaya allowed Zuwapi to pull his hand back, but not so far that his confidence would return. Rubbing it as if it had truly been burned, the Hittite gave the two officers a wounded look. Bak could not sympathize. In spite of the pain inflicted upon him, he disliked acting the bully, but the quick results testified to its effectiveness.

"Who planned the robberies?" he asked.

Zuwapi turned morose. "I was never told, but Nehi must've. Either him or Meryamon."

Bak could not credit the young priest with so important a role. "You weren't curious?"

"I was." Zuwapi spoke through gritted teeth, as if holding inside a resentment that had been building for months. "I tried many times to guess his name with no success, even tried prying the name from Nehi. I failed. He would say nothing. Nothing, I tell you."

Chapter Seventeen

Most of the cargo vessels moored along the waterfront had arrived long before the Beautiful Feast of Opet began, allowing plenty of time to unload before the temptations of the festival drew crews and workmen away from more serious endeavors. As a result, Bak thought it best to start their search for Nehi in the sacred precinct.

"It can't be true." Nebamon, overseer of the storehouses from which many of the ritual objects had been stolen, flung a perplexed look at Bak, Karoya, and Thanuny. "Meryamon was such a nice young man, so helpful. Utterly devoted to the lord Amon."

"We believe he not only took objects over an extended period of time, but he also altered the records to hide his wrongdoing and that of another man." The auditor tapped a large scroll-filled basket, so heavy the servant carrying it had both arms wrapped firmly around it. "Each and every document in this container has been tampered with."

"So many?" Nebamon gulped.

Bak glanced at Sergeant Psuro, standing in the doorway of the small walled courtyard, barring entry or exit. He did not mistrust Nebamon, but thought it best to take precautions lest he erred. "We believe Nehi, in his position as overseer of the workmen who carry offerings from incoming ships to the storehouses of Amon, was also making off with items meant to be used in the sacred rituals."

"Nehi?" Nebamon frowned, doubtful. "A most congenial man. All who know him like him."

"When I spoke with you several days ago, I told you of a red-haired man I saw you talking with while standing in the courtyard in front of Ipet-resyt. The opening procession had entered the sacred precinct and there you were, side by side, watching a group of Hittite acrobats. That man had to have been Nehi, yet when I asked, you denied knowing him."

"Did I?" Nebamon raised both hands and ran his fingers through the curly white hair above his ears. "I don't remember seeing him there—the courtyard was teeming with people, if you recall—but perhaps we exchanged a few trifling words."

"Where can we find him?"

"Come with me. We must ask the scribe who deals with these people."

"I should've guessed he dwelt here." Bak stood outside the gate through which he and Amonked had, ten days before, entered the sacred precinct to view Woserhet's body. He eyed the blank white walls of the interconnected houses that lay in the shadow of the massive wall surrounding the lord Amon's domain. He remembered well chasing the red-haired man through that confusing warren of narrow lanes. "Where do we go from here?"

Psuro could neither read nor write, but his memory was faultless. "According to the scribe, we enter the leftmost lane, turn right at the second intersection, left at the next lane, pass beneath a wooden lintel, and turn right again at the next intersecting lane. His dwelling will be behind the fourth doorway to the right."

Signaling the sergeant to lead the way, Bak followed with Karoya. A dozen of his Medjays and an equal number of harbor patrolmen hurried after them. Upon learning where Nehi dwelt, he had suggested they summon extra men.

He stopped at the lintel, while Psuro went on ahead, and

gathered the men around. "You all know what you're to do, but I must warn you." He looked from one to another, his expression stern. "He knows these lanes far better than we do. If he runs, don't follow him in a line like cattle being led to slaughter. Spread out into the surrounding lanes. We must not let him get away."

They melted into the shadows of a nearby lane, where they waited in silence until Psuro returned.

"He's home," the sergeant reported. "Sleeping late after a night of revelry, so says an old woman in the adjoining house."

Bak thanked the lord Amon that they would not have to lie in wait. "Let's go."

The sergeant and a dozen men hurried off to surround the block. Karoya took six others to close off the nearby lanes. Bak and the remainder waited. When they heard two short, sharp whistles, Psuro's signal and Karoya's, they strode toward the fourth doorway to the right. They were a dozen steps away when the red-haired man stepped into the lane, yawning, scratching his head. He saw Bak, his mouth dropped open, he spun around and leaped inside. Bak plunged into the dark dwelling, glimpsed his quarry at the top of the stairs leading to the roof. Yelling to his men to spread out and watch the doors of the other houses, he raced upward.

Nehi sped across the flat, white rooftop, leaping over baskets and bowls; bounding over fish laid out to dry; veering around small pavilions occupied by women spinning and weaving, grinding grain, and performing innumerable other household tasks while they tended their small children. He reached the opposite side of the block, looked down into the lane, saw the men below and cried out an oath. He ran to the right and looked into a side lane. Seeing more men waiting to snare him, he slumped down onto the roof, head bowed, gasping for breath. Bak called for manacles and within moments Nehi was their prisoner.

*   *   *

As soon as Bak got his first good look at Nehi, he knew the redhead had played no major role in the robberies. He was, like Meryamon, less than twenty years of age. "You knew Meryamon."

The young man wiped his eyes with the back of his hand, swallowed tears. The unexpected capture, the mere threat of burning, had completely unmanned him, turning him into the sobbing child he once had been. "We grew to manhood together. In Abedju. We were childhood playmates, the best of friends."

He seemed so lacking in guile, so genuine, that Bak almost sympathized with him. Almost. "The two of you stole many valuable objects from the lord Amon."

"We stole, yes." Sniffing back tears, Nehi spoke out readily, a young man eager to please men more senior in age and rank. "Each time I saw a ritual vessel or a jar of aromatic oil or anything else of value, if I could find a way to take it unseen, I did so. Meryamon took objects from the storehouses themselves, and he also altered the records so no one would know of his crime or mine."

"Where did you hide the items you stole?"

"I took them to a storehouse near the waterfront. There the Hittite trader Zuwapi held the goods he meant to transport to Ugarit and beyond. Meryamon stayed well clear, wanting no one to see him in the company of the foreigner."

Bak signaled Kasaya, who allowed the prisoner to scuttle backward a couple of paces away from the furnace. He wanted sufficient heat to reach the prisoner to remind him of what he faced should he fail to talk. Between the furnace, the hot breath of the lord Re reaching into the sun-baked courtyard, and the never-ending sobbing, thirst might well become a more effective threat than Nehi's fear of burning. "Why did he wish to keep his distance?"

The redhead sniffled. "He thought it best, so he said."

"How long have these thefts been going on?" Karoya asked.

"About three years. A long time."

A buzz of voices rose beneath the lean-to, where Bak's men and the harbor patrolmen knelt or sat in the shade. To steal a little from a god was a small sin, to steal so much for so long was horrendous.

Thanks to the diligence of Hori and Thanuny while searching the archives, Bak was not surprised, merely puzzled. If Karoya's expression told true, he was equally perplexed. "Meryamon dwelt within the sacred precinct and had neither property nor riches. From the appearance of your dwelling, you also are without wealth. What did the two of you gain from these robberies?"

"Our portion was being held for us in Ugarit. There we meant to end our days in luxury." Nehi burst into tears, his voice shook with anguish. "Now Meryamon has gone to the netherworld and I'm your prisoner, no doubt soon to die for taking what by rights belonged to the lord Amon. The endless fear of being caught, the constant expectation of wealth beyond measure. All for nothing."

A fitting end for men who offend the lady Maat, Bak thought, but theft, in this case, was only one of several heinous acts. "Did you slay Maruwa? The Hittite who traded in horses?"

"No," Nehi sobbed. "I didn't even know the man."

Bak signaled Kasaya, who stepped closer to the prisoner, looming over him, more threatening than words.

"I didn't slay him. I swear I didn't!"

"What of Woserhet and Meryamon?" Karoya demanded. "Did you take their lives?"

"No!" Nehi stared at the fiery embers visible within the mouth of the furnace. Tears tumbled down his cheeks. "I was appalled to hear of Woserhet's death. I knew so vile a crime would bring the wrath of the gods upon us. And when

I learned Meryamon was slain . . ." He could barely talk, so wracked was he by sobs. "He was my friend, closer than a brother."

Could a man pretend such sorrow, Bak wondered, such torment? "You dwell a short distance from the sacred precinct, with an unguarded gate close to hand. The storehouse where Woserhet died was less than a hundred paces beyond the gate, too close to bear thinking about. Meryamon was your friend, easy to lure to the shrine of the hearing ear, easier to sneak up behind and slit his throat."

"You don't understand!" Nehi cried. "Meryamon's death planted a fear in my heart greater than any I've ever before felt. I knew then that I was doomed as surely as he had been."

Bak glanced at Karoya, who nodded, indicating that he, too, shared Bak's conviction that Nehi was telling the truth, or close to the truth. The redhead—and probably Meryamon as well—was as much a victim of his own greed as he was a criminal. Which made Zuwapi a liar, a man wishing to cast suspicion away from himself. Yet how could a foreigner like Zuwapi, a seaman like Antef, plan so successful a scheme within the sacred precinct? The more questions he asked, the more convinced Bak became that someone else altogether had led this gang of thieves. "Who planned the robberies, Nehi?"

"I don't know."

"Not Meryamon?"

"No," Nehi whimpered.

Bak feigned impatience. "Do you actually know Zuwapi, or did you merely deliver the items to his storehouse?"

"He met me there each time. He had to break the seal and unlatch the door. And only he could reseal the door after we placed the objects inside."

"What of Captain Antef?"

"I learned of him by chance." Nehi swallowed a sob. "I

saw Zuwapi's trade goods being loaded onto a ship. A blind man would've guessed its captain was a party to the thefts."

"Did you ever approach him?"

"I dared not," Nehi said with a shudder. "Zuwapi would've been furious. As would Meryamon."

"If you didn't slay Maruwa or Woserhet or Meryamon . . ."

"I've slain no one! I swear to the lord Amon!"

"If you didn't take those three men's lives, who did?"

"Zuwapi. He'd slay his own mother to gain advantage."

"We need more wood, sir." Kasaya, kneeling before the furnace, was attempting to stir the fire into life. The best he could do was create a few fiery sparks that died the instant they flared.

"We could tear down the lean-to," Sergeant Mose said. He was shorter than Kasaya, but equally broad. His nose had been flattened by a blow sometime in the past, making him appear hard and cruel.

Karoya scowled his disapproval. "These buildings are the property of the royal house, Sergeant. We're accountable for their well-being."

"We can always use the cudgel, sir, or a stout stick."

Bak's eyes darted around the compound, searching for another way to intimidate the prisoners, and came to rest on the pit, a rough circle dug knee-deep into the ground, and the dried black clay at the bottom. A quick glance at the sun told him they had sufficient time. "Bring some men to break up that clay, and pour water into the pit to soften it. The threat of burning primed them to talk; with luck and the help of the gods, a fear of being smothered by mud will further their inclination to speak freely."

"More questions?" Antef glowered at Bak and Karoya. "I've already told you all I can. I hauled Zuwapi's trade goods, yes, and during the last few months I've wondered if they might be stolen, but I had absolutely no involvement in his foul scheme."

Bak's laugh was short, sharp. "You may not have been involved up to your neck, but you were certainly immersed to your knees."

The captain raised his chin high and stood as tall and straight as he could. He spoke in a haughty manner. "I must return to my ship, Lieutenant, and my crew must accompany me. I've valuable cargo on board and I fear for its safety."

Choosing not to remind him that Karoya's men had been guarding the cargo for a week, Bak asked, "Do you see that pit, Captain?"

One of Bak's Medjays knelt at the rim, pouring water over what had been rock-hard dirt, broken into clods that had been pounded to dust. A harbor patrolman waded around in mud well above his ankles, mixing in the water. Two men knelt at the edge, offering unwanted advice. A dozen or so others stood around, joking, teasing their less fortunate companion.

Antef stared, puzzled.

"We've run out of fuel for the kiln," Bak explained, "but we thought you might like a mud bath—beginning with your head."

The captain sucked in his breath and took a quick step back. "You can't do that to me. I'm a respectable man. I'll complain to the harbormaster."

"I suggest you answer our questions, sir," Karoya said. As before, his demeanor was far kinder than Bak's. "Each hour that passes makes you look more guilty in our eyes, and so the harbormaster will believe."

Bak motioned Mose to usher Antef to the pit. The sergeant was not as tall as Kasaya, but his uncompromising demeanor was more intimidating. The captain struggled to break free, but Mose's strength prevailed. The men around the pit moved out of their way, and soon they stood at the edge. Antef looked downward, his expression one of distaste and dread.

"What do you know of the other men involved in the thefts?" Bak asked.

"I did business with Zuwapi, no one else."

"You didn't know the priest Meryamon or his friend Nehi?"

"As far as I know, I never met either man."

Karoya queried Bak with a glance. The more senior of the two nodded, and the younger officer hurried across the yard to disappear around the corner of the house, behind which lay the servants' quarters.

At a command from Mose, the man in the pit scrambled out.

"Do you know the man who planned the thefts?" Bak asked. "The one who pulled the strings that made the other men dance?"

"Zuwapi did."

Bak raised a skeptical eyebrow. "Did he tell you that?"

"Not in so many words, no. He was a prosperous merchant, well placed in Hattusa, so I just assumed . . ." The words tailed off, doubt crept into Antef's voice. "He did at times take a day or two to answer my questions. Too long, I thought, but . . ." He gave Bak a sharp look. "He was no more than a tool, as I was?"

"I don't know," Bak admitted, but deep down inside the suspicion hardened that someone other than the men he had snared had planned the robberies and issued the orders.

Karoya, holding Nehi by the arm, came around the corner of the dwelling. Bak watched Antef closely. The captain looked toward the redhead but gave no sign of recognition. A patrolman appeared and took the prisoner back around the house. As Karoya approached across the yard, he shook his head, verifying Bak's impression that Nehi had failed to recognize the seaman.

"Let's speak again of Maruwa," Bak said to the captain.

"How many times must I tell you? I know nothing of his death!"

"How certain are you that he didn't notice the stolen objects mixed in with the rest of Zuwapi's cargo?"

Antef spoke as if Bak were trying his patience. "He was as transparent as rainwater, Lieutenant, and as trusting. If he'd grown suspicious, the first thing he'd have done is come to me and tell me."

"He wouldn't have thought you guilty?"

"Why would he? The goods belonged to Zuwapi, not me."

"If he's telling the truth—and I believe he is," Bak said, "he'd have had no reason to slay Maruwa."

Karoya, seated on the lower, furnace portion of a dormant kiln, looked ruefully toward the stable, where Antef had been taken. "I hate to think him innocent of all but smuggling."

Bak took a careful drink from his beer jar, trying not to stir up the sediment. "Zuwapi also claims Maruwa noticed nothing."

"If the man was as blind to the smuggling as they say, why was he slain?"

"I've slain no one!" Zuwapi stood in the pit, his feet and ankles buried in mud. Mose's big hand gripped his neck, ready to shove him onto his knees.

Bak was not sure how seriously the Hittite took the threat, but he was fully prepared to prove to him how frightening immersion would be. "One of your partners in crime says you did."

"Who? Antef?" The Hittite spat on the ground to show his contempt, whether for Bak or the captain was unclear. "He's a liar. A liar and a sneak." His expression grew sly. "I say you look at him. I'd not be surprised if he took their lives."

"He's told us he dealt solely with you, Zuwapi, and he had no knowledge of the men who stole the objects."

"He wasn't supposed to know them," Zuwapi admitted, "but he may've followed me, thinking to cut me out, to eliminate me as the man between."

"You said before that you thought Nehi slew those men," Karoya reminded him.

"Did I?" Zuwapi lifted a foot, making a sucking sound in the mud. It was too runny to form into pots, but thick enough for Bak's purpose. "He could have. He gives an impression of being weak, but he'd not be the first nor will he be the last to avoid a fight or suitable punishment by denying an accusation—or pointing a finger at someone else."

The Hittite would blame Maatkare Hatshepsut herself, Bak thought, if he believed he could make himself appear innocent. "Why would you wish Maruwa dead, Zuwapi?"

"You tell me."

Bak nodded to Mose, who struck the Hittite in the stomach, forcing a whoosh of air from his mouth, and shoved his head toward the mud.

"No!" Zuwapi struggled like a snared snake. "You'll smother me!"

"Answer my question," Bak said.

"How can I? I didn't slay him!" Mose eased the pressure slightly, allowing the Hittite to stand half bent over. "Antef swore he was too interested in the horses to pay attention to the rest of the cargo, and I believed him. If he'd thought otherwise, I'd have spotted the lie."

"If the three deaths weren't so much alike, I'd have looked to Meryamon as Woserhet's slayer. But since he was among the slain . . ." Bak let the words tail off as if he had been thinking aloud. "Who do you believe took Meryamon's life?"

"Nehi."

"Not another man? One stronger than any of you—and smarter? One who planned the robberies?"

Zuwapi stared at his interrogator, thinking hard, and a slow understanding crept onto his face. He muttered an oath in his own tongue. "One who's cut himself off from us, you mean. Severing all ties, thinking we'll take the blame while he . . ."

"Reaps the profits?" Bak laughed, as if he enjoyed the irony. "Who is he, Zuwapi?"

"I wish I knew," the Hittite growled through gritted teeth.

"Are you going to allow him to walk away free and clear, leaving you and the others as sacrificial goats?"

"Believe me, if I knew his name, I'd tell you."

"Oh, yes, I believe him." Bak accepted a beer jar from Psuro and broke out the plug. "He was too angry to lie, and can you blame him? While he and the others are put to death or suffer the hardships of a desert mine, a man no one seems to know will gain great wealth."

"I fear we've reached a dead end, sir." Karoya, looking glum, sat down on a low stool beneath the lean-to, took an open jar from Mose, and sipped from it. "If none of them knows who their leader was after three or more years, how can we hope to lay hands on him?"

"You told us Meryamon stayed away from Zuwapi's storehouse," Bak said. "Why was that?"

Nehi stood a couple of paces from the pit with Mose. The threat was obviously unnecessary. From the way his shoulders slumped, the distraught look on his face, anyone could see that he had no will to resist. "He wanted never to be seen with the trader."

"In other words, you served as the intermediary between Meryamon and Zuwapi. You knew of Antef, though you weren't supposed to."

Nehi hung his head, nodded.

"Zuwapi, in turn, served as the intermediary between you and Antef."

"Yes, sir."

"I see," Bak said, and indeed he did. The gang had been

set up as a chain, with Meryamon dealing solely with Nehi who dealt with Zuwapi, who in turn dealt with Antef. "I thought at first that Zuwapi was the key man in this little group of robbers and smugglers. Instead . . ."

Nehi, staring at the ground beneath his feet, shook his head. "As far as I know, he served no purpose other than to take the objects I gave him and trade them to men far to the north."

Bak caught the young man's chin and jerked his head up, forcing him to meet his eyes. "Who planned the robberies, Nehi? You? Have you led us to believe you're a simple thief when in fact you're the head of the gang?" The charge was ridiculous, but he had somehow to get Nehi to verify his suspicions.

"Me?" Nehi looked startled. "I've stolen objects from the lord Amon, I freely admit, but it wasn't my idea."

"Whose was it?"

"Meryamon's," he whispered.

Bak shoved the young man's head higher, forcing him to stand on his toes. "It's easy to blame a dead man."

"I swear by all the gods! He told me what they planned to do and suggested I help. He spoke of immense wealth and a life of luxury in Ugarit or some other distant land." Nehi began to sob. "Now look what I have. A promise of death for stealing from the god."

"Zuwapi said the order to slay me came from you."

Nehi gaped, stuttered, "I didn't . . ." A sudden thought struck; shock registered on his face. "Oh, no!"

"What?" Bak demanded.

"I sometimes passed messages to him, sealed scrolls Meryamon gave me."

"Earlier you used the word 'they.' Did Meryamon plan the robberies and smuggling, or did someone else lead the gang from afar?"

"Meryamon was a priest, nothing more. What would he know of transporting items of value out of the land of

Kemet, of trading such fine objects to men in faraway lands, men willing to pay dearly for them?"

Exchanging a satisfied glance with Karoya, Bak released Nehi's chin. "The one who planned the thefts, then, was another man. He was your leader, was he not?"

"Yes, sir." Nehi spoke so softly Bak could barely hear.

"Who is he?"

Nehi stared at the ground, mumbled, "Only Meryamon knew his name."

"And now your friend is dead."

Tears spilled from Nehi's eyes, he nodded.

"If you don't know who this leader of yours was, and Zuwapi and Antef don't either, how will you contact him?"

Nehi tried to meet Bak's eyes but failed. "I guess he'll contact us."

His lack of conviction made a lie of the words. He knew as well as Bak that the man had no intention of making himself known. He had slain Meryamon to break the chain, thereby assuring his safety forevermore.

Bak and Psuro walked through the gathering darkness along lanes crowded with men, women, and children, all making merry on this final night of the festival. Their Medjays had gone off with Karoya and the harbor patrolmen to escort the prisoners to the Great Prison of Waset, where they would be held until they stood before the vizier. After judgment they would return to the prison to await punishment.

"Where are you to meet our men, Psuro?" Bak asked.

"In front of Ipet-resyt. They won't be long, I'm certain." The sergeant stopped in the intersection where they must part company. A soldier stood there, holding high a flaming torch, keeping a wary eye on the people passing by, all talking and laughing, happy and excited. "Are you sure you can't come with me, sir? You've earned a night of revelry."

"I must report to Amonked, tell him of today's events." Bak nudged Psuro, and they stepped out of the way of a half-dozen sailors, sauntering arm in arm with no regard for anyone in their path. "Early tomorrow, before the festivities begin in earnest, I must go to Pentu's dwelling and point a finger at the one who became involved in the politics of Hatti. Amonked must be told what I mean to say."

"Will you not join us after you leave him, sir?"

"I'd like to, but no." Bak laid a hand on the sergeant's shoulder. "I must go somewhere to be alone and think. Something nags at me. Bits of information, statements made that slip away each time I feel them close."

Chapter Eighteen

"To what do I owe the honor of this visit, sir?" Pentu, seated in his armchair on the dais in his spacious audience hall, tried very hard to form a welcoming smile. "Especially at so early an hour."

Amonked did not return the smile. "We wished to speak with you, you and the members of your household. We knew if we came later, we'd not find you home."

From Pentu's appearance, they had caught him dressing in his festival best. He wore a calf-length kilt of fine linen and his eyes were painted, but he had not yet adorned himself with jewelry and wig. Like innumerable other people in Waset, he and his retinue were readying themselves for the short walk to Ipet-resyt. There they would watch the lord Amon leave his southern mansion and make his way to the waterfront, where he would board the sacred barge and sail north to Ipet-isut, thereby culminating the Beautiful Feast of Opet.

"Your presence is always a pleasure," Pentu said, "but we'll be far better prepared to receive you later, after the day's festivities end."

"Frankly, Pentu, the word 'pleasure' does not apply." Amonked glanced at Bak. "My young friend can explain."

A female servant, arranging flowers in a large bowl on the dais, noted his peremptory tone and glanced up at her master. Pentu's expression was stormy, his body as tense as a tautly pulled bowstring. Sensing an impending crisis, she rose quickly to her feet. She dropped a blossom, stepped on it in her haste to leave, and departed. The sweet scent of the crushed flower filled the air.

The governor scowled at Bak. "I can't imagine why you've come again, Lieutenant. I thought we were rid of you."

"I told Bak he wouldn't need my authority. I believed you to be a fair and courteous man." Amonked's voice sharpened. "It seems I erred."

Pentu flushed at the rebuke.

"We've come to reveal the name of the one who brought about your recall from Hattusa," Bak said.

"Now look here, young man . . ."

Amonked raised a hand, silencing him. "I've taken the liberty of summoning the members of your household. As soon as they arrive, we'll begin."

In less serious circumstances, Bak might have smiled. Normally unassuming in appearance and behavior, Amonked could don a cloak of power as easily as his cousin, Maatkare Hatshepsut, should the need arise. "We'll not keep you long, sir. What I have to reveal is easily explained."

"Governor Pentu has all along denied that any member of this household would foment trouble in the land of Hatti." Bak, standing with Amonked beside the dais, glanced at Pentu, who occupied the sole chair on the raised platform. The governor stared straight forward in stony silence, one hand clutching his long staff of office, the other the arm of his chair. "His refusal to believe in spite of the fact that our present envoy to Hattusa verified the accusation was one of several factors I considered when thinking over the problem."

Bak eyed the three men—Sitepehu, Netermose, and Pahure—standing before the dais, and Taharet and Meret, seated side by side on low stools. All but the priest had been interrupted in various stages of adorning themselves for the

festival. Sitepehu, who had to rise early to make the morning
offerings to the lord Inheret, wore the full-length kilt, jewelry, and robe of his priesthood; his shaven head gleamed in
the light streaming down from a high window. Netermose,
who had barely begun to dress, wore nothing but a knee-
length kilt and broad multicolored collar. Pahure wore a
long kilt, broad collar, and bracelets, but had not applied eye
paint or donned a wig.

Both women wore lovely white sheaths of the finest
linen, but there the resemblance ended. Meret was fully
groomed, bewigged, and bejeweled, ready to leave the
house. Taharet was partially made up and her hair hastily
combed. She wore no jewelry. She had obviously been
caught unprepared for guests—or for the necessary accusa-
tions. Her discomfort at having to show herself when not
looking her best was apparent, a gift from the gods Bak had
not expected.

"Of more significance," he went on, "was mistress
Taharet's sudden disapproval of me and her refusal to allow
me to speak with mistress Meret."

"You're a common soldier," Taharet said, her nose high in
the air. "Unworthy of my sister." She was clearly annoyed
at not being provided with a chair beside her husband, a position of honor due to the mistress of the house. A momen-
tary oversight on Pentu's part that Bak and Amonked had
reinforced by suggesting stools for the women.

"So you would have me believe," Bak said, bowing his
head in mock deference.

She opened her mouth as if to reply, but Meret took her
hand and squeezed it, cutting off whatever she meant to say.

"The men of the household all expressed a healthy respect
for the violence and cruelty of Hittite vengeance. Taharet
and Meret, on the other hand, offered no comments about
the Hittites' brutality even though they spoke the tongue of
Hatti, associated with the people of that wretched land, and
had to have had a knowledge of its ways."

Pentu's mouth tightened. "You're treading on dangerous ground, Lieutenant." He did not raise his voice, but none who heard him could miss the ominous tone.

"Am I?" Bak asked, directing the question at the two women.

"My wife is a fine woman, above reproach, and so is her sister. To accuse either of them of wrongdoing is an affront I'll not tolerate."

That Pentu feared his wife was the guilty party, Bak had no doubt. "I accuse one of becoming involved in the politics of the land of Hatti. How deeply embroiled the other was, I hope to discover. At the very least, she maintained a silence that brought about your recall from Hattusa."

Sitepehu sucked in his breath. Pahure muttered a curse. Netermose took a quick step forward as if to come to someone's aid. Who he should help he seemed not to know, for he looked uncertainly from Pentu to the women and back again.

The governor slammed a fist on the arm of his chair, startling everyone. "The charge is false!"

Bak studied the women, Taharet staring back defiantly, Meret sitting demurely, one hand in her lap, the other holding her sister's hand, despair clouding her face. His heart ached for her, but he could do nothing to ease her anguish. What had been done in Hattusa was too serious, threatening the throne of a king friendly to Maatkare Hatshepsut and the peaceful relations between the two lands. On a level more personal to every man and woman in Pentu's household, not one of them would have returned alive to Kemet if that king had not chosen, because he also valued that friendship, to close his eyes to the vile deed.

He pointed his baton of office at Taharet. "You, mistress, have much to account for."

"Get out!" Pentu leaped from his chair. "Get out of my house. My wife is innocent of wrongdoing, and I'll allow no more of these . . . these . . . false charges."

Bak whistled a signal. Psuro and four Medjays hurried

through the door and across the room. "Take her away," he said, pointing at Taharet.

Pentu's face paled. One did not arrest an individual for treason on a whim. Especially with Maatkare Hatshepsut's cousin serving as a witness. "No! It can't be." The worm of doubt crept into his voice, his face. "It's untrue, I tell you."

Taharet stared at him, shocked and dismayed by his waning confidence. As a Medjay reached for her, she ducked away and dropped to her knees before her husband. "I've done nothing wrong, my beloved. I swear I haven't."

He reached toward her, then slowly withdrew his hand before touching her hair. She moaned deep down inside.

Two Medjays caught her arms and lifted her to her feet. She looked wild-eyed at Bak, cried out, "You can't tear me from my home! I'm innocent, I tell you."

Bak looked upon her with pity. He was not proud of what he had to do, but it must be done. "You lived in Sile on a major trade route and learned to speak the tongues of many lands, including Hatti. Your father, a merchant, kept you and your sister by his side to serve as translators. As a result, you met all who traveled through that border city—merchants, envoys, soldiers—and you could speak to them with ease. One of you fell in love with a man from Hatti and continued your relationship when you dwelt in Hattusa." Much of what he said was conjecture, but he felt sure he was close to the truth.

Pentu stared at his wife, appalled. "You? You would be unfaithful to me? To a man who held you close, who raised you onto a plinth and worshipped you as a goddess?"

A harsh sob burst from Taharet's throat. "I've done nothing to be ashamed of. Nothing!"

Pentu's expression turned severe, cool. "You've betrayed me, woman."

"No," Taharet sobbed. "I swear I haven't."

Bak glanced at Meret, who was staring at her sister, her face whiter than the whitest of linen. He could almost feel her pain, and remorse threatened to undermine his resolve. "Take her," he said to Psuro, "to the Great Prison of Waset."

As the men pulled Taharet away from the dais, Meret sprang to her feet. "You must release her, sir. She's done nothing worse than protect me. I'm the one who became embroiled in Hittite politics."

"Meret!" Taharet cried. "Don't."

Pahure strode quickly to Meret's side. "Be silent, mistress. He knows not of what he speaks."

Meret appeared not to hear either of them. "I did what I had to do, not for myself, but for a man I cared for above all others." She looked at Bak, her distress evident. "Your assumption was correct, Lieutenant. I fell in love with a Hittite. A man of royal blood, who wished to unseat the king and replace him with another. I did nothing more than carry messages, but I knew their contents and sympathized."

Bak clamped his mouth tight, forbidding himself from urging a denial. The admission had sealed her fate and she was wise enough to realize that her life was over.

The steward placed a protective arm around her. "You must not believe her, Lieutenant. She owes to her sister all she has. She'd say anything to protect her."

Bak stood quite still, looking at the pair. He dared not look at Amonked. They had remained together long into the night, Bak explaining his conclusions and describing what he meant to do, Amonked offering suggestions and giving a final approval. Bak's plan had borne fruit, his assumption that Meret would not allow her sister to suffer in her place had proved accurate. One motive had remained uncertain, and the steward's action had answered it.

"Will you never leave me alone, Pahure?" Meret flung the steward a furious look and slid out from his grasp. "I'll not allow Taharet to suffer for my transgressions."

Pentu frowned uncertainly at the pair, whether unsure if Meret's admission was true or unsettled about his steward's behavior, Bak could not tell.

...he Hittite?" Bak asked.

...took her head. "I met him long ago in Sile. He was aide to an envoy who came and went. When my father learned of our love, he insisted I wed another. A man of Kemet. Later my husband died and my sister and I moved to Waset. After she wed Pentu, she took me into her home at Tjeny. When we went to Hattusa, I met him again and our love deepened."

"Mistress!" Pahure took her arm, tried to turn her away from Bak. Glaring at him, she stood as rigid as a tree whose roots were planted firmly in the earth, and as immovable.

Bak, well aware of what the admission must have cost her, softened his voice. "You once told me you'd loved and lost and knew not what had happened to him. You were speaking of the Hittite?"

She bit her lip, bowed her head. "Yes."

If her lover had been identified as a traitor and found to be disloyal to his king, Bak could well imagine his fate. Meret had apparently reached a similar conclusion.

"Why did you not leave us alone?" Taharet cried. "Why did you have to destroy our lives? We long ago returned from that wretched land of Hatti. The incident was forgotten. Why bring it back to life?"

Bak signaled the Medjays to release her. "A man was slain so your sister's secret would not be revealed, mistress."

"You accused Taharet, yet you've known all along I was guilty?" Meret asked.

He hardened his heart to the look of betrayal on her face. "She had too much to lose—wealth, position, security—to take such a risk. And she was far too protective of you."

"Who died for Meret's sake?" Taharet demanded. "The Hittite merchant?"

"Maruwa, yes. Whether he meant to point a finger at her, we'll never know. But someone feared he might and cut his throat to silence him."

"Neither my sister nor I took his life." Taharet glanced at

Meret, as if suddenly afraid her sister had been driven to murder. "That I swear to the lord Amon."

Bak glanced at Pentu, sitting in unrelenting silence on the dais, staring at his wife as he would at a stranger. "Men may have died because of your foolishness, mistress—many no doubt in Hattusa—but neither of you have slain a man with your own hands."

Bak caught Psuro's eye, warning him to remain alert and ready to act. "Pahure took Maruwa's life," he said.

Stunned disbelief, shocked murmurs, muffled oaths followed in quick succession. None remained unmoved except Amonked and the Medjays. The steward, though caught by surprise along with everyone else, managed a harsh, cynical laugh.

Pentu glowered disbelief. "Why would he, of all people, slay a stranger?"

"He wished to place mistress Meret in his debt, to win her hand in marriage. He wished to step up to a position of respect in your household, to become a member of the family. That he could do only through her, the sole unwed female close to you."

Meret stared at Pahure, appalled.

The steward laughed. "Don't listen to him, sir. He's desperate to uphold his reputation as a man who always lays hands on his quarry. He's found no one else to blame, so he points a finger at me."

Pentu, looking uncertain, glanced at Amonked. He found no reassurance in the grim look he received in return.

"I've heard it said that once you slay a man, a second slaying comes easier, and a third." Bak eyed the steward with contempt. "Did you find that to be true, Pahure?"

"You speak in riddles, Lieutenant."

"I speak of the auditor Woserhet and the priest Meryamon, whose lives you also took. And you ordered Zuwapi to slay me."

Pahure returned Bak's scornful look. "I've had no dealings with anyone in the sacred precinct for as long as I can remember. Why would I wish those two men dead? Or you, for that matter?"

"To save yourself from the charge of stealing ritual items from the lord Amon and smuggling them out of the land of Kemet."

Every man and woman in Pentu's household gaped.

"You know not of what you speak," Pahure scoffed. "You'd be hard pressed to prove I knew one of the three."

"You undoubtedly met Maruwa in Hattusa. You met Woserhet when he stopped in Tjeny, but I doubt you feared him at that time. You were too far removed from the scene of your crimes. Not until he became suspicious of Meryamon did he and the priest have to die."

"How would I come to know a priest?"

"Meryamon grew to manhood in Abedju, as did you. As did his friend Nehi. The town is not large. You had to know each other, and your sister's presence there along with the presence of Meryamon's parents gave you ample opportunity to meet and plan. I sent a courier downriver last night and will know for a fact within a few days."

Pahure plastered a smile on his face. "You can't prove a thing."

"He doesn't have to," Amonked said. "He has merely to take you before the vizier and state his case. My word will attest to the truth of the charge."

Baffled, the governor asked, "Pahure? Slay three men? Steal from the lord Amon? I can't believe it of him. Not for a woman with no wealth of her own."

"Mistress Meret was but a stepping-stone. Wed to her, he would be looked upon as a brother to the governor of Tjeny. He could move to Waset, to this dwelling, or to another fine dwelling in Mennufer and gradually begin to use the riches he amassed from the objects stolen from the sacred precinct. As a man of wealth and position, he could easily become ac-

quainted with those who walk in the shadow of Maatkare
Hatshepsut, and from there he could move into a position of
influence and power. Or so he believed, at any rate."

Pentu, sitting stiff and straight in his armchair, eyed
Pahure warily. "How certain are you of this charge, Lieutenant?"

Bak nodded to Psuro, who ordered two Medjays to close
in on the steward. Whistling a signal, he summoned Hori
and Kasaya from the next room.

As the pair hurried into the hall, a smiling Hori held out a
long-necked red jar like those used in the land of Amurru in
which Ugarit was the primary port. "We found this jar
buried in the garden, sir, behind the shrine of the lord Inheret. It contains scrolls describing some property held in
Ugarit and names Pahure as the owner."

Pahure rammed an elbow into the pit of one Medjay's
stomach and struck the other high between the legs with a
knee. Their spears clattered to the floor and they both bent
double, clutching their injured parts. Before anyone else
could think to act, he raced toward the door. Hori stepped
into his path. The steward plowed into the scribe with a
shoulder, knocking him against Kasaya. The jar slipped
from Hori's hands and crashed onto the floor, sending shards
and scrolls in all directions. Pahure ducked around the two
young men. Leaping across the threshold, he vanished from
sight.

Dashing after the steward, Bak yelled at Psuro and the
two unhurt Medjays to give chase. He reached the door
ahead of them and spotted his quarry on the opposite side of
an inner courtyard, vanishing through the portal at the top of
the stairs. Though Pahure had allowed his waist to thicken as
a measure of his success, he clearly had lost none of the
speed and strength honed by his life as a sailor on the Great
Green Sea.

Bak dashed across the court, passing a startled servant

carrying an armload of fresh, yeasty-smelling bread, and leaped through the door. As he plunged downward, he glimpsed Pahure racing ahead down the zigzagging stairway. The way was poorly lit, the landings cluttered with large, elongated water jars and less porous, rounder storage jars. Behind, he heard the rapid footsteps of Psuro and the Medjays. He heard a thud, a curse, the sound of a rolling jar. A triumphant shout told him one of the men had caught the container before it could tumble down the stairs.

Pahure leaped off the bottom step, shoved an elderly female servant out of his way, and raced through the door that opened into an anteroom. Certain he meant to leave the house, Bak put on an added burst of speed. The steward was too far ahead to catch. He banged open the front door, raced through, and leaped into the street, which teemed with men, women, and children streaming toward Ipet-resyt.

Bak reached the exit and glanced back. He saw Psuro and the Medjays racing out of the stairwell, with Sitepehu running after them, an unexpected sight, decked out as he was in his priestly finery. Hori followed close behind with Netermose.

Praying Pahure would not think to grab a hostage, Bak sped after him into the street, which was filled with the deep shadows of early morning. Above the two- and three-story houses that hugged both sides, ribbons of red and yellow spread out from the lord Khepre, not long risen above the eastern horizon. The smells of fresh bread, animals and their waste, humanity, and the river hung in the warm, sticky air.

Pahure dashed west toward Ipet-resyt. He shoved aside a man carrying a small boy on his shoulders, cursed three young women walking side by side, scattering them, and shouldered an elderly couple out of his way. Bubbling voices broke off at his rude passage, children half dancing at their parents' heels stopped to stare. An older boy peeked out of an open doorway. Grinning mischievously, he stuck out a foot, trying to trip the steward. Instead of the good-natured laugh he probably expected, he received a cuff across the side of his head that sent him reeling.

Bak did not break his stride. Hori, he felt confident, would summon help for anyone in need.

Dashing out of the street and onto the swath of trampled grass between the houses and the open court in front of Ipet-resyt, Pahure slowed and glanced around as if taking measure of his surroundings. He veered to the right and sped toward the northern end of the wall enclosing the court. Bak raced after him into the sunlight and he, too, took note of the world around him.

Dense crowds filled the court, awaiting the greatest of the gods and his earthly daughter and son. Those who had come too late for a prime spot from which to view the procession that would, within a short time, depart from the southern mansion were milling around the booths, seeking a better vantage point. Bak could not see the processional route beyond the court to the west, but he assumed the throng was equally large all the way to the river. There another assemblage would be massed at the water's edge, along which were moored the royal barge, the golden barge of the lord Amon, and the boats that would tow the two vessels and carry royalty and priests downriver to Ipet-isut. A flotilla of other vessels would be marking time on the river, waiting to accompany the procession downstream.

Pahure rounded the corner of the court, with Bak about thirty paces back. Ignoring the booths that had been erected north of the court, the men and women and children who wandered around them, more intent on a good time than adoring their god and sovereigns, the two men, one after the other, pounded across the northbound processional way along which the lord Amon had been carried from Ipet-isut eleven days earlier.

Trumpets blared, announcing to the world that the procession was leaving Ipet-resyt. A murmur of excitement surged through the crowded court as a dozen standard-bearers came through the pylon gateway in the massive wall in front of the god's mansion. Bak could see nothing over the spectators' heads except the sun-struck golden figures mounted on top of the standards, the long red pennants swaying gently atop the flagpoles clamped to the pylon, and a cloud of incense rising in front of the gate.

Pahure swung south around the corner of the court and raced toward the crowd standing along the westbound processional way along which the deity would be carried to the river. Surely, Bak thought, he would not be so stupid as to run into the crowd, attracting the attention of the many soldiers lining the raised thoroughfare. No sooner had the thought come and gone than Pahure turned westward to run up a broad strip of grass between the spectators and several blocks of interconnected houses, enclosed within an unbroken wall of white.

As Bak made the turn, he glanced back. He saw no sign of Psuro or the Medjays or Sitepehu. They must have tried to cut through the court and had gotten caught up in the crowd.

The grass was wet, often ankle-deep in water left by the ebbing flood. The new greenery risen out of the saturated earth was thick and luxuriant, too tempting to be ignored by residents of nearby housing blocks. A dozen or so donkeys were tied to widely spaced stakes in the ground, and an old man and a dog sat beneath an acacia, watching the crowd while tending a large flock of goats and sheep brought out to graze on the lush new foliage.

Pahure pulled up his long kilt, freeing his legs for speed, and ran toward the flock, spread out across the grass. Bak raced after him. Water erupted from beneath their pounding feet, splashing their legs. The dog began to bark, exciting the animals in the flock. A few spectators turned to look, but most were so intent on the soon to approach procession that they could not be distracted. Bak heard a second blare of trumpets and the swell of voices as the people amassed in the court greeted their sovereigns, emerging from Ipet-resyt after a week of rituals celebrating their divine birth and the renewal of their spiritual power.

A splendid white ram, the wool on his belly clumped with mud, began to trot toward the river, making the clapper tied to his neck ring, enticing his flock away from what he took to be danger. The animals bunched up to follow, forcing Pahure close to the spectators, who stood ten-deep or more all along the processional way. The dog's barking grew more frantic and it ran out into the grass. The old man stood and, shaking a fist, began to yell. The sheep and goats at the rear of the flock broke into a faster trot, pushing the others forward. People turned to look, but another blast of trumpets drew their gaze back to the court, where the lord Amon was leaving his southern mansion and the standard bearers had turned west to lead the procession toward the river.

Bak prayed Pahure would remain on the grass, staying well clear of the processional way, and that he would not turn back toward the temple. He did not wish to become entangled by priests and dancers and musicians and, above all, Maatkare Hatshepsut, Menkheperre Thutmose, and their retinue. The very least that would happen would be the steward's escape.

The dog raced toward the flock. The old man yelled more desperately, trying to call it back. Untrained, Bak guessed, and excited by the chase, it ran on, barking wildly. As it raced in among the stragglers, making them bleat in terror, the flock broke apart, with sheep and goats trotting in all directions, several threatening to run Pahure down. Forced into the crowd, he shoved men and women out of his way, raising a chorus of angry objections. Bak, also caught up in the melee, stayed behind the spectators, ducking around one animal after another, fearful of losing sight of his quarry.

The ram turned and, head down, charged the dog. With a sharp yelp and its tail between its legs, it raced away through the flock. Frightened and confused, the sheep and goats pushed in among the spectators, bumping bare legs and stepping with sharp little hooves on sandaled feet. The people began to scatter, the approaching procession no longer able to hold their attention. Men yelled and cursed and tried to beat back the animals, while children laughed with glee, thoroughly enjoying the commotion. The soldiers along the near side of the processional way broke their line to help.

The thoroughfare, a wide expanse of sparkling white limestone chips, empty of humanity all the way to the river's edge, was too inviting to resist. Pahure burst out from among the spectators to run west along this easier course.

Bak shouldered his way through the crowd, unwittingly opening a path for the ram. He glanced to the east, glimpsed the standard-bearers leading the procession toward him. With a sinking feeling in the pit of his stomach, he set off after Pahure, who was dashing along the thoroughfare, kilt held well above his knees. The waterfront lay not fifty paces ahead of him.

The line of soldiers along the south side of the processional way broke apart and the men ran onto the limestone path. Bak thought at first they meant to chase Pahure, then realized half the flock had followed the ram through the crowd and the animals were spreading out across the thoroughfare in front of the approaching procession.

Openly horrified by the potential for catastrophe, the sergeant in charge yelled to his men, "Get those wretched creatures out of here." Practically tearing out his hair, he added, "The ram. Somebody catch him. Lead him away. Cut his throat if you have to."

The soldiers, many of them innocent in the ways of animals, tried to press them back in among the spectators; instead, they set them to flight. The men and women lining the thoroughfare surely recognized the seriousness of the situation, but, following their children's example, they began to laugh. Even Bak, racing on, had to smile, though he suspected he would be the man held to account. Especially if he didn't lay hands on Pahure.

Forcing himself to greater effort, Bak gradually closed the distance between himself and his quarry. Ahead, the royal barge was moored against the riverbank at the end of the processional way. Behind the highly polished wooden craft and tethered to it by thick ropes, the golden barge of the lord Amon rocked gently on the swells. In front of the royal vessel, tied to temporary mooring posts embedded in the mudbank, were the ten boats that would tow the barges downstream, guiding them along the water's edge to Ipetisut. Each boat, bound to the vessel behind it by a long, stout rope, had been freshly oiled and painted. Colorful pennants fluttered from masts and stays.

All along the shore against which the barges and boats were moored, spearmen held the crowd back, allowing plenty of space for the royal pair and the lord Amon, the standard-bearers, priests, and musicians to board the appropriate craft for the voyage downstream.

With the sacred barge raised high upon the floodwaters, its deck above the riverbank, the priests standing on the bow had a clear view of the processional way, of the scurrying soldiers and frightened flock. Garbed all in white and shaven bald, with two men wearing leopard skins over their shoulders, they lined the rail, staring down the thoroughfare, appalled by the pandemonium.

The boatmen on the royal barge had an even better view. Rather than standing in serious expectancy while they awaited their sovereigns and their god, they were laughing heartily at the frantic gathering up of obstinate sheep and goats. The spectators waiting along the riverbank craned their necks, trying to see what was going on.

Pahure ran to the water's edge along which the royal barge was moored. He glanced over his shoulder, saw how close Bak had come. With the path ahead barred by the vessel and with any retreat cut off, he turned southward to race along the muddy shore toward the stern.

A soldier yelled, "Now look here, sir! You're not allowed . . ." He spotted Bak, blustered, "And you . . ."

"Police!" Bak ran into the open area along the river and raised his baton of office so all who looked could see. "That man's a criminal. He must be stopped."

Voices buzzed among the spectators, who pressed against the line of spearmen, eager to see. The soldiers, who might have helped Bak, given the chance, had to shove the crowd back, keeping clear the area their sovereigns and their god would, in a short time, tread.

Cursing the curiosity that so often stole away common sense, Bak ran on after Pahure. The steward, reaching the bow of the sacred barge, paused as if unsure what he should do. He glanced back at his pursuer; looked up the line of vessels tethered to the sacred craft, none of which he could hope to board and cut free; and stared out across the river at the distant shore and the flotilla of boats too far upstream to be of help. Those short moments of hesitation proved his undoing. Bak leaped at him. The steward ducked away, slipped in the mud, and half fell, half dived into the silt-laden water.

Bak, balanced precariously on the edge of the bank, came close to falling into the river with him, but scrambled back to firmer ground. Pahure surfaced just out of reach, sputtered, looked around to see where he was. The gilded bow of the barge of the lord Amon hung over him, reaching high above his head. The long, sleek prow was surmounted by a huge carved, gilded, and painted image of a ram's head emerging from the sacred lily. The horned ram, symbol of the lord Amon, wore on its head the golden disk of the sun and over its brow a rearing cobra. A large painted and gilded wooden replica of a multicolored broad collar hung below the image.

Pahure's expression clouded, as if for an instant he felt the wrath of the god breathing down his neck. He shook his head, visibly throwing off the feeling, and swam under the prow. A couple of paces beyond the vessel, he treaded water and again looked out across the river at the opposite shore, so far away few men would dare try to swim across and fewer would succeed. Especially not a man already tired after a long, hard chase. Bak, very much aware of how tired he himself was, stood poised on the riverbank, ready to swim after his quarry.

The priests on the barge, their brows furrowed by worry, peered down from the bow, looking at the man in the water and at his pursuer. Bak was as concerned as they. He could hear, over the cheering of the spectators lining the processional way, the beat of drums setting the pace of the procession, the harsher sounds of clappers and sistra. He estimated them to be about halfway between Ipet-resyt and the river, approaching the spot where last he had seen the sheep and goats. He prayed the soldiers had removed the animals from the processional way, prayed he could snare Pahure before the standard-bearers and leading priests reached the waterfront and the dual sovereigns, especially Maatkare Hatshepsut, became aware that a problem existed.

Pahure, his decision made, swam upstream, vanishing behind the far side of the golden barge. Bak pushed his dagger firmly into its sheath so he wouldn't lose it in the river, flung his baton of office away from the water's edge, and dove in after him. Rounding the hull he spotted the steward swimming south alongside the vessel at a good solid pace. The sacred barge was not large, less than fifty paces long, and its shallow hull, gilded above the waterline, lay low in the water. To a swimmer, it looked like a wall of solid gold, with scenes incised along much of its length showing Maatkare Hatshepsut praising her heavenly father.

Bak glanced up midway along the vessel, saw rising on the deck above him the gilded dais and, beneath its roof, the open shrine in which the barque of the lord Amon would be placed for its voyage to Ipet-isut. Frantic priests hung over the railing, watching him and Pahure.

He swam on, listening to the sounds of sistra and clappers and drums echoing through the water in his ears, hearing the voices of men and women on the riverbank talking excitedly, no doubt guessing where he and Pahure had gone, what the vile criminal meant to do, where the two would reappear. Bak could not imagine what Pahure hoped to gain. He could not swim across the river and the moment he set foot on the near shore, he would be taken. He was doomed one way or the other.

Ahead, the steward passed the twin rudders, each overlaid with a thin gold sheath incised with the sacred lily and the two eyes of the lord Horus, and swam beneath a second gilded ram's head mounted on the narrow stern. Spotting Bak, he dove beneath the water. Bak kicked backward to grab a rudder, fearing Pahure meant to pull him under. A half-dozen priests fluttered back and forth across the stern, peering over the sides. From their near panic, he guessed they feared he would snap off the rudder, which was much lighter and more graceful than those on working vessels.

Pahure surfaced some distance upstream and swam southward with long, fast strokes. Ignoring muscles beginning to ache from the strain, Bak shot forward through the water. The steward passed the densest part of the crowd gathered around the sacred barge and appeared to be heading toward an acacia hanging over the river's edge, a tree Bak remembered from the day he had walked along the shore with Netermose.

Even if Pahure reached the tree and pulled himself onto the mudbank, he doubted the steward would get away. Too many people were running along the shore, keeping pace. Still, he wanted to be the man to snare the vile criminal.

Pahure leaped upward and grabbed a limb, which bowed beneath his weight. As he began to pull himself out of the water, Bak swam to him and caught hold of his legs. The steward clung with both hands and tried to shake him off. The limb drooped further. Bak's hands slid down the wet legs, stopped at the ankles. He jerked as hard as he could, heard the sharp crack of breaking wood. Though not broken through, the limb bent lower, dropping Pahure into the water to his waist.

With a grim but victorious smile, Bak looked up at the man he had caught. He saw no fear on Pahure's face, only a firm determination to fight to his last breath. Beyond the steward, he glimpsed a group of spectators running toward the tree, several armed soldiers gathering around, and four nearly naked, heavily muscled men, each carrying a good-size rounded rock, identifying them as competitors in a throwing contest.

The closest soldier raised his spear and, his mouth clamped tight with determination, thrust the weapon. At the same time Bak heard a sickening thud. Pahure went limp and half slid, half fell into the water, while the spear sped harmlessly over his shoulder. As he vanished beneath the surface, Bak saw that the side of his head had been crushed.

Startled, he glanced up at the soldier, who looked equally surprised. Beyond, Bak glimpsed the rock throwers, one with a triumphant smile on his face, the others encircling him, smothering him with praise.

Chapter Nineteen

"They're coming! They're coming!"

The child's voice rang out sharp and clear, carried by some whim of the gods all across the landscape in front of Ipet-isut. Every eye turned westward, every man and woman stretched to his or her tallest, eager to see the first pair of towboats enter the canal. What had been a soft murmur of voices rose to an expectant clamor.

So many people had come to see the lord Amon return to his northern mansion that the crowd standing on the raised paths pressed against the row of royal guards lining the artificial lake in front of Ipet-isut and the canal to the river. Humble men and women unwilling or afraid to push themselves forward, people without means and accustomed to no better, stood among the trees and brush to either side in the standing water left by the retreating flood. Children perched in the trees, looking out over the multitude of heads.

Bak, having received a summons while donning clean clothing at his Medjays' quarters, had hastened to join Amonked on the raised limestone platform that overlooked the lake. Known to have the ear of his royal cousin, the Storekeeper of Amon had been given a place of distinction from which to view the approaching procession of boats. Crowded onto the platform with them were ranking priests and dignitaries from throughout the land of Kemet.

Officiating priests stood at the edge of the lake in front of the platform, some holding lustration vessels, the rest filling the air with incense that rose in a cloud, making Bak's nose itch. Four royal servants holding ostrich feather fans waited nearby. Standard-bearers stood at the lower end of the shallow stairs that led up to the processional way connecting the lake to the sacred precinct.

"He's dead?" Amonked had to shout to be heard.

Bak did not have to ask to whom he referred. "I dove down after him without delay, but even if I'd caught him before he entered the water, it would've made no difference. The rock struck him hard enough to've slain an ox."

The strident blare of a trumpet, close enough to destroy a man's hearing, rent the air. The first two towboats swung into the far end of the canal, each carrying on its bow an enshrined gilded image of the sovereign of Kemet in a symbolic pose of victory. The second pair carried similar shrines and images, as did the following vessels.

Behind the towboats, guided into the canal by men standing on the riverbank, came the long, slender royal barge on which Maatkare Hatshepsut and Menkheperre Thutmose had journeyed from Ipet-resyt. Enthroned side by side within a shrine, they were swathed in long, tight, white jubilee robes. While the barge made its slow, deliberate passage down the canal, voices rose in adoration, muting the beat of the drums marking time for the towboat oarsmen and muffling the sounds of sistra and clappers.

"What in the name of the lord Amon did he intend?" Amonked shouted.

Bak could but shrug. The question was not new. Everyone who had watched Pahure's last desperate attempt to leave the water had asked it of him. "I can only believe he thought the men on shore would be easier to evade than me. Or perhaps he hoped to die there, a quick and painless death at the hands of a soldier."

"A coward's way," Amonked said, scowling.

"Would you want to face impalement or burning?"

The golden barge of the lord Amon slipped into view. Voices swelled in a fresh round of acclaim as the long, sleek vessel was maneuvered around the tight turn into the canal. Though it was linked by rope to the royal barge, a company of soldiers stationed along the paths to either side towed the vessel in the wake of its predecessor. The task was not difficult, an honor bestowed by the royal pair.

In the lull of voices while all who watched practically held their breaths, waiting for their sovereigns' barge to touch land, Amonked said, "We know what prompted him to take Woserhet's life and Meryamon's, but did he ever say why he believed, after more than three years had passed, that Maruwa would reveal mistress Meret as a traitor?"

"He had no chance. I fear that's one question which will never be answered."

"His death was far quicker and easier than it should've been." Amonked, his expression severe, wiped the sweat from his face and neck with a square of linen. "I trust the other men involved in his foul scheme will suffer appropriate punishment."

"The chief priest will no doubt press the vizier to see justice done."

The royal barge bumped against the landing stage. Crewmen scrambled out to span the narrow gap with a gangplank, while others held the vessel steady. The dual sovereigns stepped out of the shrine and, with the dignity born of their office, removed the robes that had enshrouded them, passed them and the associated regalia to a priest and, with the help of aides, donned more appropriate attire for the final procession into Ipet-isut.

The trumpet blared again and Maatkare Hatshepsut, dressed much as she had been eleven days earlier, strode across the gangplank, head held high, the very image of grandeur. The moment her feet touched earth, the crowd roared. At the same time, Menkheperre Thutmose bounded onto the shore in two long strides. How much of the acclaim was directed toward him was impossible to tell. Bak wanted to believe the young king shared in equal measure with Maatkare Hatshepsut the adoration of his people.

The instant the barge was empty of its illustrious passengers, the crewmen jumped back on board and withdrew the gangplank so the craft could be towed out of the way, making room for the barge of the lord Amon. The priests on the landing stage stepped forward to purify with water the earth upon which their sovereigns trod and to cleanse the air around them with a scent so pungent it made Bak sneeze. The servants moved up to wave the ostrich feather fans over the heads of the royal pair.

Amonked shouted something Bak could not hear, took his arm, and ushered him off the crowded platform. The broad, open area, delineated by low walls, between the platform and Ipet-isut, hummed with the voices of priests, ranking bureaucrats, and nobility. All along both walls stood tables heaped high with offerings of food and drink and flowers, the finest produced in the land of Kemet. Sacrificial cattle, four prime black steers, stood near the northern tower of the pylon gate through which royalty and god would enter the sacred precinct. Facing the cattle across the processional route, priests held squawking geese and ducks by their wings, these also destined for sacrifice.

Slipping behind the row of royal guards who lined both sides of the processional way joining the landing stage to the sacred precinct, Bak and Amonked wove a path through the spectators to a spot not far from the live food offerings.

No sooner had they positioned themselves behind a pair of guards than Amonked went on with their conversation as if it had not been interrupted. "Pahure's thoughts were bent and twisted, his goals far out of reach."

"We all know Menkheperre Thutmose is raising men above their stations when they've proven themselves to be competent," Bak said. "I suspect the steward was extremely capable."

"In the regiments Thutmose commands, he can do what he wishes, but my cousin is more traditional in her selection of men who rise to lofty positions."

Bak noted Amonked's use of the familiar name Thutmose rather than the full, more formal Menkheperre Thutmose. He knew the Storekeeper of Amon held a special place of trust in Maatkare Hatshepsut's heart. What place, he wondered, did he hold in the heart of her youthful co-ruler? The thought was torn asunder by the approach of the standard-bearers.

Bak thanked the lord Amon for the swift progress of the procession. The faintest of breezes sporadically stirred the pennants rising above the pylons, but could not compete with the hot breath of the lord Re reaching down upon the earth, turning the crowded area in front of the sacred precinct into a kiln.

The standard-bearers came close, each holding high the golden symbol of a god or location significant to Maatkare Hatshepsut and her domain. Bak was surprised to see Netermose walking among them, representing Tjeny, the city from which had originated, according to tradition, the first sovereign of Kemet. The aide's eyes flitted toward Bak and Amonked, he tilted his head slightly in recognition, and strode on.

"I'm amazed Pentu remembered to send someone with the standard," Bak said. "The last I saw of him, he was so upset with Taharet's betrayal, her decision to help her sister at his expense, that he was thinking of nothing but the loss of his happy marriage."

"He didn't remember." Amonked tucked the square of linen under his belt. "I told Netermose to join the procession. I didn't wish to make public the dissension within the governor's household." He looked about to speak further, hesitated, then said, "I sorrow for mistress Meret, as you must."

"I do. I can't help but think her a good woman, one who

closed her eyes to the lady Maat and chose a wrong path to aid the dream of another."

"The vizier will judge her guilty."

"Yes."

Neither man wanted to voice the punishment she would no doubt face: death by her own hand. Poison.

"What of mistress Taharet?" Bak asked.

"If Pentu speaks for her, she'll probably be allowed her freedom, but I doubt she'll ever again be welcome in Waset. Certainly not in the royal house."

"Will he speak for her?"

"He's very angry now. How he'll feel in a day or two, I can't begin to guess."

As the standard-bearers passed through the pylon gate into the sacred precinct, the priests followed them across the court, shaking water onto the pathway and filling the air with a strong, musky smell. Before they could get too far ahead, a trumpeter blasted a long, shrill note. Maatkare Hatshepsut and Menkheperre Thutmose, flanked by their fan-bearers, strode up the stairs and onto the processional way. The spectators in front of Ipet-isut roared their approbation.

As the priests passed on by and the royal pair walked closer, Bak could see them clearly. He spoke without thinking. "Each time I see Maatkare Hatshepsut, she looks more like her brother, her deceased husband Ahkheperenre Thutmose."

"She does, doesn't she?" Amonked said, eyeing her with a fond smile. "She's never been beautiful—the family nose and protruding teeth have prevented that—and now she's almost as plump as he was. Too much rich food, too much comfort and ease."

She could not have heard them speaking but, almost as if she had, her eyes came to rest on Amonked. Her cousin bowed his head in obeisance. Her eyes shifted briefly to Bak, and with no change of expression whatsoever, she strode on. He understood her well enough. As long as she failed to acknowledge his presence he did not exist, and no matter how great his accomplishment she did not have to reward him with the gold of honor.

Menkheperre Thutmose, his bearing as regal as that of his aunt, looked their way. If Bak had not known better, he would have said the young man was trying hard not to laugh. Focusing again on the path ahead, he walked with his co-ruler through the towered gate and into the sacred precinct.

"Do our sovereigns know of the flock that came close to disrupting the procession?"

"I was among the spectators when the last animal, the ram, was led away. The standard-bearers were not ten paces away. They and all who walked behind them had to have seen the chaos ahead and the haste with which the guards and spectators re-formed along the processional way."

"Maatkare Hatshepsut must've been furious."

Amonked gave him a bland smile. "A rumor has begun to circulate through Waset. The lord Amon, her heavenly father, took the form of a ram and joined the procession to help bring to justice the man who stole ritual items from the sacred precinct and slew two men within its walls."

Bak forbade himself to laugh. Maatkare Hatshepsut was most adept at turning all that occurred, good and bad, to her advantage.

Saying no more, they watched the lord Amon, invisible within his covered shrine, carried high on the shoulders of the priests bearing the sacred barque. In a cloud of incense, they strode across the court and vanished behind their sovereigns through the pylon gate that rose before Ipet-isut.

The deity had returned to his earthly home, marking the end of the Beautiful Feast of Opet.